MARS, WE LOVE YOU

MARS,

WE LOVE YOU

Tales of Mars, Men, and Martians

Edited by
Jane Hipolito and Willis E. McNelly

With an Introduction by Isaac Asimov

DOUBLEDAY & COMPANY, INC., GARDEN CITY, NEW YORK, 1971

Library of Congress Catalog Card Number 77–166420
Copyright © 1971 by Jane Hipolito and Willis E. McNelly
Copyright © 1971 by Doubleday & Company, Inc.
All Rights Reserved
Printed in the United States of America
First Edition

Grateful acknowledgment is made for the use of the following material:

Excerpt from A *Princess of Mars* by Edgar Rice Burroughs. Copyright 1912 by Edgar Rice Burroughs, Inc. Copyright renewed 1939 by Edgar Rice Burroughs, Inc.

"A Martian Odyssey" by Stanley Weinbaum. Copyright 1934 by Continental Publications, Inc. Copyright renewed 1962 by Margaret Weinbaum Kay. Reprinted by arrangement with Forrest J. Ackerman.

"The Embassy" by Donald A. Wollheim. Copyright © 1942 by Street & Smith Publications, Inc. Originally published in *Astounding Science Fiction*, 1942. Reprinted by permission of the author and Forrest J. Ackerman, agent.

"Dark Mission" by Lester Del Rey. Copyright © 1943 by Street & Smith Publications, Inc. Reprinted by permission of the author and his agents, Scott Meredith Literary Agency, Inc., 580 Fifth Avenue, New York, New York 10036.

"Lost Art" by George O. Smith. Copyright © 1943 by Street & Smith Publications, Inc. Originally published in *Astounding Science Fiction*, 1943. Reprinted by permission of the author.

"The Cave" by P. Schuyler Miller. Copyright © 1943 by Street & Smith Publications, Inc. Reprinted by permission of the author and The Condé Nast Publications Inc.

"Expedition" by Anthony Boucher. Copyright © 1943 by Anthony Boucher. Reprinted by permission of Collins-Knowlton-Wing, Inc.

"Loophole" by Arthur C. Clarke. Copyright © 1946 by Street & Smith Publications, Inc. Originally published in *Astounding Science Fiction*, 1946. Reprinted by permission of the author and his agents, Scott Meredith Literary Agency, Inc., 580 Fifth Avenue, New York, New York 10036.

"Catch That Martian" by Damon Knight. Copyright © 1952 by Galaxy Publishing Corp. Originally published in *Galaxy*, March 1952. Reprinted by permission of the author.

THIS BOOK IS FOR
GEN AND TERRY
FOR OBVIOUS REASONS

CONTENTS

The Red Planet.

Mars.

John Carter, Warlord of Barsoom, Jeddak of Jeddaks.

Orson Welles and the Halloween "War of the Worlds" broadcast that terrified the major part of an entire nation.

Canals, dead sea bottoms, dying civilizations, hurtling moons, desiccated polar caps, dust storms, unending vistas of sand.

Valentine Michael Smith, a stranger from a strange land who grokked a Martian chronicle and gave to many of our youths virtually an entire way of life.

Robert A. Heinlein, Ray Bradbury, H. G. Wells, Percival Lowell, Edgar Rice Burroughs, Schiaparelli . . . the names and the ideas intertwine. Taken as a whole, they have made of our nearest planetary neighbor a modern myth that will endure even when future interplanetary probes return pictures clearer than those of Mariner 4.

For Mars is not simply a planet, fourth from the sun, diameter 4200 miles, mean distance from the sun over 141,000,000 miles, with a day forty minutes longer than ours, a year that equals nearly two of ours, and a gravity only 38 per cent that of Earth's. Mars is a symbol.

Mars is all of these things, to be sure, but she is also the object of one of the biggest bodies of literature in all of science fiction.

For hundreds of years the Red Planet has gripped the imagination of mankind. And those men whose mission it is to translate inchoate dreams into verbal reality, the science fiction writers, have produced a body of literature that would fill hundreds of books the size of this one. They have produced literally dozens of novels set on Mars, and uncountable short stories featuring Martians or men of Earth exploring the planet.

When we began assembling the stories which comprise this volume, we hoped to present as representative an anthology as possible considering both space limitations and copyright availability. It is our hope that this collection will show the chronological growth of the dream of Mars and Martians over the last hundred years. We begin with Giovanni Schiaparelli's misunderstood remarks about "channels" on the planet's surface for which the Italian word was *canali*. The myth grew from the word and provided a mystique of Mars. We progress from Percival Lowell, H. G. Wells, Edgar Rice Burroughs, and a dozen other writers to several stories and poems written expressly for this book.

The book isn't complete and it may omit your favorite Mars story, but with the writers of the past one hundred years, we hope you will be able to say with us, "Mars, We Love You!"

We would like to acknowledge our special gratitude to Harry Harrison, who has provided us professional guidance on many occasions. Damon Knight made a number of valuable suggestions to us, and Ray Bradbury helped us in choosing which of his voluminous Mars stories we would use here. Robert A. Heinlein also gave generously of his time and years of professional experience. Sherrill Felter deserves great appreciation for typing various stages of the manuscript. And we are grateful, too, to our colleagues on the staff of the English Department, California State College, Fullerton, who were understanding enough to let us do our thing.

Jane W. Hipolito

Willis E. McNelly

Short stories and pieces from the
works of famous writers showing how
the Red Planet has earned its place
in modern mythology.

THE ROMANCE OF MARS

by Isaac Asimov

This anthology begins with Giovanni Virginio Schiaparelli and
so does the modern fictional romance of Mars.

With Schiaparelli's description of the "canali" just about a century ago, came the picture of an old and sophisticated, but slowly
dying civilization on our sister planet—with its great canals, its
jeweled cities, its lovely princesses, its spindly scholars, its savage
aggressors (which author do you read?).

In science fiction, the romance has never died, as this anthology
amply witnesses. Mars is still the special planet of Ray Bradbury,
and Heinlein can still make it a plausible place of alien culture.

In real life, too, Schiaparelli started a romance. Mars had icecaps and it had an atmosphere. Surely the icecaps meant water
and the atmosphere meant oxygen and the two together meant
life. The air and water might be drifting away, else why the need
for the vast irrigation project of the canals, but surely those very
canals meant that life survived. And, if canals, surely *intelligent*
life!

At the turn of the century, H. G. Wells could, with entire jus-
tice, assume an oxygen atmosphere on Mars, and an advanced
civilization that could be driven by growing need into an invasion
of Earth.

But then the intelligences of Mars dimmed. Year by year, they
retreated—in science, if not in science fiction. No astronomer

could really duplicate Lowell's vision of the Martian canals; despite occasional glimpses, more and more began to view them as optical illusions and more and more raised their voices to say that the emperor's new clothes did not exist after all.

The closer the investigation of the Martian atmosphere, the thinner it proved, and the less likely it seemed to be terrestrial in character. If intelligent Martians existed at all, it began to be more and more likely that they were living now only under extreme difficulty. Did they live in domed cities or underground? Was it not more likely they had died out millions of years ago?

Was it not most likely, in fact, that they had never existed at all?

This, of course, did not mean that life did not exist, for intelligence is only an accidental concomitant of life and perhaps not even a very useful one. On Earth, life existed and flourished ebulliently for three billion years without anything we would call an even faint intelligence.

Then how about life-minus-intelligence on Mars? There were still the icecaps, still the atmosphere—and there was a surface that showed dark markings as well as ruddy ones. If the ruddy ones were stretches of desert, might not the dark ones be vegetation? With the change in seasons, the icecaps melted in alternation, and the dark areas spread in the hemisphere in which spring came. And if there was vegetation, ought there not to be animal life, too?

Yet successively improved studies of Mars continued to make clearer the harshness of its environment. The vision of pseudo-trees and pseudorodents gave way to something less ambitious. How about lichens? Surely there could be lichens.

So biologists took lichens and other plants that flourished in the high Himalayas and Pamirs and exposed them to what they thought the Martian environment was like—and they grew. The chance of life on Mars—at least simple life—seemed to become great indeed.

Then came the crucial year of 1965 and Mariner 4 skimmed past Mars and took photographs and sent them back to Earth. For the first time, the surface was seen better than by the best telescope.

There were no canals, but there were craters. The rugged terrain resembled that of the Moon. The lack of erosion indicated that the lack of air and water was not a new situation on Mars but extended backward through geological eons. Closer studies of the Martian atmosphere showed that it was even thinner than had been thought and that the temperature was colder. There was no oxygen at all in the atmosphere and hardly any water anywhere. The icecaps might be frozen carbon dioxide.

No intelligent life. No higher plants and lower animals. Perhaps not even lower plants or bacteria. Perhaps no life at all.

Perhaps Mars is another dead world like the Moon.

Yet can this be? Mars's gravity is 2.4 times that of the Moon. It does have a thin atmosphere. Surely there must be some water somewhere; even if the icecaps are solid carbon dioxide, there ought to be solid water mixed with it.

And if there is water, even in small quantities, might there not be life of some sort?

Hope dies hard and that part of Martian glamor will not give up the ghost. Though every step in the study of Mars has made the planet seem more unlikely as an abode of life, the hope will not entirely vanish.

Even as I write, Mariner 9 has just taken off for Mars and will go into orbit around it (we hope), mapping the surface as it has never been mapped before. Its maps will not answer the question of life on Mars, but eventually, an instrument package may make a soft landing and perhaps it will provide an answer. —And if not, there is the manned landing that must someday take place.

But why bother? Of what use is life of the primitive sort that is all that can possibly exist on Mars? Who cares about germs or viruses or bare organic remnants halfway to life but never making it?

Astronomers and biologists do!

The fact of life on another world would be the greatest and most exciting discovery in either astronomy or biology to date—no matter how simple that life might be.

All life on Earth, however various it may seem, is one. It is all related biochemically, making use of nucleic acids and proteins of the same basic sort, making use of the same vitamins, the same sets of reactions, the same scheme of metabolism. In short, the trillions of organisms on Earth make up exactly *one* ecology. And though Martian life might be so sparse in numbers and variety as to be beneath contempt from the standpoint of our own lush planet, it would form a different ecology, and the number of ecologies we could study would be exactly doubled.

The fact that life existed at all would tell us something, even if we knew not one solitary detail about that life. We can fairly make the assumption that life can exist only through molecules sufficiently complex to be capable of great versatility and flexibility of reaction; and if so we would know that the Martian environment encouraged the development of such complex molecules as soon as we knew life existed.

We know this could happen on Earth (it *did* happen) and we explain it in terms of Earth's primordial environment, but how *inevitable* was the development of life? The Martian environment will scarcely allow the development we have imagined on Earth. The temperature is so low, the radiation of the Sun so feeble, the air so thin, the water so lacking, that the chances of life-type molecules forming is only a tiny fraction of what it was on Earth.

If, nevertheless, life of any sort, however simple, formed on Mars, then the physicochemical pressures forcing it must be so strong that we can rest assured that life exists on any planet that is even approximately Earth-type in character.

If life exists—of any sort and however simple—then the next step is to discover its biochemical basis. The possibilities are two in number. The macromolecules that make it up are either proteins and/or nucleic acids, as on Earth, or (the second possibility) they are not.

If the macromolecular basis of Martian life is fundamentally different from that of Earth, then joy must surely be unconfined. Not only would we have a second ecology, but one that would be utterly new to us. It is impossible to speculate on how important this may turn out to be or what new insights into life we would gain if we could find a completely new variety of it.

If, on the other hand, Martian life were protein/nucleic acid in basis, there might still be a very good chance that there would be variations on the theme that would be extremely interesting.

There might be alternate metabolic pathways never observed on Earth; roles played by individual atoms or atom groupings unduplicated on Earth; biochemical adaptations undreamed of on Earth.

Consider one example—

All protein molecules on Earth are built up of some twenty amino acids of which all but one are capable of either a left-handed or right-handed orientation—one the mirror image of the other. Under all conditions not involving life, the two types, labeled D and L, are equally stable and equally capable of being synthesized. If an amino acid is synthesized under conditions not involving life, half the molecules are L and half are D.

In terrestrial proteins, however, with only the most insignificant and rare exceptions, all the amino acids are L. A uniform L-ness makes it possible for amino-acid chains to be built more neatly and stack more snugly, but a uniform D-ness would have done just as well.

Why, then, is terrestrial life all L? Why not all D? Or why not some life forms L and others D?

We can't be sure. Did it just happen that the first protein formed was all L? Or were L and D both formed and the L happened to win out by sheer chance? Or is there some basic asymmetry in nature that makes the L form inevitable?

Well, then, would Martian proteins be L or D? Either way it might prove something about Earthly life. If it were a mixture of both, one way or another, that might prove even more fascinating.

But suppose that Martian life existed and that it was biochemically precisely like that on Earth. Does that mean that there would be no interest in it at all? That it would be a trivial discovery—just more of the same?

Not at all.

For one thing, it would indicate that perhaps our biochemical basis was the only one that could support life, at least under conditions even faintly like that of Earth. Two cases would be far better evidence for this than one is. Secondly, if Martian life were precisely like Earthly life, but were much simpler (as surely it must be), it might be possible to discover something about the primitive basis of life that the complex life forms on Earth obscure.

In that case, Mars would be a laboratory in which we could observe the protolife that once existed on Earth and even experiment with it—as on Earth we could do only with a time machine.

Indeed, even if life did not exist on Mars, but if in its soil were half-formed molecules manifestly on their way to life in Earthly fashion, that might be helpful. It might indicate the nature of the path once taken on Earth and we would have a laboratory for prebiotic chemical evolution—with possibly incalculable consequences in the way of new knowledge of direct application to Earthly biology.

So there it is. The fictional romance of Mars continues, but the true romance is (albeit, as yet, problematically) in the future. It will come, along with results beyond what fiction may yet have imagined, when the first microscopic fragment of anything indubitably living, or even near living, is detected in the cold red soil of Mars.

MARS, WE LOVE YOU

Perhaps more than any other individual, the Italian astronomer Giovanni Schiaparelli is responsible for many of the popular illusions about Mars. Long a student of the Red Planet, Schiaparelli presented the results of his observations in his native language. When he saw grooves or channels on the surface of Mars, he used the Italian word *canali* to describe the phenomenon. The word presented no problem to astronomers who studied Schiaparelli in French or German translation. The grooves, in these languages, described bands that extended from one dark area on the planet's surface to another. Significantly Schiaparelli's works were originally translated into English from either French or German, and the word "canal" was used by these early translators to present the French or German equivalent of the Italian *canali*.

After the 1892 opposition of the planet, Schiaparelli summarized his conclusions about Mars in a long article which appeared in the Italian journal *Natura ed Arte*. This composite picture was the first direct English translation of any of Schiaparelli's works. The American astronomer William H. Pickering used the word *canals*, but only because Schiaparelli was now using two Italian words, one for *channels* and one for *canals*. He wrote first about the polar caps.

Giovanni Virginio Schiaparelli

REPORT ON *Canali*

. . . It is manifest that if the white polar spots of Mars represent snow and ice, they should continue to decrease in size with the approach of summer in those places, and increase during the winter. Now this very fact is observed in the most evident manner. In the second half of the year 1892 the southern polar cap was in full view; during that interval, and especially during the months of July and August, its rapid diminution from week to week was very evident, even to those observing with common telescopes. This snow (for we may well call it so), which in the beginning reached as far as latitude 70° and formed a cap of over 2000 kilometers [1240 miles] in diameter, progressively diminished, so that two or three months later little more of it remained than an area of perhaps 300 kilometers [185 miles] at the most, and still less was seen later in the last days of 1892. In these months the southern hemisphere of Mars had its summer; the summer solstice occurring upon October 13. Correspondingly the mass of snow surrounding the northern pole should have increased; but this fact was not observable, since that pole was situated in the hemisphere of Mars which was opposite to that facing the earth. The melting of the northern snow was seen in its turn in the years 1882, 1884, and 1886. . . .

Schiaparelli then discussed the planet's atmosphere:

In every climate, and under every zone, its atmosphere is nearly perpetually clear, and sufficiently transparent to permit one to recognize at any moment whatever, the contours of the seas and continents. . . . Here and there we see appear from time to time a few whitish spots changing their position and form, rarely extending over a very wide area. . . . It is possible that they may be layers of cloud, because the upper portions of terrestrial clouds, where they are illuminated by the Sun, appear white. But various observations lead us to think that we are dealing rather with a thin veil of fog, instead of a true nimbus cloud, carrying storms and rain. Indeed it may be merely a temporary condensation of vapor, under the form of dew or hoar frost. Accordingly, as far as we may be permitted to argue from the observed facts, the climate of Mars must resemble that of a clear day upon a high mountain. By day a very strong solar radiation hardly mitigated at all by mist or vapor, by night a copious radiation from the soil towards celestial space, and because of that a very marked refrigeration. Hence a climate of extremes, and great changes of temperature from day to night, and from one season to another.

Eventually he turned his attention to the lines he saw on the planet's surface:

All the vast extent of the continents is furrowed upon every side by a network of numerous lines or fine stripes of a more or less pronounced dark color whose aspect is very variable. They traverse the planet for long distances in regular lines, that do not at all resemble the winding courses of our streams. Some of the shorter ones do not reach 500 kilometers (300 miles), others extend for many thousands, occupying a quarter or sometimes even a third of a circumference of the planet. Some of these are very easy to see, especially the one . . . designated by the name of Nilosyrtis. Others in turn are extremely difficult, and resemble the finest thread of spider's web drawn across the disk. They are subject also to great variations in their breadth, which may reach 200 or even 300 kilometers (120 to 180 miles) for the Nilosyrtis, whilst some are scarcely 30 kilometers (18 miles) broad. . . . These lines are the famous canals of Mars. . . . Their length and arrangement are constant, or vary only between very narrow limits. Each of them always begins and ends between the same regions. But their appearance and their degree of visibility vary greatly, for all of them, from one opposition to another, and even from one week to another . . . often one or more become indistinct, or even wholly invisible, whilst others in their vicinity increase to the point of becoming conspicuous even in telescopes of moderate power. [Our map] shows all those that have been seen in a long series of observations. This does not at all correspond to the appearance of Mars at any given period, because generally only a few are visible at once. . . . The canals may intersect among themselves at all possible angles, but by preference they converge towards the small spots to which we have given the names of lakes. For example, seven are seen to converge in Lacus Phoenicis, eight in Trivium Charontis, six in Lunae Lacus, and six in Ismenius Lacus.

He particularly commented on two very prominent lines:

The two lines follow very nearly the original canal, and end in the place where it ended. One of these is often superposed as exactly upon the former line . . . but it also happens that both the lines may occupy opposite sides of the former canal, and be located upon entirely new ground. The distance between the two lines differs in different geminations, and varies from 600 kilometers (370 miles) and more, down to the smallest limit at

which two lines may appear separated in large visual telescopes—
less than an interval of 50 kilometers (30 miles).

We have already remarked that at the time of melting they
appeared surrounded by a dark zone, forming a species of temporary sea. At that time the canals of the surrounding region become blacker and wider, increasing to the point of converting,
at a certain time, all of the yellow region comprised between the
edge of the snow and the parallel of 60° north latitude, into numerous islands of small extent. Such a state of things does not
cease, until the snow, reduced to its minimum area, ceases to melt.
Then the breadth of the canals diminishes, the temporary sea
disappears, and the yellow region again returns to its former
area. The different phases of these vast phenomena are renewed
at each return of the seasons, and we have been able to observe
them in all their particulars very easily during the oppositions of
1882, 1884, and 1886, when the planet presented its northern
pole to terrestrial spectators. The most natural and the most simple interpretation is that to which we have referred, of a great
inundation produced by the melting of the snows—it is entirely
logical, and is sustained by evident analogy with terrestrial phenomena. We conclude therefore that the canals are such in fact,
and not only in name. The network formed by these was probably
determined in its origin in the geological state of the planet. . . .
It is not necessary to suppose them the work of intelligent beings,
and notwithstanding the almost geometrical appearance of all
of their system, we are now inclined to believe them to be produced by the evolution of the planet, just as on the earth we have
the English Channel and the Channel of Mozambique.

Finally, he presents his last comments on the planet:

For my person I have not yet succeeded in formulating an organic whole of logical and credible thoughts about the phenomena
of Mars, which are perhaps somewhat more complicated than Dr.
Arrhenius believes. . . . I believe with him that the lines and
bands on Mars (the name "canals" should be avoided) can be explained as the results of physical and chemical forces, always ex-
cepting certain periodical color changes which are likely to be the

result of organic events of large magnitude, like the flowering of the steppes on earth and similar phenomena. I am also of the opinion that the regular and geometric lines (the existence of which is still denied by many persons) do not yet teach us anything about the existence of intelligent beings on this planet. But I think it worthwhile if somebody collected everything . . . that can reasonably be said in favor of their existence.

No other single writer has so influenced contemporary thinking about Mars as has the late astronomer Percival Lowell. Gifted with rare imagination, Lowell extrapolated from the few facts known about Mars at the turn of the century to create a mystique that lives today. Reading Lowell for the first time, one is amazed to realize that he wrote before Burroughs, Weinbaum, and almost every other science fiction writer. And if Lowell seems familiar, even on first reading, credit the many writers who were inspired by him, and realize that they weren't original, and that Lowell was. In addition to being the first to speak of dead sea bottoms, dying civilizations, life-giving canals on a desert planet, and many other Martian features, Lowell wrote of Mars with a highly charged emotional prose that is effective sixty years later. We hope this selection from *Mars as the Abode of Life* will stimulate a Lowell revival.

Percival Lowell

MARS AS THE ABODE OF LIFE

Beautiful as the opaline tints of the planet look, down the far vista of the telescope-tube, the deserts represent a really terrible reality. To the bodily eye, the aspect of the disk is lovely beyond compare; but to the mind's eye, its import is horrible. That rose-ochre enchantment is but a mind mirage. A vast expanse of arid ground, world-wide in its extent, girdling the planet completely in circumference, and stretching in places almost from pole to pole, is what those opaline glamours signify. All deserts, seen from a safe distance, have something of this charm of tint. Their bare rock gives them color, from yellow marl through ruddy sandstone to blue slate. And color shows across space for the massing due to great extent. But this very color, unchanging in its hue, means the extinction of life. Pitilessly persistent, the opal here bears out its attributed sinister intent.

To let one's thoughts dwell on these Martian Saharas is gradually to enter into the spirit of the spot, and so to gain comprehension of what the essence of Mars consists. Without such background always omnipresent in the picture, the lesser and more pregnant features fail of effect in their true value for want of setting off. To conceive of this great buckler of brazen sand and rock, level as a polished shield, and stretching to the far distance, to stand sharp-cut there by the horizon of a sky, unrelieved by so much as mountain-notching of its blue, is to realize in part what life on it must mean. Where days and months of travel would bring one no nearer to its edge, despair might well settle on the mind. And the sun in its daily course rises from out the stony waste only to set in it again.

Pitiless indeed, yet to this condition the earth itself must come, if it last so long. With steady, if stealthy, stride, Saharas, as we have seen, are even now possessing themselves of its surface. The outcome is doubtless yet far off, but it is as fatalistically sure as that tomorrow's sun will rise, unless some other catastrophe anticipate the end. It is perhaps not pleasing to learn the manner of our death. But science is concerned only with the fact, and Mars we have to thank for its presentment.

Before the final stage in the long life drama of a planet is thus brought to its close, there will come a time when the water, having left the surface, still lingers for a little in the air. For the atmosphere is the pathway the water takes to the sky. Insufficient in amount to leave a surplus on the ground in the shape of oceans, or even lakes and ponds, a certain quantity will still hover up above.

With regard to the distribution of the humidity, what scant moisture the desert-born equatorial winds might possess would be deposited northward as they cooled, in part impermanently in the forties, in part more permanently at the poles. The return flow of air in winter, being steadily warmed, would not tend to deposit moisture down the disk; nor in summer either, to any extent, although from the melting of the cap such winds would then be more charged with vapor. Unlike our own earth, therefore, moisture would proceed poleward, to remain there. Not only, therefore, is the water much less in amount on Mars, but what is there tends to be kept about the poles. The only available supply lies in the arctic and antarctic regions, stationary on the ground or else is in process of journeying round to it again.

In this last stage of temporizing, the water that once as such bespread Mars's face now is. The well-nigh total disappearance

of the one cap, and the entire extinction of the other, show how
each summer melts what the winter had deposited, and that in
both cases this is nearly the sum total of the cap. Covering as each
does so much territory, one might suppose the water not scanty,
but comparable in quantity to the earth's supply. If we calculate it,
however, we shall find this anything but the case. At Point Barrow, in Alaska, in latitude 71° N., where the temperature is below
freezing from September 1 to June 15, 75 inches of snow fall during the nine and a half months. Ten inches of snow are equal to
one inch of water. This quantity, then, measures the amount of
the Earth's impermanent cap, and forms a basis for comparison
with the depth of the snow-cap melted on Mars. It seems, too, not
an improbable value for what occurs there; for though on the one
hand it is likely that day by day the snowfall is greater at Point
Barrow than on Thyle, in Mars, at the same latitude, on the other,
the winter season is there twice as long. To be lavish, we may estimate that the equivalent of 100 inches of snow fall on Thyle. That
would mean 10 inches of water. Now, the southern cap of Mars,
the larger of the two, covers 96° across at its greatest, which makes
its area equal to one-fifth of the whole surface of the planet. To
this we need not add the other cap, since it at the time stretches
over only 6°, a vanishing quantity in comparison. On earth, oceans
cover 72 per cent of the surface, and are, on the average, 2100
fathoms deep. Calculation from these data gives the amount of
water on the earth as 189,000 times that on Mars. We said rightly,
then, that Mars was badly off for water.

In consequence of this state of things, the water supply of the
planet is both scant in amount and tethered at that. For it is
tied up during the greater part of the year at one pole or the other.
For a few weeks only of each six months it stands unlocked, first
in the arctic, then in the antarctic, zone. Then, and then only,
may this deposit, meagre as it is, be drawn upon. Mars is indebted
for the staff of life to a polar pittance sparsely doled out, and that
only at appointed times.

Study of the natural features of the planet leaves us, then, this
picture of its present state—a world-wide desert where fertile
spots are the exception, not the rule, and where water everywhere
is scarce. So scanty is this organic essential, that over the greater

part of the surface there is none to quicken vegetation or to support life. Only here and there by nature are possible those processes which make our earth the habitable, homelike place we know. In our survey of Mars, then, we behold the saddening picture of a world athirst, where, as in our own Saharas, water is the one thing needful, and yet where by nature it cannot be got. But one line of salvation is open to it, and that lies in the periodic unlocking of the remnant of water that each year gathers as snow and ice about its poles.

The evidence of observation thus bears out what we might suspect from the planet's smaller size: that it is much farther along in its planetary career than is our earth. This aging in its own condition must have its effect upon any life it may previously have brought forth. That life at the present moment would be likely to be of a high order. For whatever its actual age, any life now existent on Mars must be in the land stage of its development, on the whole a much higher one than the marine. But, more than this, it should probably have gone much farther if it exist at all, for in its evolving of terra firma, Mars has far outstripped the earth. Mars's surface is now all land. Its forms of life must be not only terrestrial as against aquatic, but even as opposed to terraqueous ones. They must have reached not simply the stage of land-dwelling, where the possibilities are greater for those able to embrace them, but that further point of pinching poverty where brain is needed to survive at all.

The struggle for existence in their planet's decrepitude and decay would tend to evolve intelligence to cope with circumstances growing momentarily more and more adverse. But, furthermore, the solidarity that the conditions prescribed would conduce to a breadth of understanding sufficient to utilize it. Intercommunication over the whole globe is made not only possible, but obligatory. This would lead to the easier spreading over it of some dominant creature,—especially were this being of an advanced order of intellect,—able to rise above its bodily limitations to amelioration of the conditions through exercise of mind. What absence of seas would thus entail, absence of mountains would further. These two obstacles to distribution removed, life there would tend the quicker to reach a highly organized stage. Thus Martian conditions themselves make for intelligence.

Our knowledge of it would likewise have its likelihood increased. Not only could any beings there disclose their presence only through their works, but from the physical features the planet presents, we are led to believe that such disclosure would be distinctly more probable than in the case of the earth. Any markings made by mind should there be more definite, more uniform, and more widespread than those human ones with which we are familiar. More dominant of its domicile, it should so have impressed itself upon its habitat as to impress us across intervening space.

What the character of such markings might be, we shall best conceive by letting the pitiless forbiddingness of the Martian surface take hold upon our thought. Between the two polar husbandings of the only water left, stands the pathless desert—pathless even to the water semiannually set free. Only overhead does the moisture find natural passage to its winter sojourn at the other pole. Untraversable without water to organic life, and uninhabitable, the Sahara cuts off completely the planet's hemispheres from each other, barring surface commerce by sundering its supplies. Thirst—the thirst of the desert—comes to us as we realize the situation, parching our throat as we think of a thirst impossible of quenching except in the far-off and by nature unattainable polar snows.

To interpret now the successive growth of the canals latitudinally down the disk is our next concern. We saw that it started at the edges of the polar cap. Now, such an origin in place at once suggests an origin of causation as well, and furthermore precludes all other. For the origin of time was after the melting of the cap. First the cap melted, and then the canals began to appear. Those nearest to the cap did so first, and then the others in their order of distance from it, progressing in a stately march down over the face of the disk.

Thus we reach the deduction that water liberated from the polar cap and thence carried down the disk in regular progression is the cause of the latitudinal quickening of the canals. A certain delay in the action, together with the amount of darkening that takes place, seems to negative the supposition that what we see is the water itself.

On the other hand, vegetation would respond only after a lapse of time necessary for it to sprout,—a period of, say, two weeks,—and such tarrying would account for the observed delay.

Vegetation, then, explains the behavior of the canals. Not transference of water merely, but transformation consequent upon transference, furnishes the key to the meaning of the cartouches. Not the body of water, but the quickened spirit to which it gives rise, produces the result we see. Set free from its winter storage by the unlocking of the bonds of its solid state, the water, accumulated as snow, begins to flow and starts vegetation, which becomes responsible for the increased visibility of the canals.

Part and parcel of this information is the order of intelligence involved in the beings thus disclosed. Peculiarly impressive is the thought that life on another world should thus have made its presence known by its exercise of mind. That intelligence should thus mutely communicate its existence to us across the far stretches of space, itself remaining hid, appeals to all that is highest and most far-reaching in man himself. More satisfactory than strange this; for in no other way could the habitation of the planet have been revealed. It simply shows again the supremacy of mind. Men live after they are dead by what they have written while they were alive, and the inhabitants of a planet tell of themselves across space as do individuals athwart time, by the same imprinting of their mind.

Thus, not only do the observations we have scanned lead us to the conclusion that Mars at this moment is inhabited, but they land us at the further one that these denizens are of an order whose acquaintance was worth the making. Whether we ever shall come to converse with them in any more instant way is a question upon which science at present has no data to decide. More important to us is the fact that they exist, made all the more interesting by their precedence of us in the path of evolution. Their presence certainly ousts us from any unique or self-centred position in the solar system, but so with the world did the

Copernican system the Ptolemaic, and the world survived this deposing change. So may man. To all who have a cosmoplanetary breadth of view it cannot but be pregnant to contemplate extramundane life and to realize that we have warrant for believing that such life now inhabits the planet Mars.

A sadder interest attaches to such existence: that it is, cosmically speaking, soon to pass away. To our eventual descendants life on Mars will no longer be something to scan and interpret. It will have lapsed beyond the hope of study or recall. Thus to us it takes on an added glamour from the fact that it has not long to last. For the process that brought it to its present pass must go on to the bitter end, until the last spark of Martian life goes out. The drying up of the planet is certain to proceed until its surface can support no life at all. Slowly but surely time will snuff it out. When the last ember is thus extinguished, the planet will roll a dead world through space, its evolutionary career forever ended.

While Schiaparelli and Lowell pictured Mars on their pages, it remained for Herbert George Wells to make Martians real to men. With the publication of Wells's *War of the Worlds* in 1898, the Martians did indeed invade Earth. Wells's precisely detailed descriptions of Martian anatomy and technology, based on the best scientific data of the time, seemed at once so plausible and so terrible that his readers could not forget them. Indeed Wells's work was all the more devastating because it showed humans to be even more frightening than the octopuslike Martians: Wells's Martian attack particularly exposed human arrogance, stupidity, and incompetence.

Perhaps the best measure of the Martians' effectiveness is the fact that today, more than seventy years after they arrived on our scene, they are still very much with us. In Orson Welles's celebrated 1938 Halloween radio broadcast, George Pal's film, and several of the stories included in *Mars, We Love You*—not to mention the hundreds of other plays, films, and stories modeled after *War of the Worlds*—the first Martians live on. Yet impressive as all of the later invaders are, none has surpassed Wells's memorable Martians in illuminating both the Red Planet and Earth to ourselves.

H. G. Wells

WAR OF THE WORLDS

No one would have believed in the last years of the nineteenth century that this world was being watched keenly and closely by intelligences greater than man's and yet as mortal as his own; that as men busied themselves about their various concerns they were scrutinised and studied, perhaps almost as narrowly as a man with a microscope might scrutinise the transient creatures that swarm and multiply in a drop of water. With infinite complacency men went to and fro over this globe about their little affairs, serene in their assurance of their empire over matter. It is possible that the infusoria under the microscope do the same. No one gave a thought to the older worlds of space as sources of human danger, or thought of them only to dismiss the idea of life upon them as impossible or improbable. It is curious to recall some of the mental habits of those departed days. At most, terrestrial men fancied there might be other men upon Mars, perhaps inferior to themselves and ready to welcome a missionary enterprise. Yet across the gulf of space, minds that are to our minds as ours are to those of the beasts that perish, intellects vast and cool and unsympathetic, regarded this earth with envious eyes, and slowly and surely drew their plans against us. And early in the twentieth century came the great disillusionment.

The planet Mars, I scarcely need remind the reader, revolves about the sun at a mean distance of 140,000,000 miles, and the light and heat it receives from the sun is barely half of that received by this world. It must be, if the nebular hypothesis has any truth, older than our world; and long before this earth ceased to be molten, life upon its surface must have begun its course. The fact that it is scarcely one seventh of the volume of the earth must have accelerated its cooling to the temperature at which life could begin. It has air and water and all that is necessary for the support of animated existence.

Yet so vain is man, and so blinded by his vanity, that no writer, up to the very end of the nineteenth century, expressed any idea that intelligent life might have developed there far, or indeed at all, beyond its earthly level. Nor was it generally understood that since Mars is older than our earth, with scarcely a quarter of the superficial area and remoter from the sun, it necessarily follows that it is not only more distant from life's beginning but nearer its end.

The secular cooling that must someday overtake our planet has already gone far indeed with our neighbour. Its physical condition is still largely a mystery, but we know now that even in its equatorial region the midday temperature barely approaches that of our coldest winter. Its air is much more attenuated than ours, its oceans have shrunk until they cover but a third of its surface, and as its slow seasons change huge snowcaps gather and melt about either pole and periodically inundate its temperate zones. That last stage of exhaustion, which to us is still incredibly remote, has become a present-day problem for the inhabitants of Mars. The immediate pressure of necessity has brightened their intellects, enlarged their powers, and hardened their hearts. And looking across space with instruments, and intelligences such as we have scarcely dreamed of, they see, at its nearest distance only 35,000,000 of miles sunward of them, a morning star of hope, our own warmer planet, green with vegetation and grey with water, with a cloudy atmosphere eloquent of fertility, with glimpses through its drifting cloud wisps of broad stretches of populous country and narrow, navy-crowded seas.

And we men, the creatures who inhabit this earth, must be to them at least as alien and lowly as are the monkeys and lemurs to us. The intellectual side of man already admits that life is an incessant struggle for existence, and it would seem that this too is the belief of the minds upon Mars. Their world is far gone in its cooling and this world is still crowded with life, but crowded only with what they regard as inferior animals. To carry warfare sunward is, indeed, their only escape from the destruction that, generation after generation, creeps upon them.

And before we judge of them too harshly we must remember what ruthless and utter destruction our own species has wrought, not only upon animals, such as the vanished bison and the dodo, but upon its inferior races. The Tasmanians, in spite of their human likeness, were entirely swept out of existence in a war of extermination waged by European immigrants, in the space of fifty years. Are we such apostles of mercy as to complain if the Martians warred in the same spirit?

The Martians seem to have calculated their descent with amazing subtlety—their mathematical learning is evidently far in excess of ours—and to have carried out their preparations with a well-nigh perfect unanimity. Had our instruments permitted it, we might have seen the gathering trouble far back in the nineteenth century. Men like Schiaparelli watched the red planet—it is odd, by-the-bye, that for countless centuries Mars has been the star of war—but failed to interpret the fluctuating appearances of the markings they mapped so well. All that time the Martians must have been getting ready.

During the opposition of 1894 a great light was seen on the illuminated part of the disk, first at the Lick Observatory, then by Perrotin of Nice, and then by other observers. English readers heard of it first in the issue of *Nature* dated August 2. I am inclined to think that this blaze may have been the casting of the huge gun, in the vast pit sunk into their planet, from which their shots were fired at us. Peculiar markings, as yet unexplained, were seen near the site of that outbreak during the next two oppositions.

The storm burst upon us six years ago now. As Mars approached opposition, Lavelle of Java set the wires of the astronomical exchange palpitating with the amazing intelligence of a huge outbreak of incandescent gas upon the planet. It had occurred towards midnight of the twelfth; and the spectroscope, to which he had at once resorted, indicated a mass of flaming gas, chiefly hydrogen, moving with an enormous velocity towards this earth. This jet of fire had become invisible about a quarter past twelve. He compared it to a colossal puff of flame suddenly and violently squirted out of the planet, "as flaming gases rushed out of a gun."

A singularly appropriate phrase it proved. Yet the next day there was nothing of this in the papers except a little note in the *Daily Telegraph*, and the world went in ignorance of one of the gravest dangers that ever threatened the human race. I might not have heard of the eruption at all had I not met Ogilvy, the well-known astronomer, at Ottershaw. He was immensely excited at the news, and in the excess of his feelings invited me up to take a turn with him that night in a scrutiny of the red planet.

In spite of all that has happened since, I still remember that vigil very distinctly: the black and silent observatory, the shadowed lantern throwing a feeble glow upon the floor in the corner, the steady ticking of the clockwork of the telescope, the little slit in the roof—an oblong profundity with the stardust streaked across it. Ogilvy moved about, invisible but audible. Looking through the telescope, one saw a circle of deep blue and the little round planet swimming in the field. It seemed such a little thing, so bright and small and still, faintly marked with transverse stripes, and slightly flattened from the perfect round. But so little it was, so silvery warm—a pin's-head of light! It was as if it quivered, but really this was the telescope vibrating with the activity of the clockwork that kept the planet in view.

As I watched, the planet seemed to grow larger and smaller and to advance and recede, but that was simply that my eye was tired. Forty millions of miles it was from us—more than forty millions of miles of void. Few people realise the immensity of vacancy in which the dust of the material universe swims.

Near it in the field, I remember, were three faint points of light, three telescopic stars infinitely remote, and all around it was the unfathomable darkness of empty space. You know how that blackness looks on a frosty starlight night. In a telescope it seems far profounder. And invisible to me because it was so remote and small, flying swiftly and steadily towards me across that incredible distance, drawing nearer every minute by so many thousands of miles, came the Thing they were sending us, the Thing that was to bring so much struggle and calamity and death to the earth. I never dreamed of it then as I watched; no one on earth dreamed of that unerring missile.

That night, too, there was another jetting out of gas from the distant planet. I saw it. A reddish flash at the edge, the slightest projection of the outline just as the chronometer struck midnight; and at that I told Ogilvy and he took my place. The night was warm and I was thirsty, and I went, stretching my legs clumsily and feeling my way in the darkness, to the little table where the siphon stood, while Ogilvy exclaimed at the streamer of gas that came out towards us.

That night another invisible missile started on its way to the earth from Mars, just a second or so under twenty-four hours after the first one. I remember how I sat on the table there in the blackness, with patches of green and crimson swimming before my eyes. I wished I had a light to smoke by, little suspecting the meaning of the minute gleam I had seen and all that it would presently bring me. Ogilvy watched till one, and then gave it up; and we lit the lantern and walked over to his house. Down below in the darkness were Ottershaw and Chertsey and all their hundreds of people, sleeping in peace.

He was full of speculation that night about the condition of Mars, and scoffed at the vulgar idea of its having inhabitants who were signalling us. His idea was that meteorites might be falling in a heavy shower upon the planet, or that a huge volcanic explosion was in progress. He pointed out to me how unlikely it was that organic evolution had taken the same direction in the two adjacent planets.

"The chances against anything manlike on Mars are a million to one," he said.

Hundreds of observers saw the flame that night and the night after about midnight, and again the night after; and so for ten nights, a flame each night. Why the shots ceased after the tenth no one on earth has attempted to explain. It may be the gases of the firing caused the Martians inconvenience. Dense clouds of smoke or dust, visible through a powerful telescope on earth as little grey, fluctuating patches, spread through the clearness of the planet's atmosphere and obscured its more familiar features.

Even the daily papers woke up to the disturbances at last, and popular notes appeared here, there, and everywhere concerning the volcanoes upon Mars. The seriocomic periodical *Punch*, I remember, made a happy use of it in the political cartoon. And, all unsuspected, those missiles the Martians had fired at us drew earthward, rushing now at a pace of many miles a second through the empty gulf of space, hour by hour and day by day, nearer and nearer. It seems to me now almost incredibly wonderful that, with that swift fate hanging over us, men could go about their petty concerns as they did. I remember how jubilant Markham was at securing a new photograph of the planet for the illustrated paper he edited in those days. People in these latter times scarcely realise the abundance and enterprise of our nineteenth-century papers. For my own part, I was much occupied in learning to ride the bicycle, and busy upon a series of papers discussing the probable developments of moral ideas as civilisation progressed.

One night (the first missile then could scarcely have been 10,000,000 miles away) I went for a walk with my wife. It was starlight, and I explained the Signs of the Zodiac to her, and pointed out Mars, a bright dot of light creeping zenithward, towards which so many telescopes were pointed. It was a warm night. Coming home, a party of excursionists from Chertsey or Isleworth passed us singing and playing music. There were lights in the upper windows of the houses as the people went to bed. From the railway station in the distance came the sound of shunting trains, ringing and rumbling, softened almost into melody by the distance. My wife pointed out to me the brightness of the red, green, and yellow signal lights hanging in a framework against the sky. It seemed so safe and tranquil.

Then came the night of the first falling star. It was seen early in the morning, rushing over Winchester eastward, a line of flame high in the atmosphere. Hundreds must have seen it, and taken it for an ordinary falling star. Albin described it as leaving a greenish streak behind it that glowed for some seconds. Denning, our greatest authority on meteorites, stated that the height of its first appearance was about ninety or one hundred miles. It seemed to him that it fell to earth about one hundred miles east of him.

I was at home at that hour and writing in my study; and although my French windows face towards Ottershaw and the blind was up (for I loved in those days to look up at the night sky), I saw nothing of it. Yet this strangest of all things that ever came to earth from outer space must have fallen while I was sitting there, visible to me had I only looked up as it passed. Some of those who saw its flight say it travelled with a hissing sound. I myself heard nothing of that. Many people in Berkshire, Surrey, and Middlesex must have seen the fall of it, and, at most, have thought that another meteorite had descended. No one seems to have troubled to look for the fallen mass that night.

But very early in the morning poor Ogilvy, who had seen the shooting star and who was persuaded that a meteorite lay somewhere on the common between Horsell, Ottershaw, and Woking, rose early with the idea of finding it. Find it he did, soon after dawn, and not far from the sand pits. An enormous hole had been made by the impact of the projectile, and the sand and gravel had been flung violently in every direction over the heath, forming heaps visible a mile and a half away. The heather was on fire eastward, and a thin blue smoke rose against the dawn.

When I returned to the common the sun was setting. Scattered groups were hurrying from the direction of Woking, and one or two persons were returning. The crowd about the pit had increased, and stood out black against the lemon yellow of the sky— a couple of hundred people, perhaps. There were raised voices, and some sort of struggle appeared to be going on about the pit.

Strange imaginings passed through my mind. As I drew nearer I heard Stent's voice:

"Keep back! Keep back!"

A boy came running towards me.

"It's a-movin'," he said to me as he passed; "a-screwin' and a-screwin' out. I don't like it. I'm a-goin' 'ome, I am."

I went on to the crowd. There were really, I should think, two or three hundred people elbowing and jostling one another, the one or two ladies there being by no means the least active.

"He's fallen in the pit!" cried some one.

"Keep back!" said several.

The crowd swayed a little, and I elbowed my way through. Every one seemed greatly excited. I heard a peculiar humming sound from the pit.

"I say!" said Ogilvy; "help keep these idiots back. We don't know what's in the confounded thing, you know!"

I saw a young man, a shop assistant in Woking I believe he was, standing on the cylinder and trying to scramble out of the hole again. The crowd had pushed him in.

The end of the cylinder was being screwed out from within. Nearly two feet of shining screw projected. Somebody blundered against me, and I narrowly missed being pitched onto the top of the screw. I turned, and as I did so the screw must have come out, for the lid of the cylinder fell upon the gravel with a ringing concussion. I stuck my elbow into the person behind me, and turned my head towards the Thing again. For a moment that circular cavity seemed perfectly black. I had the sunset in my eyes.

I think everyone expected to see a man emerge—possibly something a little unlike us terrestrial men, but in all essentials a man. I know I did. But, looking, I presently saw something stirring within the shadow: greyish billowy movements, one above another, and then two luminous disks—like eyes. Then something resembling a little grey snake, about the thickness of a walking stick, coiled up out of the writhing middle, and wriggled in the air towards me—and then another.

A sudden chill came over me. There was a loud shriek from a woman behind. I half turned, keeping my eyes fixed upon the cylinder still, from which other tentacles were now projecting, and began pushing my way back from the edge of the pit. I saw astonishment giving place to horror on the faces of the people about me. I heard inarticulate exclamations on all sides. There was a general movement backwards. I saw the shopman struggling still on the edge of the pit. I found myself alone, and saw the people on the other side of the pit running off, Stent among them. I looked again at the cylinder, and ungovernable terror gripped me. I stood petrified and staring.

A big greyish rounded bulk, the size, perhaps, of a bear, was rising slowly and painfully out of the cylinder. As it bulged up and caught the light, it glistened like wet leather.

Two large dark-coloured eyes were regarding me steadfastly. The mass that framed them, the head of the thing, was rounded, and had, one might say, a face. There was a mouth under the eyes, the lipless brim of which quivered and panted, and dropped saliva. The whole creature heaved and pulsated convulsively. A lank tentacular appendage gripped the edge of the cylinder, another swayed in the air.

Those who have never seen a living Martian can scarcely imagine the strange horror of its appearance. The peculiar V-shaped mouth with its pointed upper lip, the absence of brow ridges, the absence of a chin beneath the wedgelike lower lip, the incessant quivering of this mouth, the Gorgon groups of tentacles, the tumultuous breathing of the lungs in a strange atmosphere, the evident heaviness and painfulness of movement due to the greater gravitational energy of the earth—above all, the extraordinary intensity of the immense eyes—were at once vital, intense, inhuman, crippled and monstrous. There was something fungoid in the oily brown skin, something in the clumsy deliberation of the tedious movements unspeakably nasty. Even at this first encounter, this first glimpse, I was overcome with disgust and dread.

Suddenly the monster vanished. It had toppled over the brim of the cylinder and fallen into the pit, with a thud like the fall of a great mass of leather. I heard it give a peculiar thick cry, and forthwith another of these creatures appeared darkly in the deep shadow of the aperture.

I turned and, running madly, made for the first group of trees, perhaps a hundred yards away; but I ran slantingly and stumbling, for I could not avert my face from these things.

There, among some young pine trees and furze bushes, I stopped, panting, and waited further developments. The common round the sand pits was dotted with people, standing like myself in a half-fascinated terror, staring at these creatures, or rather at the heaped gravel at the edge of the pit in which they lay. And then, with a renewed horror, I saw a round, black object bobbing up and down on the edge of the pit. It was the head of the shop-man who had fallen in, but showing as a little black object against the hot western sky. Now he got his shoulder and knee up, and again he seemed to slip back until only his head was visible. Suddenly he vanished, and I could have fancied a faint shriek had reached me. I had a momentary impulse to go back and help him that my fears overruled.

Everything was then quite invisible, hidden by the deep pit and the heap of sand that the fall of the cylinder had made. Anyone coming along the road from Chobham or Woking would have been amazed at the sight—a dwindling multitude of perhaps a hundred people or more standing in a great irregular circle, in ditches, behind bushes, behind gates and hedges, saying little to one another and that in short, excited shouts, and staring, staring hard at a few heaps of sand. The barrow of ginger beer stood, a queer derelict, black against the burning sky, and in the sand pits was a row of deserted vehicles with their horses feeding out of nosebags or pawing the ground.

Edgar Rice Burroughs wrote his first Mars story in 1911 when Lowell's speculations were front-page news. He called it "Under the Moons of Mars," and it was an instant success. The Mars of Lowell's canals and dead sea bottoms was transformed into John Carter's Barsoom of red men, tharks, thoats, and "the incomparable Dejah Thoris." In book form the story became *A Princess of Mars*, the first in nearly a dozen novels that have sold, in the past fifty-eight years, millions of copies.

Shortly after the opening of the novel, John Carter of Virginia, sometime captain in the Army of the Confederate States of America, has been trapped by hostile Indians in an Arizona cave. Safe for the moment, he turns his attention to the Arizona landscape.

Edgar Rice Burroughs

A PRINCESS OF MARS

Few western wonders are more inspiring than the beauties of an Arizona moonlit landscape; the silvered mountains in the distance, the strange lights and shadows upon hog back and arroyo, and the grotesque details of the stiff, yet beautiful cacti form a picture at once enchanting and inspiring; as though one were catching for the first time a glimpse of some dead and forgotten world, so different is it from the aspect of any other spot upon our earth.

As I stood thus meditating, I turned my gaze from the landscape to the heavens where the myriad stars formed a gorgeous and fitting canopy for the wonders of the earthly scene. My attention was quickly riveted by a large red star close to the distant horizon. As I gazed upon it I felt a spell of overpowering fascination—it was Mars, the god of war, and for me, the fighting man, it had always held the power of irresistible enchantment. As I gazed at it on that far-gone night it seemed to call across the unthinkable void, to lure me to it, to draw me as the lodestone attracts a particle of iron.

My longing was beyond the power of opposition; I closed my

eyes, stretched out my arms toward the god of my vocation and felt myself drawn with the suddenness of thought through the trackless immensity of space. There was an instant of extreme cold and utter darkness.

I opened my eyes upon a strange and weird landscape. I knew that I was on Mars; not once did I question either my sanity or my wakefulness. I was not asleep, no need for pinching here; my inner consciousness told me as plainly that I was upon Mars as your conscious mind tells you that you are upon Earth. You do not question the fact; neither did I.

I found myself lying prone upon a bed of yellowish, moss-like vegetation which stretched around me in all directions for interminable miles. I seemed to be lying in a deep, circular basin, along the outer verge of which I could distinguish the irregularities of low hills.

It was midday, the sun was shining full upon me and the heat of it was rather intense upon my naked body, yet no greater than would have been true under similar conditions on an Arizona desert. Here and there were slight outcroppings of quartz-bearing rock which glistened in the sunlight; and a little to my left, perhaps a hundred yards, appeared a low, walled enclosure about four feet in height. No water, and no other vegetation than the moss was in evidence, and as I was somewhat thirsty I determined to do a little exploring.

Springing to my feet I received my first Martian surprise, for the effort, which on Earth would have brought me standing upright, carried me into the Martian air to the height of about three yards. I alighted softly upon the ground, however, without appreciable shock or jar. Now commenced a series of evolutions which even then seemed ludicrous in the extreme. I found that I must learn to walk all over again, as the muscular exertion which carried me easily and safely upon Earth played strange antics with me upon Mars.

Instead of progressing in a sane and dignified manner, my attempts to walk resulted in a variety of hops which took me clear of the ground a couple of feet at each step and landed me sprawling upon my face or back at the end of each second or third hop. My muscles, perfectly attuned and accustomed to the force of gravity on Earth, played the mischief with me in attempting for the first time to cope with the lesser gravitation and lower air pressure on Mars.

I was determined, however, to explore the low structure which was the only evidence of habitation in sight, and so I hit upon the unique plan of reverting to first principles in locomotion, creeping. I did fairly well at this and in a few moments had reached the low, encircling wall of the enclosure.

There appeared to be no doors or windows upon the side nearest me, but as the wall was but about four feet high I cautiously gained my feet and peered over the top upon the strangest sight it had ever been given me to see.

The roof of the enclosure was of solid glass about four or five inches in thickness, and beneath this were several hundred large eggs, perfectly round and snowy white. The eggs were nearly uniform in size being about two and one-half feet in diameter.

Five or six had already hatched and the grotesque caricatures which sat blinking in the sunlight were enough to cause me to doubt my sanity. They seemed mostly head, with little scrawny bodies, long necks and six legs, or, as I afterward learned, two legs and two arms, with an intermediary pair of limbs which could be used at will either as arms or legs. Their eyes were set at the extreme sides of their heads a trifle above the center and protruded in such a manner that they could be directed either forward or back and also independently of each other, thus permitting this queer animal to look in any direction, or in two directions at once, without the necessity of turning the head.

The ears, which were slightly above the eyes and closer together, were small, cup-shaped antennae, protruding not more than an inch on these young specimens. Their noses were but longitudinal slits in the center of their faces, midway between their mouths and ears.

There was no hair on their bodies, which were of a very light yellowish-green color. In the adults, as I was to learn quite soon, this color deepens to an olive green and is darker in the male than in the female. Further, the heads of the adults are not so out of proportion to their bodies as in the case of the young.

The iris of the eyes is blood red, as in Albinos, while the pupil is dark. The eyeball itself is very white, as are the teeth. These latter add a most ferocious appearance to an otherwise fearsome and terrible countenance, as the lower tusks curve upward to sharp points which end about where the eyes of earthly human beings are located. The whiteness of the teeth is not that of ivory, but of the snowiest and most gleaming of china. Against the dark background of their olive skins their tusks stand out in a most striking manner, making these weapons present a singularly formidable appearance.

Most of these details I noted later, for I was given but little time to speculate on the wonders of my new discovery. I had seen that the eggs were in the process of hatching, and as I stood watching the hideous little monsters break from their shells I failed to note the approach of a score of full-grown Martians from behind me.

Coming, as they did, over the soft and soundless moss, which covers practically the entire surface of Mars with the exception of the frozen areas at the poles and the scattered cultivated districts, they might have captured me easily, but their intentions were far more sinister. It was the rattling of the accouterments of the foremost warrior which warned me.

On such a little thing my life hung that I often marvel that I escaped so easily. Had not the rifle of the leader of the party swung from its fastenings beside his saddle in such a way as to strike against the butt of his great metal shod spear I should have snuffed out without ever knowing that death was near me. But the little sound caused me to turn, and there upon me, not ten feet from my breast, was the point of that huge spear, a spear forty feet long, tipped with gleaming metal, and held low at the side of a mounted replica of the little devils I had been watching.

But how puny and harmless they now looked beside this huge and terrific incarnation of hate, of vengeance and of death. The man himself, for such I may call him, was fully fifteen feet in height and, on Earth, would have weighed some four hundred pounds. He sat his mount as we sit a horse, grasping the animal's barrel with his lower limbs, while the hands of his two right arms held his immense spear low at the side of his mount; his two left arms were outstretched laterally to help preserve his balance, the thing he rode having neither bridle nor reins of any description for guidance.

And his mount! How can earthly words describe it! It towered ten feet at the shoulder; had four legs on either side; a broad flat tail, larger at the tip than at the root, and which it held straight out behind while running; a gaping mouth which split its head from its snout to its long, massive neck.

Like its master, it was entirely devoid of hair, but was of a dark slate color and exceeding smooth and glossy. Its belly was white, and its legs shaded from the slate of its shoulders and hips to a vivid yellow at the feet. The feet themselves were heavily padded and nailless, which fact had also contributed to the noiselessness of their approach, and, in common with a multiplicity of legs, is a characteristic feature of the fauna of Mars. The highest type of man and one other animal, the only mammal existing on Mars, alone have well-formed nails, and there are absolutely no hoofed animals in existence there.

Behind this first charging demon trailed nineteen others, similar in all respects, but, as I learned later, bearing individual characteristics peculiar to themselves; precisely as no two of us are identical although we are all cast in a similar mold. This picture, or rather materialized nightmare, which I have described at length, made but one terrible and swift impression on me as I turned to meet it.

John Carter's earthly muscles enable him to escape this immediate danger. He is captured by the green men, however, who take him to the nearest Barsoomian city.

We had gone perhaps ten miles when the ground began to rise very rapidly. We were, as I was later to learn, nearing the edge of one of Mars' long-dead seas, in the bottom of which my encounter with the Martians had taken place.

In a short time we gained the foot of the mountains, and after traversing a narrow gorge came to an open valley, at the far extremity of which was a low table land upon which I beheld an enormous city. Toward this we galloped, entering it by what appeared to be a ruined roadway leading out from the city, but only to the edge of the table land, where it ended abruptly in a flight of broad steps.

Upon closer observation I saw as we passed them that the buildings were deserted, and while not greatly decayed had the appearance of not having been tenanted for years, possibly for ages. Toward the center of the city was a large plaza, and upon this and in the buildings immediately surrounding it were camped some nine or ten hundred creatures of the same breed as my captors, for such I now considered them despite the suave manner in which I had been trapped.

With the exception of their ornaments all were naked. The women varied in appearance but little from the men, except that their tusks were much larger in proportion to their height, in some instances curving nearly to their high-set ears. Their bodies were smaller and lighter in color, and their fingers and toes bore the rudiments of nails, which were entirely lacking among the males. The adult females ranged in height from ten to twelve feet.

The children were light in color, even lighter than the women, and all looked precisely alike to me, except that some were taller than others; older, I presumed.

I saw no signs of extreme age among them, nor is there any appreciable difference in their appearance from the age of maturity, about forty, until, at about the age of one thousand years, they go voluntarily upon their last strange pilgrimage down the river Iss, which leads no living Martian knows whither and from whose bosom no Martian has ever returned, or would be allowed to live did he return after once embarking upon its cold, dark waters.

Only about one Martian in a thousand dies of sickness or disease, and possibly about twenty take the voluntary pilgrimage. The other nine hundred and seventy-nine die violent deaths in duels, in hunting, in aviation and in war; but perhaps by far the greatest death loss comes during the age of childhood, when vast numbers of the little Martians fall victims to the great white apes of Mars.

The average life expectancy of a Martian after the age of maturity is about three hundred years, but would be nearer the one-thousand mark were it not for the various means leading to violent death. Owing to the waning resources of the planet it evidently became necessary to counteract the increasing longevity which their remarkable skill in therapeutics and surgery produced, and so human life has come to be considered but lightly on Mars, as is evidenced by their dangerous sports and the almost continual warfare between the various communities.

There are other and natural causes tending toward a diminution of population, but nothing contributes so greatly to this end as the fact that no male or female Martian is ever voluntarily without a weapon of destruction.

As we neared the plaza and my presence was discovered we were immediately surrounded by hundreds of the creatures who seemed anxious to pluck me from my seat behind my guard. A word from the leader of the party stilled their clamor, and we proceeded at a trot across the plaza to the entrance of as magnificent an edifice as mortal eye has rested upon.

The building was low, but covered an enormous area. It was constructed of gleaming white marble inlaid with gold and brilliant stones which sparkled and scintillated in the sunlight. The main entrance was some hundred feet in width and projected from the building proper to form a huge canopy above the entrance hall. There was no stairway, but a gentle incline to the first floor of the building opened into an enormous chamber encircled by galleries.

On the floor of this chamber, which was dotted with highly carved wooden desks and chairs, were assembled about forty or fifty male Martians around the steps of a rostrum. On the platform proper squatted an enormous warrior heavily loaded with metal ornaments, gay-colored feathers and beautifully wrought leather trappings ingeniously set with precious stones. From his shoulders depended a short cape of white fur lined with brilliant scarlet silk.

What struck me as most remarkable about this assemblage and the hall in which they were congregated was the fact that the creatures were entirely out of proportion to the desks, chairs, and other furnishings; these being of a size adapted to human beings such as I, whereas the great bulks of the Martians could scarcely have squeezed into the chairs, nor was there room beneath the desks for their long legs. Evidently, then, there were other denizens on Mars than the wild and grotesque creatures into whose hands I had fallen, but the evidences of extreme antiquity which showed all around me indicated that these buildings might have belonged to some long-extinct and forgotten race in the dim antiquity of Mars.

Carter soon discovers that Barsoomian mammals are viviparous whose young are raised in incubators. There are other differences. Martians are also telepathic, and Carter explains this power as he is about to join an expedition to visit one of the incubators.

I found the entire community engaged in watching or helping at the harnessing of huge mastodonian animals to great three-wheeled chariots. There were about two hundred and fifty of these vehicles, each drawn by a single animal, any one of which, from their appearance, might easily have drawn the entire wagon train when fully loaded.

The chariots themselves were large, commodious, and gorgeously decorated. In each was seated a female Martian loaded with ornaments of metal, with jewels and silks and furs, and upon the back of each of the beasts which drew the chariots was perched a young Martian driver. Like the animals upon which the warriors were mounted, the heavier draft animals wore neither bit nor bridle, but were guided entirely by telepathic means.

This power is wonderfully developed in all Martians, and accounts largely for the simplicity of their language and the relatively few spoken words exchanged even in long conversations. It is the universal language of Mars, through the medium of which the higher and lower animals of this world of paradoxes are able to communicate to a greater or less extent, depending upon the intellectual sphere of the species and the development of the individual.

As the cavalcade took up the line of march in single file, Sola dragged me into an empty chariot and we proceeded with the procession toward the point by which I had entered the city the day before. At the head of the caravan rode some two hundred warriors, five abreast, and a like number brought up the rear, while twenty-five or thirty outriders flanked us on either side.

Every one but myself—men, women, and children—were heavily armed, and at the tail of each chariot trotted a Martian hound, my own beast following closely behind ours; in fact, the faithful creature never left me voluntarily during the entire ten years I spent on Mars. Our way led out across the little valley before the city, through the hills, and down into the dead sea bottom which I had traversed on my journey from the incubator to the plaza. The incubator, as it proved, was the terminal point of our journey this day, and, as the entire cavalcade broke into a mad gallop as soon as we reached the level expanse of sea bottom, we were soon within sight of our goal.

The journey gives Burroughs another opportunity to exercise his fertile imagination, presenting his explanation of the care and education of young Martians, at least those of the green race.

The work of rearing young, green Martians consists solely in teaching them to talk, and to use the weapons of warfare with which they are loaded down from the very first year of their lives. Coming from eggs in which they have lain for five years, the period of incubation, they step forth into the world perfectly developed except in size. Entirely unknown to their own mothers, who, in turn, would have difficulty in pointing out the fathers with any degree of accuracy, they are the common children of the community, and their education devolves upon the females who chance to capture them as they leave the incubator.

Their foster mothers may not even have had an egg in the incubator, as was the case with Sola, who had not commenced to lay, until less than a year before she became the mother of another woman's offspring. But this counts for little among the green Martians, as parental and filial love is as unknown to them as it is common among us. I believe this horrible system which has been carried on for ages is the direct cause of the loss of all the finer feelings and higher humanitarian instincts among these poor creatures. From birth they know no father or mother love, they know not the meaning of the word home; they are taught that they are only suffered to live until they can demonstrate by their physique and ferocity that they are fit to live. Should they prove deformed or defective in any way they are promptly shot; nor do they see a tear shed for a single one of the many cruel hardships they pass through from earliest infancy.

I do not mean that the adult Martians are unnecessarily or intentionally cruel to the young, but theirs is a hard and pitiless struggle for existence upon a dying planet, the natural resources of which have dwindled to a point where the support of each additional life means an added tax upon the community into which it is thrown.

By careful selection they rear only the hardiest specimens of each species, and with almost supernatural foresight they regulate the birth rate to merely offset the loss by death. Each adult Martian female brings forth about thirteen eggs each year, and those which meet the size, weight, and specific gravity tests are hidden in the recesses of some subterranean vault where the temperature is too low for incubation. Every year these eggs are carefully examined by a council of twenty chieftains, and all but about one hundred of the most perfect are destroyed out of each yearly supply. At the end of five years about five hundred almost perfect eggs have been chosen from the thousands brought forth. These are then placed in the almost air-tight incubators to be hatched by the sun's rays after a period of another five years. The hatching which we had witnessed today was a fairly representative event of its kind, all but about one per cent of the eggs hatching in two days. If the remaining eggs ever hatched we knew nothing of the fate of the little Martians. They were not wanted, as their offspring might inherit and transmit the tendency to prolonged incubation, and thus upset the system which has maintained for ages and which permits the adult Martians to figure the proper time for return to the incubators, almost to an hour.

The incubators are built in remote fastnesses, where there is little or no likelihood of their being discovered by other tribes. The result of such a catastrophe would mean no children in the community for another five years. I was later to witness the results of the discovery of an alien incubator.

The community of which the green Martians with whom my lot was cast formed a part was composed of some thirty thousand souls. They roamed an enormous tract of arid and semi-arid land between forty and eighty degrees south latitude, and bounded on the east and west by two large fertile tracts. Their headquarters lay in the southwest corner of this district, near the crossing of two of the so-called Martian canals.

As the incubator had been placed far north of their own territory in a supposedly uninhabited and unfrequented area, we had before us a tremendous journey, concerning which I, of course, knew nothing.

After our return to the dead city I passed several days in comparative idleness. On the day following our return all the warriors had ridden forth early in the morning and had not returned until just before darkness fell. As I later learned, they had been to the subterranean vaults in which the eggs were kept and had transported them to the incubator, which they had then walled up for another five years, and which, in all probability, would not be visited again during that period.

The vaults which hid the eggs until they were ready for the incubator were located many miles south of the incubator, and would be visited yearly by the council of twenty chieftains. Why they did not arrange to build their vaults and incubators nearer home has always been a mystery to me, and, like many other Martian mysteries, unsolved and unsolvable by earthly reasoning and customs.

Science fiction fans—or anybody else, for that matter—who read Stanley Weinbaum's "A Martian Odyssey" for the first time are immediately impressed
with its scope, its humanity, and its modernity. Thus it comes as a shock to
many readers to learn that "A Martian Odyssey" predates even John W. Campbell's long tenure as editor of *Astounding-Analog*, having been written in 1934.
It's also sad for them to learn that Weinbaum died over twenty-five years ago,
the brilliant promise of a great writing career fulfilled only in a few stories like
"A Martian Odyssey." Yet this one tale would be enough to insure Weinbaum
science fiction immortality. It is drenched with color, realistic dialog, and characters who were not prototypes when Weinbaum created them. Most of all,
the tale boasts a most engaging Martian, the ostrichlike Tweel who is obviously much more intelligent than man because he learns more about Earthmen than we learn about him.

Stanley Weinbaum

A MARTIAN ODYSSEY

Jarvis stretched himself as luxuriously as he could in the cramped
general quarters of the *Ares*.

"Air you can breathe!" he exulted. "It feels as thick as soup
after the thin stuff out there!" He nodded at the Martian landscape
stretching flat and desolate in the light of the nearer moon, beyond the glass of the port.

The other three stared at him sympathetically—Putz, the engineer, Leroy, the biologist, and Harrison, the astronomer and captain of the expedition. Dick Jarvis was chemist of the famous crew,
the *Ares* expedition, first human beings to set foot on the mysterious neighbor of the earth, the planet Mars. This, of course, was in
the old days, less than twenty years after the mad American
Doheny perfected the atomic blast at the cost of his life, and only
a decade after the equally mad Cardoza rode on it to the moon.
They were true pioneers, these four of the *Ares*. Except for a half-
dozen moon expeditions and the ill-fated de Lancey flight aimed at
the seductive orb of Venus, they were the first men to feel other
gravity than earth's, and certainly the first successful crew to leave

the earth-moon system. And they deserved that success when one considers the difficulties and discomforts—the months spent in acclimatization chambers back on earth, learning to breathe the air as tenuous as that of Mars, the challenging of the void in the tiny rocket driven by the cranky reaction motors of the twenty-first century, and mostly the facing of an absolutely unknown world.

Jarvis stretched and fingered the raw and peeling tip of his frost-bitten nose. He sighed again contentedly.

"Well," exploded Harrison abruptly, "are we going to hear what happened? You set out all shipshape in an auxiliary rocket, we don't get a peep for ten days, and finally Putz here picks you out of a lunatic ant-heap with a freak ostrich as your pal! Spill it, man!"

"Speel?" queried Leroy perplexedly. "Speel what?"

"He means '*spiel*'," explained Putz soberly. "It iss to tell."

Jarvis met Harrison's amused glance without the shadow of a smile. "That's right, Karl," he said in grave agreement with Putz. "*Ich spiel es!*" He grunted comfortably and began.

"According to orders," he said, "I watched Karl here take off toward the North, and then I got into my flying sweat-box and headed South. You'll remember, Cap—we had orders not to land, but just scout about for points of interest. I set the two cameras clicking and buzzed along, riding pretty high—about two thousand feet—for a couple of reasons. First, it gave the cameras a greater field, and second, the under-jets travel so far in this half-vacuum they call air here that they stir up dust if you move low."

"We know all that from Putz," grunted Harrison. "I wish you'd saved the films, though. They'd have paid the cost of this junket; remember how the public mobbed the first moon pictures?"

"The films are safe," retorted Jarvis. "Well," he resumed, "as I said, I buzzed along at a pretty good clip; just as we figured, the wings haven't much lift in this air at less than a hundred miles per hour, and even then I had to use the under-jets.

"So, with the speed and the altitude and the blurring caused by the under-jets, the seeing wasn't any too good. I could see enough, though, to distinguish that what I sailed over was just more of this grey plain that we'd been examining the whole week since our landing—same blobby growths and the same eternal carpet of crawling little plant-animals, or biopods, as Leroy calls them. So I sailed along, calling back my position every hour as instructed, and not knowing whether you heard me."

"I did!" snapped Harrison.

"A hundred and fifty miles south," continued Jarvis imperturbably, "the surface changed to a sort of low plateau, nothing but desert and orange-tinted sand. I figured that we were right in our guess, then, and this grey plain we dropped on was really the Mare Cimmerium which would make my orange desert the region called Xanthus. If I were right, I ought to hit another grey plain, the Mare Chronium in another couple of hundred miles, and then another orange desert, Thyle I or II. And so I did."

"Putz verified our position a week and a half ago!" grumbled the captain. "Let's get to the point."

"Coming!" remarked Jarvis. "Twenty miles into Thyle—believe it or not—I crossed a canal!"

"Putz photographed a hundred! Let's hear something new!"

"And did he also see a city?"

"Twenty of 'em, if you call those heaps of mud cities!"

"Well," observed Jarvis, "from here on I'll be telling a few things Putz didn't see!" He rubbed his tingling nose, and continued. "I knew that I had sixteen hours of daylight at this season, so eight hours—eight hundred miles—from here, I decided to turn back. I was still over Thyle, whether I or II I'm not sure, not more than twenty-five miles into it. And right there, Putz's pet motor quit!"

"Quit? How?" Putz was solicitous.

"The atomic blast got weak. I started losing altitude right away, and suddenly there I was with a thump right in the middle of Thyle! Smashed my nose on the window, too!" He rubbed the injured member ruefully.

"Did you maybe try vashing der combustion chamber mit acid sulphuric?" inquired Putz. "Sometimes der lead giffs a secondary radiation—"

"Naw!" said Jarvis disgustedly. "I wouldn't try that, of course—not more than ten times! Besides, the bump flattened the landing gear and busted off the under-jets. Suppose I got the thing working—what then? Ten miles with the blast coming right out of the bottom and I'd have melted the floor from under me!" He rubbed his nose again. "Lucky for me a pound only weighs seven ounces here, or I'd have been mashed flat!"

"I could have fixed!" ejaculated the engineer. "I bet it vas not serious."

"Probably not," agreed Jarvis sarcastically. "Only it wouldn't fly. Nothing serious, but I had my choice of waiting to be picked up or trying to walk back—eight hundred miles, and perhaps twenty days before we had to leave! Forty miles a day! Well," he concluded, "I chose to walk. Just as much chance of being picked up, and it kept me busy."

"We'd have found you," said Harrison.

"No doubt. Anyway, I rigged up a harness from some seat straps, and put the water tank on my back, took a cartridge belt and revolver, and some iron rations, and started out."

"Water tank!" exclaimed the little biologist, Leroy. "She weigh one-quarter ton!"

"Wasn't full. Weighed about two hundred and fifty pounds earth-weight, which is eighty-five here. Then, besides, my own personal two hundred and ten pounds is only seventy on Mars, so, tank and all, I grossed a hundred and fifty-five, or fifty-five pounds less than my everyday earth-weight. I figured on that when I undertook the forty-mile daily stroll. Oh—of course I took a thermo-skin sleeping bag for these wintry Martian nights.

"Off I went, bouncing along pretty quickly. Eight hours of daylight meant twenty miles or more. It got tiresome, of course—plugging along over a soft sand desert with nothing to see, not even Leroy's crawling biopods. But an hour or so brought me to the canal—just a dry ditch about four hundred feet wide, and straight as a railroad on its own company map.

"There'd been water in it sometime, though. The ditch was covered with what looked like a nice green lawn. Only, as I approached, the lawn moved out of my way!"

"Eh?" said Leroy.

"Yeah, it was a relative of your biopods. I caught one—a little grass-like blade about as long as my finger, with two thin, stemmy legs."

"He is where?" Leroy was eager.

"He is let go! I had to move, so I plowed along with the walking grass opening in front and closing behind. And then I was out on the orange desert of Thyle again.

"I plugged steadily along, cussing the sand that made going so tiresome, and, incidentally, cussing that cranky motor of yours, Karl. It was just before twilight that I reached the edge of Thyle, and looked down over the grey Mare Chronium. And I knew there was seventy-five miles of *that* to be walked over, and then a couple of hundred miles of that Xanthus desert, and about as much more Mare Cimmerium. Was I pleased? I started cussing you fellows for not picking me up!"

"We were trying, you sap!" said Harrison.

"That didn't help. Well, I figured I might as well use what was left of daylight in getting down the cliff that bounded Thyle. I found an easy place, and down I went. Mare Chronium was just the same sort of place as this—crazy leafless plants and a bunch of crawlers; I gave it a glance and hauled out my sleeping bag. Up to that time, you know, I hadn't seen anything worth worrying about on this half-dead world—nothing dangerous, that is."

"Did you?" queried Harrison.

"*Did I!* You'll hear about it when I come to it. Well, I was just about to turn in when suddenly I heard the wildest sort of shenanigans!"

"Vot iss shenanigans?" inquired Putz.

"He says, '*Je ne sais quoi*,'" explained Leroy. "It is to say, 'I don't know what.'"

"That's right," agreed Jarvis. "I didn't know what, so I sneaked over to find out. There was a racket like a flock of crows eating a bunch of canaries—whistles, cackles, caws, trills, and what have you. I rounded a clump of stumps, and there was Tweel!"

"Tweel?" said Harrison, and "Tveel?" said Leroy and Putz.

"That freak ostrich," explained the narrator. "At least, Tweel is as near as I can pronounce it without sputtering. He called it something like 'Trrrweerrlll.'"

"What was he doing?" asked the Captain.

"He was being eaten! And squealing, of course, as any one would."

"Eaten! By what?"

"I found out later. All I could see then was a bunch of black ropy arms tangled around what looked like, as Putz described it to you, an ostrich. I wasn't going to interfere, naturally; if both creatures were dangerous, I'd have one less to worry about.

"But the bird-like thing was putting up a good battle, dealing vicious blows with an eighteen-inch beak, between screeches. And besides, I caught a glimpse or two of what was on the end of those arms!" Jarvis shuddered. "But the clincher was when I noticed a little black bag or case hung about the neck of the bird-thing! It was intelligent! That or tame, I assumed. Anyway, it clinched my decision. I pulled out my automatic and fired into what I could see of its antagonist.

"There was a flurry of tentacles and a spurt of black corruption, and then the thing, with a disgusting sucking noise, pulled itself and its arms into a hole in the ground. The other let out a series of clacks, staggered around on legs about as thick as golf sticks, and turned suddenly to face me. I held my weapon ready, and the two of us stared at each other.

"The Martian wasn't a bird, really. It wasn't even bird-like, except just at first glance. It had a beak all right, and a few feathery appendages, but the beak wasn't really a beak. It was somewhat flexible; I could see the tip bend slowly from side to side; it was almost like a cross between a beak and a trunk. It had four-toed feet, and four fingered things—hands, you'd have to call them, and a little roundish body, and a long neck ending in a tiny head—and that beak. It stood an inch or so taller than I, and—well, Putz saw it!"

The engineer nodded. "*Ja!* I saw!"

Jarvis continued. "So—we stared at each other. Finally the creature went into a series of clackings and twitterings and held out its hands toward me, empty. I took that as a gesture of friendship."

"Perhaps," suggested Harrison, "it looked at that nose of yours and thought you were its brother!"

"Huh! You can be funny without talking! Anyway, I put up my gun and said 'Aw, don't mention it,' or something of the sort, and the thing came over and we were pals.

"By that time, the sun was pretty low and I knew that I'd better build a fire or get into my thermo-skin. I decided on the fire. I picked a spot at the base of the Thyle cliff, where the rock could reflect a little heat on my back. I started breaking off chunks of this desiccated Martian vegetation, and my companion caught the idea and brought in an armful. I reached for a match, but the Martian fished into his pouch and brought out something that looked like a glowing coal; one touch of it, and the fire was blazing—and you all know what a job we have starting a fire in this atmosphere!

"And that bag of his!" continued the narrator. "That was a manufactured article, my friends; press an end and she popped open—press the middle and she sealed so perfectly you couldn't see the line. Better than zippers.

"Well, we stared at the fire a while and I decided to attempt some sort of communication with the Martian. I pointed at myself and said 'Dick'; he caught the drift immediately, stretched a bony claw at me and repeated 'Tick.' Then I pointed at him, and he gave that whistle I called Tweel; I can't imitate his accent. Things were going smoothly; to emphasize the names, I repeated 'Dick,' and then, pointing at him, 'Tweel.'

"There we stuck! He gave some clacks that sounded negative, and said something like 'P-p-p-root.' And that was just the beginning; I was always 'Tick,' but as for him—part of the time he was 'Tweel,' and part of the time he was 'P-p-p-proot,' and part of the time he was sixteen other noises!

"We just couldn't connect. I tried 'rock,' and I tried 'star,' and 'tree,' and 'fire,' and Lord knows what else, and try as I would, I couldn't get a single word! Nothing was the same for two successive minutes, and if that's a language, I'm an alchemist! Finally I gave it up and called him Tweel, and that seemed to do.

"But Tweel hung on to some of my words. He remembered a couple of them, which I suppose is a great achievement if you're used to a language you have to make up as you go along. But I couldn't get the hang of his talk; either I missed some subtle point or we just didn't *think* alike—and I rather believe the latter view.

"I've other reasons for believing that. After a while I gave up the language business, and tried mathematics. I scratched two plus two equals four on the ground, and demonstrated it with pebbles. Again Tweel caught the idea, and informed me that three plus three equals six. Once more we seemed to be getting somewhere.

"So, knowing that Tweel had at least a grammar school education, I drew a circle for the sun, pointing first at it, and then at the last glow of the sun. Then I sketched in Mercury, and Venus, and Mother Earth, and Mars, and finally, pointing to Mars, I swept my hand around in a sort of inclusive gesture to indicate that Mars was our current environment. I was working up to putting over the idea that my home was on the earth.

"Tweel understood my diagram all right. He poked his beak at it, and with a great deal of trilling and clucking, he added Deimos and Phobos to Mars, and then sketched in the earth's moon!

"Do you see what that proves? It proves that Tweel's race uses telescopes—that they're civilized!"

"Does not!" snapped Harrison. "The moon is visible from here as a fifth magnitude star. They could see its revolution with the naked eye."

"The moon, yes!" said Jarvis. "You've missed my point. Mercury isn't visible! And Tweel knew of Mercury because he placed the Moon at the *third* planet, not the second. If he didn't know Mercury, he'd put the earth second, and Mars third, instead of fourth! See?"

"Humph!" said Harrison.

"Anyway," proceeded Jarvis, "I went on with my lesson. Things were going smoothly, and it looked as if I could put the idea over. I pointed at the earth on my diagram, and then at myself, and then, to clinch it, I pointed to myself and then to the earth itself shining bright green almost at the zenith.

"Tweel set up such an excited clacking that I was certain he understood. He jumped up and down, and suddenly he pointed at himself and then at the sky, and then at himself and at the sky again. He pointed at his middle and then at Arcturus, at his head and then at Spica, at his feet and then at half a dozen stars, while I just gaped at him. Then, all of a sudden, he gave a tremendous leap. Man, what a hop! He shot straight up into the starlight, seventy-five feet if an inch! I saw him silhouetted against the sky, saw him turn and come down at me head first, and land smack on his beak like a javelin! There he stuck square in the center of my sun-circle in the sand—a bull's eye!"

"Nuts!" observed the captain. "Plain nuts!"

"That's what I thought, too! I just stared at him open-mouthed while he pulled his head out of the sand and stood up. Then I figured he'd missed my point, and I went through the whole blamed rigamarole again, and it ended the same way, with Tweel on his nose in the middle of my picture!"

"Maybe it's a religious rite," suggested Harrison.

"Maybe," said Jarvis dubiously. "Well, there we were. We could exchange ideas up to a certain point, and then—blooey! Something in us was different, unrelated; I don't doubt that Tweel thought me just as screwy as I thought him. Our minds simply looked at the world from different viewpoints, and perhaps his viewpoint is as true as ours. But—we couldn't get together, that's all. Yet, in spite of all difficulties, I *liked* Tweel, and I have a queer certainty that he liked me."

"Nuts!" repeated the captain. "Just daffy!"

"Yeah? Wait and see. A couple of times I've thought that perhaps we—" He paused, and then resumed his narrative. "Anyway, I finally gave it up, and got into my thermo-skin to sleep. The fire hadn't kept me any too warm, but that damned sleeping bag did. Got stuffy five minutes after I closed myself in. I opened it a little and bingo! Some eighty-below-zero air hit my nose, and that's when I got this pleasant little frostbite to add to the bump I acquired during the crash of my rocket.

"I don't know what Tweel made of my sleeping. He sat around, but when I woke up, he was gone. I'd just crawled out of my bag, though, when I heard some twittering, and there he came, sailing down from that three-story Thyle cliff to alight on his beak beside me. I pointed to myself and toward the north, and he pointed at himself and toward the south, but when I loaded up and started away, he came along.

"Man, how he traveled! A hundred and fifty feet at a jump, sailing through the air stretched out like a spear, and landing on his beak. He seemed surprised at my plodding, but after a few moments he fell in beside me, only every few minutes he'd go into one of his leaps, and stick his nose into the sand a block ahead of me. Then he'd come shooting back at me; it made me nervous at first to see that beak of his coming at me like a spear, but he always ended in the sand at my side.

"So the two of us plugged along across the Mare Chronium. Same sort of place as this—same crazy plants and same little green biopods growing in the sand, or crawling out of your way. We talked—not that we understood each other, you know, but just for company. I sang songs, and I suspect Tweel did too; at least, some of his trillings and twitterings had a subtle sort of rhythm.

"Then, for variety, Tweel would display his smattering of English words. He'd point to an outcropping and say 'rock,' and point to a pebble and say it again; or he'd touch my arm and say 'Tick,' and then repeat it. He seemed terrifically amused that the same word meant the same thing twice in succession, or that the same word could apply to two different objects. It set me wondering if perhaps his language wasn't like the primitive speech of some earth people—you know, Captain, like the Negritoes, for instance, who haven't any generic words. No word for food or water or man —words for good food and bad food, or rain water and sea water, or strong man and weak man—but no names for general classes. They're too primitive to understand that rain water and sea water are just different aspects of the same thing. But that wasn't the case with Tweel; it was just that we were somehow mysteriously different—our minds were alien to each other. And yet—we *liked* each other!"

"Looney, that's all," remarked Harrison. "That's why you two were so fond of each other."

"Well, I like *you!*" countered Jarvis wickedly. "Anyway," he resumed, "don't get the idea that there was anything screwy about Tweel. In fact, I'm not so sure but that he couldn't teach our highly praised human intelligence a trick or two. Oh, he wasn't an intellectual superman, I guess; but don't overlook the point that he managed to understand a little of my mental workings, and I never even got a glimmering of his."

"Because he didn't have any!" suggested the captain, while Putz and Leroy blinked attentively.

"You can judge of that when I'm through," said Jarvis. "Well,

we plugged along across the Mare Chronium all that day, and all
the next. Mare Chronium—Sea of Time! Say, I was willing to
agree with Schiaparelli's name by the end of that march! Just that
grey, endless plain of weird plants, and never a sign of any other
life. It was so monotonous that I was even glad to see the desert
of Xanthus toward the evening of the second day.

"I was fair worn out, but Tweel seemed as fresh as ever, for all
I never saw him drink or eat. I think he could have crossed the
Mare Chronium in a couple of hours with those block-long nose
dives of his, but he stuck along with me. I offered him some water
once or twice; he took the cup from me and sucked the liquid
into his beak, and then carefully squirted it all back into the cup
and gravely returned it.

"Just as we sighted Xanthus, or the cliffs that bounded it, one of
those nasty sand clouds blew along, not as bad as the one we had
here, but mean to travel against. I pulled the transparent flap of
my thermo-skin bag across my face and managed pretty well, and
I noticed that Tweel used some feathery appendages growing like
a mustache at the base of his beak to cover his nostrils, and some
similar fuzz to shield his eyes."

"He is a desert creature!" ejaculated the little biologist, Leroy.

"Huh? Why?"

"He drink no water—he is adapt' for sand storm—"

"Proves nothing! There's not enough water to waste any
where on this desiccated pill called Mars. We'd call all of it desert
on earth, you know." He paused. "Anyway, after the sand storm
blew over, a little wind kept blowing in our faces, not strong
enough to stir the sand. But suddenly things came drifting along
from the Xanthus cliffs—small, transparent spheres, for all the
world like glass tennis balls! But light—they were almost light
enough to float even in this thin air—empty, too; at least, I cracked
open a couple and nothing came out but a bad smell. I asked
Tweel about them, but all he said was 'No, no, no,' which I took
to mean that he knew nothing about them. So they went bouncing by like tumbleweeds, or like soap bubbles, and we plugged
on toward Xanthus. Tweel pointed at one of the crystal balls once
and said 'rock,' but I was too tired to argue with him. Later I discovered what he meant.

"We came to the bottom of the Xanthus cliffs finally, when there wasn't much daylight left. I decided to sleep on the plateau if possible; anything dangerous, I reasoned, would be more likely to prowl through the vegetation of the Mare Chronium than the sand of Xanthus. Not that I'd seen a single sign of menace, except the rope-armed black thing that had trapped Tweel, and it apparently didn't prowl at all, but lured its victims within reach. It couldn't lure me while I slept, especially as Tweel didn't seem to sleep at all, but simply sat patiently around all night. I wondered how the creature had managed to trap Tweel, but there wasn't any way of asking him. I found that out too, later; it's devilish!

"However, we were ambling around the base of the Xanthus barrier looking for an easy spot to climb. At least, I was. Tweel could have leaped it easily, for the cliffs were lower than Thyle—perhaps sixty feet. I found a place and started up, swearing at the water tank strapped to my back—it didn't bother me except when climbing—and suddenly I heard a sound that I thought I recognized!

"You know how deceptive sounds are in this thin air. A shot sounds like the pop of a cork. But this sound was the drone of a rocket, and sure enough, there went our second auxiliary about ten miles to westward, between me and the sunset!"

"Vas me!" said Putz. "I hunt for you."

"Yeah; I knew that, but what good did it do me? I hung on to the cliff and yelled and waved with one hand. Tweel saw it too, and set up a trilling and twittering, leaping to the top of the barrier and then high into the air. And while I watched, the machine droned on into the shadows to the south.

"I scrambled to the top of the cliff. Tweel was still pointing and trilling excitedly, shooting up toward the sky and coming down head-on to stick upside down on his beak in the sand. I pointed toward the south and at myself, and he said, 'Yes—Yes —Yes'; but somehow I gathered that he thought the flying thing was a relative of mine, probably a parent. Perhaps I did his intellect an injustice; I think now that I did.

"I was bitterly disappointed by the failure to attract attention. I pulled out my thermo-skin bag and crawled into it, as the night chill was already apparent. Tweel stuck his beak into the sand and drew up his legs and arms and looked for all the world like one of those leafless shrubs out there. I think he stayed that way all night."

"Protective mimicry!" ejaculated Leroy. "See? He is desert creature!"

"In the morning," resumed Jarvis, "we started off again. We hadn't gone a hundred yards into Xanthus when I saw something queer! This is one thing Putz didn't photograph, I'll wager!

"There was a line of little pyramids—tiny ones, not more than six inches high, stretching across Xanthus as far as I could see! Little buildings made of pygmy bricks, they were, hollow inside and truncated, or at least broken at the top and empty. I pointed at them and said 'What?' to Tweel, but he gave some negative twitters to indicate, I suppose, that he didn't know. So off we went, following the row of pyramids because they ran north, and I was going north.

"Man, we trailed that line for hours! After a while, I noticed another queer thing: they were getting larger. Same number of bricks in each one, but the bricks were larger.

"By noon they were shoulder high. I looked into a couple—all just the same, broken at the top and empty. I examined a brick or two as well; they were silica, and old as creation itself!"

"How you know?" asked Leroy.

"They were weathered—edges rounded. Silica doesn't weather easily even on earth, and in this climate—!"

"How old you think?"

"Fifty thousand—a hundred thousand years. How can I tell? The little ones we saw in the morning were older—perhaps ten times as old. Crumbling. How old would that make *them*? Half a million years? Who knows?" Jarvis paused a moment. "Well," he resumed, "we followed the line. Tweel pointed at them and said 'rock' once or twice, but he'd done that many times before. Besides, he was more or less right about these.

"I tried questioning him. I pointed at a pyramid and asked 'People?' and indicated the two of us. He set up a negative sort of clucking and said, 'No, no, no. No one-one-two. No two-two-four,' meanwhile rubbing his stomach. I just stared at him and he went through the business again. 'No one-one-two. No two-two-four.' I just gaped at him."

"That proves it!" exclaimed Harrison. "Nuts!"

"You think so?" queried Jarvis sardonically. "Well, I figured it out different! 'No one-one-two!' You don't get it, of course, do you?"

"Nope—nor do you!"

"I think I do! Tweel was using the few English words he knew to put over a very complex idea. What, let me ask, does mathematics make you think of?"

"Why—of astronomy. Or—or logic!"

"That's it! 'No one-one-two!' Tweel was telling me that the builders of the pyramids weren't people—or that they weren't intelligent, that they weren't reasoning creatures! Get it?"

"Huh! I'll be damned!"

"You probably will."

"Why," put in Leroy, "he rub his belly?"

"Why? Because, my dear biologist, that's where his brains are! Not in his tiny head—in his middle!"

"*C'est impossible!*"

"Not on Mars, it isn't! This flora and fauna aren't earthly; your biopods prove that!" Jarvis grinned and took up his narrative. "Anyway, we plugged along across Xanthus and in about the middle of the afternoon, something else queer happened. The pyramids ended."

"Ended!"

"Yeah; the queer part was that the last one—and now they were ten-footers—was capped! See? Whatever built it was still inside; we'd trailed 'em from their half-million-year-old origin to the present.

"Tweel and I noticed it about the same time. I yanked out my automatic (I had a clip of Boland explosive bullets in it) and Tweel, quick as a sleight-of-hand trick, snapped a queer little glass revolver out of his bag. It was much like our weapons, except that the grip was larger to accommodate his four-taloned hand. And we held our weapons ready while we sneaked up along the lines of empty pyramids.

"Tweel saw the movement first. The top tiers of bricks were

heaving, shaking, and suddenly slid down the sides with a thin crash. And then—something—something was coming out!

"A long, silvery-grey arm appeared, dragging after it an armored body. Armored, I mean, with scales, silver-grey and dull-shining. The arm heaved the body out of the hole; the beast crashed to the sand.

"It was a nondescript creature—body like a big grey cask, arm and a sort of mouth-hole at one end; stiff, pointed tail at the other—and that's all. No other limbs, no eyes, ears, nose—nothing! The thing dragged itself a few yards, inserted its pointed tail in the sand, pushed itself upright, and just sat.

"Tweel and I watched it for ten minutes before it moved. Then, with a creaking and rustling like—oh, like crumpling stiff paper —its arm moved to the mouth-hole and out came a brick! The arm placed the brick carefully on the ground, and the thing was still again.

"Another ten minutes—another brick. Just one of Nature's bricklayers. I was about to slip away and move on when Tweel pointed at the thing and said 'rock'! I went 'huh?' and he said it again. Then, to the accompaniment of some of his trilling, he said, 'No—no—,' and gave two or three whistling breaths.

"Well, I got his meaning, for a wonder! I said, 'No breath?' and demonstrated the word. Tweel was ecstatic; he said, 'Yes, yes, yes! No, no, no breet!' Then he gave a leap and sailed out to land on his nose about one pace from the monster!

"I was startled, you can imagine! The arm was going up for a brick, and I expected to see Tweel caught and mangled, but— nothing happened! Tweel pounded on the creature, and the arm took the brick and placed it neatly beside the first. Tweel rapped on its body again, and said 'rock,' and I got up nerve enough to take a look myself.

"Tweel was right again. The creature *was* rock, and it didn't breathe!"

"How you know?" snapped Leroy, his black eyes blazing interest.

"Because I'm a chemist. The beast was made of silica! There must have been pure silicon in the sand, and it lived on that. Get it? We, and Tweel, and those plants out there, and even the biopods are *carbon* life; this thing lived by a different set of chemical reactions. It was silicon life!"

"*La vie silicieuse!*" shouted Leroy. "I have suspect, and now it is proof! I must go see! *Il faut que je—*"

"All right! All right!" said Jarvis. "You can go see. Anyhow, there the thing was, alive and yet not alive, moving every ten minutes, and then only to remove a brick. Those bricks were its waste matter. See, Frenchy? We're carbon, and our waste is carbon dioxide, and this thing is silicon, and *its* waste is silicon dioxide —silica. But silica is a solid, hence the bricks. And it builds itself in, and when it is covered, it moves over to a fresh place to start over. No wonder it creaked! A living creature half a million years old!"

"How you know how old?" Leroy was frantic.

"We trailed its pyramids from the beginning, didn't we? If this weren't the original pyramid builder, the series would have ended somewhere before we found him, wouldn't it?—ended and started over with the small ones. That's simple enough, isn't it?

"But he reproduces, or tries to. Before the third brick came out, there was a little rustle and out popped a whole stream of those little crystal balls. They're his spores, or eggs, or seeds—call 'em what you want. They went bouncing by across Xanthus just as they'd bounced by us back in the Mare Chronium. I've a hunch how they work, too—this is for your information, Leroy. I think the crystal shell of silica is no more than a protective covering, like an eggshell, and that the active principle is the smell inside. It's some sort of gas that attacks silicon, and if the shell is broken near a supply of that element, some reaction starts that ultimately develops into a beast like that one."

"You should try!" exclaimed the little Frenchman. "We must break one to see!"

"Yeah? Well, I did. I smashed a couple against the sand. Would you like to come back in about ten thousand years to see if I planted some pyramid monsters? You'd most likely be able to tell by that time!" Jarvis paused and drew a deep breath. "Lord! That queer creature! Do you picture it? Blind, deaf, nerveless, brainless—just a mechanism, and yet—immortal! Bound to go on making bricks, building pyramids, as long as silicon and oxygen exist, and even afterwards it'll just stop. It won't be dead. If the accidents of a million years bring it its food again, there it'll be, ready to run again, while brains and civilizations are part of the past. A queer beast—yet I met a stranger one!"

"If you did, it must have been in your dreams!" growled Harrison.

"You're right!" said Jarvis soberly. "In a way, you're right. The dream-beast! That's the best name for it—and it's the most fiendish, terrifying creation one could imagine! More dangerous than a lion, more insidious than a snake!"

"Tell me!" begged Leroy. "I must go see!"

"Not *this* devil!" He paused again. "Well," he resumed, "Tweel and I left the pyramid creature and plowed along through Xanthus. I was tired and a little disheartened by Putz's failure to pick me up, and Tweel's trilling got on my nerves, as did his flying nosedives. So I just strode along without a word, hour after hour across that monotonous desert.

"Toward mid-afternoon we came in sight of a low dark line on the horizon. I knew what it was. It was a canal; I'd crossed it in the rocket and it meant that we were just one-third of the way across Xanthus. Pleasant thought, wasn't it? And still, I was keeping up to schedule.

"We approached the canal slowly; I remembered that this one was bordered by a wide fringe of vegetation and that Mudheap City was on it.

"I was tired, as I said. I kept thinking of a good hot meal, and then from that I jumped to reflections of how nice and home-like even Borneo would seem after this crazy planet, and from that, to thoughts of little old New York, and then to thinking about a girl I know there—Fancy Long. Know her?"

"Vision entertainer," said Harrison. "I've tuned her in. Nice blonde—dances and sings on the *Yerba Mate* hour."

"That's her," said Jarvis ungrammatically. "I know her pretty well—just friends, get me?—though she came down to see us off in the *Ares*. Well, I was thinking about her, feeling pretty lonesome, and all the time we were approaching that line of rubbery plants.

"And then—I said, 'What 'n Hell!' and stared. And there she

was—Fancy Long, standing plain as day under one of those crack-brained trees, and smiling and waving just the way I remembered her when we left!"

"Now you're nuts, too!" observed the captain.

"Boy, I almost agreed with you! I stared and pinched myself and closed my eyes and then stared again—and every time, there was Fancy Long smiling and waving! Tweel saw something, too; he was trilling and clucking away, but I scarcely heard him. I was bounding toward her over the sand, too amazed even to ask myself questions.

"I wasn't twenty feet from her when Tweel caught me with one of his flying leaps. He grabbed my arm, yelling, 'No—no—no!' in his squeaky voice. I tried to shake him off—he was as light as if he were built of bamboo—but he dug his claws in and yelled. And finally some sort of sanity returned to me and I stopped less than ten feet from her. There she stood, looking as solid as Putz's head!"

"Vot?" said the engineer.

"She smiled and waved, and waved and smiled, and I stood there dumb as Leroy, while Tweel squeaked and chattered. I *knew* it couldn't be real, yet—there she was!

"Finally I said, 'Fancy! Fancy Long!' She just kept on smiling and waving, but looking as real as if I hadn't left her thirty-seven million miles away.

"Tweel had his glass pistol out, pointing it at her. I grabbed his arm, but he tried to push me away. He pointed at her and said, 'No breet! No breet!' and I understood that he meant that the Fancy Long thing wasn't alive. Man, my head was whirling!

"Still, it gave me the jitters to see him pointing his weapon at her. I don't know why I stood there watching him take careful aim, but I did. Then he squeezed the handle of his weapon; there was a little puff of steam, and Fancy Long was gone! And in her place was one of those writhing, black, rope-armed horrors like the one I'd saved Tweel from!

"The dream-beast! I stood there dizzy, watching it die while Tweel trilled and whistled. Finally he touched my arm, pointed at the twisting thing, and said, 'You one-one-two, he one-one-two.' After he'd repeated it eight or ten times, I got it. Do any of you?"

"*Oui!*" shrilled Leroy. "*Moi—je le comprends!* He mean you think of something, the beast he know, and you see it! *Un chien* —a hungry dog, he would see the big bone with meat! Or smell it —not?"

"Right!" said Jarvis. "The dream-beast uses its victim's longings and desires to trap its prey. The bird at nesting season would see its mate, the fox, prowling for its own prey, would see a helpless rabbit!"

"How he do?" queried Leroy.

"How do I know? How does a snake back on earth charm a bird into its very jaws? And aren't there deep-sea fish that lure their victims into their mouths? Lord!" Jarvis shuddered. "Do you see how insidious the monster is? We're warned now—but henceforth we can't trust even our eyes. You might see me—I might see one of you—and back of it may be nothing but another of those black horrors!"

"How'd your friend know?" asked the captain abruptly.

"Tweel? I wonder! Perhaps he was thinking of something that couldn't possibly have interested me, and when I started to run, he realized that I saw something different and was warned. Or perhaps the dream-beast can only project a single vision, and Tweel saw what I saw—or nothing. I couldn't ask him. But it's just another proof that his intelligence is equal to ours or greater."

"He's daffy, I tell you!" said Harrison. "What makes you think his intellect ranks with the human?"

"Plenty of things! First, the pyramid-beast. He hadn't seen one before; he said as much. Yet he recognized it as a dead-alive automaton of silicon."

"He could have heard of it," objected Harrison. "He lives around here, you know."

"Well how about the language? I couldn't pick up a single idea of his and he learned six or seven words of mine. And do you realize what complex ideas he put over with no more than those six or seven words? The pyramid-monster—the dream-beast! In a single phrase he told me that one was a harmless automaton and the other a deadly hypnotist. What about that?"

"Huh!" said the captain.

"*Huh* if you wish! Could you have done it knowing only six words of English? Could you go even further, as Tweel did, and tell me that another creature was of a sort of intelligence so different from ours that understanding was impossible—even more impossible than that between Tweel and me?"

"Eh? What was that?"

"Later. The point I'm making is that Tweel and his race are worthy of our friendship. Somewhere on Mars—and you'll find I'm right—is a civilization and culture equal to ours, and maybe more than equal. And communication is possible between them and us; Tweel proves that. It may take years of patient trial, for their minds are alien, but less alien than the next minds we encountered—if they *are* minds."

"The next ones? What next ones?"

"The people of the mud cities along the canals." Jarvis frowned, then resumed his narrative. "I thought the dream-beast and the silicon-monster were the strangest beings conceivable, but I was wrong. These creatures are still more alien, less understandable than either and far less comprehensible than Tweel, with whom friendship is possible, and even, by patience and concentration, the exchange of ideas.

"Well," he continued, "we left the dream-beast dying, dragging itself back into its hole, and we moved toward the canal. There was a carpet of that queer walking-grass scampering out of our way, and when we reached the bank, there was a yellow trickle of water flowing. The mound city I'd noticed from the rocket was a mile or so to the right and I was curious enough to want to take a look at it.

"It had seemed deserted from my previous glimpse of it, and if any creatures were lurking in it—well, Tweel and I were both armed. And by the way, that crystal weapon of Tweel's was an interesting device; I took a look at it after the dream-beast episode. It fired a little glass splinter, poisoned, I suppose, and I guess it held at least a hundred of 'em to a load. The propellent was steam—just plain steam!"

"Shteam!" echoed Putz. "From vot come, shteam?"

"From water, of course! You could see the water through the transparent handle and about a gill of another liquid, thick and yellowish. When Tweel squeezed the handle—there was no trigger—a drop of water and a drop of the yellow stuff squirted into the firing chamber, and the water vaporized—pop!—like that. It's not so difficult; I think we could develop the same principle. Concentrated sulphuric acid will heat water almost to boiling, and so will quicklime, and there's potassium and sodium—

"Of course, his weapon hadn't the range of mine, but it wasn't so bad in this thin air, and it *did* hold as many shots as a cowboy's gun in a Western movie. It was effective, too, at least against Martian life; I tried it out, aiming at one of the crazy plants, and darned if the plant didn't wither up and fall apart! That's why I think the glass splinters were poisoned.

"Anyway, we trudged along toward the mud-heap city and I began to wonder whether the city builders dug the canals. I pointed to the city and then at the canal, and Tweel said 'No—no—no!' and gestured toward the south. I took it to mean that some other race had created the canal system, perhaps Tweel's people. I don't know; maybe there's still another intelligent race on the planet, or a dozen others. Mars is a queer little world.

"A hundred yards from the city we crossed a sort of road—just a hard-packed mud trail, and then, all of a sudden, along came one of the mound builders!

"Man, talk about fantastic beings! It looked rather like a barrel trotting along on four legs with four other arms or tentacles. It had no head, just body and members and a row of eyes completely around it. The top end of the barrel-body was a diaphragm stretched as tight as a drum head, and that was all. It was pushing a little coppery cart and tore right past us like the proverbial bat out of Hell. It didn't even notice us, although I thought the eyes on my side shifted a little as it passed.

"A moment later another came along, pushing another empty cart. Same thing—it just scooted past us. Well, I wasn't going to be ignored by a bunch of barrels playing train, so when the third one approached, I planted myself in the way—ready to jump, of course, if the thing didn't stop.

"But it did. It stopped and set up a sort of drumming from the diaphragm on top. And I held out both hands and said, 'We are friends!' And what do you suppose the thing did?"

"Said, 'Pleased to meet you,' I'll bet!" suggested Harrison.

"I couldn't have been more surprised if it had! It drummed on its diaphragm, and then suddenly boomed out, 'We are v-r-r-riends!' and gave its pushcart a vicious poke at me! I jumped aside, and away it went while I stared dumbly after it.

"A minute later another one came hurrying along. This one didn't pause, but simply drummed out, 'We are v-r-r-riends!' and scurried by. How did it learn the phrase? Were all of the creatures in some sort of communication with each other? Were they all parts of some central organism? I don't know, though I think Tweel does.

"Anyway, the creatures went sailing past us, every one greeting us with the same statement. It got to be funny; I never thought to find so many friends on this God-forsaken ball! Finally I made a puzzled gesture to Tweel; I guess he understood, for he said, 'One-one-two—yes!—two-two-four—no!' Get it?"

"Sure," said Harrison. "It's a Martian nursery rhyme."

"Yeah! Well, I was getting used to Tweel's symbolism, and I figured it out this way. 'One-one-two—yes!' The creatures were intelligent. 'Two-two-four—no!' Their intelligence was not of our order, but something different and beyond the logic of two and two is four. Maybe I missed his meaning. Perhaps he meant that their minds were of low degree, able to figure out the simple things—'One-one-two—yes!'—but not more difficult things—'Two-two-four—no!' But I think from what we saw later that he meant the other.

"After a few moments, the creatures came rushing back—first one, then another. Their pushcarts were full of stones, sand, chunks of rubbery plants, and such rubbish as that. They droned out their friendly greeting, which didn't really sound so friendly, and dashed on. The third one I assumed to be my first acquaintance and I decided to have another chat with him. I stepped into his path again and waited.

"Up he came, booming out his 'We are v-r-r-riends' and stopped. I looked at him; four or five of his eyes looked at me. He tried his password again and gave a shove on his cart, but I stood firm. And then the—the dashed creature reached out one of his arms, and two finger-like nippers tweaked my nose!"

"Haw!" roared Harrison. "Maybe the things have a sense of beauty!"

"Laugh!" grumbled Jarvis. "I'd already had a nasty bump and a mean frostbite on that nose. Anyway, I yelled 'Ouch!' and jumped aside and the creature dashed away; but from then on, their greeting was 'We are v-r-r-riends! Ouch!' Queer beasts!

"Tweel and I followed the road squarely up to the nearest mound. The creatures were coming and going, paying us not the slightest attention, fetching their loads of rubbish. The road simply dived into an opening, and slanted down like an old mine, and in and out darted the barrel-people, greeting us with their eternal phrase.

"I looked in; there was a light somewhere below, and I was curious to see it. It didn't look like a flame or torch, you understand, but more like a civilized light, and I thought that I might get some clue as to the creatures' development. So in I went and Tweel tagged along, not without a few trills and twitters, however.

"The light was curious; it sputtered and flared like an old arc light, but came from a single black rod set in the wall of the corridor. It was electric, beyond doubt. The creatures were fairly civilized, apparently.

"Then I saw another light shining on something that glittered and I went on to look at that, but it was only a heap of shiny sand. I turned toward the entrance to leave, and the Devil take me if it wasn't gone!

"I suppose the corridor had curved, or I'd stepped into a side passage. Anyway, I walked back in that direction I thought we'd come, and all I saw was more dimlit corridor. The place was a labyrinth! There was nothing but twisting passages running every way, lit by occasional lights, and now and then a creature running by, sometimes with a pushcart, sometimes without.

"Well, I wasn't much worried at first. Tweel and I had only come a few steps from the entrance. But every move we made after that seemed to get us in deeper. Finally I tried following one of the creatures with an empty cart, thinking that he'd be going out for his rubbish, but he ran around aimlessly, into one passage and out another. When he started dashing around a pillar like one of these Japanese waltzing mice, I gave up, dumped my water tank on the floor, and sat down.

"Tweel was as lost as I. I pointed up and he said 'No—no—no!' in a sort of helpless trill. And we couldn't get any help from the natives. They paid no attention at all, except to assure us they were friends—ouch!

"Lord! I don't know how many hours or days we wandered around there! I slept twice from sheer exhaustion; Tweel never seemed to need sleep. We tried following only the upward corridors, but they'd run uphill a ways and then curve downwards. The temperature in that damned ant hill was constant; you couldn't tell night from day and after my first sleep I didn't know whether I'd slept one hour or thirteen, so I couldn't tell from my watch whether it was midnight or noon.

"We saw plenty of strange things. There were machines running in some of the corridors, but they didn't seem to be doing anything—just wheels turning. And several times I saw two barrel-beasts with a little one growing between them, joined to both."

"Parthenogenesis!" exulted Leroy. "Parthenogenesis by budding like *les tulipes!*"

"If you say so, Frenchy," agreed Jarvis. "The things never noticed us at all, except, as I say, to greet us with 'We are v-r-r-riends! Ouch!' They seemed to have no home-life of any sort, but just scurried around with their pushcarts, bringing in rubbish. And finally I discovered what they did with it.

"We'd had a little luck with a corridor, one that slanted upwards for a great distance. I was feeling that we ought to be close to the surface when suddenly the passage debouched into a domed chamber, the only one we'd seen. And man!—I felt like dancing when I saw what looked like daylight through a crevice in the roof.

"There was a—a sort of machine in the chamber, just an enormous wheel that turned slowly, and one of the creatures was in the act of dumping his rubbish below it. The wheel ground it with a crunch—sand, stones, plants, all into powder that sifted away somewhere. While we watched, others filed in, repeating the process, and that seemed to be all. No rhyme nor reason to the whole thing—but that's characteristic of this crazy planet. And there was another fact that's almost too bizarre to believe.

"One of the creatures, having dumped his load, pushed his cart aside with a crash and calmly shoved himself under the wheel! I watched him being crushed, too stupefied to make a sound, and a moment later, another followed him! They were perfectly methodical about it, too; one of the cartless creatures took the abandoned pushcart.

"Tweel didn't seem surprised; I pointed out the next suicide to him, and he just gave the most human-like shrug imaginable, as much as to say, 'What can I do about it?' He must have known more or less about these creatures.

"Then I saw something else. There was something beyond the wheel, something shining on a sort of low pedestal. I walked over; there was a little crystal about the size of an egg, fluorescing to beat Tophet. The light from it stung my hands and face, almost like a static discharge, and then I noticed another funny thing. Remember that wart I had on my left thumb? Look!" Jarvis extended his hand. "It dried up and fell off—just like that! And my abused nose—say, the pain went out of it like magic! The thing had the property of hard ex-rays or gamma radiations, only more so; it destroyed diseased tissue and left healthy tissue unharmed!

"I was thinking what a present *that'd* be to take back to Mother Earth when a lot of racket interrupted. We dashed back to the other side of the wheel in time to see one of the pushcarts ground up. Some suicide had been careless, it seems.

"Then suddenly the creatures were booming and drumming all around us and their noise was decidedly menacing. A crowd of them advanced toward us; we backed out of what I thought was the passage we'd entered by, and they came rumbling after us, some pushing carts and some not. Crazy brutes! There was a whole chorus of 'We are v-r-r-riends! Ouch!' I didn't like the 'ouch'; it was rather suggestive.

"Tweel had his glass gun out and I dumped my water tank for greater freedom and got mine. We backed up the corridor with the barrel-beasts following—about twenty of them. Queer thing—the ones coming in with loaded carts moved past us inches away without a sign.

"Tweel must have noticed that. Suddenly, he snatched out that glowing coal cigar-lighter of his and touched a cart-load of plant limbs. Puff! The whole load was burning—and the crazy beast pushing it went right along without a change of pace! It created some disturbance among our 'v-r-r-riends,' however—and then I noticed the smoke eddying and swirling past us, and sure enough, there was the entrance!

"I grabbed Tweel and out we dashed and after us our twenty pursuers. The daylight felt like Heaven, though I saw at first glance that the sun was all but set, and that was bad, since I couldn't live outside my thermo-skin bag in a Martian night—at least, without a fire.

"And things got worse in a hurry. They cornered us in an angle between two mounds, and there we stood. I hadn't fired nor had Tweel; there wasn't any use in irritating the brutes. They stopped a little distance away and began their booming about friendship and ouches.

"Then things got still worse! A barrel-brute came out with a pushcart and they all grabbed into it and came out with handfuls of foot-long copper darts—sharp-looking ones—and all of a sudden one sailed past my ear—zing! And it was shoot or die then.

"We were doing pretty well for a while. We picked off the ones next to the pushcart and managed to keep the darts at a minimum, but suddenly there was a thunderous booming of 'v-r-r-riends' and 'ouches,' and a whole army of 'em came out of their hole.

"Man! We were through and I knew it! Then I realized that Tweel wasn't. He could have leaped the mound behind us as easily as not. He was staying for me!

"Say, I could have cried if there'd been time! I'd liked Tweel from the first, but whether I'd have had gratitude to do what he was doing—suppose I *had* saved him from the first dream-beast—he'd done as much for me, hadn't he? I grabbed his arm, and said 'Tweel,' and pointed up, and he understood. He said, 'No—no—no, Tick!' and popped away with his glass pistol.

"What could I do? I'd be a goner anyway when the sun set, but I couldn't explain that to him. I said, 'Thanks, Tweel. You're a man!' and felt that I wasn't paying him any compliment at all. A man! There are mighty few men who'd do that.

"So I went 'bang' with my gun and Tweel went 'puff' with his, and the barrels were throwing darts and getting ready to rush us, and booming about being friends. I had given up hope. Then suddenly an angel dropped right down from Heaven in the shape of Putz, with his under-jets blasting the barrels into very small pieces!

"Wow! I let out a yell and dashed for the rocket; Putz opened the door and in I went, laughing and crying and shouting! It was a moment or so before I remembered Tweel; I looked around in time to see him rising in one of his nosedives over the mound and away.

"I had a devil of a job arguing Putz into following! By the time we got the rocket aloft, darkness was down; you know how it comes here—like turning off a light. We sailed out over the desert and put down once or twice. I yelled 'Tweel!' and yelled it a hundred times, I guess. We couldn't find him; he could travel like the wind and all I got—or else I imagined it—was a faint trilling and twittering drifting out of the south. He'd gone, and damn it! I wish—I wish he hadn't!"

The four men of the *Ares* were silent—even the sardonic Harrison. At last little Leroy broke the stillness.

"I should like to see," he murmured.

"Yeah," said Harrison. "And the wart-cure. Too bad you missed that; it might be the cancer cure they've been hunting for a century and a half."

"Oh, that!" muttered Jarvis gloomily. "That's what started the fight!" He drew a glistening object from his pocket.

"Here it is."

Donald Wollheim is one of the most respected editors and writers in the entire science fiction field. His editorial abilities as an anthologist and a director of Ace paperbacks have overshadowed his talents as a writer. This little story, "The Embassy," is an example of a classic science fiction yarn. It has pace, complications, just enough gimmickry to sustain it, and a surprise ending worthy of O. Henry. All in all, reading "The Embassy" makes you wish there were two Wollheims, one to edit and one to write.

Donald A. Wollheim

THE EMBASSY

"I came to New York," said Grafius, "because I am sure that there are Martians here." He leaned back to blow a smoke ring, followed it to its dissolution in the air-conditioning outlet with his cool, gray eyes.

"Iron Man!" bawled Broderick, quick as the snap of a relay. He backed around behind his chair as the office door opened and the formidable Mr. Doolan appeared, fists cocked on the ready.

"It's a whack," declared Broderick, pointing at Grafius. "It says there are Martians in New York."

Doolan, probably the most muscular, certainly the dumbest, cop ever kicked out of the police department, eyed Grafius dimly as he clamped the caller's shoulder in a colossal vise of a hand. "Make with the feet," he said, groping for his words. "Hit the main, but heavy."

"He means 'get out,'" explained Broderick. "I echo his sentiments completely."

Grafius, rising leisurely, fished in his breast pocket and chucked a sharkskin wallet onto the desk. "Look it over," he said. "Well worth your time." He stood impassively as Broderick drew from the wallet several large bills.

"Holy-holy," whispered the inspector general as he fingered the money. "I didn't think you cared." Briskly he seated himself again and waved away Doolan.

"Naturally," he explained, toying with Grafius' card, "I'm loath to part with all this lettuce. Your remark about our little speckled friends, the Martians, I shall ignore. This is a small, young agency, new to the art of private investigation. Martians are outside our ken at this moment of the year 1942, but if there's anything in a more conventional line we can do for you—"

"Nothing at all, thank you," said Grafius of Springfield. He recovered his wallet and card from the desk. "However, if you'd care to listen with an open mind—"

"Open wider than the gates of hell," said the private detective, his eyes on the vanishing currency. "Tell your tale."

Grafius crushed out his cigar. "Suppose you were a Martian," he said.

Broderick snickered. "One of the small ones with three tails, or the nasty size with teeth to match?" he asked amiably.

"I'm sorry," said the man from Springfield. "My data doesn't go as far as that, but in a moment I'll give you a reasonable description of the Martians that are in New York.

"When I say Martian, of course, the meaning is 'extraterrestrial of greater civilization than ours.' They may not be Martians. They may even be from another galaxy. But assume you are what I call a Martian, and that you want to keep in touch with Earthly civilization and advancement. Just where would you go?"

"Coney Island?" helplessly suggested the detective.

"Naturally not," said Grafius severely. "Nor to Sea Breeze, Kansas. Nor to Nome, Alaska. Nor to Equatorial Africa. You wouldn't go to some small town. You wouldn't go to some out-of-the-way part of the world where living is anywhere from twenty to several hundred years behind human progress. This will eliminate Asia and Africa. It will eliminate almost all of Europe and South America."

"I get it," said Broderick. "The Martians would head for the U. S. A."

"Exactly. The United States today is the most technically and culturally advanced nation on Earth. And, further, if you came to the United States, you'd come to New York. You would come because it's the largest human concentration on the globe. It's the economic capital of the continent—the very hemisphere! You agree?"

"Sure," said Broderick. "And you wouldn't be in London because of the war. You can't observe human culture while the shells are popping."

"Exactly. But I still haven't proved anything. To continue: it's quite clear to me that we Earth people aren't the only intelligent, civilized race in the Universe. Out of the infinitude of stars and planets there most definitely, mathematically *must* be others. Mars—to continue with my example—is older than Earth geologically; if there were Martians, and if their evolutionary history corresponded with ours, they would certainly be further advanced than we.

"And I will make one more hypothesis: it is that we Earth people are today on the verge of space conquest, and that any race further advanced than we must have already mastered space flight."

"Go on," said Broderick, who was beginning to look scared. He was a naturally apprehensive type, and the thought that Martians might be just around the corner didn't help him.

"Certainly. But you needn't look so worried, for the Martians won't show up in your office. They must work strictly under cover, since from their point of view—advanced, you will remember— it would be foolish to make themselves known to us as long as we humans are a military, predatory race. It would be a risk which no advanced mentality would take."

"How long has this been going on?" asked Broderick agitatedly.

"Judging from the geology of Mars, some hundreds of years," replied Grafius dreamily. "They've been watching, waiting—"

"You said you could describe them," snapped the detective. "What do they look like?"

"I can't describe their appearance," said Grafius, down to Earth again. "But this is what they most probably are: a group of ordinary-appearing people who live together. In downtown New York, close to newspapers, publishers, news cables, communication centers and the financial powers of Wall Street. They would have no obvious means of support, for all their time must be taken up with the observation that is their career. They almost certainly live in a private house, without prying janitors who would get curious about their peculiar radio equipment.

"And our best bet—they are sure to receive every major paper and magazine, in all the languages of the world."

"I get it," said Broderick. "Very sweet and simple. But what's your reason for wanting to meet up with the Martians, social, if I may ask?"

"Call it curiosity," smiled Grafius. "Or an inflated ego. Or merely the desire to check my logic."

"Sure," said Broderick. "I can offer you the following services of my bureau: bodyguard—that's Iron Man, outside. Think you'll need him?"

"Certainly not," said Grafius of Springfield. "You have no right to suppose that the Martians would stoop to violence. Remember their advanced mentality."

"I won't insist," said the detective. "Second, I can check on all subscription departments of the big papers and magazines. Third, the radio parts lead. Fourth, renting agents. Fifth, sixth and seventh, correlation of these. Eighth, incidentals. It should come to about—" He named a figure. The remainder of the interview was purely financial in character.

Iron Man Doolan wasn't very bright. He knew how to walk, but occasionally he forgot and would try to take both feet off the ground at once. This led to minor contusions of the face and extremities, bruises and gashes that the ex-cop never noticed. He was underorganized.

It taxed him seriously, this walking about in a strange neighborhood. There were hydrants and traffic signals in his way, and each one was a problem in navigation to be solved. Thus it took him half an hour to walk the city block he had been shown to by Broderick, who was waiting nervously, tapping his feet, in a cigar store.

"He's dull—very dull," confided the detective to Grafius, who sipped a coke at the soda fountain. "But the only man for a job like this. Do you think they'll make trouble for him?"

Grafius gurgled through the straw apologetically. "Perhaps," he said. "If it is No. 108—" He brooded into his glass, not finishing the sentence.

"It certainly is," said Broderick decidedly. "What could it be but the Martian embassy that takes everything from *Pic* to the Manchester *Guardian?*"

"Polish revolutionaries," suggested the man from Springfield. "Possibly an invalid. We haven't watched the place for more than a couple of weeks. We really haven't any data worth the name."

The detective hiccupped with nervousness, hastily swallowed a pepsin tablet. Then he stared at his client fixedly. "You amaze me," he stated at last. "You come at me with a flit-git chain of possibilities that you're staking real cash on. And once we hit a solid train you refuse to believe your own eyes. Man, what do you want—a sworn statement from your Martians that they live in No. 108?"

"Let's take a look," said Grafius. "I hope your Mr. Doolan gets a bite."

"Iron Man, I repeat, is not very bright. But he's pushed buttons before, and if somebody answers the door he's going to push the button on his minicam. I drilled that into his—"

He broke off at the sound of a scream, a shriek, a lance of thin noise that sliced down the street. Then there was a crash of steel on concrete. The two dashed from the shop and along the sidewalk.

They stopped short at the sight of Iron Man Doolan's three hundred pounds of muscle grotesquely spattered and slimed underneath a ponderous safe. A colored girl, young and skinny, was wailing in a thin monotone, to herself: "First he squashed and then it fell. First he squashed and then—"

Broderick grabbed her by the shoulders. "What happened?" he yelled hoarsely. "What did you see?"

She stopped her wail and looked directly and simply at him. In an explanatory tone she said: "First he squashed—and *then* it fell." Broderick, feeling sick, let go of her, vaguely heard her burst into hysterical tears as he took Grafius by the arm and walked him away down the street.

Somewhere on Riverside Drive that evening the detective declared: "I know it sounds like a damned childish trick, but I'm going to get drunk, because I had a lot of affection for Doolan. He would understand it as a fitting tribute."

"He was, in his way, the perfect expression of a brutal ideal," mused Grafius. "In an earlier, less sophisticated day he would have been a sort of deity. I'll go with you, if you don't mind."

In a place whose atmosphere was Chinese they drank libations to the departed Iron Man, then moved on down the street. Midnight found Broderick pie-eyed, but with a tense control over his emotions that he was afraid to break through.

It was Grafius at last who suggested calmly: "They are a menace. What shall we do about them?"

Broderick knew just exactly what the man from Springfield meant. With a blurred tongue he replied: "Lay off of them. Keep out of their way. If we make trouble, it's curtains for us—what they did to Doolan is all the proof I need. I know when I'm licked."

"Yes," said Grafius. "That's the trouble with you. Doolan didn't know—" He collapsed softly over the table. Broderick stared at him for a long moment, then gulped the rest of his drink and poked his client in the shoulder.

Grafius came up fighting. "Martians," he shrilled. "Dirty, dusty, dry sons of—"

"Take it easy," said the detective. He eyed a girl sitting solo at a nearby table, who eyed him back with a come-on smile.

Grafius stared at the interchange broodingly. "Keep away from her," he said at last. "She may be one of the Martians—filth they are—unspeakable things—bone-dry monsters from an undead world—" He canted over the table again.

The liquor hit Broderick then like a padded tent maul. He remembered conducting a fantastically polite Gallup poll of the customers in the saloon, inquiring their precise sentiments toward "our little feathered friends of the Red Planet."

He should have known better than to act up in Skelley's Skittle House. Skelley was a restaurateur slow to wrath, but he had his license to take care of, as well as his good name. And Skelley, like so many of his kind, got a big kick out of seeing what a Mickey Finn could do.

Grafius was completely unconscious when Broderick, with elaborate protestations of gratitude, accepted the "last one on the house." He tossed down the rye and quaffed the chaser. Skelley, ever the artist, had stirred the chloral into the larger glass.

The stuff took effect on Broderick like a keg of gunpowder. After the first few spasms he was utterly helpless, poisoned to within an inch of his life, lying heaving on the floor, his eye whites rolling and yellowed, pouring sweat from every hair, actually and literally wishing he were dead and out of his internal agony. That is what a skilled practitioner can do with the little bottle behind the bar.

He saw the waiter and Skelley go through Grafius' pockets, calling for witnesses among the customers that they were taking no more than their due. The customers heartily approved; a woman whose face was baggy and chalked said: "Peeble wh' dunno hodda drink li' gennlem'n shunt drink 't all!" She hiccupped violently, and a waitress led her to the powder room for treatment.

Skelley laboriously read the calling card in Grafius' vest. "That ain't no help," he declared wittily. "It don't say which Springfield."

Broderick saw and felt himself being rolled over, his pockets being dipped into. The spasms began again, ending suddenly as he heard the voice of his host declare: "No. 108! Snooty neighborhood for a lush like that."

The detective tried to explain, tried to tell the man that it wasn't his address but the address of the Martians he'd chanced on in his pockets. But all the voice he could summon up was a grunt that broke to a peep of protest as he was hauled up and carried out in Skelley's strong and practiced arms.

He and Grafius were dumped into a taxi; between spasms he heard the restaurateur give the hackie the Martians' address.

Broderick was going through a physical and mental hell, lying there in the back of the cab. He noted through his nauseous haze the street lights sliding by, noted the passage of Washington Square, sensed the auto turning up Fifth Avenue. His agony lessened by Fiftieth Street, and for a moment he could talk. Hoarsely he called to the cabby to stop. Before he could amplify and explain, the retching overtook him again, and he was helpless.

He passed out completely at a long traffic-light stop; he never felt the car turn right. The next thing he knew the cabby was bundling him out of the rear, leaning him beside Grafius against the door of No. 108. The cabby leaned against the buzzer for a moment, then drove off.

Broderick could only stare with dumb agony as the door opened. "Dear, dear!" said the soft, shocked voice of a woman.

"Are they anyone we know, Florence?" demanded a man.

"Unfortunate creatures, whoever they are," said the woman.

Broderick got a glimpse of a handsome, ruddy face as the man carried him into the hall, the woman following with Grafius. The man from Springfield awoke suddenly, stared into the face of the woman, then set up a shrill screaming that did not end until she had punched him twice in the jaw.

"Shame!" she declared. "We're kind enough to take you two sots in out of the cold and then you get the D. T.'s!" There was a warm smile lurking in the corners of her mouth.

The man opened a door somewhere, and Broderick apprehended a smooth, continuous clicking sound, very much faster and more rhythmical than a typewriter.

"There's something familiar about this boy, Florence," declared the man as he studied the helpless detective.

She wrinkled her brows prettily. "Of course!" she cried at last with a delighted smile. "It's that Broderick!"

"Yes. That Broderick," said the man. "And this other one—"

"Oh!" cried the woman, in tones of ineffable loathing. "*Oh!*" She turned her head away as though sickened.

"Yes," said the man, his face wrinkled and writhing with unspeakable disgust. "This other one is the Grafius he was so often thinking about."

The woman turned again, her face raging angry, black with the blackest passion. Her high French heels ground into the face of the dead-drunk Grafius again and again; the man had to pull her off at last. It was plain that he himself was exercising will power of the highest order in control of an impulse to smash and mangle the despised one.

"Grafius!" he said at last, as though the word were a lump of vileness in his mouth. "That Venusian!" He spat.

The woman broke free from his grasp, kicked the mutilated face. Broderick heard the teeth splintering in the abused mouth.

One of the most remarkable developments in science fiction has been the increasing co-operation between science fiction literature and the science fiction film. Usually we think of this as a one-way relationship, with science fiction books being adapted into movies. But from the first science fiction film, Melies' 1902 *Trip to the Moon*, to such recent cinematic spectaculars as Pal's *War of the Worlds* and Kubrick's *2001*, the science fiction movie has held the fascinated eyes and ears of a world-wide audience. And science fiction writers have tended to find more and more inspiration on the movie screen. So, for example, Lester Del Rey's "Dark Mission," which is a superbly successful short story, succeeds chiefly because it uses cinematic techniques. Like a well-made war movie, "Dark Mission" is above all visual—a clearly focused, forcefully kinetic dramatization of a Martian invasion. Reading Del Rey's words, we can actually see the mysterious Martians, even to the pigmentation of their skin. And we can see, too, how fearfully near they have come to us.

Lester Del Rey

DARK MISSION

The rays of the Sun lanced down over the tops of the trees and into the clearing, revealing a scene of chaos and havoc. Yesterday there had been a wooden frame house there, but now only pieces of it remained. One wall had been broken away, as by an explosion, and lay on the ground in fragments; the roof was crushed in, as if some giant had stepped on it and passed on.

But the cause of the damage was still there, lying on the ruins of the house. A tangled mass of buckled girders and metal plates lay mixed with a litter of laboratory equipment that had been neatly arranged in one room of the house, and parts of a strange engine lay at one side. Beyond was a tube that might have been a rocket. The great metal object that lay across the broken roof now only hinted at the sleek cylinder it had once been, but a trained observer might have guessed that it was the wreck of a rocketship. From the former laboratory, flames were licking up at the metal hull, and slowly spreading toward the rest of the house.

In the clearing, two figures lay outstretched, of similar size and build, but otherwise unlike. One was of a dark man of middle age, completely naked, with a face cut and battered beyond all recognition. The odd angle of the head was unmistakable proof that his neck was broken. The other man might have been a brawny sea viking of earlier days, both from his size and appearance, but his face revealed something finer and of a higher culture. He was fully clothed, and the slow movement of his chest showed that there was still life in him. Beside him, there was a broken beam from the roof, a few spots of blood on it. There was more blood on the man's head, but the cut was minor, and he was only stunned.

Now he stirred uneasily and groped uncertainly to his feet, shaking his head and fingering the cut on his scalp. His eyes traveled slowly across the clearing and to the ruins that were burning merrily. The corpse claimed his next attention, and he turned it over to examine the neck. He knit his brows and shook his head savagely, trying to call back the memories that eluded him.

They would not come. He recognized what his eyes saw, but his mind produced no words to describe them, and the past was missing. His first memory was of wakening to find his head pounding with an ache that was almost unbearable. Without surprise, he studied the rocket and saw that it had come down on the house, out of control, but it evoked no pictures in his mind, and he gave up. He might have been in the rocket or the house at the time; he had no way of telling which. Probably the naked man had been asleep at the time in the house.

Something prickled gently in the back of his mind, growing stronger and urging him to do something. He must not waste time here, but must fulfill some vital mission. What mission? For a second, he almost had it, and then it was gone again, leaving only the compelling urge that must be obeyed. He shrugged and started away from the ruins toward the little trail that showed through the trees.

Then another impulse called him back to the corpse, and he obeyed it because he knew of nothing else to do. Acting without conscious volition, he tugged at the corpse, found it strangely heavy, and dragged it toward the house. The flames were everywhere now, but he found a place where the heat was not too great and pulled the corpse over a pile of combustibles.

With the secondary impulse satisfied, the first urge returned, and he set off down the trail, moving slowly. The shoes hurt his feet, and his legs were leaden, but he kept on grimly, while a series of questions went around his head in circles. Who was he, where, and why?

Whoever had lived in the house, himself or the corpse, had obviously chosen the spot for privacy; the trail seemed to go on through the woods endlessly, and he saw no signs of houses along it. He clumped on mechanically, wondering if there was no end, until a row of crossed poles bearing wires caught his eye. Ahead, he made out a broad highway, with vehicles speeding along it in both directions, and hastened forward, hoping to meet someone.

Luck was with him. Pulled up at the side of the road was one of the vehicles, and a man was doing something at the front end of the car. Rough words carried back to him suggesting anger. He grinned suddenly and hastened toward the car, his eyes riveted on the man's head. A tense feeling shot through his brain and left, just as he reached the machine.

"Need help?" The words slipped out unconsciously, and now other words came pouring into his head, along with ideas and knowledge that had not been there before. But the sight of the man, or whatever had restored that section of his memory, had brought back no personal knowledge, and that seemed wrong somehow. The driving impulse he felt was still unexplained.

The man had looked up at his words, and relief shot over the sweating face. "Help's the one thing I need," he replied gratefully. "I been fussing with this blasted contraption darned near an hour, and nobody's even stopped to ask, so far. Know anything about it?"

"Um-m-m." The stranger, as he was calling himself for want of a better name, tested the wires himself, vaguely troubled at the simplicity of the engine. He gave up and went around to the other side, lifting the hood and inspecting the design. Then sureness came to him as he reached for the tool kit. "Probably the . . . um . . . timing pins," he said.

It was. A few minutes later the engine purred softly and the driver turned to the stranger. "O. K. now, I guess. Good thing you came along; worst part of the road and not a repair shop for miles. Where you going?"

"I—" The stranger caught himself. "The big city," he said, for want of a better destination.

"Hop in, then. I'm going to Elizabeth, right on your way. Glad to have you along; gets so a man talks to himself on these long drives, unless he has something to do. Smoke?"

"Thank you, no. I never do." He watched the other light up, feeling uncomfortable about it. The smell of the smoke, when it reached him, was nauseous, as were the odor of gasoline and the man's own personal effluvium, but he pushed them out of his mind as much as possible. "Have you heard or read anything about a rocketship of some kind?"

"Sure. Oglethorpe's, you mean? I been reading what the papers had to say about it." The drummer took his eyes off the road for a second, and his beady little eyes gleamed. "I been wondering a long time why some of these big-shot financiers don't back up the rockets, and finally Oglethorpe does. Boy, now maybe we'll find out something about this Mars business."

The stranger grinned mechanically. "What does his ship look like?"

"Picture of it in the *Scoop*, front page. Find it back of the seat, there. Yeah, that's it. Wonder what the Martians look like?"

"Hard to guess," the stranger answered. Even rough halftones of the picture showed that it was not the ship that had crashed, but radically different. "No word of other rockets?"

"Nope, not that I know of. You know, I kinda feel maybe the Martians might look like us. Sure." He took the other's skepticism for granted without looking around. "Wrote a story about that once, for one of these science-fiction magazines, but they sent it back. I figured out maybe a long time ago there was a civilization on Earth—Atlantis, maybe—and they went over and settled on Mars. Only Atlantis sunk on them, and there they were, stranded. I figured maybe one day they came back, sort of lost out for a while, but popped up again and started civilization humming. Not bad, eh?"

"Clever," the stranger admitted. "But it sounds vaguely familiar. Suppose we said instead there was a war between the mother world and Mars that wrecked both civilizations, instead of your Atlantis sinking. Wouldn't that be more logical?"

"Maybe, I dunno. Might try it, though mostly they seem to want freaks— Darned fool, passing on a hill!" He leaned out to shake a pudgy fist, then came back to his rambling account. "Read one the other day with two races, one like octopuses, the others twenty feet tall and all blue."

Memory pricked tantalizingly and came almost to the surface. Blue— Then it was gone again, leaving only a troubled feeling. The stranger frowned and settled down in the seat, answering in monosyllables to the other's monologue, and watching the patchwork of country and cities slip by.

"There's Elizabeth. Any particular place you want me to drop you?"

The stranger stirred from the half-coma induced by the cutting ache in his head, and looked about. "Any place," he answered. Then the urge in the back of his mind grabbed at him again, and he changed it. "Some doctor's office."

That made sense, of course. Perhaps the impulse had been only the logical desire to seek medical aid, all along. But it was still there, clamoring for expression, and he doubted the logic of anything connected with it. The call for aid could not explain the sense of disaster that accompanied it. As the car stopped before a house with a doctor's shingle, his pulse was hammering with frenzied urgency.

"Here we are." The drummer reached out toward the door handle, almost brushing one of the other's hands. The stranger jerked it back savagely, avoiding contact by a narrow margin, and a cold chill ran up his back and quivered its way down again. If that hand had touched him— The half-opened door closed again, but left one fact impressed on him. Under no conditions must he suffer another to make direct contact with his body, lest something horrible should happen! Another crazy angle, unconnected with the others, but too strong for disobedience.

He climbed out, muttering his thanks, and made up the walk toward the office of Dr. Lanahan, hours 12:00 to 4:00.

The doctor was an old man, with the seamed and rugged goodnature of the general practitioner, and his office fitted him. There was a row of medical books along one wall, a glass-doored cabinet containing various medicaments, and a clutter of medical instruments. He listened to the stranger's account quietly, smiling encouragement at times, and tapping the desk with his pencil.

"Amnesia, of course," he agreed, finally. "Rather peculiar in some respects, but most cases of that are individual. When the brain is injured, its actions are usually unpredictable. Have you considered the possibility of hallucinations in connection with those impulses you mention?"

"Yes." He had considered it from all angles, and rejected the solutions as too feeble. "If they were ordinary impulses, I'd agree with you. But they're far deeper than that, and there's a good reason for them, somewhere. I'm sure of that."

"Hm-m-m." The doctor tapped his pencil again and considered. The stranger sat staring at the base of his neck, and the tense feeling in his head returned, as it had been when he first met the drummer. Something rolled around in his mind and quieted. "And you have nothing on you in the way of identification?"

"Uh!" The stranger grunted, feeling foolish, and reached into his pockets. "I hadn't thought of that." He brought out a package of cigarettes, a stained handkerchief, glasses, odds and ends that meant nothing to him, and finally a wallet stuffed with bills. The doctor seized on that and ran through its contents quickly.

"Evidently you had money. . . . Hm-m-m, no identification card, except for the letters L. H. Ah, here we are; a calling card." He passed it over, along with the wallet, and smiled in self-satisfaction. "Evidently you're a fellow physician, Dr. Lurton Haines. Does that recall anything?"

"Nothing." It was good to have a name, in a way, but that was his only response to the sight of the card. And why was he carrying glasses and cigarettes for which he had no earthly use?

The doctor was hunting through his pile of books, and finally came up with a dirty red volume. "Who's Who," he explained. "Let's see. Hm-m-m! Here we are. 'Lurton R. Haines, M. D.' Odd, I thought you were younger than that. Work along cancer research. No relatives mentioned. The address is evidently that of the house you remember first—'Surrey Road, Danesville.' Want to see it?"

He passed the volume over, and the stranger—or Haines—scanned it carefully, but got no more out of it than the other's summary, except for the fact that he was forty-two years old. He put the book back on the desk, and reached for his wallet, laying a bill on the pad where the other could reach it.

"Thank you, Dr. Lanahan." There was obviously nothing more the doctor could do for him, and the odor of the little room and the doctor were stifling him; apparently he was allergic to the smell of other men. "Never mind the cut on the head—it's purely superficial."

"But—"

Haines shrugged and mustered a smile, reached for the door, and made for the outside again. The urge was gone now, replaced by a vast sense of gloom, and he knew that his mission had ended in failure.

They knew so little about healing, though they tried so hard. The entire field of medicine ran through Haines' mind now, with all its startling successes and hopeless failures, and he knew that even his own problem was beyond their ability. And the knowledge, like the sudden return of speech, was a mystery; it had come rushing into his mind while he stared at the doctor, at the end of the sudden tenseness, and a numbing sense of failure had accompanied it. Strangely, it was not the knowledge of a specialist in cancer research, but such common methods as a general practitioner might use.

One solution suggested itself, but it was too fantastic for belief. The existence of telepaths was suspected, but not ones who could steal whole pages of knowledge from the mind of another, merely by looking at him. No, that was more illogical than the sudden wakening of isolated fields of memory by the sight of the two men.

He stopped at a corner, weary under the load of despondency he was carrying, and mulled it over dully. A newsboy approached hopefully. "*Time* a' *News* out!" the boy singsonged his wares. "*Scoop* 'n' *Juhnal!* Read awl about the big train wreck! Paper, mister?"

Haines shrugged dully. "No paper!"

"Blonde found moidehed in bathtub," the boy insinuated. "Mahs rocket account!" The man must have an Achilles' heel somewhere.

But the garbled jargon only half registered on Haines' ears. He started across the street, rubbing his temples, before the second driving impulse caught at him and sent him back remorselessly to the paper boy. He found some small change in his pocket, dropped a nickel on the pile of papers, disregarding the boy's hand, and picked up a copy of the *Scoop*. "Screwball," the boy decided aloud, and dived for the nickel.

The picture was no longer on the front page of the tabloid, but Haines located the account with some effort. "Mars Rocket Take-off Wednesday," said the headline in conservative twenty-four-point type, and there was three-quarters of a column under it. "Man's first flight to Mars will not be delayed, James Oglethorpe told reporters here today. Undismayed by the skepticism of the scientists, the financier is going ahead with his plans, and expects his men to take off for Mars Wednesday, June 8, as scheduled. Construction has been completed, and the rocket machine is now undergoing tests."

Haines scanned down the page, noting the salient facts. The writer had kept his tongue in his cheek, but under the faintly mocking words there was the information he wanted. The rocket might work; man was at last on his way toward the conquests of the planets. There was no mention of another rocket. Obviously then, that one must have been built in secret in a futile effort to beat Oglethorpe's model.

But that was unimportant. The important thing was that he must stop the flight! Above all else, man must not make that trip! There was no sanity to it, and yet somehow it was beyond mere sanity. It was his duty to prevent any such voyage, and that duty was not to be questioned.

He returned quickly to the newsboy, reached out to touch his shoulder, and felt his hand jerk back to avoid the touch. The boy seemed to sense it, though, for he turned quickly. "Paper?" he began brightly before recognizing the stranger. "Oh, it's you. Watcha want?"

"Where can I find a train to New York?" Haines pulled a quarter from his pocket and tossed it on the pile of papers.

The boy's eyes brightened again.

"Four blocks down, turn right, and keep going till you come to the station. Can't miss it. Thanks, mister."

The discovery of the telephone book as a source of information was Haines' single major triumph, and the fact that the first Oglethorpe he tried was a colored street cleaner failed to take the edge off it. Now he trudged uptown, counting the numbers that made no sense to him; apparently the only system was one of arithmetical progression, irrespective of streets.

His shoulders were drooping, and the lines of pain around his eyes had finally succeeded in drawing his brows together. A coughing spell hit him, torturing his lungs for long minutes, and then passed. That was a new development, as was the pressure around his heart. And everywhere was the irritating aroma of men, gasoline, and tobacco, a stale mixture that he could not escape. He thrust his hands deeper into his pockets to avoid chance contact with someone on the street, and crossed over toward the building that bore the number for which he was searching.

Another man was entering the elevator, and he followed mechanically, relieved that he would not have to plod up the stairs. "Oglethorpe?" he asked the operator, uncertainly.

"Fourth floor, Room 405." The boy slid the gate open, pointing, and Haines stepped out and into the chromium-trimmed reception room. There were half a dozen doors leading from it, but he spotted the one marked "James H. Oglethorpe, Private," and slouched forward.

"Were you expected, sir?" The girl popped up in his face, one hand on the gate that barred his way. Her face was a study in frustration, which probably explained the sharpness of her tone. She delivered an Horatius-guarding-the-bridge formula. "Mr. Oglethorpe is busy now."

"Lunch," Haines answered curtly. He had already noticed that men talked more freely over food.

She flipped a little book in her hand and stared at it. "There's no record here of a luncheon engagement, Mr.—"

"Haines. Dr. Lurton Haines." He grinned wryly, wiggling a

twenty-dollar bill casually in one hand. Money was apparently the one disease to which nobody was immune. Her eyes dropped to it, and hesitation entered her voice as she consulted her book.

"Of course, Mr. Oglethorpe might have made it some time ago and forgotten to tell me—" She caught his slight nod, and followed the bill to the corner of the desk. "Just have a seat, and I'll speak to Mr. Oglethorpe."

She came out of the office a few minutes later, and winked quickly. "He'd forgotten," she told Haines, "but it's all right now. He'll be right out, Dr. Haines. It's lucky he's having lunch late today."

James Oglethorpe was a younger man than Haines had expected, though his interest in rocketry might have been some clue to that. He came out of his office, pushing a Homburg down on curly black hair, and raked the other with his eyes. "Dr. Haines?" he asked, thrusting out a large hand. "Seems we have a luncheon engagement."

Haines rose quickly and bowed before the other had a chance to grasp his hand. Apparently Oglethorpe did not notice, for he went on smoothly. "Easy to forget these telephone engagements, sometimes. Aren't you the cancer man? One of your friends was in a few months ago for a contribution to your work."

They were in the elevator then, and Haines waited until it opened and they headed for the lunchroom in the building before answering. "I'm not looking for money this time, however. It's the rocket you're financing that interests me. I think it may work."

"It will, though you're one of the few that believes it." Caution, doubt, and interest were mingled on Oglethorpe's face. He ordered before turning back to Haines. "Want to go along? If you do, there's still room for a physician in the crew."

"No, nothing like that. Toast and milk only, please—" Haines had no idea of how to broach the subject, with nothing concrete to back up his statements. Looking at the set of the other's jaw and the general bulldog attitude of the man, he gave up hope and only continued because he had to. He fell back on imagination, wondering how much of it was true.

"Another rocket made that trip, Mr. Oglethorpe, and returned.

But the pilot was dying before he landed. I can show you the wreck of his machine, though there's not much left after the fire—perhaps not enough to prove it was a rocketship. Somewhere out on Mars there's something man should never find. It's—"

"Ghosts?" suggested Oglethorpe, brusquely.

"Death! I'm asking you—"

Again Oglethorpe interrupted. "Don't. There was a man in to see me yesterday who claimed he'd been there—offered to show me the wreck of *his* machine. A letter this morning explained that the Martians had visited the writer and threatened all manner of things. I'm not calling you a liar, Dr. Haines, but I've heard too many of those stories; whoever told you this one was either a crank or a horror-monger. I can show you a stack of letters that range from astrology to zombies, all explaining why I can't go, and some offer photographs for proof."

"Suppose I said I'd made the trip in that rocket?" The card in the wallet said he was Haines, and the wallet had been in the suit he was wearing; but there had also been the glasses and cigarettes for which he had no use.

Oglethorpe twisted his lips, either in disgust or amusement. "You're an intelligent man, Dr. Haines; let's assume I am, also. It may sound ridiculous to you, but the only reason I had for making the fortune I'm credited with was to build that ship, and it's taken more work and time than the layman would believe. If a green ant, seven feet high, walked into my office and threatened Armageddon, I'd still go."

Even the impossible impulse recognized the impossible. Oglethorpe was a man who did things first and worried about them when the mood hit him—and there was nothing moody about him. The conversation turned to everyday matters and Haines let it drift as it would, finally dragging out into silence.

At least, he was wiser by one thing: he knew the location of the rocket ground and the set-up of guards around it—something even the newspapermen had failed to learn, since all pictures and information had come through Oglethorpe. There could no longer be any question of his ability to gain desired information by some hazy telepathic process. Either he was a mental freak, or the accident had done things to him that should have been surprising but weren't.

Haines had taken a cab from the airport, giving instructions that caused the driver to lift his eyebrows; but money was still all-powerful. Now they were slipping through country even more desolate than the woods around Haines' house, and the end of the road came into view, with a rutted muddy trail leading off, marked by the tires of the trucks Oglethorpe had used for his freighting. The cab stopped there.

"This the place?" the driver asked uncertainly.

"It is." Haines added a bill to what had already been paid and dismissed him. Then he dragged his way out to the dirt road and followed it, stopping for rest frequently. His ears were humming loudly now, and each separate little vertebra of his back protested at his going on. But there was no turning back; he had tried that, at the airport and found the urge strong enough to combat his weakening will.

"Only a little rest!" he muttered thickly, but the force in his head lifted his leaden feet and sent them marching toward the rocket camp. Above him the gray clouds passed over the Moon, and he looked up at Mars shining in the sky. Words from the lower part of the drummer's vocabulary came into his throat, but the effort of saying them was more than the red planet merited. He plowed on in silence.

Mars had moved over several degrees in the sky when he first sighted the camp, lying in a long, narrow valley. At one end were the shacks of the workmen, at the other a big structure that housed the rocket from chance prying eyes. Haines stopped to cough out part of his lungs, and his breath was husky and labored as he worked his way down.

The guards should be strung out along the edge of the valley. Oglethorpe was taking no chances with the cranks who had written him letters and denounced him as a godless fool leading his men to death. Rockets at best were fragile things, and only a few men would be needed to ruin the machine once it was discovered. Haines ran over the guards' positions, and skirted through the underbrush, watching for periods when the Moon was darkened. Once he almost tripped an alarm, but missed it in time.

Beyond, there was no shrubbery, but his suit was almost the shade of the ground in the moonlight, and by lying still between dark spells, he crawled forward toward the rocket shed, undetected. He noticed the distance of the houses and the outlying guards and nodded to himself; they should be safe from any explosion.

The coast looked clear. Then, in the shadow of the building, a tiny red spark gleamed and subsided slowly; a man was there, smoking a cigarette. By straining his eyes, Haines made out the long barrel of a rifle against the building. This guard must be an added precaution, unknown to Oglethorpe.

A sudden rift in the thickening clouds came, and Haines slid himself flat against the ground, puzzling over the new complication. For a second he considered turning back, but realized that he could not—his path now was clearly defined, and he had no choice but to follow it. As the Moon slid out of sight again, he came to his feet quietly and moved toward the figure waiting there.

"Hello!" His voice was soft, designed to reach the man at the building but not the guards behind in the outskirts. "Hello, there. Can I come forward? Special inspector from Oglethorpe."

A beam of light lanced out from the shadow, blinding him, and he walked forward at the best pace he could muster. The light might reveal him to the other guards, but he doubted it; their attention was directed outward, away from the buildings.

"Come ahead," the answer came finally. "How'd you get past the others?" The voice was suspicious, but not unusually so. The rifle, Haines saw, was directed at his mid-section, and he stopped a few feet away, where the other could watch him.

"Jimmy Durham knew I was coming," he told the guard. According to the information he had stolen from Oglethorpe's mind, Durham was in charge of the guards. "He told me he hadn't had time to notify you, but I took a chance."

"Hm-m-m. Guess it's all right, since they let you through; but you can't leave here until somebody identifies you. Keep your hands up." The guard came forward cautiously to feel for concealed weapons. Haines held his hands up out of the other's reach, where there was no danger of a direct skin to skin contact. "O. K., seems all right. What's your business here?"

"General inspection; the boss got word there might be a little trouble brewing and sent me here to make sure guard was being kept, and to warn you. All locked up here?"

"Nope. A lock wouldn't do much good on this shack; that's why I'm here. Want I should signal Jimmy to come and identify you so you can go?"

"Don't bother." Conditions were apparently ideal, except for one thing. But he would not murder the guard! There must be some other way, without adding that to the work he was forced to do. "I'm in no hurry, now that I've seen everything. Have a smoke?"

"Just threw one away. 'Smatter, no matches? Here."

Haines rubbed one against the friction surface of the box and lit the cigarette gingerly. The raw smoke stung against his burning throat, but he controlled the cough, and blew it out again; in the dark, the guard could not see his eyes watering, nor the grimaces he made. He was waging a bitter fight with himself against the impulse that had ordered the smoke to distract the guard's attention, and he knew he was failing. "Thanks!"

One of the guard's hands met his, reaching for the box. The next second the man's throat was between the stranger's hands, and he was staggering back, struggling to tear away and cry for help. Surprise confused his efforts for the split second necessary, and one of Haines' hands came free and out, then chopped down sharply to strike the guard's neck with the edge of the palm. A low grunt gurgled out, and the figure went limp.

Impulse had conquered again! The guard was dead, his neck broken by the sharp blow. Haines leaned against the building, catching his breath and fighting back the desire to lose his stomach's contents. When some control came back, he picked up the guard's flashlight, and turned into the building. In the darkness, the outlines of the great rocketship were barely visible.

With fumbling fingers Haines groped forward to the hull, then struck a match and shaded it in his hands until he could make out the airport, standing open. Too much light might show through a window and attract attention.

Inside, he threw the low power of the flashlight on and moved forward, down the catwalk and toward the rear where the power machinery would be housed. It had been simple, after all, and only the quick work of destruction still remained.

He traced the control valves easily, running an eye over the uncovered walls and searching out the pipes that led from them. From the little apparatus he saw, this ship was obviously inferior to the one that had crashed, yet it had taken years to build and drained Oglethorpe's money almost to the limit. Once destroyed, it might take men ten more years to replace it; two was the minimum, and in those two years—

The thought slipped from him, but some memories were coming back. He saw himself in a small metal room, fighting against the inexorable exhaustion of fuel, and losing. Then there had been a final burst from the rockets, and the ship had dropped sickeningly through the atmosphere. He had barely had time to get to the air locks before the crash. Miraculously, as the ship's fall was cushioned by the house, he had been thrown free into the lower branches of a tree, to catch, and lose momentum before striking Earth.

The man who had been in the house had fared worse; he had been thrown out with the wrecked wall, already dead. Roughly, the stranger remembered a hasty transfer of clothing from the corpse, and then the beam had dropped on him, shutting out his memory in blackness. So he was not Haines, after all, but someone from the rocket, and his story to Oglethorpe had been basically true.

Haines—he still thought of himself under that name—caught himself as his knees gave under him, and hauled himself up by the aid of a protruding bar. There was work to be done; after that, what happened to his own failing body was another matter. It seemed now that from his awakening he had expected to meet death before another day, and had been careless of the fact.

He ran his eyes around the rocket room again, until he came to a tool kit that lay invitingly open with a large wrench sticking up from it. That would serve to open the valves. The flashlight lay on the floor where he had dropped it, and he kicked it around with his foot to point at the wall, groping out for the wrench. His fingers were stiff as they clasped around the handle.

And, in the beam of light, he noticed his hand for the first time in hours. Dark-blue veins rose high on the flesh that was marked with a faint pale-blue. He considered it dully, thrusting out his other hand and examining it; there, too, was the blue flush, and on his palms, as he turned them upward, the same color showed. Blue!

The last of his memory flashed through his brain in a roaring wave, bringing a slow tide of pictures with it. With one part of his mind, he was working on the valves with the wrench, while the other considered the knowledge that had returned to him. He saw the streets of a delicate, fairy city, half deserted, and as he seemed to watch, a man staggered out of a doorway, clutching at his throat with blue hands, to fall writhing to the ground! The people passed on quickly, avoiding contact with the corpse, fearful even to touch each other.

Everywhere, death reached out for the people. The planet was riddled with it. It lay on the skin of an infected person, to be picked up by the touch of another, and passed on to still more. In the air, a few seconds sufficed to kill the germs, but new ones were being sent out from the pores of the skin, so that there were always a few active ones lurking there. On contact, the disease began an insidious conquest, until, after months without a sign, it suddenly attacked the body housing it, turned it blue, and brought death in a few painful hours.

Some claimed it was the result of an experiment that had gone beyond control, others that it had dropped as a spore from space. Whatever it was, there was no cure for it on Mars. Only the legends that spoke of a race of their people on the mother world of Earth offered any faint hope, and to that they had turned when there was no other chance.

He saw himself undergoing examinations that finally resulted in his being chosen to go in the rocket they were building feverishly. He had been picked because his powers of telepathy were unusual, even to the mental science of Mars; the few remaining weeks had been used in developing that power systematically, and implanting in his head the duties that he must perform, so long as a vestige of life remained to him.

Haines watched the first of the liquid from the fuel pipes splash out, and dropped the wrench. Old León Dagh had doubted his ability to draw knowledge by telepathy from a race of a different culture, he reflected; too bad the old man had died without knowing of the success his methods had met, even though the mission had been a failure, due to man's feeble knowledge of the curative sciences. Now his one task was to prevent the race of this world from dying in the same manner.

He pulled himself to his feet again and went staggering down the catwalk, muttering disconnected sentences. The blue of his skin was darker now, and he had to force himself across the space from the ship to the door of the building, grimly commanding his failing muscles, to the guard's body that still lay where he had left it.

Most of the strength left him was useless against the pull of this heavier planet and the torture movement had become. He tried to drag the corpse behind him, then fell on hands and knees and backed toward the ship, using one arm and his teeth on the collar to pull it after him. He was swimming in a world that was bordering on unconsciousness, now, and once darkness claimed him; he came out of it to find himself inside the rocket, still dragging his burden, the implanted impulses stronger than his will.

Bit by bit, he dragged his burden behind him down the catwalk, until the engine room was reached, and he could drop it on the floor, where the liquid fuel had made a thin film. The air was heavy with vapors, and chilled by the evaporation, but he was only partly conscious of that. Only a spark was needed now, and his last duty would be finished.

Inevitably, a few of the dead on Mars would be left unburned, where men might find the last of that unfortunate race, and the germs would still live within them. Earthmen must not face that. Until such a time as the last Martian had crumbled to dust and released the plague into the air to be destroyed, the race of Earth must remain within the confines of its own atmosphere, and safe.

There was only himself and the corpse he had touched left here to carry possible germs, and the ship to carry the men to other sources of infection; all that was easily remedied.

The stranger from Mars groped in his pocket for the guard's match box, smiling faintly. Just before the final darkness swept over him, he drew one of the matches from the box and scraped it across the friction surface. Flame danced from the point and outward—

Although H. G. Wells suggested in 1898 that the Martians were supreme technicians, it was not until the Age of Campbell overtook science fiction a generation later that writers began to avail themselves of the full possibilities of Martian technology. With John W. Campbell's active editorial encouragement, many science fiction authors of the 1930s and 1940s abandoned the romantically impressionistic Marsscapes of Percival Lowell and Edgar Rice Burroughs for an altogether different kind of Mars story. These new Martian narratives centered on Campbell's favorite "hard" sciences—mathematics, chemistry, physics, engineering. They described a Mars rich in technological marvels, lively with the adventurous exploits of engineers rather than the gymnastics of space-age Tarzans. One of the finest of the technological stories is George O. Smith's "Lost Art," which envisions the Martians as master builders and Mars as a scientific paradise. If you like machines, you'll love Smith's Mars.

George O. Smith

LOST ART

Sargon of Akkad was holding court in all of his splendor in the Mesopotamia area, which he thought to be the center of the Universe. The stars to him were but holes in a black bowl which he called the sky. They were beautiful then, as they are now, but he thought that they were put there for his edification only; for was he not the ruler of Akkadia?

After Sargon of Akkad, there would come sixty centuries of climbing before men reached the stars and found not only that there had been men upon them, but that a civilization on Mars had reached its peak four thousand years before Christ and was now but a memory and a wealth of pictographs that adorned the semipreserved Temples of Canalopsis.

And sixty centuries after, the men of Terra wondered about the ideographs and solved them sufficiently to piece together the wonders of the long-dead Martian Civilization.

Sargon of Akkad did not know that the stars that he beheld carried on them wonders his mind would not, could not, accept.

Altas, the Martian, smiled tolerantly at his son. The young man boasted on until Altas said: "So you have memorized the contents of my manual? Good, Than, for I am growing old and I would be pleased to have my son fill my shoes. Come into the workshop that I may pass upon your proficiency."

Altas led Than to the laboratory that stood at the foot of the great tower of steel; Altas removed from a cabinet a replacement element from the great beam above their heads, and said: "Than, show me how to hook this up!"

Than's eyes glowed. From other cabinets he took small auxiliary parts. From hooks upon the wall, Than took lengths of wire. Working with a brilliant deftness that was his heritage as a Martian, Than spent an hour attaching the complicated circuits. After he was finished, Than stepped back and said: "There—and believe it or not, this is the first time you have permitted me to work with one of the beam elements."

"You have done well," said Altas with that same cryptic smile. "But now we shall see. The main question is: Does it work?"

"Naturally," said Than in youthful pride. "Is it not hooked up exactly as your manual says? It will work."

"We shall see," repeated Altas. "We shall see."

Barney Carroll and James Baler cut through the thin air of Mars in a driver-wing flier at a terrific rate of speed. It was the only kind of flier that would work on Mars with any degree of safety since it depended upon the support of its drivers rather than the wing surface. They were hitting it up at almost a thousand miles per hour on their way from Canalopsis to Lincoln Head; their trip would take an hour and a half.

As they passed over the red sand of Mars, endlessly it seemed, a glint of metal caught Barney's eye, and he shouted.

"What's the matter, Barney?" asked Jim.

"Roll her over and run back a mile or so," said Barney. "I saw something down there that didn't belong in this desert."

Jim snapped the plane around in a sharp loop that nearly took their heads off, and they ran back along their course.

"Yop," called Barney, "there she is!"

"What?"

"See that glint of shiny metal? That doesn't belong in this mess of erosion. Might be a crash."

"Hold tight," laughed Jim. "We're going down."

They did. Jim's piloting had all of the aspects of a daredevil racing pilot's, and Barney was used to it. Jim snapped the nose of the little flier down and they power-dived to within a few yards of the sand before he set the plane on its tail and skidded flatwise to kill speed. He leveled off, and the flier came screaming in for a perfect landing not many feet from the glinting object.

"This is no crash," said Baler. "This looks like the remains of an air-lane beacon of some sort."

"Does it? Not like any I've ever seen. It reminds me more of some of the gadgets they find here and there—the remnants of the Ancients. They used to build junk like this."

"Hook up the sand-blower," suggested Jim Baler. "We'll clear some of this rubble away and see what she really looks like. Can't see much more than what looks like a high-powered searchlight."

Barney hauled equipment out of the flier and hitched it to a small motor in the plane. The blower created a small storm for an hour or so, its blast directed by suit-clad Barney Carroll. Working with experience gained in uncovering the remains of a dozen dead and buried cities, Barney cleared the shifting sand from the remains of the tower.

The head was there, preserved by the dry sand. Thirty feet below the platform, the slender tower was broken off. No delving could find the lower portion.

"This is quite a find," said Jim. "Looks like some of the carvings on the Temple of Science at Canalopsis—that little house on the top of the spire with the three-foot runway around it; then this dingbat perched on top of the roof. Never did figure out what it was for."

"We don't know whether the Martians' eyes responded as ours do," suggested Barney. "This might be a searchlight that puts out with Martian visible spectrum. If they saw with infrared, they wouldn't be using Terran fluorescent lighting. If they saw with long heat frequencies, they wouldn't waste power with even a tungsten filament light, but would have invented something that cooked its most energy in the visible spectrum, just as we have in the last couple of hundred years."

"That's just a guess, of course."

"Naturally," said Barney. "Here, I've got the door cracked. Let's be the first people in this place for six thousand years Terran. Take it easy, this floor is at an angle of thirty degrees."

"I won't slide. G'wan in. I'm your shadow."

They entered the thirty-foot circular room and snapped on their torches. There was a bench that ran almost around the entire room. It was empty save for a few scraps of metal and a Martian book of several hundred metal pages.

"Nuts," said Barney, "we would have to find a thing like this but empty. That's our luck. What's the book, Jim?"

"Some sort of text, I'd say. Full of diagrams and what seems to be mathematics. Hard to tell, of course, but we've established the fact that mathematics is universal, though the characters can not possibly be."

"Any chance of deciphering it?" asked Barney.

"Let's get back in the flier and try. I'm in no particular hurry."

"Nor am I. I don't care whether we get to Lincoln Head tonight or the middle of next week."

"Now let's see that volume of diagrams," he said as soon as they were established in the flier.

Jim passed the book over, and Barney opened the book to the first page. "If we never find anything else," he said, "this will make us famous. I am now holding the first complete volume of Martian literature that anyone has ever seen. The darned thing is absolutely complete, from cover to cover!"

"That's a find," agreed Jim. "Now go ahead and transliterate it —you're the expert on Martian pictographs."

For an hour, Barney scanned the pages of the volume. He made copious notes on sheets of paper which he inserted between the metal leaves of the book. At the end of that time, during which Jim Baler had been inspecting the searchlight-thing on the top of the little house, he called to his friend, and Jim entered the flier lugging the thing on his shoulders.

"What'cha got?" he grinned. "I brought this along. Nothing else in that shack, so we're complete except for the remnants of some very badly corroded cable that ran from this thing to a flapping end down where the tower was broken."

Barney smiled and blinked. It was strange to see this big man working studiously over a book; Barney Carroll should have been leading a horde of Venusian engineers through the Palanortis country instead of delving into the artifacts of a dead civilization.

"I think that this thing is a sort of engineer's handbook," he said. "In the front there is a section devoted to mathematical tables. You know, a table of logs to the base twelve which is because the Martians had six fingers on each hand. There is what seems to be a table of definite integrals—at least if I were writing a handbook I'd place the table of integrals at the last part of the math section. The geometry and trig is absolutely recognizable because of the designs. So is the solid geom and the analyt for the same reason. The next section seems to be devoted to chemistry; the Martians used a hexagonal figure for a benzene ring, too, and so that's established. From that we find the key to the Periodic Chart of the Atoms which is run vertically instead of horizontally, but still unique. These guys were sharp, though; they seem to have hit upon the fact that isotopes are separate elements though so close in grouping to one another that they exhibit the same properties. Finding this will uncover a lot of mystery."

"Yeah," agreed Baler, "from a book of this kind we can decipher most anything. The keying on a volume of physical constants is perfect and almost infinite in number. What do they use for Pi?"

"Circle with a double dot inside."

"And Planck's Constant?"

"Haven't hit that one yet. But we will. But to get back to the meat of this thing, the third section deals with something strange. It seems to have a bearing on this gadget from the top of the tower. I'd say that the volume was a technical volume on the construction, maintenance, and repair of the tower and its functions—whatever they are."

Barney spread the volume out for Jim to see. "That dingbat is some sort of electronic device. Or, perhaps subelectronic. Peel away that rusted side and we'll look inside."

Jim peeled a six-inch section from the side of the big metal tube, and they inspected the insides. Barney looked thoughtful for a minute and then flipped the pages of the book until he came to a diagram.

"Sure," he said exultantly, "this is she. Look, Jim, they draw a cathode like this, and the grids are made with a series of fine parallel lines. Different, but more like the real grid than our symbol of a zigzag line. The plate is a round circle instead of a square, but that's so clearly defined that it comes out automatically. Here's your annular electrodes, and the . . . call 'em deflection plates. I think we can hook this do-boodle up as soon as we get to our place in Lincoln Head."

"Let's go then. Not only would I like to see this thing work, but I'd give anything to know what it's for!"

"You run the crate," said Barney, "and I'll try to decipher this mess into voltages for the electrode-supply and so on. Then we'll be in shape to go ahead and hook her up."

The trip to Lincoln Head took almost an hour. Barney and Jim landed in their landing yards and took the book and the searchlight-thing inside. They went to their laboratory, and called for sandwiches and tea. Jim's sister brought in the food a little later and found them tinkering with the big beam tube.

"What have you got this time?" she groaned.

"Name it and it's yours," laughed Barney.

"A sort of gadget that we found on the Red Desert."

"What does it do?" asked Christine Baler.

"Well," said Jim, "it's a sort of a kind of a dingbat that does things."

"Uh-huh," said Christine. "A dololly that plings the inghams."

"Right!"

"You're well met, you two. Have your fun. But for Pete's sake don't forget to eat. Not that you will, I know you, but a girl has got to make some sort of attempt at admonishment. I'm going to the moompicher. I'll see you when I return."

"I'd say stick around," said Barney. "But I don't think we'll have anything to show you for hours and hours. We'll have something by the time you return."

Christine left, and the men applied themselves to their problem. Barney had done wonders in unraveling the unknown. Inductances, he found, were spirals; resistance were dotted lines; capacitances were parallel squares.

"What kind of stuff do we use for voltages?" asked Jim.

"That's a long, hard trail," laughed Barney. "Basing my calculations on the fact that their standard voltage cell was the same as ours, we apply the voltages as listed on my schematic here."

"Can you assume that their standard is the same as ours?"

"Better," said Barney. "The Terran Standard Cell—the well-known Weston Cell—dishes out what we call 1.0183 volts at twenty degrees C. Since the Martian description of their Standard Cell is essentially the same as the Terran, they are using the same thing. Only they use sense and say that a volt is the unit of a standard cell, period. Calculating their figures on the numerical base of twelve is tricky, but I've done it."

"You're doing fine. How do you assume their standard is the same?"

"Simple," said Barney in a cheerful tone. "Thank God for their habit of drawing pictures. Here we have the well-known H tube. The electrodes are signified by the symbols for the elements used. The Periodic Chart in the first section came in handy here. But look, master mind, this dinky should be evacuated, don't you think?"

"If it's electronic or subelectronic, it should be. We can solder up this breach here and apply the hyvac pump. Rig us up a power supply whilst I repair the blowout."

"Where's the BFO?"

"What do you want with that?" asked Jim.

"The second anode takes about two hundred volts worth of eighty-four cycles," explained Barney. "Has a sign that seems to signify 'In Phase,' but I'll be darned if I know with what. Y'know, Jim, this dingbat looks an awful lot like one of the drivers we use in our spaceships and driver-wing fliers."

"Yeah," drawled Jim. "About the same recognition as the difference between Edison's first electric light and a twelve-element, electron multiplier, a power output tube. Similarity: They both have cathodes."

"Edison didn't have a cathode—"

"Sure he did. Just because he didn't hang a plate inside of the bottle doesn't stop the filament from being a cathode."

Barney snorted. "A monode, hey?"

"Precisely. After which come diodes, triodes, tetrodes, pentodes, hexodes, heptodes—"

"—and the men in the white coats. How's your patching job?"

"Fine. How's your power-supply job?"

"Good enough," said Barney. "This eighty-four cycles is not going to be a sine wave at two hundred volts; the power stage of the BFO overloads just enough to bring in a bit of second harmonic."

"A beat-frequency-oscillator was never made to run at that level," complained Jim Baler. "At least, not this one. She'll tick on a bit of second, I think."

"Are we ready for the great experiment?"

"Yup, and I still wish I knew what the thing was for. Go ahead, Barney. Crack the big switch!"

Altas held up a restraining hand as Than grasped the main power switch. "Wait," he said. "Does one stand in his sky flier and leave the ground at full velocity? Or does one start an internal combustion engine at full speed?"

"No," said the youngster. "We usually take it slowly."

"And like the others, we must tune our tube. And that we cannot do under full power. Advance your power lever one-tenth step and we'll adjust the deflection anodes."

"I'll get the equipment," said Than. "I forgot that part."

"Never mind the equipment," smiled Altas. "Observe."

Altas picked up a long screwdriverlike tool and inserted it into the maze of wiring that surrounded the tube. Squinting in one end of the big tube, he turned the tool until the cathode surface brightened slightly. He adjusted the instrument until the cathode was at its brightest, and then withdrew the tool.

"That will do for your experimental set-up," smiled Altas. "The operation in service is far more critical and requires equipment. As an experiment, conducted singly, the accumulative effect cannot be dangerous, though if the deflection plates are not properly served with their supply voltages, the experiment is a failure. The operation of the tube depends upon the perfection of the deflection-plate voltages."

"No equipment is required, then?"

"It should have been employed," said Altas modestly. "But in my years as a beam-tower attendant, I have learned the art of aligning the plates by eye. Now, son, we may proceed from there."

Barney Carroll took a deep breath and let the power switch fall home. Current meters swung across their scales for an instant, and then the lights went out in the house!

"Fuse blew," said Barney shortly. He fumbled his way through the dark house and replaced the fuse. He returned smiling. "Fixed that one," he told Jim. "Put a washer behind it."

"O.K. Hit the switch again."

Barney cranked the power over, and once more the meters climbed up across the scales. There was a groaning sound from the tube, and the smell of burning insulation filled the room. One meter blew with an audible sound as the needle hit the end stop, and immediately afterward the lights in the entire block went out.

"Fix that one by hanging a penny behind it," said Jim with a grin.

"That's a job for Martian Electric to do," laughed Barney.

Several blocks from there, an attendant in the substation found the open circuit-breaker and shoved it in with a grim smile. He looked up at the power-demand meter and grunted. High for this district, but not dangerous. Duration, approximately fifteen seconds. Intensity, higher than usual but not high enough to diagnose any failure of the wiring in the district. "Ah, well," he thought, "we can crank up the blow-point on this breaker if it happens again."

He turned to leave and the crashing of the breaker scared him out of a week's growth. He snarled and said a few choice words not fit for publication. He closed the breaker and screwed the blow-point control up by two-to-one. "That'll hold 'em," he thought, and then the ringing of the telephone called him to his office, and he knew that he was in for an explanatory session with some people who wanted to know why their lights were going on and off.

He composed a plausible tale on his way to the phone. Meanwhile, he wondered about the unreasonable demand and concluded that one of the folks had just purchased a new power saw or something for their home workshop.

"Crack the juice about a half," suggested Barney. "That'll keep us on the air until we find out what kind of stuff this thing takes. The book claims about one tenth of the current-drain for this unit. Something we've missed, no doubt."

"Let's see that circuit," said Jim. After a minute, he said: "Look, guy, what are these screws for?"

"They change the side plate voltages from about three hundred to about three hundred and fifty. I've got 'em set in the middle of the range."

"Turn us on half voltage and diddle one of 'em."

"That much of a change shouldn't make the difference," objected Barney.

"Brother, we don't know what this thing is even for," reminded Jim. "Much less do we know the effect of anything on it. Diddle, I say."

"O.K., we diddle." Barney turned on half power and reached into the maze of wiring and began to tinker with one of the screws. "Hm-m-m," he said after a minute. "Does things, all right. She goes through some kind of resonance point or something. There is a spot of minimum current here. There! I've hit it. Now for the other one."

For an hour, Barney tinkered with first one screw and then the other one. He found a point where the minimum current was really low; the two screws were interdependent and only by adjusting them alternately was he able to reach the proper point on each. Then he smiled and thrust the power on full. The current remained at a sane value.

"Now what?" asked Barney.

"I don't know. Anything coming out of the business end?"

"Heat."

"Yeah, and it's about as lethal as a sun lamp. D'ye suppose the Martians used to artificially assist their crops by synthetic sunshine?"

Barney applied his eye to a spectroscope. It was one of the

newer designs that encompassed everything from short ultraviolet to long infrared by means of fluorescent screens at the invisible wave lengths. He turned the instrument across the spectrum and shook his head. "Might be good for a chest cold," he said, "but you wouldn't get a sunburn off of it. It's all in the infra. Drops off like a cliff just below the deep red. Nothing at all in the visible or above. Gee," he said with a queer smile, "you don't suppose that they died off because of a pernicious epidemic of colds and they tried chest-cooking *en masse?*"

"I'd believe anything if this darned gadget were found in a populated district," said Jim. "But we know that the desert was here when the Martians were here, and that it was just as arid as it is now. They wouldn't try farming in a place where iron oxide abounds."

"Spinach?"

"You don't know a lot about farming, do you?" asked Jim.

"I saw a cow once."

"That does not qualify you as an expert on farming."

"I know one about the farmer's daughter, and—"

"Not even an expert on dirt farming," continued Jim. "Nope, Barney, we aren't even close."

Barney checked the book once more and scratched his nose.

"How about that eighty-four cycle supply," asked Jim.

"It's eighty-four, all right. From the Martian habit of using twelve as a base, I've calculated the number to be eighty-four."

"Diddle that, too," suggested Jim.

"O.K.," said Barney. "It doesn't take a lot to crank that one around from zero to about fifteen thousand c.p.s. Here she goes!"

Barney took the main dial of the beat-frequency oscillator and began to crank it around the scale. He went up from eighty-four to the top of the dial and then returned. No effect. Then he passed through eighty-four and started down toward zero.

He hit sixty cycles and the jackpot at the same time!

At exactly sixty cycles, a light near the wall dimmed visibly. The wallpaper scorched and burst into a smoldering flame on a wall opposite the dimmed light.

Barney removed the BFO from the vicinity of sixty cycles and Jim extinguished the burning wallpaper.

"Now we're getting somewhere," said Barney.

"This is definitely some sort of weapon," said Jim. "She's not very efficient right now, but we can find out why and then we'll have something hot."

"What for?" asked Barney. "Nobody hates anybody any more."

"Unless the birds who made this thing necessary return," said Jim soberly. His voice was ominous. "We know that only one race of Martians existed, and they were all amicable. I suspect an inimical race from outer space—"

"Could be. Some of the boys are talking about an expedition to Centauri right now. We could have had a visitor from somewhere during the past."

"If you define eternity as the time required for everything to happen once, I agree. In the past or in the future, we have or will be visited by a super race. It may have happened six thousand years ago."

"Did you notice that the electric light is not quite in line with the axis of the tube?" asked Barney.

"Don't turn it any closer," said Jim. "In fact, I'd turn it away before we hook it up again."

"There she is. Completely out of line with the light. Now shall we try it again?"

"Go ahead."

Barney turned the BFO gingerly, and at sixty cycles the thing seemed quite sane. Nothing happened. "Shall I swing it around?"

"I don't care for fires as a general rule," said Jim. "Especially in my own home. Turn it gently, and take care that you don't focus the tube full on that electric light."

Barney moved the tube slightly, and then with a cessation of noise, the clock on the wall stopped abruptly. The accustomed ticking had not been noticed by either man, but the unaccustomed lack-of-ticking became evident at once. Barney shut off the BFO immediately and the two men sat down to a head-scratching session.

"She's good for burning wallpaper, dimming electric lights, and stopping clocks," said Barney. "Any of which you could do without a warehouse full of cockeyed electrical equipment. Wonder if she'd stop anything more powerful than a clock."

"I've got a quarter-horse motor here. Let's wind that up and try it."

The motor was installed on a bench nearby, and the experiment was tried again. At sixty cycles the motor groaned to a stop, and the windings began to smolder. But at the same time the big tube began to exhibit the signs of strain. Meters raced up their scales once more, reached the stops and bent. Barney shut off the motor, but the strains did not stop in the tube. The apparent overload increased linearly and finally the lights went out all over the neighborhood once more.

"Wonderful," said Barney through the darkness. "As a weapon, this thing is surpassed by everything above a fly swatter."

"We might be able to cook a steak with it—if it would take the terrific overload," said Jim. "Or we could use it as an insect exterminator."

"We'd do better by putting the insect on an anvil and hitting it firmly with a five-pound hammer," said Barney. "Then we'd only have the anvil and hammer to haul around. This thing is like hauling a fifty-thousand-watt radio transmitter around. Power supplies, BFO, tube, meters, tools, and a huge truck full of spare fuses for the times when we miss the insect. Might be good for a central heating system."

"Except that a standard electric unit is more reliable and considerably less complicated. You'd have to hire a corps of engineers to run the thing."

The lights went on again, and the attendant in the substation screwed the blow-point control tighter. He didn't know it, but his level was now above the rating for his station. But had he known it he might not have cared. At least, his station was once more in operation.

"Well," said Barney, getting up from the table, "what have we missed?"

Altas said: "Now your unit is operating at its correct level. But, son, you've missed one thing. It is far from efficient. Those two leads must be isolated from one another. Coupling from one to the other will lead to losses."

"Gosh," said Than, "I didn't know that."

"No, for some reason the books assume that the tower engineer has had considerable experience in the art. Take it from me, son, there are a lot of things that are not in the books. Now isolate those leads from one another and we'll go on."

"While you're thinking," said Jim, "I'm going to lockstitch these cables together. It'll make this thing less messy." Jim got a roll of twelve-cord from the cabinet and began to bind the many supply leads into a neat cable.

Barney watched until the job was finished, and then said: "Look, chum, let's try that electric-light trick again."

They swung the tube around until it was in the original position, and turned the juice on. Nothing happened.

Barney looked at Jim, and then reached out and pointed the big tube right at the electric light.

Nothing happened.

"Check your anode voltages again."

"All O.K."

"How about that aligning job?"

Barney fiddled with the alignment screws for minutes, but his original setting seemed to be valid.

"Back to normal," said Barney. "Rip out your cabling."

"Huh?"

"Sure. You did something. I don't know what. But rip it out and fan out the leads. There is something screwy in the supply lines. I've been tied up on that one before; this thing looks like electronics, as we agree, and I've had occasion to remember coupling troubles."

"All right," said Jim, and he reluctantly ripped out his lockstitching. He fanned the leads and they tried it again.

Obediently the light dimmed and the wallpaper burned.

"Here we go again," said Jim, killing the circuits and reaching for a small rug to smother the fire. "No wonder the Martians had this thing out in the middle of the desert. D'ye suppose that they were trying to find out how it works, too?"

"Take it easier this time and we'll fan the various leads," said Barney. "There's something tricky about the lead placement."

"Half power," announced Barney. "Now, let's get that sixty cycles."

The light dimmed slightly and a sheet of metal placed in front of the tube became slightly warm to the touch. The plate stopped the output of the tube, for the wallpaper did not scorch. Jim began to take supply line after supply line from the bundle of wiring. About halfway through the mess he hit the critical lead, and immediately the light went out completely, and the plate grew quite hot.

"Stop her!" yelled Barney.

"Why?"

"How do we know what we're overloading this time?"

"Do we care?"

"Sure. Let's point this thing away from that light. Then we can hop it up again and try it at full power."

"What do you want to try?"

"This energy-absorption thing."

"Wanna burn out my motor?"

"Not completely. This dingbat will stop a completely mechanical gadget like a clock. It seems to draw power from electric lights. It stops electromechanical power. I wonder just how far it will go toward absorbing power. And also I want to know where the power goes."

The tube was made to stop the clock again. The motor groaned under the load put upon it by the tube. Apparently the action of the tube was similar to a heavy load being placed on whatever its end happened to point to. Barney picked up a small metal block and dropped it over the table.

"Want to see if it absorbs the energy of a falling object— Look at that!"

The block fell until it came inside of the influence of the tube. Then it slowed in its fall and approached the table slowly. It did not hit the table, it touched and came to rest.

"What happens if we wind up a spring and tie it?" asked Jim.

They tried it. Nothing happened.

"Works on kinetic energy, not potential energy," said Barney.

He picked up a heavy hammer and tried to hit the table. "Like swinging a club through a tub of water," he said.

"Be a useful gadget for saving the lives of people who are falling," said Jim thoughtfully.

"Oh, sure. Put it on a truck and rush it out to the scene of the suicide."

"No. How about people jumping out of windows on account of fires? How about having one of the things around during a flier-training course? Think of letting a safe down on one of these beams, or taking a piano from the fifth floor of an apartment building."

"The whole apartment full of furniture could be pitched out of a window," said Barney.

"Mine looks that way now," said Jim, "and we've only moved a couple of times. No, Barney, don't give 'em any ideas."

Jim picked up the hammer and tried to hit the table. Then, idly, he swung the hammer in the direction of the tube's end.

Barney gasped. In this direction there was no resistance. Jim's swing continued, and the look on Jim's face indicated that he was trying to brake the swing in time to keep from hitting the end of the tube. But it seemed as though he were trying to stop an avalanche. The swing continued on and on and finally ended when the hammer head contacted the end of the tube.

There was a burst of fire. Jim swung right on through, whirling around off balance and coming to a stop only when he fell to the floor. He landed in darkness again. The burst of fire emanated from the insulation as it flamed under the heat of extreme overload.

This time the lights were out all over Lincoln Head. The whole city was in complete blackout!

Candles were found, and they inspected the tube anxiously. It seemed whole. But the hammer head was missing. The handle was cut cleanly, on an optically perfect surface.

Where the hammer head went, they couldn't say. But on the opposite wall there was a fracture in the plaster that Jim swore hadn't been there before. It extended over quite an area, and after some thought, Barney calculated that if the force of Jim's hammer blow had been evenly distributed over that area on the wall, the fracturing would have been just about that bad.

"A weapon, all right," said Barney.

"Sure. All you have to do is to shoot your gun right in this end and the force is dissipated over quite an area out of that end. In the meantime you blow out all of the powerhouses on the planet. If a hammer blow can raise such merry hell, what do you think the output of a sixteen-inch rifle would do? Probably stop the planet in its tracks. D'ye know what I think?"

"No, do you?"

"Barney, I think that we aren't even close as to the operation and use of this device."

"For that decision, Jim, you should be awarded the Interplanetary Award for Discovery and Invention—posthumously!"

"So what do we do now?"

"Dunno. How soon does this lighting situation get itself fixed?"

"You ask me . . . I don't know either."

"Well, let's see what we've found so far."

"That's easy," said Jim. "It might be a weapon, but it don't weap. We might use it for letting elevators down easy, except that it would be a shame to tie up a room full of equipment when the three-phase electric motor is so simple. We could toast a bit of bread, but the electric toaster has been refined to a beautiful piece of breakfast furniture that doesn't spray off and scorch the wallpaper. We could use it to transmit hammer blows, or to turn out electric lights, but both of those things have been done very simply; one by means of sending the hammerer to the spot, and the other by means of turning the switch. And then in the last couple of cases, there is little sense in turning out a light by short circuiting the socket and blowing all the fuses."

"That is the hard way," smiled Barney. "Like hitting a telephone pole to stop the car, or cutting the wings off a plane to return it to the ground."

"So we have a fairly lucid book that describes the entire hook-up of the thing except what it's for. It gives not only the use of this device, but also variations and replacements. Could we figure it out by sheer deduction?"

"I don't see how. The tower is in the midst of the Red Desert.

There is nothing but sand that assays high in iron oxide between Canalopsis, at the junction of the Grand Canal and Lincoln Head. Might be hid, of course, just as this one was, and we'll send out a crew of expert sub-sand explorers with under-surface detectors to cover the ground for a few hundred miles in any direction from the place where we found this. Somehow, I doubt that we'll find much."

"And how do you . . . ah, there's the lights again . . . deduce that?" asked Jim.

"This gadget is or was of importance to the Martians. Yet in the Temple of Science and Industry at Canalopsis, there is scant mention of the towers."

"Not very much, hey?"

"Very little, in fact. Of course the pictographs on the Temple at Canalopsis show one tower between what appeared to be two cities. Wavy lines run from one city to the tower and to the other city. Say! I'll bet a cooky that this is some sort of signaling device!"

"A beam transmitter?" asked Jim skeptically. "Seems like a lot of junk for just signaling. Especially where such a swell job can be done with standard radio equipment. A good civilization—such as the Martians must have had—wouldn't piddle around with relay stations between two cities less than a couple of thousand miles apart. With all the juice this thing can suck, they'd be more than able to hang a straight broadcast station and cover halfway around the planet as ground-wave area. What price relay station?"

"Nevertheless, I'm going to tinker up another one of these and see if it is some sort of signaling equipment."

The door opened and Christine Baler entered. She waved a newspaper before her brother's eyes and said: "Boy, have you been missing it!"

"What?" asked Barney.

"Pixies or gremlins loose in Lincoln Head."

"Huh-huh. Read it," said Jim.

"Just a bunch of flash headlines. Fire on Manley Avenue. Three planes had to make dead-tube landings in the center of the city; power went dead for no good reason for about ten minutes.

Façade of the City Hall caved in. Power plants running wild all over the place. Ten thousand dollars' worth of electrical equipment blown out. Automobiles stalled in rows for blocks."

Jim looked at Barney. "Got a bear by the tail," he said.

"Could be," admitted Barney.

"Are you two blithering geniuses going to work all night?" asked Christine.

"Nope. We're about out of ideas. Except the one that Barney had about the gadget being some sort of signaling system."

"Why don't you fellows call Don Channing? He's the signaling wizard of the Solar System."

"Sure, call Channing. Every time someone gets an idea, everyone says, 'Call Channing!' He gets called for everything from Boy Scout wigwag ideas to super-cyclotronic-electron-stream beams to contact the outer planets. Based upon the supposition that people will eventually get there, of course."

"Well?"

"Well, I . . . we, I mean . . . found this thing and we're jolly well going to tinker it out. In spite of the fact that it seems to bollix up everything from electric lights to moving gears. I think we're guilty of sabotage. Façade of the City Hall, et cetera. Barney, how long do you think it will take to tinker up another one of these?"

"Few hours. They're doggoned simple things in spite of the fact that we can't understand them. In fact, I'm of the opinion that the real idea would be to make two; one with only the front end for reception, one for the rear end for transmission, and the one we found for relaying. That's the natural bent, I believe."

"Could be. Where are you going to cut them?"

"The transmitter will start just before the cathode and the receiver will end just after the . . . uh, cathode."

"Huh?"

"Obviously the cathode is the baby that makes with the end product. She seems to be a total intake from the intake end and a complete output from the opposite end. Right?"

"Right, but it certainly sounds like heresy."

"I know," said Barney thoughtfully, "but the thing is obviously different from anything that we know today. Who knows how she works?"

"I give up."

Christine, who had been listening in an interested manner, said: "You fellers are the guys responsible for the ruckus that's been going on all over Lincoln Head?"

"I'm afraid so."

"Well, brother warlocks, unless you keep your activities under cover until they're worth mentioning, you'll both be due for burning at the stake."

"O.K., Chris," said Jim. "We'll not let it out."

"But how are you going to tinker up that transmitter-relay-receiver system?"

"We'll take it from here to Barney's place across the avenue and into his garage. That should do it."

"O.K., but now I'm going to bed."

"Shall we knock off, too?" asked Jim.

"Yup. Maybe we'll dream a good thought."

"So long then. We'll leave the mess as it is. No use cleaning up now, we'll only have to mess it up again tomorrow with the same junk."

"And I'll have that—or those—other systems tinkered together by tomorrow noon. That's a promise," said Barney. "And you," he said to Christine, "will operate the relay station."

Altas said to Than: "Now that your system is balanced properly, and we have proved the worth of this tube as a replacement, we shall take it to the roof and install it. The present tube is about due for retirement."

"I've done well, then?" asked Than.

"Considering all, you've done admirably. But balancing the device in the tower, and hooked into the circuit as an integral part is another thing. Come, Than. We shall close the line for an hour whilst replacing the tube."

"Is that permissible?"

"At this time of the night the requirements are small. No damage will be done; they can get along without us for an hour. In fact, at this time of night, only the people who are running the city will know that we are out of service. And it is necessary that the tube be maintained at full capability. We can not chance a weakened tube; it might fail when it is needed the most."

Than carried the tube to the top of the tower, and Altas remained to contact the necessary parties concerning the shut-off for replacement purposes. He followed Than to the top after a time and said: "Now disconnect the old tube and put it on the floor. We shall replace the tube immediately, but it will be an hour before it is properly balanced again."

It was not long before Than had the tube connected properly. "Now," said Altas, "turn it on one-tenth power and we shall align it."

"Shall I use the meters?"

"I think it best. This requires perfect alignment now. We've much power and considerable distance, and any losses will create great amounts of heat."

"All right," said Than. He left the tower top to get the meters.

Barney Carroll spoke into a conveniently placed microphone. "Are you ready?" he asked.

"Go ahead," said Christine.

"We're waiting," said Jim.

"You're the bird on the transmitter," said Barney to Jim. "You make with the juice."

Power rheostats were turned up gingerly, until Jim shouted to stop. His shout was blotted out by cries from the other two. They met in Barney's place to confer.

"What's cooking?" asked Jim.

"The meters are all going crazy in my end," said Barney. "I seem to be sucking power out of everything in line with my tube."

"The so-called relay station is firing away at full power and doing nothing but draining plenty of power from the line," complained Christine.

"And on my end, I was beginning to scorch the wallpaper again. I don't understand it. With no receiver-end, how can I scorch wallpaper?"

"Ask the Martians. They know."

"You ask 'em. What shall we do, invent a time machine and go back sixty centuries?"

"Wish we could," said Barney. "I'd like to ask the bird that left this textbook why they didn't clarify it more."

"Speaking of Don Channing again," said Jim, "I'll bet a hat that one of his tube-replacement manuals for the big transmitters out on Venus Equilateral do not even mention that the transmitter requires a receiver before it is any good. We think we're modern. We are, and we never think that some day some poor bird will try to decipher our technical works. Why, if Volta himself came back and saw the most perfect machine ever invented—the transformer —he'd shudder. No connection between input and output, several kinds of shorted loops of wire; and instead of making a nice simple electromagnet, we short the lines of force and on top of that we use a lot of laminations piled on top of one another instead of a nice, soft iron core. We completely short the input, et cetera, but how do we make with a gadget like that?"

"I know. We go on expecting to advance. We forget the simple past. Remember the lines of that story: 'How does one chip the flint to make the best arrowhead?' I don't know who wrote it any more than I know how to skin a boar, but we do get on without making arrowheads or skinning boars or trimming birch-bark canoes."

"All right, but there's still this problem."

"Remember how we managed to align this thing? I wonder if it might not take another alignment to make it work as a relay."

"Could be," said Jim. "I'll try it. Christine, you work these screws at the same time we do, and make the current come out as low as we can."

They returned to their stations and began to work on the alignment screws. Jim came out first on the receiver. Christine was second on the transmitter, while Barney fumbled for a long time with the relay tube.

Then Christine called: "Fellows, my meter readings are climbing up again. Shall I diddle?"

"Wait a minute," said Barney. "That means I'm probably taking power out of that gadget you have in there. Leave 'em alone."

He fiddled a bit more, and then Jim called: "Whoa, Nellie.

Someone just lost me a millimeter. She wound up on the far end."

"Hm-m-m," said Barney, "so we're relaying."

"Go ahead," said Jim. "I've got a ten-ampere meter on here now."

Barney adjusted his screws some more.

"Wait a minute," said Jim. "I'm going to shunt this meter up to a hundred amps."

"What?" yelled Barney.

"Must you yell?" asked Christine ruefully. "These phones are plenty uncomfortable without some loud-mouthed bird screaming."

"Sorry, but a hundred amps . . . *whoosh!* What have we got here, anyway?"

"Yeah," said Christine. "I was about to say that my input meter is running wild again."

"Gone?"

"Completely. You shouldn't have hidden it behind that big box. I didn't notice it until just now, but she's completely gone."

"I'll be over. I think we've got something here."

An hour passed, during which nothing of any great importance happened. By keying the transmitter tube, meters in the receiver tube were made to read in accordance. Then they had another conclave.

"Nothing brilliant," said Jim. "We could use super-output voice amplifiers and yell halfway across the planet if we didn't have radio. We can radio far better than this cockeyed system of signaling."

"We might cut the power."

"Or spread out quite a bit. I still say, however, that this is no signaling system."

"It works like one."

"So can a clothesline be made to serve as a transmitter of intelligence. But it's prime function is completely different."

"S'pose we have a super-clothesline here?" asked Christine.

"The way that hammer felt last night, I'm not too sure that this might not be some sort of tractor beam," said Jim.

"Tractor beams are mathematically impossible."

"Yeah, and they proved conclusively that a bird cannot fly," said Jim. "That was before they found the right kind of math. Up until Clerk Maxwell's time, radio was mathematically impossible. Then he discovered the electromagnetic equations, and we're squirting signals across the Inner System every day. And when math and fact do not agree, which changes?"

"The math. Galileo proved that. Aristotle said that a heavy stone will fall faster. Then Galileo changed the math of that by heaving a couple of boulders off the Leaning Tower. But what have we here?"

"Has anyone toyed with the transmission of power?"

"Sure. A lot of science-fiction writers have their imaginary planets crisscrossed with transmitted power. Some broadcast it, some have it beamed to the consumer. When they use planes, they have the beam coupled to an object-finder so as to control the direction of the beam. I prefer the broadcasting, myself. It uncomplicates the structure of the tale."

"I mean actually?"

"Oh, yes. But the losses are terrific. Useful power transmission is a minute percentage of the total output of the gadget. Absolutely impractical, especially when copper and silver are so plentiful to string along the scenery on steel towers. No good."

"But look at this cockeyed thing. Christine puts in a couple of hundred amps; I take them off my end. Believe it or not, the output meter at my end was getting a lot more soup than I was pouring in."

"And my gadget was not taking anything to speak of," said Barney.

"Supposing it was a means of transmitting power. How on Mars did they use a single tower there in the middle of the Red Desert? We know there was a Martian city at Canalopsis, and another one not many miles from Lincoln Head. Scribbled on the outer cover of this book is the legend: 'Tower Station, Red Desert,' and though the Martians didn't call this the 'Red Desert,' the terminology will suffice for nomenclature."

"Well?" asked Jim.

"You notice they did not say: 'Station No. 1,' or '3' or '7.' That means to me that there was but one."

"Holy Smoke! Fifteen hundred miles with only one station? On Mars the curvature of ground would put such a station below the electrical horizon—" Jim thought that one over for a minute and then said: "Don't tell me they bent the beam?"

"Either they did that or they heated up the sand between," said Barney cryptically. "It doesn't mind going through nonconducting walls, but a nice, fat ground . . . blooey, or I miss my guess. That'd be like grounding a high line."

"You're saying that they did bend— *Whoosh*, again!"

"What was that alignment problem? Didn't we align the deflecting anodes somehow?"

"Yeah, but you can't bend the output of a cathode-ray tube externally of the deflection plates."

"But this is not electron-beam stuff," objected Barney. "This is as far ahead of cathode-ray tubes as they are ahead of the Indian signal drum or the guy who used to run for twenty-four miles from Ghent to Aix."

"That one was from Athens to Sparta," explained Christine, "the Ghent to Aix journey was a-horseback, and some thousand-odd years after."

"Simile's still good," said Barney. "There's still a lot about this I do not understand."

"A masterpiece of understatement, if I ever heard one," laughed Jim. "Well, let's work on it from that angle. Come on, gang, to horse!"

"Now," said Altas, "you will find that the best possible efficiency is obtained when the currents in these two resistances are equal and opposite in direction. That floats the whole tube on the system, and makes it possible to run the tube without any external power source. It requires a starter-source for aligning and for standby service, and for the initial surge; then it is self-sustaining. Also the in-phase voltage can not better be obtained than by exciting the phasing anode with some of the main-line power. That must always be correctly phased. We now need the frequency generator no longer, and by increasing the power rheostat to full, the tube will take up the load. Watch the meters, and when they read full power, you may throw the cut-over switch and make the tube self-sustaining. Our tower will then be in perfect service, and you and I may return to our home below."

Than performed the operations, and then they left, taking the old tube with them.

And on Terra, Sargon of Akkad watched ten thousand slaves carry stone for one of his public buildings. He did not know that on one of the stars placed in the black bowl of the evening sky for his personal benefit, men were flinging more power through the air than the total output of all of his slaves combined. Had he been told, he would have had the teller beheaded for lying because Sargon of Akkad couldn't possibly have understood it—

"You know, we're missing a bet," said Jim. "This in-phase business here. Why shouldn't we hang a bit of the old wall-socket juice in here?"

"That might be the trick," said Barney.

Jim made the connections, and they watched the meters read up and up and up—and from the street below them a rumbling was heard. Smoke issued from a crevasse in the pavement, and then with a roar, the street erupted and a furrow three feet wide and all the way across the street from Jim Baler's residence to Barney Carroll's garage lifted out of the ground. It blew straight up and fell back, and from the bottom of the furrow the smoldering of burned and tortured wiring cast a foul smell.

"*Wham!*" said Barney, looking at the smoking trench. "What was that?"

"I think we'll find that it was the closest connection between our places made by the Electric Co.," said Jim.

"But what have we done?"

"I enumerate," said Christine, counting off on her fingers. "We've blasted in the façade of the City Hall. We've caused a couple of emergency flier-landings within the city limits. We've blown fuses and circuit breakers all the way from here to the main powerhouse downtown. We've stalled a few dozen automobiles. We've torn or burned or cut the end off of one hammer and have fractured the wall with it . . . where did that go, anyway, the hammerhead? We've burned wallpaper. We've run our electric bill up to about three hundred dollars, I'll bet. We've bunged up a dozen meters. And now we've ripped up a trench in the middle of the street."

"Somewhere in this set-up, there is a return circuit," said Jim thoughtfully. "We've been taking power out of the line, and I've been oblivious of the fact that a couple of hundred amperes is too high to get out of our power line without trouble. What we've been doing is taking enough soup out of the public utility lines to supply the losses only. The power we've been seeing on our meters is the build-up, recirculated!"

"Huh?"

"Sure. Say we bring an amp in from the outside and shoot it across the street. It goes to the wires and comes back because of some electrical urge in our gadgets here, and then goes across the street inphase with the original. That makes two amps total crossing our beam. The two come back and we have two plus two. Four come back, and we double again and again until the capability of our device is at saturation. All we have to do is to find the ground-return and hang a load in there. We find the transmitter-load input, and supply that with a generator. Brother, we can beam power all the way from here to Canalopsis on one relay tower!"

Barney looked at his friend. "Could be."

"Darned right. What other item can you think of that fits this tower any better? We've run down a dozen ideas, but this works. We may be arrested for wrecking Lincoln Head, but we'll get out as soon as this dingbat hits the market. Brother, what a find!"

"Fellows, I think you can make your announcement now," smiled Christine. "They won't burn you at the stake if you can bring electric power on a beam of pure nothing. This time you've hit the jackpot!"

It is six thousand Terran Years since Sargon of Akkad held court that was lighted by torch. It is six thousand years, Terran, since Than and Altas replaced the link in a power system that tied their cities together.

It is six thousand years since the beam tower fell into the Red Desert and the mighty system of beamed power became lost as an art. But once again the towers dot the plains, not only of Mars, but of Venus and Terra, too.

And though they are of a language understood by the peoples of three worlds, the manuals of instruction would be as cryptic to Than as his manual was to Barney Carroll and Jim Baler.

People will never learn.

P. Schuyler Miller's "The Cave" has the fascinations of the two-faced Janus. Like that Roman god, Miller's story looks both backward and forward, to the past and to the future. From the past "The Cave" takes Schiaparelli's and Lowell's descriptions of Martian geography, translating those earlier views of Mars into crisp, precise modern prose. For the future "The Cave" introduces the "grak" in an intriguing foreshadowing of the "grok" later made famous by Robert A. Heinlein in his Martian novel, *Stranger in a Strange Land.* But of course "The Cave" has a great deal more to recommend it than its literary predecessors and successors. Miller's story is beautifully styled and tightly plotted. Moreover, it is one of the most daring Mars tales ever written, for instead of keeping a safe distance and painting the Red Planet in an impressionistic fog, "The Cave" boldly takes a microscopically close focus on Mars and the Martians.

P. Schuyler Miller

THE CAVE

The cave measured less than a hundred feet from end to end. It opened at the base of a limestone ridge which rose like a giant, rounded fin out of the desert. Its mouth was a flat oval, a shallow alcove scoured out of the soft stone by wind and sand. Near one end a smooth-walled tunnel sloped gently back into the ridge. Twenty feet from the entrance it turned sharply to the right and in a few feet swung back to the left, paralleling its original course. Here it levelled out into a broad, flat channel not more than four feet high. This was the main chamber of the cave.

The big room, like the rest of the cave, had been leached out of the limestone by running water, long before. The water had followed a less resistant seam in the rock, dissolving out a passage whose low ceiling rose and fell a little with irregularities in the harder stratum overhead, whose floor was flat and water-polished in spots and in others buried under a fine yellow clay. A little past the midpoint, the room opened out into a kind of inverted funnel in which a tall man could stand erect, a tapering chimney which quickly dwindled to a shaft barely big enough to admit a man's hand. Here the floor of the cave was lower and the walls, which had drawn together until they were less than ten feet apart, were ribbed and terraced with flowstone.

Beyond the chimney the ceiling dropped suddenly to within a few inches of the floor. By lying flat on his face and squirming along between the uneven layers of rock a thin man might have entered here. After measuring his length perhaps three times he would have been able to raise himself on one elbow and twist into a sitting position, his back against the end wall of the cave and his head and shoulders wedged into a crevice which cut across the main passage at right angles. This crevice lay directly under the highest part of the ridge and vanished into darkness above and on either side. Water must at one time have flowed through it, for the harder silicious layers in the limestone stood out on the walls in low relief like fine ruled lines drawn in sooty black. Not even air stirred in it now.

Twenty feet in the winding entry—six or eight feet at the bend—another thirty to the chimney and fifteen or twenty more to the back wall; it was a small cave. It was also very old.

The limestone of which the ridge was formed was perhaps the oldest exposed rock on the surface of that small old world. It had been laid down in fairly deep water at a time when there were seas where there were only deserts now. There had been life in those seas; where wind or water had worn away the softer lime, their fossil bodies stood out from the surface of the grey stone. There were fluted shells like glistening black trumpets—swarms of tiny big-eyed things with fantastically shaped armour and many sprawling arms—long ropes of delicate, saw-edged weed whose fossil tissues were still stained a dull purple—occasionally fragments of some larger thing like an armoured, blunt-headed fish. They had been alive, swarming and breeding in the shallow sea, when Earth was no more than a scabbed-over globe of slowly jelling flame.

The cave itself was very old. It had been made by running water, and it was a long time since there was much water on the dying world. Water, sour with soil acids leached from the black humus of a forest floor, had seeped down into the network of joint-planes which intersected the flat-lying limestone beds, eating away the soft stone, widening cracks into crannies and crannies into high-arched rooms, rushing along the harder strata and tunnelling through the softer ones, eventually bursting out into the open again at the base of a mossy ledge and babbling away over the rocks to join a brook, a river, or the sea.

Millions of years had passed since there were rivers and seas on Mars.

Things change slowly underground. After a cave has died—after the sources of moisture which created it have shifted or dried up—it may lie without changing for centuries. A man may set his foot in the clay of its floor and go away, and another man may come a hundred or a thousand or ten thousand years afterwards and see his footprint there, as fresh as though it had been made yesterday. A man may write on the ceiling with the smoke of a torch, and if there is still a little life in the cave and moisture in the rock, what he has written will gradually film over with clear stone and last forever. Rock may fall from the ceiling and bury portions of the floor, or seal off some rooms completely. Water may return and wash away what has been written or coat it with slime. But if a cave has died—if water has ceased to flow and its walls and ceiling are dry—things seldom change.

Most of the planet's surface had been desert for more millions of years than anyone has yet estimated. From the mouth of the cave its dunes and stony ridges stretched away like crimson ripples left on a beach after a wave has passed. They were dust rather than sand: red, ferric dust ground ever finer by the action of grain against grain, milling over and over through the centuries. It lay in a deep drift in the alcove and spilled down into the opening of the cave; it carpeted the first twenty-foot passage as with a strip of red velvet, and a little of it passed around the angle in the tunnel into the short cross-passage. Only the very finest powder, wellnigh impalpable, hung in the still air long enough to pass the second bend and reach the big room. Enough had passed to lay a thin, rusty mantle over every horizontal surface in the cave. Even in the black silt at the very back of the cave, where the air never stirred, there was a soft red bloom on the yellow flowstone.

The cave was old. Animals had sheltered in it. There were trails trodden into the dry clay, close to the walls, made before the clay had dried. There was no dust on these places—animals still followed them when they needed to. There was a mass of draggled, shredded stalks and leaves from some desert plant, packed into the cranny behind a fallen rock and used as a nest. There were little piles of excreta, mostly the chitinous shells of insectlike creatures and the indigestible cellulose of certain plants. Under the chimney the ceiling was blackened by smoke, and there were shards of charcoal and burned bone mixed with the dust of the floor. There were places where the clay had been chipped and dug away to give more headroom, or to make a flat place where a bowl could be set down. There were other signs as well.

The *grak* reached the cave a little after dawn. He had been run-ning all night, and as the sun rose he had seen the shadow of the ridge drawn in a long black line across the crimson dunes, and turned towards it. He ran with the tireless lope of the desert people, his splayed feet sinking only a little way into the soft dust where a man of his weight would have floundered ankle deep.

He was a young male, taller than most of his kind, better mus-cled and fatter. His fur was sleek and thick, jet black with a pat-tern of rich brown. The colours in his cheek patches were fresh and bright, and his round black eyes shone like discs of polished coal.

He had been a hunter for less than one season. His tribe was one of the marauding bands which summered in the northern oases, raiding down into the lowlands in winter when the dry plateau became too cold and bare even for their hardy breed. It had fared better than most, for it had had little contact with man. The *grak* carried a knife which he had made for himself out of an eight-inch bar of beryllium copper, taken in his first raid. It was the only human thing he owned. Its hilt was of bone, intri-cately carved with the clan symbols of his father-line; its burnished blade was honed to a wicked double edge. It was the finest knife any of the desert folk had ever seen, and he had had to fight for it more than once. The desert tribes retained the old skills of metal working which the softer-living pastoral greenlanders had forgotten, and his tribe, the *Begar*, were among the best of the dryland smiths.

He wore the knife tucked into the short kilt of plaited leather which was his only garment. The Old One of his father-line had given it to him on the day he became a hunter and could no longer run naked like a cub. It was soft and pliable with long wear and oiled to a mahogany brown almost as dark and rich as his own chest patterns. There were black stains on it which he knew were blood, for the Old One had been one of the fiercest slayers of his line and the kilt had come down to him from an even greater warrior in his own youth. The very pattern in which the thin strips of *zek* hide were woven had lost its meaning, though it undoubtedly had been and still was of great virtue.

It was cold in the shadow of the ridge, and the *grak's* long fur fluffed out automatically to provide extra insulation. He looked like a big black owl as he stood scanning the western sky, sniffing the wind with his beaklike nose. There was a tawny band low on the horizon, brightening as the sun rose. He had smelled a storm early in the night, for he had all the uncanny weather-wiseness of his race and was sensitive to every subtle change in the quality of the atmosphere. He had started for the nearest arm of the greenlands, intending to claim the hospitality of the first village he could find, but the storm front was moving faster than he could run. He had seen the ridge only just in time.

He had recognized the place as he approached, though he had never seen it and none of his tribe had visited this part of the desert for many seasons. Such landmarks were part of the education of every dryland cub, and until they had become thoroughly ingrained in his wrinkled young brain he could not hope to pass the hunter's tests and win a hunter's rights. The cave was where he had known it would be, and he chuckled softly with satisfaction as he saw the weathered symbol carved in the stone over the opening. The desert people had long ago discarded the art of writing, having no use for it, but the meaning of certain signs had been passed down as a very practical part of their lore. This was a cave which the *grak's* own forefathers had used and marked.

He studied the signs in the dust around the entrance of the cave. He was not the first to seek shelter there. The feathery membranes of his nose unfolded from their horny sheath, recording the faint scents which still hung in the thin air. They confirmed what his eyes had told him. The cave was occupied.

The wind was rising fast. Red dust devils whirled ahead of the advancing wall of cloud. Red plumes were streaming from the summit of every dune. Making the sign of peace-coming, the *grak* stooped and entered the cave. Beyond the second bend in the passage was darkness which not even his owl's eyes, accustomed to the desert nights, could penetrate. However, he did not need to see. The sensitive organs of touch which were buried in the gaudy skin of his cheek patches picked up infinitesimal vibrations in the still air and told him accurately where there were obstacles. His ears were pricked for the slightest sound. His nose picked up a mixture of odours—his own characteristic scent, the dry and slightly musty smell of the cave itself, and the scents of the other creatures with which he would have to share it.

He identified them, one by one. There were four or five small desert creatures which had more to fear from him than he from them. There was one reptilian thing which under other circumstances might be dangerous, and which still might be if the peace were broken. And there was a *zek*.

The carnivore was as big and nearly as intelligent as the tribesman himself. Its kind waged perpetual war on the flocks of the greenland people, and rarely visited the oases, but when one did wander into the desert it was the most dreaded enemy of the dryland tribes. It stole their cubs from beside their very campfires and attacked full-grown hunters with impunity. Its mottled pelt was the choicest prize a hunter could bring back as proof of his prowess. To some of the more barbaric tribes of the north it was more than just a beast—it was His emissary.

A sudden gust from the passage at his back told the *grak* that the storm was breaking. In a matter of minutes the air would be unbreathable outside. Softly, so as not to arouse the savage beast's suspicions, he began to murmur the ritual of the peace. His fingers were on the hilt of his knife as he began, but as the purring syllables went out into the hollow darkness, his nostrils told him that the fear-odour was diminishing. Somewhere in the dark a horny paw scuffed on the dry clay and there was an instant reek of terror from some of the smaller things, but the *zek* made no sign. It was satisfied to keep the peace. Moving cautiously, the *grak* found a hollow in the wall near the entry and sat down to wait, squatting with his knees tucked up close under his furry belly, the hard rock at his back. The knife he laid on the floor beside his hand where it would be ready if he needed it. For a time his senses remained keyed to fever pitch, but gradually his tenseness eased. They were all *grekka* here—all living things, united in the common battle for existence against a cruel and malignant Nature. They knew the law and the brotherhood, and they would keep the truce as long as the storm lasted. Gradually the nictitating lids slipped across his open eyes and he sank into a half-sleep.

Harrigan blundered into the cave by pure luck. He knew nothing about Mars or its deserts except what the Company put in its handbook, and that was damn little. He was a big man and a strong man, born in the mountains with a more than ordinary tolerance for altitude, and he had had to spend less than a week in the dome before they shifted him to the new post in the eastern Sabaeus. He did what he was told and no more than he was told, laid away his pay every week in anticipation of one almighty spree when they brought him in at the next opposition, and had nothing but contempt for the native Martians. *Grekka* they were called, and that was all he knew or cared about them. To him they looked like animals and they were animals, in spite of the fact that they could talk and build houses and kept herds of peg-legged monstrosities which seemed to serve as cattle. Hell—parrots could talk and ants kept cattle!

Harrigan had been a miner on Earth. He was that here, but he couldn't get used to the idea that plants could be more valuable than all the copper and tungsten and carnotite in the world. The desert and its barren red hills nagged at him, and whenever he could get time off he explored them. The fact that he found only rocks and sand did nothing to extinguish his sullen conviction that there was treasure incalculable here somewhere if only the damned natives would talk or the Company would listen to a man who knew minerals better than the big shots knew the swing of their secretaries' hips.

The fact was, of course, as the Company knew very well, that Martian mineral deposits had been exhausted by a native Martian civilization pursuing its inevitable way to an inevitable end at a time when Adam and Eve probably had tails. That the descendants of that civilization were still alive, even on a basis of complete savagery, spoke volumes for the stamina of the native race. Such arguments, however, would have meant less than nothing to a man of Harrigan's type. There were mines on Earth. There were mines on the Moon. Hell—there were mines on Mars!

This time he had overstayed his luck. To him the low yellow wall of cloud on the western horizon was only a distant range of hills which he might some day visit and where he might find wealth enough to set him up in liquor for the rest of his life. He had spent the night in the cab of his sand car, and it was not until the clouds were a sullen precipice towering half-way up the sky that he understood what he was heading into. He swung around and headed back, but by then it was too late.

When the storm hit it was like night. The air was a semi-solid mass through which the sand car wallowed blindly with only its instrument board to show where it was going. Dust swiftly clogged the air intake and he had to take out the filters, put on his mask, and hope for the best. It didn't come. In seconds the air inside the cab was a reddish mist and dust was settling like fine red pepper on every exposed surface. The wind seized the squat machine and rocked it like a skiff in a typhoon, but Harrigan could only hang on, peer red-eyed through dust-coated goggles at his dust-covered instruments, and wonder where he was.

The floundering car climbed painfully to the top of a monster dune, pushed its blunt snout out over the steep leading edge, slewed violently around and started down. Harrigan yanked despairingly at the steering levers; they were packed tight with dust and refused to move. He did not see the ridge until the car smashed head on into it. There was a despairing gurgle from the engine, a last clatter of broken bearings, and the car stopped. At once sand began to pile up behind and around it, and Harrigan, picking himself up off the floor of the cab, saw that if he didn't get out fast he would be buried where he sat.

He struggled out on the lee side of the car into a gale that bit into him like an icy knife. He could not see the car when he had taken one step away from it. The dust drove through every seam and patch of his clothes and filtered in around the edges of his mask. It was sucked into his mouth and nose and gritted under his swollen eyelids. It was everywhere, and in no time it would smother him.

The car was lost, though he was probably less than ten feet from it. The wind screamed past him in unholy glee, tearing at every loose flap on his coat, chilling him to the bone. He took half a dozen blundering steps, knee-deep in the soft dust, stumbled, and came down on his knees at the foot of the cliff. His outthrust hands met solid rock. He struggled forward on his knees and peered at it through crusted goggles. It was limestone, and where there was limestone there might be a cave. Foot by foot he felt his way along the uneven surface of the ridge until suddenly it dropped away in front of him, he staggered forward, and fell on his hands and knees in the entrance of the cave.

His head had clipped the low overhang as he fell and it was a minute or two before he realized where he was. Almost automatically, then, he crawled ahead until his skull rammed hard into another wall. He sat gingerly back on his heels and clawed at his mask. It was completely plugged with dust and utterly useless. He lifted it off his face and took a slow breath. There was dust in the air—plenty of it—but he could breathe.

He groped about him in the pitch dark, found an opening in the right-hand wall, and crawled in. Almost immediately there was another sharp turn and the passage suddenly opened out on either side and left him crouching at the entrance of what he knew must be a good-sized room.

Harrigan knew caves too well to take chances with them. What lay ahead might be a room or it might be a pit dropping to some lower level. He had a feeling that it was big. He found the corner where the left-hand wall swung back, moved up against it, moistened his lips with a thick, dry tongue, and shouted:

"Hoy!"

The echo rattled back at him like gunfire. The place was big, but not too big. What he needed now was water and a light.

He had both. Dust had worked in around the stopper of his canteen until he could barely start the threads, but one last savage twist of his powerful fingers did the trick. There wasn't much left. He let a few drops trickle over his tongue and down his throat, wiped the caked dust off the threads with a finger, and screwed the cap back on. These storms lasted for days sometimes, and it was all the water in the world as far as he was concerned.

Light came next. Harrigan had spent too much time underground to be afraid of the dark, but it was plain common sense to want to see what you were getting into. Harrigan hated mysteries. If he knew what he was facing he could fight his way through anything, but he hated blind fumbling and he hated the dark.

Enough water had evaporated from the open canteen in the minute or two he had had the cap off appreciably to raise the moisture content of the cave—at least for the Martians. To their acute senses it was the equivalent of a heavy fog. A few feet away in the blackness the *grak* awoke with a start. Farther back in the cave one of the small animals stirred eagerly. And the *zek* sneezed.

Harrigan's blundering approach had roused the occupants of the cave, and every eye, ear and nose had been trained on him when he appeared. One rodentlike creature made a panicky rush as it got his scent, only to freeze in terror as it nearly bumped into the *zek*. The peace, for the moment, was suspended—a new factor had entered the situation and a new equilibrium must be reached. They quietly awaited developments.

Harrigan had missed all this preliminary activity in his efforts to find out where he was, rub the dust out of his eyes, and get a few drops of water down his parched gullet. But when the *zek* sneezed, the sudden sound was like an explosion in his ears. In the dead silence which followed he could clearly hear the sound of quiet breathing. It was close to him, and it came from more than one place. He had to have a light!

There should have been a torch in the pocket of his coverall. There wasn't. He had lost it or left it in the car. He had a lighter, though. He ripped feverishly at the zipper of his coverall. It slid

open a few inches with a sound like the crackle of lightning and
jammed. Sweat dripping from his forehead he sat back on his
heels and fumbled for his gun, but there was no movement from
the things in the dark. Slowly and softly he slipped two fingers
into his pocket and found the lighter. Levelling the gun at the
blank blackness in front of him he lifted the lighter above his
head and flipped off the cap.

The burst of yellow flame was dazzling. Then he saw their eyes—
dozens of little sparks of green and red fire staring out of the dark.
As his own eyes adjusted he saw the *grak*, huddled like a woolly
black gargoyle in his corner. The Martian's huge round eyes were
watching him blankly, his grinning mouth was slightly open over
a saw-edged line of teeth, and his pointed ears were spread wide
to catch every sound. His beaklike, shining nose and bright red
cheek patches gave him the look of a partly plucked owl. He had
a wicked-looking knife in his spidery fingers.

Harrigan's gaze flickered around the circle of watching beasts.
He knew nothing of Martian animals, except for the few domesti-
cated creatures the greenlanders kept, and they made a weird
assortment. They were mostly small, ratty things with big eyes
and feathery antennae in place of noses. Some of them were furred
and some had horny or scaly armour. All of them were vari-
ously decorated with fantastic collections of coloured splotches,
crinkled horns, and faceted spines which presumably were at-
tractive to themselves or their mates. At the far end of the cave,
curled up in a bed of dry grass, was a lean splotched thing almost
as big as the little native which stared at him with malevolent
red eyes set close together over a grinning, crocodilian snout. As
he eyed it, it yawned hideously and dropped its head on its
crossed forepaws—paws like naked, taloned hands. It narrowed
its eyes to crimson slits and studied him insolently from under
the pallid lids. It looked nasty, and his fingers closed purposefully
over the butt of his gun.

The *grak's* cackle of protest stopped him. The only word he
could make out was *bella*—peace. He knew that because he had
a woman named Bella back in New York, or he had had before he
signed on with the Company. Besides, it was part of the spiel
you were supposed to rattle off every time you talked to one

of the damned little rats. It was all the Martian he knew, so he
spat it out, keeping one eye on the other beast.

This was the first man the *grak* had ever seen. It was a mon-
strous-looking thing, wrapped in layer after layer of finely plaited
fabric which must have taken his mates many years to weave, even
if their clumsy fingers were as deft as those of the greenlanders,
who occasionally did such things. A thrilling philosophical problem
was teasing the *grak's* young brain. Was or was not this man of
the *grekka?*

To a native Martian the term *grekka* means literally "living
things". Any creature native to the planet is a *grak;* all of them,
separately or collectively, are *grekka.* The first men to come in
contact with the native race heard the word used to designate the
Martians themselves and assumed that it was the Martian equivalent of "men". Graziani, of course, as an anthropologist of note,
immediately realized the truth of the matter—the situation is
duplicated again and again among human aborigines—but the
label stuck. Nor did that matter too much, for *grekka* did include
the natives and made perfectly good sense when it was used as
men proceeded to use it. What did matter was that the word was
also the key to the whole elaborate structure of Martian psychology.

Millions of years of unceasing struggle with the forces of an
inclement environment on a swiftly maturing and rapidly dying
planet have ingrained in the native Martian race, greenlanders
and drylanders alike, the fundamental concept that Nature is
their undying enemy. Life for them is a bitter fight against overwhelming odds, with an invisible foe who will use every possible
means to grind out the little spark of ego in each round, furry Martian skull. You find it in the oldest legends: always the wily native
hero is outwitting—there is no other word for it—the evil purposes
of the personified, malignant Universe.

Grekka is the ultimate expression of this grim philosophy. In
the battle for life all living things—all *grekka*—are brothers. No
Martian would ever dispute the theory of evolution—it is the
very core of his existence that all beasts are brothers. That is a
somewhat oversimplified statement of the fact, for from there on

grekka becomes entangled in the most elaborate maze of quali-
fications and exceptions which a once highly civilized race has
been able to devise over a period of millions of years. Your native
Martian, drylander or greenlander, will help his brother beast
whenever the latter is clearly losing out in a battle with Nature,
but there are certain things which the individual is supposed to
be able to do for himself if he is not to give unholy satisfaction
to Him—the Great Evil One—the personification of the universal
doom which pours unending misfortune on all *grekka* alike.

The distinction is one of those things which no logician will
ever be able to work out. It is one thing for the desert tribes and
something else for the lowlanders. The *Begar* will draw the line
at something which is a sacred duty of every *Gorub*, in spite of
the fact that the two tribes have lived side by side on a more or
less friendly basis for generations. One clan—even one father-
line—may and must act in ways which no other clan on Mars may
duplicate without eternally losing a varying number of points in
its game with Him and His aides.

What puzzled the young *grak* of the cave was whether man—
specifically Harrigan—was *grekka*. If he was, he was an innate
member of the brotherhood of living things and subject to its
laws. If he wasn't, then he could only be a personification or extension of the inimical First Principle Himself, and hence an
inherent enemy. Since the time of Graziani and the Flemming
expedition every Martian native, individual by individual and
tribe by tribe, has had to make this decision for himself, and by
it govern his further relations with humanity. The *Begar* had had
too little contact with mankind to have needed to make such a
decision as a tribe. Now the young *grak* decided to reserve judg-
ment, keep his eyes open, and let the man prove himself by his
further actions.

Harrigan, of course, knew absolutely nothing of all this. It would
probably not have mattered if he had. What some damned animal
thought about the Universe was nothing to him.

For a moment there had been death in the air. Now the tension
was vanishing. The smaller animals were settling down again, the
little *grak* grinning and nodding as he squatted down in the cor-

ner. Only the *zek's* slitted eyes were still studying him with cold indifference. The damned nightmare was curled up in the one place in the cave where a man could stand up! Harrigan gave it eye for eye, and all the little furry and scaly creatures lifted their heads and watched them while the *grak* blinked worriedly. They could all smell the hostility between the two. The *zek* yawned again, showing an evil double line of knife-edged fangs and a leprous white gullet, and flexed the mighty muscles which lay like slabs of moulded steel across its massive shoulders. Harrigan sat glumly down where he was, his back against the cold stone, his gun on the floor beside him, the lighter wedged into a crack in the rock between his feet.

Outside the storm was at its height. The far-off screaming of the wind echoed and re-echoed in the big room. Puffs of red dust drifted in out of the darkness, and the flame of the lighter wavered and danced. In the occasional lulls, the only sound in the cave was their steady breathing. Every eye, Harrigan knew, was on him. He was the intruder here, and they were wary of him. Let 'em be! A man was something to *be* afraid of on this damned little dried-up world!

He glowered back at them, making up malicious fantasies about their probable habits. There were plenty of fancy stories going the rounds about how these Martians went at things. He grinned sardonically at the little *grak* as he recalled one particularly outrageous libel. The *grak* smiled reassuringly back at him. This man was a hideous travesty of a thing, but he was keeping the peace.

Harrigan sized up the cave. It wasn't a bad hole as caves went. It was dry, the angle in the passage kept the dust out, and it was big enough so a man could stretch. With a fire and water he could last as long as the storm would.

There had been a fire, he noticed, under the chimney at the far end of the cave. There was soot on the ceiling, and the rock had the crumbled look of burned limestone. It was too close to the big beast for comfort, though. That was a wicked-looking brute if there ever was one. Better leave him be—but if he tried to start anything, James Aloysius Harrigan would show him who was tough!

A gust stronger than any that had come before bent the thin

flame of the lighter far over, drawing it out into a feeble yellow thread. Harrigan bent quickly and sheltered it with his cupped palms. It seemed smaller and duller than when he had first lit it. He picked up the lighter and shook it close to his ear. It was almost dry! He snapped down the cap.

The darkness which fell was stifling. The invisible walls of the cave seemed to be closing in on him, compressing the thin air, making it hard to breathe. The dust got into his nose and throat. It had a dry metallic taste. Iron in it. It shrivelled the membranes of his throat like alum. He cleared his throat noisily and ran his tongue over his thick lips. What he needed was a drink. Just a couple of drops. He unscrewed the canteen and lifted it to his lips.

Somewhere in the blackness something moved. It made only the very smallest sound—the tick of a claw on the rock—but he heard it. Instantly he was on the alert. So that was their game! Well, let 'em come! They were as blind as he was in this hole, and he had yet to see the day when any animal could outsmart him!

He set the canteen carefully down behind a block of stone. It would be safer there if there was a scrap, and it might hit against something and give him away if he carried it. Shifting his gun to his left hand, he began cautiously to work his way along the wall, stopping every few inches to listen. He could hear nothing but the rhythmic, ghostly whisper of the creatures' breathing. Whatever it was that had moved, it was quiet now.

His fingers found the first of the slabs of fallen limestone which lay half buried in the clay along the right-hand wall. They reached almost to the chimney, but about fifteen feet from where he had been sitting there was a break in the line, and the wall dropped back into a shallow alcove no more than two feet high. In there he would have solid rock on all sides of him, and he would be directly opposite the pile of dried weeds in which the *zek* was lying. He would have a clear shot at the ugly brute between two of the fallen blocks.

His groping hand came down on something cold and scaly that wriggled hastily away under the rocks. There was an answering squeal of terror and a patter of scampering feet as panic-stricken little creatures scattered in front of him. Something as heavy as a cat landed on his back and clung there, chattering madly. He batted at it and knocked it to the floor. Then, only a few feet ahead in the darkness, he heard the stealthy click of claw on stone again. The *zek!*

He had to have light! It was suicide to face that monster in pitch blackness! He had slipped the lighter back into the outside pocket of his coverall. He fumbled for it. It was gone!

The panic went out of Harrigan in a flash. He sat back on his heels and curled his fingers lovingly around the butt of his gun. The tougher things got, the better he liked them. The lighter must have dropped out of his open pocket; he could find it when he needed it by going back over the ground he had just covered. It wasn't lost. But he didn't need it. The dark was his protection, not his enemy. They couldn't see him in the dark.

He dropped back on all fours. Everything was quiet again. He'd hear them if they tried anything. He was almost at the alcove, and then they'd have to blast to get at him. He could pick 'em off one by one if they tried to get in.

The clay was hard as brick and full of little chunks of broken stone that gouged at his knees, even through the heavy suit. The roof was lower, too; he had to get down on his elbows and hitch along, almost flat on his face.

His heart was thumping like mad. He was working too hard in this thin air. He rolled over on his side, his back against one of the big blocks, and stared into the blackness. Another few feet and he could lie down and wait for them. He needed time out. He had to have a clear head. He cursed his stupidity in not bringing an oxygen flask from the car. One shot of that stuff and he'd be ready to take 'em on all at once, barehanded!

As he started on again something tinkled on the stone beside him. He groped for it: it was the lighter. It had been in his back pocket. Damn fool—letting the darkness rattle him! Animals were all afraid of fire. He could smoke 'em out any time he wanted to. He was boss of this cave! A grin of satisfaction spread over his grimy face as he shuffled along on knees and elbows through the dust.

One big slab almost blocked the hole he was looking for. It was a tight squeeze, but he wriggled through and found plenty of room behind it. He felt for the crack between the blocks that was opposite the nest, slid his gun cautiously into position, and flashed the lighter. Now!

The nest was empty.

With a curse Harrigan rolled to the other opening. The flame of the lighter showed him the far end of the cave—the *grak* crouching wide-eyed in his niche—the black arch of the entrance—and the *zek!*

The thing had slipped past him in the dark. It stood where he had been sitting a moment ago, by the entrance. It stared back at him over its shoulder—a hideous thing like a giant reptile-snouted weasel, mottled with leprous grey. It grinned at him, its red eyes mocking, then stretched out a handlike paw and picked up his canteen!

Harrigan's first shots spattered against the rock above the monster's head; the light blinded him. His next clipped through the coarse mane on the back of its thick neck. His last was fired point-blank into its snarling face. Then the lighter went spinning away across the floor and talons like steel clamps closed on his arm.

The rocks saved him then. The thing had him by the arm, but his body was protected. He still had the gun; he twisted around in the beast's grim grasp and emptied it into the darkness. Its grip loosened and he snatched his arm free. It was bleeding where the *zek's* claws had bitten into the flesh. Then, through the crack on his right, he saw a sheet of white flame go up as the lighter touched the powder-dry mass of weeds in the beast's nest.

The cave was lit up as bright as day. Harrigan saw the *zek*, blood streaming from a ragged wound in its broad chest, its face a bloody mask of fury. One shot had plowed a long furrow across the side of his head. It gathered its powerful hind legs under it, seized a corner of the great block which barred the opening with paws like human hands, and pulled. The muscles stood out in knotted ropes on its arms and shoulders as it worried at the massive stone. Then the packed clay at its base crumbled and the great block slowly tipped. The way was open. His sanctuary had become a trap.

There was one way out. Harrigan took it. Desperately he lunged forward, out of the cranny straight into the thing's arms. He clamped both hands over its narrow lower jaw and forced its slavering snout straight back with all the power of his own broad back. It rose on its haunches, hugging him to it, then toppled over, dragging him with it into the open, raking at him with its cruel hind claws. He set his jaw and felt his arms stiffen and straighten as the evil head was driven back—back. As through a red mist he saw the *grak's* owl eyes staring at him over the monster's shoulder —saw the coppery gleam of firelight on a shining knife. He felt the *zek* shudder as the keen blade was driven home in its back. It began to cough—great racking coughs that shook its whole frame. Its arms tightened convulsively about him and its claws clenched in his back as the copper knife drove home again and again. Then, slowly, they began to loosen. The beast was dead.

The burning weeds had dimmed to a dull flicker. The dust that had been stirred up in their struggle hung like a red veil in the air. Harrigan lay staring up through it at the little native, sucking the thin air painfully into his tortured lungs. The damned little rat had saved his life! He wiped the blood and dust off his face with his sleeve and got slowly to his feet. He had to stoop to clear the ceiling. That knife—that was a man's weapon. Wonder where the *grak* got it—

He took one step towards the *grak*. Before he could take another the knife went smoothly into his belly, just under the breastbone, driving upwards to the heart.

Squatting in the darkness, listening to the distant murmur of the storm, the *grak* wondered what would have happened in the cave if the man had not come there. The *zek* had been a treacherous ally: sooner or later it might have broken the peace. Once its blood-rage had been aroused it had, of course, been necessary to kill it. But if the man had not come that necessity might have been averted.

The man had been very clever. The *grak* had been almost certain that he was what he pretended to be. But as always there was one thing—one very little thing—to betray him. He did not know the law of water.

In every doubtful situation, the *grak* reflected smugly, there was some trivial matter in which the Source of Evil or His emissaries would reveal themselves. Some one thing in which the true *grak* was clearly distinguishable from the forces of Nature against which he must forever fight. One must be quick to see such discrepancies—and quick to act on them.

The matter of water lay at the very root of the law by which all *grekka*—all living things—existed. It was the thing which all must have, which none, under the law, could withhold from another. Without it there could be no life. With it every living thing was given strength to battle on against the eternal foe.

The man had brought water to the cave. Under the law all *grekka* must share in it according to their need. But when the *zek* had gone to take its share, the man had tried to kill it. By that small thing he revealed himself—no *grak*, but one of His evil things. So he had died. So, once more, was victory won for the brotherhood of living things against the Universe.

He would make a song about this thing, and sing it by the fires of his tribe. He would cut a sign in the stone over the entrance of the cave, after the storm was over, so that others who came there would know of it. And the cave itself, where his forefathers had come and lit their fires, would keep the bodies of the *zek* and the man thus, side by side, as witness forever.

When Anthony Boucher first published "Expedition" in 1943, Martians had been invading earthly science fiction for almost half a century. Furthermore, the rate of their invasions had greatly increased after Orson Welles's 1938 radio dramatization of *War of the Worlds*, so that by the beginning of the 1940s virtually every science fiction magazine and every science fiction anthology contained at least one Martian army. Although he wrote "Expedition" at the very height of the Martian flood, Anthony Boucher somehow managed to give it a freshness which (deceptively) suggested that it was the first and only story about the Martian coming. This almost miraculous ability to spice even the stalest tales with the delightful flavor of novelty was one of the late Mr. Boucher's finest talents. But Anthony Boucher was a writer of many gifts. As "Expedition" clearly reveals, he was more than master of the difficult arts of suspense, comedy, and pathos; he invariably endowed his characters with interesting personalities as well as amusing dialogue; and he is still the unquestioned champion among science fiction authors at playing hilarious games with linguistic patterns and literary allusions. And to cap its excellences, "Expedition" combines all these charms within that most challenging story form, the epistolary.

Anthony Boucher

EXPEDITION

The following is a transcript of the recorded two-way messages between Mars and the field expedition to the satellite of the third planet.

First Interplanetary Exploratory Expedition to Central Receiving Station:

What has the Great One achieved?

Murvin, Central Receiving Station, to First Interplanetary Exploratory Expedition:

All right, boys. I'll play games. What *has* the Great One achieved? And when are we going to get a report on it?

Falzik, First Interplanetary Exploratory Expedition, to Murvin, Central Receiving Station:

Haven't you any sense of historical moments? That was the first interplanetary message ever sent. It had to be worthy of the occasion. Trubz spent a long time working on the psychology of it while I prepared the report. Those words are going to live down through the ages of our planet.

Murvin to Falzik:

All right. Swell. You'll be just as extinct while they live on. Now how's about that report?

Report of First Interplanetary Exploratory Expedition, presented by Falzik, specialist in reporting:

The First Interplanetary Exploratory Expedition has landed successfully upon the satellite of the third planet. The personnel of this expedition consists of Karnim, specialist in astrogation; Halov, specialist in life sciences; Trubz, specialist in psychology; Lilil, specialist in the art; and Falzik, specialist in reporting.

The trip itself proved unimportant for general reporting. Special aspects of difficulties encountered and overcome will appear in the detailed individual report of Karnim after the return of the expedition. The others, in particular Trubz and Lilil, were largely unaware of these difficulties. To anyone save the specialist in astrogation, the trip seemed nowise different, except in length, from a vacation excursion to one of our own satellites.

The majority theory is apparently vindicated here on this satellite of the third planet. It does not sustain life. According to Halov, specialist in life sciences, it is not a question of can not; since life of some strange sort might conceivably exist under any conditions save those of a perfect vacuum. But so far as can be ascertained there is no life of any remotely recognizable form upon this satellite.

This globe is dead. It is so dead that one may say the word without fear. The euphemism *extinct* would be too mild for the absolute and utter deadness here. It is so dead that the thought of death is not terrifying.

Trubz is now working on the psychology of that.

Observation checks the previous calculations that one face of this satellite is always turned towards its world and one always from it, the period of rotation coinciding exactly with the orbital period. There seems to be no difference in nature between the two sides; but obviously the far side is the proper site for the erection of our temporary dome. If the hypothetical inhabitants of the third planet have progressed to the use of astronomical instruments, we do not wish to give them warning of our approach by establishing ourselves in the full sight of those instruments.

The absence of life on this satellite naturally proved a serious disappointment to Halov, but even more so to Lilil, who felt inspired to improvise a particularly ingenious specimen of his art. Fortunately the stores of the ship had provided for such an emergency and the resultant improvisation was one of the greatest triumphs of Lilil's great career. We are now about to take our first rest after the trip, and our minds are aglow with the charm and beauty of his exquisite work.

Murvin to Falzik:

All right. Report received and very welcome. But can't you give us more color? Physical description of the satellite—minerals present—exploitation possibilities—anything like that? Some of us are more interested in those than in Trubz's psychology or even Lilil's practice of the art.

Falzik to Murvin:

What are you asking for? You know as well as I do the purpose of this expedition: to discover other intelligent forms of life. And you know the double purpose behind that purpose: to verify by comparison the psychological explanation of our race-dominant fear of death (if this were a formal dispatch I'd censor that to "extinction"), and to open up new avenues of creation in the art.

That's why the personnel of this expedition, save for the astrogator, was chosen for its usefulness *if* we discover life. Until we do, our talents as specialists are wasted. We don't know about minerals and topography. Wait for the next expedition's report on them.

If you want color, our next report should have it. It will come from the third planet itself. We've established our temporary base here easily, and are blasting off very soon for what our scientists have always maintained is the most probable source of life in this system.

Murvin to Falzik:

All right. And if you find life, I owe you a sarbel dinner at Noku's.

Falzik to Murvin:

Sarbel for two, please! Though what we've found, the Great One only—but go on to the report.

Report of First Interplanetary Exploratory Expedition, presented by Falzik, specialist in reporting:

The site of the Expedition's landing on the third planet was chosen more or less at random. It is situated on the third in size of the five continents, not far from the shore of the largest ocean. It is approximately indicated by the coordinates——and——[1] in Kubril's chart of the planet.

In the relatively slow final period of our approach, we were able to observe that the oceans of the third planet are indeed true liquids and not merely beds of molten metal, as has been conjectured by some of our scientists. We were more elated to observe definite signs of intelligent life. We glimpsed many structures which only the most unimaginative materialist could attribute to natural accident, and the fact that these structures tend to cluster together in great numbers indicates an organized and communal civilization.

That at least was our first uplifting emotional reaction, as yet not completely verified. The place of our landing is free from such structures, and from almost everything else. It is as purely arid a desert as the region about Krinavizhd, which in some respects it strongly resembles.

At first we saw no signs of life whatsoever, which is as we could have wished it. An exploratory expedition does not want a welcoming committee, complete with spoken speeches and seven-string sridars. There was a sparse amount of vegetation, apparently

[1] The mathematical signs indicating these coordinates are, unfortunately, typographically impossible to reproduce.—*Editor.*

in an untended state of nature, but nothing to indicate the presence of animal life until we saw the road.

It was an exceedingly primitive and clumsy road, consisting of little more than a ribbon of space from which the vegetation had been cleared; but it was a sign, and we followed it, to be rewarded shortly by our first glimpse of moving life. This was some form of apodal being, approximately one-fifth of the length of one of us, which glided across the road and disappeared before we could make any attempt at communication.

We continued along the road for some time, suffering severely from the unaccustomed gravity and the heavy atmosphere, but spurred on by the joyous hope of fulfilling the aim of the expedition. Lilil in particular evinced an inspired elation at the hope of finding new subjects for his great compositions.

The sun, markedly closer and hotter here on the third planet, was setting when at last we made our first contact with third-planet life. This being was small, about the length of the first joint of one's foreleg, covered with fur of pure white, save for the brown dust of the desert, and quadrupedal. It was frisking in a patch of shade, seeming to rejoice in the setting of the sun and the lowering of the temperature. With its forelegs it performed some elaborate and to us incomprehensible ritual with a red ball.

Halov approached it and attracted its attention by a creaking of his wing-rudiments. It evinced no fear, but instantly rolled the red ball in his direction. Halov deftly avoided this possible weapon. (We later examined it and found it to be harmless, at least to any form of life known to us; its purpose remains a mystery. Trubz is working on the psychology of it.) He then—optimistically, but to my mind foolishly—began the fifth approach, the one developed for beings of a civilization roughly parallel to our own.

It was a complete failure. The white thing understood nothing of what Halov scratched in the ground, but persisted in trying to wrench from his digits the stick with which he scratched. Halov reluctantly retreated through the approaches down to approach one (designed for beings of the approximate mental level of the Narbian aborigines) but the creature paid no heed to them and insisted upon performing with the moving stick some ritual similar to that which it had practiced with the ball.

By this time we were all weary of these fruitless efforts, so that it came as a marked relief when Lilil announced that he had been inspired to improvise. The exquisite perfection of his art refreshed us and we continued our search with renewed vitality, though not before Halov had examined the corpse of the white creature and determined that it was indubitably similar to the mammals, though many times larger than any form of mammalian life has ever become on our planet.

Some of us thought whimsically of that favorite fantasy of the science-fiction composers—the outsize mammals who will attack and destroy our race. But we had not yet seen anything.

Murvin to Falzik:

That's a fine way to end a dispatch. You've got me all agog. Has the Monster Mammal King got you in his clutches?

Falzik to Murvin:

Sorry. I didn't intend to be sensational. It is simply that we've been learning so much here through—well, yes, you can call him the Monster Mammal King, though the fictionists would be disappointed in him—that it's hard to find time enough for reports. But here is more.

Report of First Interplanetary Exploratory Expedition, presented by Falzik, specialist in reporting:

The sun was almost down when we saw the first intelligent being ever beheld by one of our race outside of our planet. He (for we learned afterwards that he was male, and it would be unjust to refer to an intelligent being as *it*) was lying on the ground in the shade of a structure—a far smaller structure than those we had glimpsed in passing, and apparently in a sad state of dilapidation.

In this posture the fact was not markedly noticeable, but he is a biped. Used as we are on our own planet to many forms of life— octopods (though the Great One be thanked that those terrors are nearly wiped out), ourselves hexapods, and the pesky little mammalian tetrapods—a biped still seems to us something strange and mythical. A logical possibility, but not a likelihood. The length of body of this one is approximately that of a small member of our own race.

He held a container apparently of glass in one foreleg (there must be some other term to use of bipeds, since the front limbs are not used as legs) and was drinking from it when he spied us. He choked on his drink, looked away, then returned his gaze to us and stared for a long time. At last he blinked his eyes, groaned aloud, and hurled the glass container far away.

Halov now advanced toward him. He backed away, reached one forelimb inside the structure, and brought it out clasping a long metal rod, with a handle of some vegetable material. This he pointed at Halov, and a loud noise ensued. At the time some of us thought this was the being's speech, but now we know it came from the rod, which apparently propelled some form of metal missile against Halov.

The missile, of course, bounced harmlessly off Halov's armor (he prides himself on keeping in condition) and our specialist in life sciences continued to advance toward the biped, who dropped the rod and leaned back against the structure. For the first time we heard his voice, which is extraordinarily low in pitch. We have not yet fully deciphered his language, but I have, as instructed, been keeping full phonetic transcriptions of his every remark. Trubz has calculated psychologically that the meaning of this remark must be:

"Ministers of the Great One, be gracious to me!"

The phonetic transcription is as follows:[1]

AND THEY TALK ABOUT PINK ELEPHANTS!

He watched awestruck as Halov, undaunted by his former experience, again went directly into the fifth approach. The stick in Halov's digits traced a circle in the dirt with rays coming out of it, then pointed up at the setting sun.

The biped moved his head forward and back and spoke again. Trubz's conjecture here is:

"The great sun, the giver of life."

Phonetic transcription:

BUGS THAT DRAW PRETTY PICTURES YET!

---

[1] For the convenience of the reader, these transcriptions have been retranscribed into the conventional biped spelling.—*Editor.*

Then Halov drew a series of concentric ellipses of dotted lines about the figure of the sun. He drew tiny circles on these orbits to indicate the first and second planets, then larger ones to indicate the third and our own. The biped was by now following the drawing with intense absorption.

Halov now pointed to the drawing of the third planet, then to the biped, and back again. The biped once more moved his head forward, apparently as a gesture of agreement. Finally Halov in like manner pointed to the fourth planet, to himself, and back again, and likewise in turn for each of us.

The biped's face was blank for a moment. Then he himself took a stick and pointed from the fourth planet to Halov, saying, according to Trubz:

"This is really true?"

Transcription:

YOU MEAN YOU'RE MARTIANS?

Halov imitated the head movement of agreement. The biped dropped his stick and gasped out sounds which Trubz is sure were the invocation of the name of a potent deity. Transcription:

ORSON WELLES!

We had all meanwhile been groping with the biped's thought patterns, though no success had attended our efforts. In the first place, his projection was almost nil; his race is apparently quite unaccustomed to telepathic communication. In the second place, of course, it is next to impossible to read alien thought patterns without some fixed point of reference.

Just as we could never have deciphered the ancient writings of the Khrugs without the discovery of the Burdarno Stone which gave the same inscription in their language and in an antique form of our own, so we could not attempt to decode this biped's thought patterns until we knew what they were like on a given known subject.

We now began to perceive some of his patterns of the Solar System and for our respective worlds. Halov went on to the second stage of the fifth approach. He took a group of small rocks, isolated one, held up one digit, and drew the figure one in the dirt. The biped seemed puzzled. Then Halov added another rock to the first, held up two digits, and drew the figure two, and so on for three and four. Now the biped seemed enlightened and made his agreement gesture. He also held up one digit and drew a figure beside Halov's.

His *one* is the same as ours—a not too surprising fact. Trubz has been working on the psychology of it and has decided that the figure one is probably a simple straight line in almost any numerical system. His other figures differed markedly from ours, but his intention was clear and we could to some extent follow his patterns.

Using both forelegs, Halov went on to five, six, and seven with the biped writing down his number likewise. Then Halov held up all his digits and wrote a one followed by the dot which represents zero and is the essence of any mathematical intelligence. This was the crucial moment—did these bipeds know how to calculate or was their numerical system purely primitive?

The biped held up eight digits and wrote a new figure, a conjoined pair of circles. Halov, looking worried, added another rock to his group and wrote down two ones. The biped wrote a circle with a tail to it. Halov added another rock and wrote a one followed by a two. The biped wrote a one followed by a circle.

Then Halov understood. We have always used an octonary system, but our mathematicians have long realized the possibility of others: a system of two, for instance, in which 11 would mean three, a system of four (the folk speech even contains survivals of such a system) in which 11 would mean five. For 11 means simply the first power of the number which is your base, plus one. This system of the bipeds obviously employs a decimal base.

(Trubz has been working on the psychology of this. He explains it by the fact that the bipeds have five digits on each forelimb, or a total of ten, whereas we have four each, a total of eight.)

Halov now beckoned to Karnim, who as astrogator is the best mathematician among us, and asked him to take over. He studied for a moment the biped's numbers, adjusted his mind rapidly to the (for the layman) hopeless confusion of a decimal system, and went ahead with simple mathematical operations. The biped followed him not unskillfully, while the rest of us concentrated on his thought patterns and began to gather their shape and nature.

The growing darkness bothered the biped before it incommoded Karnim. He rose from his squatting position over the numerals and went into the structure, the interior of which was soon alight. He came back to the doorway and beckoned us to enter. As we did so, he spoke words which Trubz conjectures to mean:

"Enter my abode and stay in peace, O emissaries from the fourth planet."

Phonetic transcription:

YOU'LL BE GONE IN THE MORNING AND WILL I HAVE A HEAD!

Murvin to Falzik:

What a yarn! A planet of intelligent beings! What a future for the art! Maybe I never was sold on this expedition, but I am now. Keep the reports coming. And include as much phonetic transcription as you can—the specialists are working on what you've sent and are inclined to doubt some of Trubz' interpretations. Also tell Trubz to get to work as soon as possible on the psychological problem of extinction. If this being's a mammal, he should help.

[Several reports are omitted here, dealing chiefly with the gradually acquired skill of the expedition in reading a portion of the biped's thought patterns and in speaking a few words of his language.]

Report of First Interplanetary Exploratory Expedition, presented by Falzik, specialist in reporting:

Halov and Trubz agree that we should stay with this *man* (for such we have by now learned is the name of his race) until we have learned as much from him as we can. He has accepted us now and is almost at ease with us, though the morning after our arrival, for some peculiar reason, he seemed even more surprised to see us than when we first appeared.

We can learn much more from him, now that he is used to us, than we could from the dwellers in the large massed structures, and after we are well-versed in his civilization we stand much more chance of being accepted peaceably.

We have been here now for three of the days of this planet, absorbed in our new learning. (All save Lilil, who is fretful because he has not practiced his art for so long. I have occasionally seen him eying the *man* speculatively.) By using a mixture of telepathy, sign language, and speech, we can by now discuss many things, though speech comes with difficulty to one who has used it only on formal and fixed occasions.

For instance we have learned why this *man* lives alone far from his fellows. His specialty is the making of pictures with what he calls a *camera*, a contrivance which records the effect of different intensities of light upon a salt of silver—a far more complex method than our means of making pictures with photosensitized elduron, but one producing much the same results. He has taken pictures of us, though he seems doubtful that any other *man* will ever believe the record of his *camera*.

At present he is engaged in a series of pictures of aspects of the desert, an undertaking which he seems to regard not as a useful function but as an art of some strange sort. Trubz is working on the psychology of it and says that a reproductive and imitative art is conceivable, but Lilil is scornful of the notion.

Today he showed us many pictures of other *mans* and of their cities and structures. *Man* is a thin-skinned and almost hairless animal. This *man* of ours goes almost naked, but that is apparently because of the desert heat. Normally a *man* makes up for his absence of hair by wearing a sort of artificial fur of varying shapes known as *clothes*. To judge from the pictures shown us by the *man*, this is true only of the male of the species. The female never covers her bare skin in any way.

Examination of these pictures of females shown us by our *man* fully confirms our theory that the animal *man* is a mammal.

The display of pictures ended with an episode still not quite clear to us. Ever since our arrival, the *man* has been worrying and talking about something apparently lost—something called a *kitten*. The thought pattern was not familiar enough to gather its nature, until he showed us a picture of the small white beast which we had first met and we recognized in his mind this *kitten-*

pattern. He seemed proud of the picture, which showed the beast in its ritual with the ball, but still worried, and asked us, according to Trubz, if we knew anything of its whereabouts. Transcription:

YOU WOULDN'T ANY OF YOU BIG BUGS KNOW WHAT THE DEVIL'S BECOME OF THAT KITTEN, WOULD YOU?

Thereupon Lilil arose in his full creative pride and led the *man* to the place where we had met the *kitten*. The corpse was by now withered in the desert sun, and I admit that it was difficult to gather from such a spectacle the greatness of Lilil's art, but we were not prepared for the *man's* reaction.

His face grew exceedingly red and a fluid formed in his eyes. He clenched his digits and made curious gestures with them. His words were uttered brokenly and exceedingly difficult to transcribe. Trubz has not yet conjectured their meaning, but the transcription reads:

YOU DID THAT? TO A POOR HARMLESS LITTLE KITTEN? WHY, YOU—[1]

His attitude has not been the same toward us since. Trubz is working on the psychology of it.

Murvin to Falzik:

Tell Trubz to work on the major psychological problem. Your backers are getting impatient.

Falzik to Murvin:

I think that last report was an aspect of it. But I'm still puzzled. See what you can make of this one.

Report of First Interplanetary Exploratory Expedition, presented by Falzik, specialist in reporting:

Tonight Halov and Trubz attempted to present the great psychological problem to the *man*. To present such a problem in our confusion of thoughts, language and gesture is not easy, but I think that to some extent they succeeded.

[1] The remainder of this transcription has been suppressed for this audience. —*Editor.*

They stated it in its simplest form: Our race is obsessed by a terrible fear of extinction. We will each of us do anything to avoid his personal extinction. No such obsession has ever been observed among the minute mammalian pests of our planet.

Now, is our terror a part of our intelligence? Does intelligence necessarily imply and bring with it a frantic clinging to the life that supports us? Or does this terror stem from our being what we are, rather than mammals? A mammal brings forth its young directly; the young are a direct continuation of the life of the old. But with us a half dozen specialized individuals bring forth all the young. The rest of us have no part in it; our lives are dead ends, and we dread the approach of that blank wall.

Our psychologists have battled over this question for generations. Would another—say, a mammalian—form of intelligent life have such an obsession? Here we had an intelligent mammal. Could he answer us?

I give the transcription of his answer, as yet not fully deciphered:

I THINK I GET WHAT YOU MEAN. AND I THINK THE ANSWER IS A LITTLE OF BOTH. O.K., SO WE'RE INTELLIGENT MAMMALS. WE HAVE MORE FEAR OF DEATH THAN THE UNINTELLIGENT, LIKE THE POOR LITTLE KITTEN YOU BUTCHERED; BUT CERTAINLY NOT SUCH A DOMINANT OBSESSION AS I GATHER YOUR RACE HAS.

Trubz thinks that this was an ambiguous answer, which will not satisfy either party among our specialists in psychology.

We then proposed, as a sub-question, the matter of the art. Is it this same psychological manifestation that has led us to develop such an art? That magnificent and highest of arts which consists in the extinction with the greatest esthetic subtlety of all other forms of life?

Here the *man's* reactions were as confusing as they had been beside the corpse of the *kitten*. He said:

SO THAT'S WHAT HAPPENED TO SNOWPUSS? ART . . . ! ART, YOU CALL IT YET! AND YOU'VE COME HERE TO PRACTICE THAT ART ON THIS WORLD? I'LL SEE YOU FRIED CRISP ON BOTH SIDES ON HADES' HOTTEST GRIDDLE FIRST!

Trubz believes that the extremely violent emotion expressed was shock at realization of the vast new reaches of esthetic experience which lay before him.

Later, when he thought he was alone, I overheard him talking to himself. There was something so emphatically inimical in his thought-patterns that I transcribed his words though I have not yet had a chance to secure Trubz' opinion on them. He beat the clenched digits of one forelimb against the other and said:

SO THAT'S WHAT YOU'RE UP TO! WE'LL SEE ABOUT THAT. BUT HOW? HOW . . . ? GOT IT! THOSE PICTURES I TOOK FOR THE PUBLIC HEALTH CAMPAIGN . . .

I am worried. If this attitude indicated by his thought-patterns persists, we may have to bring about his extinction and proceed at once by ourselves. At least it will give Lilil a chance to compose one of his masterpieces.

Final report of the First Interplanetary Exploratory Expedition, presented by Falzik, specialist in reporting:

How I could so completely have misinterpreted the *man's* thought-patterns I do not understand. Trubz is working on the psychology of it. Far from any hatred or enmity, the *man* was even then resolving to save our lives. The First Interplanetary Exploratory Expedition owes him a debt which it can never repay.

It was after sun-up the next day that he approached us with his noble change of heart. As I describe this scene I cannot unfortunately give his direct words; I was too carried away by my own emotions to remember to transcribe. Such phrases as I attribute to him here are reconstructed from the complex of our intercourse, and were largely a matter of signs and pictures.

What he did first was to show us one of his pictures. We stared at it, and drew back horrified. For it represented a being closely allied to us, almost to be taken for one of us, meeting extinction beneath a titanic weapon wielded by what was obviously the characteristic five-digited forelimb of a *man*. And that forelimb was many, many times the size of the being resembling us.

"I've been keeping this from you," he informed us. "I'll admit I've been trying to trap you. But the truth is: I'm a dwarf *man*.

The real ones are as much bigger than me as you are bigger than the *kitten*. More, even. And their favorite pastime—only they call it a sport, not art—is killing bugs like you."

We realized now what should have struck us before—the minute size of his structure compared with those which we had seen before. Obviously he spoke the truth—he was a dwarf specimen of his race.

Then he produced more pictures—horrible, terrifying, monstrous pictures, all showing something perturbingly like us meeting cruel extinction at the whim of a *man*.

"I've just been keeping you here," he said, "until some real members of my race could come and play with you. They'd like it. But I haven't got the heart to do it. I like you, and what you told me about your art convinces me that you don't deserve extinction like that. So I'm giving you your chance: Clear out of here and stay away from this planet. It's the most unsafe place in the universe for your kind. If you dread extinction, stay away from the third planet!"

His resolve to spare our lives had made him happy. His face kept twisting into the grimace we had learned to recognize as a sign of *man's* pleasure. But we hardly watched him or even listened to him. Our eyes kept returning with awful fascination to those morbidly terrifying pictures. Then our thoughts fused into one, and with hardly a word of farewell to our savior we sped back to the ship.

This is our last report. We are now on the temporary base established on the satellite and will return as soon as we have recovered from the shock of our narrow escape. Lilil has achieved a new composition with a captive pergut from the ship which has somewhat solaced us.

Murvin to First Interplanetary Exploratory Expedition:

You dopes! You low mammalian idiots! It's what comes of sending nothing but specialists on an expedition. I tried to convince them you needed a good general worker like me, but no. And look at you!

It's obvious what happened. On our planet, mammals are minute pests and the large intelligent beings are arthropodal hexapods. All right. On the third planet things have worked out the other way round. *Bugs*, as the *man* calls our kin, are tiny insignificant things. You saw those pictures and thought the *mans* were enormous; actually they meant only that the *bugs* were minute!

That *man* tricked you unpardonably, and I like him for it. Specialists . . . ! You deserve extinction for this, and you know it. But Vardanek has another idea. Stay where you are. Develop the temporary base in any way you can. We'll send others to help you. We'll build up a major encampment on that side of the satellite, and in our own sweet time we can invade the third planet with enough sensible ones to counteract the boners of individual specialists.

We can do it too. We've got all the time we need to build up our base, even if that *man* has warned his kind—who probably wouldn't believe him anyway. Because remember this always, and feel secure: *No being on the third planet ever knows what is happening on the other side of its satellite.*

Arthur C. Clarke's "Loophole" plainly illustrates why the short story has long been the most popular form of science fiction writing. It also illustrates why Clarke has long been acclaimed by mainstream and science fiction critics alike. Within its incredibly brief word span "Loophole" provides more humor, terror, and surprise than the average novel; deceptively slight in size and light in tone, it packs a major wallop. In this tale, written at the close of the Second World War, Clarke envisions the Martians as super-Nazis, determined to rule the solar system by their master plan. Gifted technicians, sophisticated politicians, and responsible guardians of galactic peace, Clarke's Martians seem truly to be the superior race they believe themselves. But there's a loophole in the almost perfect Martian program, and through that loophole slip the Martians' bumbling, quarrelsome, bumptious enemies, the Earthmen, on their way from 1946 to 2001.

Arthur C. Clarke

LOOPHOLE

From: President.
To: Secretary, Council of Scientists.

I have been informed that the inhabitants of Earth have succeeded in releasing atomic energy and have been making experiments with rocket propulsion. This is most serious. Let me have a full report immediately. And make it *brief* this time.

K.K. IV.

From: Secretary, Council of Scientists.
To: President.

The facts are as follows. Some months ago our instruments detected intense neutron emission from Earth, but an analysis of radio programs gave no explanation at the time. Three days ago a second emission occurred and soon afterwards all radio transmissions from Earth announced that atomic bombs were in use in the current war. The translators have not completed their interpretation, but it appears that the bombs are of considerable power. Two have so far been used. Some details of their construction have been released, but the elements concerned have not yet been identified. A fuller report will be forwarded as soon as possible. For the moment all that is certain is that the inhabitants of Earth *have* liberated atomic power, so far only explosively.

Very little is known concerning rocket research on Earth. Our astronomers have been observing the planet carefully ever since radio emissions were detected a generation ago. It is certain that long-range rockets of some kind are in existence on Earth, for there have been numerous references to them in recent military broadcasts. However, no serious attempt has been made to reach interplanetary space. When the war ends, it is expected that the inhabitants of the planet may carry out research in this direction. We will pay very careful attention to their broadcasts and the astronomical watch will be rigorously enforced.

From what we have inferred of the planet's technology, it should require about twenty years before Earth develops atomic rockets capable of crossing space. In view of this, it would seem that the time has come to set up a base on the Moon, so that a close scrutiny can be kept on such experiments when they commence.

Trescon.

(Added in manuscript.)

The war on Earth has now ended, apparently owing to the intervention of the atomic bomb. This will not affect the above arguments but it may mean that the inhabitants of Earth can devote themselves to pure research again more quickly than expected. Some broadcasts have already pointed out the application of atomic power to rocket propulsion.

T.

From: President.
To: Chief of Bureau of Extra-Planetary Security. (C.B.E.P.S.).
You have seen Trescon's minutes.
Equip an expedition to the satellite of Earth immediately. It is to keep a close watch on the planet and to report at once if rocket experiments are in progress.

The greatest care must be taken to keep our presence on the Moon a secret. You are personally responsible for this. Report to me at yearly intervals, or more often if necessary.

K.K. IV.

From: President.
To: C.B.E.P.S.
  Where is the report on Earth?! !

K.K. IV.

From: C.B.E.P.S.
To: President.
  The delay is regretted. It was caused by the breakdown of the ship carrying the report.
  There have been no signs of rocket experimenting during the past year, and no reference to it in broadcasts from the planet.

Ranthe.

From: C.B.E.P.S.
To: President.
  You will have seen my yearly reports to your respected father on this subject. There have been no developments of interest for the past seven years, but the following message has just been received from our base on the Moon:
  Rocket projectile, apparently atomically propelled, left Earth's atmosphere today from Northern land-mass, traveling into space for one quarter diameter of planet before returning under control.

Ranthe.

From: President.
To: Chief of State.
  Your comments, please.

K.K. V.

From: Chief of State.
To: President.

This means the end of our traditional policy.

The only hope of security lies in preventing the Terrestrials from making further advances in this direction. From what we know of them, this will require some overwhelming threat.

Since its high gravity makes it impossible to land on the planet, our sphere of action is restricted. The problem was discussed nearly a century ago by Anvar, and I agree with his conclusions. We must act *immediately* along those lines.

F.K.S.

From: President.
To: Secretary of State.

Inform the Council that an emergency meeting is convened for noon tomorrow.

K.K. V.

From: President.
To: C.B.E.P.S.

Twenty battleships should be sufficient to put Anvar's plan into operation. Fortunately there is no need to arm them—yet. Report progress of construction to me weekly.

K.K. V.

From: C.B.E.P.S.
To: President.

Nineteen ships are now completed. The twentieth is still delayed owing to hull failure and will not be ready for at least a month.

Ranthe.

From: President.
To: C.B.E.P.S.

Nineteen will be sufficient. I will check the operational plan with you tomorrow. Is the draft of our broadcast ready yet?

K.K. V.

From: C.B.E.P.S.
To: President.

Draft herewith:

People of Earth!

We, the inhabitants of the planet you call Mars, have for many years observed your experiments towards achieving interplanetary travel. *These experiments must cease.* Our study of your race has convinced us that you are not fitted to leave your planet in the present state of your civilization. The ships you now see floating above your cities are capable of destroying them utterly, and will do so unless you discontinue your attempts to cross space.

We have set up an observatory on your Moon and can immediately detect any violation of these orders. If you obey them, we will not interfere with you again. Otherwise, one of your cities will be destroyed every time we observe a rocket leaving the Earth's atmosphere.

By order of the President and Council of Mars.

Ranthe.

From: President.
To: C.B.E.P.S.

I approve. The translation can go ahead.

I shall not be sailing with the fleet, after all. You will report to me in detail immediately on your return.

K.K. V.

From: C.B.E.P.S.
To: President.

I have the honor to report the successful completion of our mission. The voyage to Earth was uneventful: radio messages from the planet indicated that we were detected at a considerable distance and great excitement had been aroused before our arrival. The fleet was dispersed according to plan and I broadcast the ultimatum. We left immediately and no hostile weapons were brought to bear against us.

I shall report in detail within two days.

Ranthe.

From: Secretary, Council of Scientists.
To: President.

The psychologists have completed their report, which is attached herewith.

As might be expected, our demands at first infuriated this stubborn and high-spirited race. The shock to their pride must have been considerable, for they believed themselves to be the only intelligent beings in the Universe.

However, within a few weeks there was a rather unexpected change in the tone of their statements. They had begun to realize that we were intercepting all their radio transmissions, and some messages have been broadcast directly to us. They state that they have agreed to ban all rocket experiments, in accordance with our wishes. This is as unexpected as it is welcome. Even if they are trying to deceive us, we are perfectly safe now that we have established the second station just outside the atmosphere. They cannot possibly develop spaceships without our seeing them or detecting their tube radiation.

The watch on Earth will be continued rigorously, as instructed.

Trescon.

From: C.B.E.P.S.
To: President.

Yes, it is quite true that there have been no further rocket experiments in the last ten years. We certainly did not expect Earth to capitulate so easily!

I agree that the existence of this race now constitutes a permanent threat to our civilization and we are making experiments along the lines you suggest. The problem is a difficult one, owing to the great size of the planet. Explosives would be out of the question, and a radioactive poison of some kind appears to offer the greatest hope of success.

Fortunately, we now have an indefinite time in which to complete this research, and I will report regularly.

Ranthe.

End of Document

From: Lieutenant Commander Henry Forbes, Intelligence Branch, Special Space Corps.

To: Professor S. Maxton, Philological Department, University of Oxford.

Route: Transender II (via Schenectady).

The above papers, with others, were found in the ruins of what is believed to be the capital Martian city. (Mars Grid KL302895.) The frequent use of the ideograph for "Earth" suggests that they may be of special interest and it is hoped that they can be translated. Other papers will be following shortly.

H. Forbes, Lt/Cdr.

(Added in manuscript.)

Dear Max,

Sorry I've had no time to contact you before. I'll be seeing you as soon as I get back to Earth.

Gosh! Mars *is* in a mess! Our co-ordinates were dead accurate and the bombs materialized right over their cities, just as the Mount Wilson boys predicted.

We're sending a lot of stuff back through the two small machines, but until the big transmitter is materialized we're rather restricted, and, of course, none of us can return. So hurry up with it!

I'm glad we can get to work on rockets again. I may be old-fashioned, but being squirted through space at the speed of light doesn't appeal to me!

Yours in haste,

Henry.

There is a continuing popular delusion that science fiction is merely a collection of thrilling wonder tales designed to excite morons and perverts. Yet for decades science fiction readers have known that the field offers a great deal more than mindless escapism—that in fact science fiction contains much of the brightest comedy and boldest speculation in modern literature. Certainly no one has done more to preserve the decency of science fiction than Damon Knight. Throughout his long career as author, editor, and mentor of Science Fiction Writers of America, Mr. Knight has worked to better both the working conditions and the reputations of science fiction writers. In "Catch that Martian" he gives us splendid proof of his own argument that true science fiction is very good indeed. For "Catch that Martian" is purely, brilliantly funny, a superb piece of humorous writing. And fittingly enough, Knight's Martians are above all comedians, bringing laughter to a befuddled Earth.

Damon Knight

CATCH THAT MARTIAN

The first person who got on the Martian's nerves, according to a survey I made just recently, was a Mrs. Frances Economy, about forty-two, five foot three, heavy-set, with prominent mole on left cheek, formerly of 302 West 46th Street, Manhattan. Mrs. Economy went to a neighborhood movie on the night of September 5th, and halfway through the first feature, just as she was scrambling for the last of her popcorn, zip—she wasn't there any more.

That is, she was only half there. She could still see the screen, but it was like a television with the sound off. The way she realized something had happened to her, she started stomping her feet, like you do when the sound goes off or the picture stops, and her feet didn't make any noise.

In fact, she couldn't feel the floor, just some kind of rubbery stuff that seemed to be holding her up. Same way with the arms of her chair. They weren't there, as far as her feeling them went.

Everything was dead still. She could hear her own breathing, and the gulp when she swallowed that last mouthful, and her heart beating if she listened close. That was all. When she got up and went out, she didn't step on anybody's feet—and she tried to.

Of course I asked her who was sitting next to her when it happened, but she doesn't remember. She didn't notice. It was like that with everybody.

Not to keep you in suspense, the Martian did it. We figured that out, later, and there still isn't any proof but it has to be that way. This Martian, the way it figures, looks just like anybody else. He could be the little guy with the derby hat and the sour expression, or the girl with the china-blue eyes, or the old gent with the chin spinach and glasses on a string—or anybody.

But he's a Martian. And being a Martian, he's got this power that people haven't got. If he feels like it, he just looks at you cockeyed, and zip—you're in some other dimension. I don't know what the scientists would call it, the Fourth or Fifth Dimension, or what, but I call it the next-door dimension because it seems it's right next door—you can see into it. In other words, it's a place where other people can see you, but they can't hear you or touch you, unless they're ghosts, too, and there's nothing but some kind of cloudy stuff to walk around on. I don't know if that sounds good or what. It stinks. It's just plain dull.

One more thing. He annoys easy. You crunch popcorn in his ear, he doesn't like that. You step on his toe, same thing. Say, "Hot enough for you?" or slap him on the back when he's got sunburn, serve him a plate of soup with your finger in it—zip.

The way we figured out it's a Martian, who else could it be? And nobody ever noticed him, so it must be he looks like anybody else. The way we know he annoys easy, there was eighteen "ghosts" wandering around when it first came to the attention of the public, during the early morning of September 6th. That was about eleven hours after he got Mrs. Economy.

Thirteen of them were up at Broadway and 49th, walking through traffic. They went right through the cars. By nine o'clock there were two wrecks on that corner and a busted hydrant gushing water all over. The ghost people walked through it and didn't get wet.

Three more showed up in front of a big delicatessen near 72nd Street and Amsterdam Avenue, just looking in the window.

Every once in a while one of them would reach in through the glass and grab for something, but it was always no dice.

The other two were sailors. They were out in the harbor, walking on water and thumbing their noses at petty officers aboard the ships that were anchored there.

The first eight patrolmen who reported all this got told they would be fired if they ever came on duty drunk again. But by ten-thirty it was on the radio, and then WPIX sent a camera crew up, and by the time the afternoon papers came out there were so many people in Times Square that we had to put a cordon around the ghosts and divert traffic.

The delicatessen window up on Amsterdam got busted from the crowd leaning against it, or some guy trying to put his hand through the way the three ghosts did, we never figured out which. There were about sixty tugs, launches and rowboats in the harbor, trying to get close enough to the sailors—and three helicopters.

One thing we know, the Martian must have been in that crowd on Times Square, because between one and one-thirty P.M., seven more ghosts wandered through the barrier and joined the other ones. You could tell they were mad, but of course you couldn't tell what they were saying.

Then there were some more down by Macy's in the afternoon, and a few in Greenwich Village, and by evening we had lost count. The guesses in the papers that night ran from three hundred to a thousand. It was the *Times* that said three hundred.

The next day there was just nothing else at all in the papers, or on the radio or TV. Bars did an all-time record business. So did churches.

The Mayor appointed a committee to investigate. The Police Commissioner called out special reserves to handle the mobs. The Governor was understood to say he was thinking about declaring a statewide emergency, but all he got in most papers was half a column on page four. Later on he denied the whole thing.

Everybody had to be asked what he thought, from Einstein to Martin and Lewis. Some people said mass hysteria, some said the end of the world, some said the Russians.

Winchell was the first one to say in print that it was a Martian.

I had the same idea myself, but by the time I got it all worked out, I was too late to get the credit.

I was handicapped, because all this time I still hadn't seen one of the ghosts yet. I was on Safe, Loft and Truck—just promoted last spring from a patrolman—and while I was on duty I never got near any of the places where they were congregating. In the evening I had to take care of my mother.

But my brain was working. I had this Martian idea, and I kept thinking, thinking, all the time.

I knew better than to mention this to Captain Rifkowicz. All I would have to do was mention to him that I was thinking, and he would say, "With what, Dunlop, with what?" or something sarcastic like that. As for asking him to get me transferred to Homicide or Missing Persons, where I might get assigned to the ghost case, that was out. Rifkowicz says I should have been kept on a beat long enough for my arches to fall, in order to leave more room on top for brains.

So I was on my own. And that evening, when they started announcing the rewards, I knew I had to get the Martian. There was fifteen hundred dollars, voted by the City Council that afternoon, for whoever would find out what was making the ghosts and stop it. Because if it didn't stop, there would be eighteen thousand ghosts in a month, and over two hundred thousand in a year.

Then there was a bunch of private rewards, running from twenty-five bucks to five hundred, offered by people that had relatives among the departed. There was a catch to those, though—you had to get the relatives back.

All together, they added up to nearly five thousand. With that dough, I could afford to hire somebody to take care of Ma and maybe have some private life of my own. There was a cute waitress down on Varick Street, where I had lunch every day, and for a long time I had been thinking if I asked her to go out, maybe she would say yes. But what was the use of me asking her, if all I could do was have her over to listen to Ma talk?

The first thing I did, I got together all the newspaper stuff about the ghosts. I spread it out on the living room table and sorted it and started pasting it into a scrapbook. Right away

I saw I had to have more information. What was in the papers was mostly stories about the crowds and the accidents and traffic tieups, plus interviews with people that didn't know anything.

What I wanted to know was—what were all these people doing when the Martian got them? If I knew that, maybe I could figure out some kind of a pattern, like if the Martian's pet peeve was back-slappers, or people who make you jump a foot when they sneeze, or whatever.

Another thing. I wanted to know all the times and places. From that, I could figure out what the Martian's habits were, if he had any, and with all of it together I could maybe arrange to be on the spot whenever he got sore. Then anybody except me who was there every time would have to be him.

I explained all this to Ma, hoping she would make a sacrifice and let me get Mrs. Proctor from across the hall to sit with her a few evenings. She didn't seem to get the picture. Ma never believes anything she reads in the papers, anyway, except the astrology column. The way it struck her, the whole thing was some kind of a plot, and I would be better to stay away from it.

I made one try, emphasizing about the money I would get, but all she said was, "Well, then why don't you just *tell* that Captain Rifkowicz he's got to *let* you earn that reward?"

Ma has funny ideas about a lot of things. She came over here from England when she was a girl, and it looks like she never did get to understand America. I knew that if I kept after her, she would start crying and telling me about all the things she did for me when I was a baby. That breaks me down every time.

So what I did next, I took the bull by the horns. I waited till Ma went to sleep and then I just walked out and hopped an uptown bus on Seventh Avenue. If I couldn't get off during the daytime, I would cut down my sleep for a while, that was all.

I was heading for Times Square, but at 27th I saw a crowd on the sidewalk. I got out and ran over there. Sure enough, in the middle of the crowd were two of the ghosts, a fat man with a soupstrainer mustache and a skinny woman with cherries on her hat. You could tell they were ghosts because the people were waving their hands through them. Aside from that, there was no difference.

I took the lady first, to be polite. I flashed the badge, and then I hauled out my notebook and wrote, "Name and address please," and shoved it at her.

She got the idea and looked through her bag for a pencil and an envelope. She scribbled, "Mrs. Edgar F. Walters, Schenectady, N. Y."

I asked her, "When did this happen to you and where?"

She wrote it was about one P.M. the afternoon before, and she was in Schrafft's on Broadway near 37th, eating lunch with her husband. I asked her if the fat man was her husband, and she said he was.

I then asked her if she could remember exactly what the two of them were doing right at the moment when it happened. She thought a while and then said she was talking and her husband was dunking his doughnut in his coffee. I asked her if it was the kind with powdered sugar and she said yes.

I knew then that I was on the right track. She was one of those little women with big jaws that generally seem to have loud voices and like to use them; and I always hated people who dunk those kind of doughnuts, myself.

I thanked them and went on uptown. When I got home that night, about four A.M. the next morning, I had fifteen interviews in my book. The incidents had taken place all over the midtown area. Six got theirs for talking, four on crowded sidewalks—probably for jostling or stepping on corns—two for yelling on a quiet street at two in the morning, one for dunking, one for singing to himself on a subway, one, judging by the looks of him, for not being washed, and one for coming in late to a Broadway play. The six talkers broke down to three in restaurants, two in a newsreel movie, and one in Carnegie Hall while a concert was going on.

Nobody remembered who they were next to at the time, but I was greatly encouraged. I had a hunch I was getting warm already.

I got through the next day, the eighth, in a kind of daze, and don't think Rifkowicz didn't call my attention to it. I suppose I wasn't worth more than a nickel to the City that day, but I promised myself I would make it up later. For the moment, I ignored Rifkowicz.

On the radio and TV, there were two new developments. In my head, there was one.

First, the radio and TV. I ate lunch in a saloon so as to catch the latest news, even though I had to give up my daily glimpse of the waitress in the beanery. Two things were new. One, people had started noticing that a few things had turned into ghosts—besides people, I mean. Things like a barrel organ, and an automobile that had its horn stuck, and like that.

That made things twice as bad, of course, because anybody was liable to try to touch one of these ghost things and jump to the conclusion they were a ghost, themselves.

Two, the TV reporters were interviewing the ghosts, the same way I did, with paper and pencil. I picked up four more sets of questions and answers just while I was eating lunch.

The ghosts came over fine on TV, by the way. Somehow it looked even creepier on the screen, when you saw somebody's hand disappear into them, than it did when you saw it with your own eyes.

The development in my head was like this. Out of the fifteen cases I already had, and the four I got from TV, there were eight that happened on the street or in subways or buses, five in restaurants, and six in places of entertainment. Four *different* places of entertainment. Now, at first glance, that may not look like it means much. But I said to myself, what does this Martian do? He travels around from one place to another—that's normal. He eats—that's normal. But he goes to four different shows that I know about in three days—and I know just nineteen cases out of maybe a thousand!

It all fitted together. Here is this Martian, he's never been here before—we know that because he just now started making trouble. The way I see it, these Martians look us over for a while from a distance, and then they decide to send one Martian down to New York to study us close up. Well, what's the first thing he does, being that he wants to find out all about us? He goes to the movies. And concerts and stage plays too, of course, because he wants to try everything once. But probably he sees two or three double features a day. It stands to reason.

So there he is in the movie, watching and listening so he shouldn't miss anything important, and some customer in the next seat starts making loud comments to her boy friend, rattling cellophane, and snapping her bag open and shut every five seconds to find a Kleenex. So he flips her into the next dimension where she can make all the noise she wants without bothering him.

And that's the reason why there are so many ghosts that got theirs in the movies and places like that. On the streets of New York City you can walk for miles without running into more than two or three really obnoxious characters. But in any kind of theater there's *always* somebody talking, or coughing, or rattling paper. It stands to reason.

I went even further than that. I checked with my notes and then looked in a copy of *Cue* magazine to find out what was playing at each of these theaters when the Martian was there.

I found out that the play was a long-run musical—the concert was musical, naturally—and one of the two movies was a Hollywood remake of a musical comedy. The other was a newsreel.

There it was—I as good as had him. Then I got another idea and went back through my notes to find out where the theater victims had been sitting. The guy in Carnegie Hall had been in the balcony; that's where you hear best, I guess. But the other five had all been sitting down front, in the first four rows.

The little guy was nearsighted.

That's the way I was thinking about him now—a little nearsighted guy who liked music better than Westerns, and was used to some place where everybody's careful not to bother anybody else. It was hard not to feel sorry for him; after all, some people that come from places closer than Mars have a hard time in New York.

But it was me against him. That night the total rewards were up to almost twenty thousand dollars.

I thought of one thing I could do right away. I could write to the Mayor to make an announcement that if people didn't want to be ghosts, they should keep from making unnecessary noise or being pests, especially in theaters. But one, he probably wouldn't pay any attention to me, and two, if he did, twenty thousand other guys would be following my lead before I could turn around, and one of them would probably catch the Martian before I did.

That night, I did the same as before. I waited till Ma was sleeping, then went out to a movie on Broadway. It was a first-run house, they had a musical playing, and I sat down front.

But nothing happened. The Martian wasn't there.

I felt pretty discouraged when I got home. My time was running out and there are over three hundred theaters in Manhattan. I had to start working faster.

I lay awake for a long while, worrying about it in my head, and finally I came to one of the most important decisions in my life. The next morning I was going to do something I never did before—call in and pretend like I was sick. And I was going to stay sick until I found the Martian.

I felt bad about it and I felt even worse in the morning, when Rifkowicz told me to take it easy till I got well.

After breakfast, I got the papers and made a list of shows on my way uptown. I went to one on 42nd Street first—it was a musical picture about some composer named Handel, and the second feature was a comedy, but it had Hoagy Carmichael in it, so I figured I should stay for that too. I sat in the fifth row. There was plenty of coughing going on, but nobody got turned into a ghost. I enjoyed both pictures.

Then I had lunch and went to another musical, on Broadway. I drew another blank.

My eyes were beginning to bother me a little from sitting so close to the screen, so I thought I would just go to a newsreel movie and then walk around a while before dinner. But when I got out of the newsreel I began to feel jittery, and I went straight to another double feature. The Martian wasn't there, either.

I had seen plenty of ghosts standing around on the streets, but they were all just standing there looking kind of lost and bewildered, the way they did after a while. You could tell a new victim because he would be rushing here and there, shoving his hands through things, trying to talk to people, and so on.

One thing I forgot to mention. Everybody was wondering now how these ghosts got along without eating. In this dimension where they were, there wasn't any food—there wasn't *anything*, just the stuff like rubbery clouds that they were standing on. But they all claimed they weren't hungry or thirsty, and they all seemed to be in good shape. Even the ones that had been ghosts now for four days.

When I got out of that last movie, it was about eight in the evening. I was feeling low in my mind, but I still had a healthy appetite. I started wandering around the side streets of Broadway, looking for a restaurant that wasn't too crowded or too expensive. I passed a theater that was on my list, except I knew I was too late to get a ticket for it. It was the premiere of the newest Rodgers and Hammerstein show, and the lobby and half the sidewalk were full of customers.

I went on past, feeling gloomier because of all the bright lights and excitement, and then I heard something funny. Without paying any attention, I had been listening to one of those raspy-voiced barkers inside the lobby going, "GETcha program here." Now, all of a sudden, he said, "GETch—" and stopped.

I turned around, with a funny prickling up the back of my spine. The voice didn't start up again. Just as I started back toward the lobby, a ghost came out of the crowd. There was no doubt about him being a ghost—he ran through people.

He had a bunch of big booklets with slick covers under his arm, and his mouth was wide open like he was shouting. Then he showed his teeth, and his face got all red, and he lifted the booklets in both hands and threw them away as hard as he could. *They* went through people, too.

The ghost walked away with his hands shoved into his pockets. I didn't try to stop him. I ran into that lobby, I shoved my badge at the ticket taker, and told him to find me the manager, quick.

When the manager came up, I grabbed him by the lapels and said, "I got reason to believe there's a dangerous criminal going to be in this audience tonight. With your cooperation, we'll get him." He looked worried, so I said, "There won't be any trouble. You just put me where I can see the front pews and leave the rest to me."

He said, "I can't give you a seat. The house is completely sold out."

I told him, "Okay, put me back in the wings, or whatever you call them."

He argued, but that's what he did. We went down the side aisle, through the orchestra pit and through a little door that went under the stage. Then we went up a little stairway to backstage, and he put me right at the edge of the stage, up front, where I could peek out at the audience.

There was a million people running back there behind the curtain, actors and chorus girls, guys in their shirt sleeves and guys in overalls. I could hear the hum out front—people were beginning to fill the seats—and I wanted that curtain to go up the worst way.

It took about a century, but finally the actors took their places, and the band suddenly started playing, and the curtain went up.

I understand that show is still playing to standing room only, even with all the trouble that's happened since then, but I didn't pay any attention to it and I couldn't even tell you what it was about. I was watching the front four rows, trying to memorize every face I saw.

Right in the middle there were three that I paid more attention to than the rest. One of them was a young blond girl with blue eyes like the color of Ma's fancy china that she brought with her from the old country. Another was an old gent with chin spinach and glasses on a string. The third was a little guy with a sour expression and a derby hat.

I don't know why I picked out those three, except maybe it was a hunch. Maybe I was looking at the blond girl just because she was pretty, but then again, I never saw eyes just that color before or since. It could be that Martians have china-blue eyes; how would I know? I might have had some wild idea that the old guy could be the Martian and was wearing the frizzy white whiskers because Martians don't have chins exactly like us. And I think I picked on the little guy because he fitted the picture I already had in my head. And the way he was clutching that derby in his lap, like it was made of gold—I was thinking to myself, maybe he's got some kind of ray gun built into that hat; maybe that's how he does it.

I admit that I wasn't thinking very logical—I was too excited—but I never took my eyes off that audience for a second.

I was waiting for somebody to start coughing or something and get turned into a ghost. When that happened, I would be watching the people, and if I was lucky I might see who was looking at the victim when it happened.

That's what I was waiting for. What I got was a sniff of smoke and then somebody screaming and yelling, "*Fire!*"

Half the audience was on their feet in a second. I looked up, and sure enough there was smoke pouring out at the back of the room. Some more women screamed and the stampede was on.

The girls on stage stopped dancing and the band stopped playing. Somebody—some actor—ran out on the stage and started saying, "Ladies and gentlemen, your attention please. *Walk*, do not run, to the nearest exit. There is no danger. *Walk*, do not run—"

I lost my head. Not on account of the fire—I knew the actor was right, and the only bad thing that could happen would be people trampling each other to death to get out of there. But the seats were emptying fast and it struck me all of a sudden that I didn't know my way through that tangle of scenery backstage—by the time I got down the stairs and out into the auditorium, the Martian might be gone.

I felt cold all over. I didn't even stop to remember that I didn't have to go back the way I came, because there were little steps right at the side of the stage. I ran out from behind the wings and started to jump over the musicians. At that, I would have made it if I hadn't caught my toe in that little trough where the footlights are.

I had worse luck than that, even. I landed smack in the middle of the bass drum.

You never heard such a sound in your life. It sounded like the ceiling caved in. Sitting there, with my legs and arms sticking out of that drum, I saw the people turn around and look at me like they had been shot. I saw them all, the girl with the china-blue eyes, the old gent with the whiskers, the little guy with the derby, and a lot more. And then, suddenly, all the sounds stopped like when you turn off a radio.

The guy who owned the drum leaned over and tried to pull me out of it. He couldn't.

His hands went right through me.

It's like I said, this Martian annoys easy. I don't know what he did about all those women screaming—maybe he figured there was a good reason for that and left them alone. But when I hit that bass drum, it must have burned him good. You know, when you're excited already, a loud noise will make you jump twice as far.

That's about the only satisfaction I got—that I probably annoyed him the worst of anybody in New York City.

That and being so close to catching him.

The company here is nothing to brag about—women that will talk your arm off and half your shoulder, and guys that say, "Peaceful enough for you?" and back-slappers, and people that hum to themselves—

Besides that, the place is dull as dishwater. Clouds to stand on, nothing to eat even if you wanted to eat, and nothing to do except stand around and watch the new ones come through. We can't even see much of New York any more, because it keeps getting mistier all the time—fading away, kind of, like maybe this dimension is getting a little farther away from the ordinary one every day.

I asked Mr. Dauth yesterday how he thought the whole thing would wind up. Mr. Dauth isn't bad. He's a big, cheerful guy, about fifty. The kind that likes good food and good beer and a lot of it. But he doesn't complain. He admits that his habit of sucking his teeth is aggravating and says maybe he deserved what he got, which you'll admit is big of him. So I talk to him a lot, and the other day, when we were watching a new batch that had just come through, I asked him where he thought it would all end.

He pursed his lips and frowned like he was thinking it over, and then said that as far as he could see, there wasn't any human being that was perfect. Anybody is liable to do something aggravating sooner or later. That's the way people are.

"And this Martian of yours seems to be thorough," he said. "Very thorough. It might take him years to get through studying the Earth."

"And then what?" I asked him.

"Well," he said, "eventually, if he keeps it up long enough, we'll *all* be over here."

I hope he's right. Now that I come to think of it, that cute waitress I mentioned has a habit of setting down a coffee cup so half of it slops into the saucer. . . .

If he's right, all I've got to do is wait.

It stands to reason.

How to learn from a civilization long dead has always been a challenging problem to science fiction writers. The late H. Beam Piper has provided one of the most ingenious solutions, one that is logical, practical, indeed inevitable. Here is a story about men on Mars that does not strain the imagination; the people are believable, the situation foreseeable. "Omnilingual" praises the slow, tedious, careful work of scientists in many fields who attempt to uncover the secrets of lost civilizations. Archeology, philology, psychology, and chemistry are some of the sciences utilized in this very human Martian story. In addition, however, "Omnilingual" presents a panoply of characters that are well-delineated human beings. It lets us know that the original explorers of Mars or of the third planet of, say, Canopus, will share the foibles, the eccentricities, the very humanity of all Earthmen.

H. Beam Piper

OMNILINGUAL

Martha Dane paused, looking up at the purple-tinged copper sky. The wind had shifted since noon, while she had been inside, and the dust storm that was sweeping the high deserts to the east was now blowing out over Syrtis. The sun, magnified by the haze, was a gorgeous magenta ball, as large as the sun of Terra, at which she could look directly. Tonight, some of that dust would come sifting down from the upper atmosphere to add another film to what had been burying the city for the last fifty thousand years.

The red loess lay over everything, covering the streets and the open spaces of park and plaza, hiding the small houses that had been crushed and pressed flat under it and the rubble that had come down from the tall buildings when roofs had caved in and walls had toppled outward. Here where she stood, the ancient streets were a hundred to a hundred and fifty feet below the surface; the breach they had made in the wall of the building behind her had opened into the sixth story. She could look down on the cluster of prefabricated huts and sheds, on the brush-grown flat that had been the waterfront when this place had been a seaport on the ocean that was now Syrtis Depression; already, the bright metal was thinly coated with red dust. She thought, again, of what clearing this city would mean, in terms of time and labor, of people and supplies and equipment brought across fifty million miles of space. They'd have to use machinery; there was no other way it could be done. Bulldozers and power shovels and draglines; they were fast, but they were rough and indiscriminate. She remembered the digs around Harappa and Mohenjo-Daro, in the Indus Valley, and the careful, patient native laborers—the painstaking foremen, the pickmen and spademen, the long files of basketmen carrying away the earth. Slow and primitive as the civilization whose ruins they were uncovering, yes, but she could count on the fingers of one hand the times one of her pickmen had damaged a valuable object in the ground. If it hadn't been for the underpaid and uncomplaining native laborer, archaeology would still be back where Wincklemann had found it. But on Mars there was no native labor; the last Martian had died five hundred centuries ago.

Something started banging like a machine gun, four or five hundred yards to her left. A solenoid jackhammer; Tony Lattimer must have decided which building he wanted to break into next. She became conscious, then, of the awkward weight of her equipment, and began redistributing it, shifting the straps of her oxytank pack, slinging the camera from one shoulder and the board and drafting tools from the other, gathering the notebooks and sketchbooks under her left arm. She started walking down the road, over hillocks of buried rubble, around snags of wall jutting up out of the loess, past buildings still standing, some of them already breached and explored, and across the brush-grown flat to the huts.

There were ten people in the main office room of Hut One when she entered. As soon as she had disposed of her oxygen equipment, she lit a cigarette, her first since noon, then looked from one to another of them. Old Selim von Ohlmhorst, the Turco-German, one of her two fellow archaeologists, sitting at the end of the long table against the farther wall, smoking his big curved pipe and going through a looseleaf notebook. The girl ordnance officer, Sachiko Koremitsu, between two droplights at the

other end of the table,
bert Penrose, the Space
ligence officer, listening to
returned from his afternoo
ants from Signals, going o
to be transmitted to the Cy
planet and relayed from thei
lain, the Trans-Space News
Selim and herself, he was a
with a white shirt and a sl
Lindemann, the engineer office
ing over some plans on a draft
pint of hot water to wash her ha
they were doing something about t   ner face, that

She started to carry the notebooks and sketchbooks over to where Selim von Ohlmhorst was sitting, and then, as she always did, she turned aside and stopped to watch Sachiko. The Japanese girl was restoring what had been a book, fifty thousand years ago; her eyes were masked by a binocular loup, the black headband invisible against her glossy black hair, and she was picking delicately at the crumbled page with a hair-fine wire set in a handle of copper tubing. Finally, loosening a particle as tiny as a snowflake, she grasped it with tweezers, placed it on the sheet of transparent plastic on which she was reconstructing the page, and set it with a mist of fixitive from a little spraygun. It was a sheer joy to watch her; every movement was as graceful and precise as though done to music after being rehearsed a hundred times.

"Hello, Martha. It isn't cocktail time yet, is it?" The girl at the table spoke without raising her head, almost without moving her lips, as though she were afraid that the slightest breath would disturb the flaky stuff in front of her.

"No, it's only fifteen-thirty. I finished my work, over there. I didn't find any more books, if that's good news for you."

Sachiko took off the loup and leaned back in her chair, her palms cupped over her eyes.

"No, I like doing this. I call it micro-jigsaw puzzles. This book, here, really is a mess. Selim found it lying open, with some heavy

were simply crushed." She hesitated

an something, after I did it."

tly critical overtone to that. As she replied,

she was being defensive.

day. Look how long it took to read Egyptian hi-

, even after they had the Rosetta Stone."

o smiled. "Yes, I know. But they did have the Rosetta

e."

"And we don't. There is no Rosetta Stone, not anywhere on Mars. A whole race, a whole species, died while the first Crô-Magnon cave-artist was daubing pictures of reindeer and bison, and across fifty thousand years and fifty million miles there was no bridge of understanding.

"We'll find one. There must be something, somewhere, that will give us the meaning of a few words, and we'll use them to pry meaning out of more words, and so on. We may not live to learn this language, but we'll make a start, and some day somebody will."

Sachiko took her hands from her eyes, being careful not to look toward the unshaded lights, and smiled again. This time Martha was sure that it was not the Japanese smile of politeness, but the universally human smile of friendship.

"I hope so, Martha; really I do. It would be wonderful for you to be the first to do it, and it would be wonderful for all of us to be able to read what these people wrote. It would really bring this dead city to life again." The smile faded slowly. "But it seems so hopeless."

"You haven't found any more pictures?"

Sachiko shook her head. Not that it would have meant much if she had. They had found hundreds of pictures with captions; they had never been able to establish a positive relationship between any pictured object and any printed word. Neither of them said anything more, and after a moment Sachiko replaced the loup and bent her head forward over the book.

Selim von Ohlmhorst looked up from his notebook, taking his pipe out of his mouth.

"Everything finished, over there?" he asked, releasing a puff of smoke.

"Such as it was." She laid the notebooks and sketches on the table. "Captain Gicquel's started airsealing the building from the fifth floor down, with an entrance on the sixth; he'll start putting in oxygen generators as soon as that's done. I have everything cleared up where he'll be working."

Colonel Penrose looked up quickly, as though making a mental note to attend to something later. Then he returned his attention to the pilot, who was pointing something out on a map.

Von Ohlmhorst nodded. "There wasn't much to it, at that," he agreed. "Do you know which building Tony has decided to enter next?"

"The tall one with the conical thing like a candle extinguisher on top, I think. I heard him drilling for the blasting shots over that way."

"Well, I hope it turns out to be one that was occupied up to the end."

The last one hadn't. It had been stripped of its contents and fittings, a piece of this and a bit of that, haphazardly, apparently over a long period of time, until it had been almost gutted. For centuries, as it had died, this city had been consuming itself by a process of auto-cannibalism. She said something to that effect.

"Yes. We always find that—except, of course, at places like Pompeii. Have you seen any of the other Roman cities in Italy?" he asked. "Minturnae, for instance? First the inhabitants tore down this to repair that, and then, after they had vacated the city, other people came along and tore down what was left, and burned the stones for lime, or crushed them to mend roads, till there was nothing left but the foundation traces. That's where we are fortunate; this is one of the places where the Martian race perished, and there were no barbarians to come later and destroy what they had left." He puffed slowly at his pipe. "Some of these days, Martha, we are going to break into one of these buildings and find that it was one in which the last of these people died. Then we will learn the story of the end of this civilization."

And if we learn to read their language, we'll learn the whole story, not just the obituary. She hesitated, not putting the thought into words. "We'll find that, sometime, Selim," she said, then looked at her watch. "I'm going to get some more work done on my lists, before dinner."

For an instant, the old man's face stiffened in disapproval; he started to say something, thought better of it, and put his pipe back into his mouth. The brief wrinkling around his mouth and the twitch of his white mustache had been enough, however; she knew what he was thinking. She was wasting time and effort, he believed; time and effort belonging not to herself but to the expedition. He could be right, too, she realized. But he had to be wrong; there had to be a way to do it. She turned from him silently and went to her own packing-case seat, at the middle of the table.

Photographs, and photostats of restored pages of books, and transcripts of inscriptions, were piled in front of her, and the notebooks in which she was compiling her lists. She sat down, lighting a fresh cigarette, and reached over to a stack of unexamined material, taking off the top sheet. It was a photostat of what looked like the title page and contents of some sort of a periodical. She remembered it; she had found it herself, two days before, in a closet in the basement of the building she had just finished examining.

She sat for a moment, looking at it. It was readable, in the sense that she had set up a purely arbitrary but consistently pronounceable system of phonetic values for the letters. The long vertical symbols were vowels. There were only ten of them; not too many, allowing separate characters for long and short sounds. There were twenty of the short horizontal letters, which meant that sounds like -ng or -ch or -sh were single letters. The odds were millions to one against her system being anything like the original sound of the language, but she had listed several thousand Martian words, and she could pronounce all of them.

And that was as far as it went. She could pronounce between three and four thousand Martian words, and she couldn't assign a meaning to one of them. Selim von Ohlmhorst believed that she never would. So did Tony Lattimer, and he was a great deal less reticent about saying so. So, she was sure, did Sachiko Kore-mitsu. There were times, now and then, when she began to be afraid that they were right.

The letters on the page in front of her began squirming and dancing, slender vowels with fat little consonants. They did that, now, every night in her dreams. And there were other dreams, in which she read them as easily as English; waking, she would try desperately and vainly to remember. She blinked, and looked away from the photostated page; when she looked back, the letters were behaving themselves again. There were three words at the top of the page, over-and-underlined, which seemed to be the Martian method of capitalization. *Mastharnorvod Tadavas Sorn-hulva*. She pronounced them mentally, leafing through her note-books to see if she had encountered them before, and in what contexts. All three were listed. In addition, *masthar* was a fairly common word, and so was *norvod*, and so was *nor*, but *-vod* was a suffix and nothing but a suffix. *Davas*, was a word, too, and *ta-* was a common prefix; *sorn* and *hulva* were both common words. This language, she had long ago decided, must be something like German; when the Martians had needed a new word, they had just pasted a couple of existing words together. It would prob-ably turn out to be a grammatical horror. Well, they had pub-lished magazines, and one of them had been called *Mastharnorvod Tadavas Sornhulva*. She wondered if it had been something like the *Quarterly Archaeological Review*, or something more on the order of *Sexy Stories*.

A smaller line, under the title, was plainly the issue number and date; enough things had been found numbered in series to enable her to identify the numerals and determine that a decimal system of numeration had been used. This was the one thousand and seven hundred and fifty-fourth issue, for Doma, 14837; then Doma must be the name of one of the Martian months. The word had turned up several times before. She found herself puffing furiously on her cigarette as she leafed through notebooks and piles of already examined material.

Sachiko was speaking to somebody, and a chair scraped at the end of the table. She raised her head, to see a big man with red hair and a red face, in Space Force green, with the single star of a major on his shoulder, sitting down. Ivan Fitzgerald, the medic. He was lifting weights from a book similar to the one the girl ordnance officer was restoring.

"Haven't had time, lately," he was saying, in reply to Sachiko's question. "The Finchley girl's still down with whatever it is she has, and it's something I haven't been able to diagnose yet. And I've been checking on bacteria cultures, and in what spare time I have, I've been dissecting specimens for Bill Chandler. Bill's finally found a mammal. Looks like a lizard, and it's only four inches long, but it's a real warm-blooded, gamogenetic, placental, viviparous mammal. Burrows, and seems to live on what pass for insects here."

"Is there enough oxygen for anything like that?" Sachiko was asking.

"Seems to be, close to the ground." Fitzgerald got the head-band of his loup adjusted, and pulled it down over his eyes. "He found this thing in a ravine down on the sea bottom— Ha, this page seems to be intact; now, if I can get it out all in one piece—"

He went on talking inaudibly to himself, lifting the page a little at a time and sliding one of the transparent plastic sheets under it, working with minute delicacy. Not the delicacy of the Japanese girl's small hands, moving like the paws of a cat washing her face, but like a steam-hammer cracking a peanut. Field archaeology requires a certain delicacy of touch, too, but Martha watched the pair of them with envious admiration. Then she turned back to her own work, finishing the table of contents.

The next page was the beginning of the first article listed; many of the words were unfamiliar. She had the impression that this must be some kind of scientific or technical journal; that could be because such publications made up the bulk of her own periodical reading. She doubted if it were fiction; the paragraphs had a solid, factual look.

At length, Ivan Fitzgerald gave a short, explosive grunt.

"Ha! Got it!"

She looked up. He had detached the page and was cementing another plastic sheet onto it.

"Any pictures?" she asked.

"None on this side. Wait a moment." He turned the sheet. "None on this side, either." He sprayed another sheet of plastic to sandwich the page, then picked up his pipe and relighted it.

"I get fun out of this, and it's good practice for my hands, so don't think I'm complaining," he said, "but, Martha, do you honestly think anybody's ever going to get anything out of this?"

Sachiko held up a scrap of the silicone plastic the Martians had used for paper with her tweezers. It was almost an inch square.

"Look; three whole words on this piece," she crowed. "Ivan, you took the easy book."

Fitzgerald wasn't being sidetracked. "This stuff's absolutely meaningless," he continued. "It had a meaning fifty thousand years ago, when it was written, but it has none at all now."

She shook her head. "Meaning isn't something that evaporates with time," she argued. "It has just as much meaning now as it ever had. We just haven't learned how to decipher it."

"That seems like a pretty pointless distinction," Selim von Ohlmhorst joined the conversation. "There no longer exists a means of deciphering it."

"We'll find one." She was speaking, she realized, more in self-encouragement than in controversy.

"How? From pictures and captions? We've found captioned pictures, and what have they given us? A caption is intended to explain the picture, not the picture to explain the caption. Suppose some alien to our culture found a picture of a man with a white beard and mustache sawing a billet from a log. He would think the caption meant, 'Man Sawing Wood.' How would he know that it was really 'Wilhelm II in Exile at Doorn?'"

Sachiko had taken off her loup and was lighting a cigarette.

"I can think of pictures intended to explain their captions," she said. "These picture language-books, the sort we use in the Service—little line drawings, with a word or phrase under them."

"Well, of course, if we found something like that," von Ohlmhorst began.

"Michael Ventris found something like that, back in the Fifties," Hubert Penrose's voice broke in from directly behind her.

She turned her head. The colonel was standing by the archaeologists' table; Captain Field and the airdyne pilot had gone out.

"He found a lot of Greek inventories of military stores," Penrose continued. "They were in Cretan Linear B script, and at the head of each list was a little picture, a sword or a helmet or a cooking tripod or a chariot wheel. That's what gave him the key to the script."

"Colonel's getting to be quite an archaeologist," Fitzgerald commented. "We're all learning each others' specialties, on this expedition."

"I heard about that long before this expedition was even contemplated." Penrose was tapping a cigarette on his gold case. "I heard about that back before the Thirty Days' War, at Intelligence School, when I was a lieutenant. As a feat of cryptanalysis, not an archaeological discovery."

"Yes, cryptanalysis," von Ohlmhorst pounced. "The reading of a known language in an unknown form of writing. Ventris' lists were in the known language, Greek. Neither he nor anybody else ever read a word of the Cretan language until the finding of the Greek-Cretan bilingual in 1963, because only with a bilingual text, one language already known, can an unknown ancient language be learned. And what hope, I ask you, have we of finding anything like that here? Martha, you've been working on these Martian texts ever since we landed here—for the last six months. Tell me, have you found a single word to which you can positively assign a meaning?"

"Yes, I think I have one." She was trying hard not to sound too exultant. "*Doma.* It's the name of one of the months of the Martian calendar."

"Where did you find that?" von Ohlmhorst asked. "And how did you establish—?"

"Here." She picked up the photostat and handed it along the table to him. "I'd call this the title page of a magazine."

He was silent for a moment, looking at it. "Yes. I would say so, too. Have you any of the rest of it?"

"I'm working on the first page of the first article, listed there. Wait till I see; yes, here's all I found, together, here." She told him where she had gotten it. "I just gathered it up, at the time, and gave it to Geoffrey and Rosita to photostat; this is the first I've really examined it."

The old man got to his feet, brushing tobacco ashes from the front of his jacket, and came to where she was sitting, laying the title page on the table and leafing quickly through the stack of photostats.

"Yes, and here is the second article, on page eight, and here's the next one." He finished the pile of photostats. "A couple of pages missing at the end of the last article. This is remarkable; surprising that a thing like a magazine would have survived so long."

"Well, this silicone stuff the Martians used for paper is pretty durable," Hubert Penrose said. "There doesn't seem to have been any water or any other fluid in it originally, so it wouldn't dry out with time."

"Oh, it's not remarkable that the material would have survived. We've found a good many books and papers in excellent condition. But only a really vital culture, an organized culture, will publish magazines, and this civilization had been dying for hundreds of years before the end. It might have been a thousand years before the time they died out completely that such activities as publishing ended."

"Well, look where I found it; in a closet in a cellar. Tossed in there and forgotten, and then ignored when they were stripping the building. Things like that happen."

Penrose had picked up the title page and was looking at it.

"I don't think there's any doubt about this being a magazine, at all." He looked again at the title, his lips moving silently. "*Mastharnorvod Tadavas Sornhulva.* Wonder what it means. But you're right about the date—*Doma* seems to be the name of a month. Yes, you have a word, Dr. Dane."

Sid Chamberlain, seeing that something unusual was going on, had come over from the table at which he was working. After examining the title page and some of the inside pages, he began whispering into the stenophone he had taken from his belt.

"Don't try to blow this up to anything big, Sid," she cautioned. "All we have is the name of a month, and Lord only knows how long it'll be till we even find out which month it was."

"Well, it's a start, isn't it?" Penrose argued. "Grotefend only had the word for 'king' when he started reading Persian cuneiform."

"But I don't have the word for month; just the name of a month. Everybody knew the names of the Persian kings, long before Grotefend."

"That's not the story," Chamberlain said. "What the public back on Terra will be interested in is finding out that the Martians published magazines, just like we do. Something familiar; make the Martians seem more real. More human."

Three men had come in, and were removing their masks and helmets and oxy-tanks, and peeling out of their quilted coveralls. Two were Space Force lieutenants; the third was a youngish civilian with close-cropped blond hair, in a checked woolen shirt. Tony Lattimer and his helpers.

"Don't tell me Martha finally got something out of that stuff?" he asked, approaching the table. He might have been commenting on the antics of the village half-wit, from his tone.

"Yes; the name of one of the Martian months." Hubert Penrose went on to explain, showing the photostat.

Tony Lattimer took it, glanced at it, and dropped it on the table.

"Sounds plausible, of course, but just an assumption. That word may not be the name of a month, at all—could mean 'published' or 'authorized' or 'copyrighted' or anything like that. Fact is, I don't think it's more than a wild guess that that thing's anything like a periodical." He dismissed the subject and turned to Penrose. "I picked out the next building to enter; that tall one with the conical thing on top. It ought to be in pretty good shape inside; the conical top wouldn't allow dust to accumulate, and from the outside nothing seems to be caved in or crushed. Ground level's higher than the other one, about the seventh floor. I found a good place and drilled for the shots; tomorrow I'll blast a hole in it, and if you can spare some people to help, we can start exploring it right away."

"Yes, of course, Dr. Lattimer. I can spare about a dozen, and I suppose you can find a few civilian volunteers," Penrose told him. "What will you need in the way of equipment?"

"Oh, about six demolition-packets; they can all be shot together. And the usual thing in the way of lights, and breaking and digging tools, and climbing equipment in case we run into broken or doubtful stairways. We'll divide into two parties. Nothing ought to be entered for the first time without a qualified archaeologist along. Three parties, if Martha can tear herself away from this catalogue of systematized incomprehensibilities she's making long enough to do some real work."

She felt her chest tighten and her face become stiff. She was pressing her lips together to lock in a furious retort when Hubert Penrose answered for her.

"Dr. Dane's been doing as much work, and as important work, as you have," he said brusquely. "More important work, I'd be inclined to say."

Von Ohlmhorst was visibly distressed; he glanced once toward Sid Chamberlain, then looked hastily away from him. Afraid of a story of dissension among archaeologists getting out.

"Working out a system of pronunciation by which the Martian language could be transliterated was a most important contribution," he said. "And Martha did that almost unassisted."

"Unassisted by Dr. Lattimer, anyway," Penrose added. "Captain Field and Lieutenant Koremitsu did some work, and I helped out a little, but nine-tenths of it she did herself."

"Purely arbitrary," Lattimer disdained. "Why, we don't even know that the Martians could make the same kind of vocal sounds we do."

"Oh, yes, we do," Ivan Fitzgerald contradicted, safe on his own ground. "I haven't seen any actual Martian skulls—these people seem to have been very tidy about disposing of their dead—but from statues and busts and pictures I've seen, I'd say that their vocal organs were identical with our own."

"Well, grant that. And grant that it's going to be impressive to rattle off the names of Martian notables whose statues we find, and that if we're ever able to attribute any place names, they'll sound a lot better than this horse-doctors' Latin the old astronomers splashed all over the map of Mars," Lattimer said. "What I object to is her wasting time on this stuff, of which nobody will ever be able to read a word if she fiddles around with those lists till there's another hundred feet of loess on this city, when there's so much real work to be done and we're as shorthanded as we are."

That was the first time that had come out in just so many words. She was glad Lattimer had said it and not Selim von Ohlmhorst.

"What you mean," she retorted, "is that it doesn't have the publicity value that digging up statues has."

For an instant, she could see that the shot had scored. Then Lattimer, with a side glance at Chamberlain, answered:

"What I mean is that you're trying to find something that any archaeologist, yourself included, should know doesn't exist. I don't object to your gambling your professional reputation and making a laughing stock of yourself; what I object to is that the blunders of one archaeologist discredit the whole subject in the eyes of the public."

That seemed to be what worried Lattimer most. She was framing a reply when the communication-outlet whistled shrilly, and then squawked: "Cocktail time! One hour to dinner; cocktails in the library, Hut Four!"

The library, which was also lounge, recreation room, and general gathering-place, was already crowded; most of the crowd was at the long table topped with sheets of glasslike plastic that had been wall panels out of one of the ruined buildings. She poured herself what passed, here, for a martini, and carried it over to where Selim von Ohlmhorst was sitting alone.

For a while, they talked about the building they had just finished exploring, then drifted into reminiscences of their work on Terra—von Ohlmhorst's in Asia Minor, with the Hittite Empire, and hers in Pakistan, excavating the cities of the Harappa Civilization. They finished their drinks—the ingredients were plentiful; alcohol and flavoring extracts synthesized from Martian vegetation—and von Ohlmhorst took the two glasses to the table for refills.

"You know, Martha," he said, when he returned, "Tony was right about one thing. You are gambling your professional standing and reputation. It's against all archaeological experience that a language so completely dead as this one could be deciphered. There was a continuity between all the other ancient languages —by knowing Greek, Champollion learned to read Egyptian; by knowing Egyptian, Hittite was learned. That's why you and your colleagues have never been able to translate the Harappa hieroglyphics; no such continuity exists there. If you insist that this utterly dead language can be read, your reputation will suffer for it."

"I heard Colonel Penrose say, once, that an officer who's afraid to risk his military reputation seldom makes much of a reputation. It's the same with us. If we really want to find things out, we have to risk making mistakes. And I'm a lot more interested in finding things out than I am in my reputation."

She glanced across the room, to where Tony Lattimer was sitting with Gloria Standish, talking earnestly, while Gloria sipped one of the counterfeit martinis and listened. Gloria was the leading contender for the title of Miss Mars, 1996, if you liked big bosomy blondes, but Tony would have been just as attentive to her if she'd looked like the Wicked Witch in "The Wizard of Oz," because Gloria was the Pan-Federation Telecast System commentator with the expedition.

"I know you are," the old Turco-German was saying. "That's why, when they asked me to name another archaeologist for this expedition, I named you."

He hadn't named Tony Lattimer; Lattimer had been pushed onto the expedition by his university. There'd been a lot of high-level string-pulling to that; she wished she knew the whole story. She'd managed to keep clear of universities and university politics; all her digs had been sponsored by nonacademic foundations or art museums.

"You have an excellent standing; much better than my own, at your age. That's why it disturbs me to see you jeopardizing it by this insistence that the Martian language can be translated. I can't, really, see how you can hope to succeed."

She shrugged and drank some more of her cocktail, then lit another cigarette. It was getting tiresome to try to verbalize something she only felt.

"Neither do I, now, but I will. Maybe I'll find something like the picture-books Sachiko was talking about. A child's primer, maybe; surely they had things like that. And if I don't, I'll find something else. We've only been here six months. I can wait the rest of my life, if I have to, but I'll do it sometime."

"I can't wait so long," von Ohlmhorst said. "The rest of my life will only be a few years, and when the *Schiaparelli* orbits in, I'll be going back to Terra on the *Cyrano*."

"I wish you wouldn't. This is a whole new world of archaeology. Literally."

"Yes." He finished the cocktail and looked at his pipe as though wondering whether to re-light it so soon before dinner, then put it in his pocket. "A whole new world—but I've grown old, and it isn't for me. I've spent my life studying the Hittites. I can speak the Hittite language, though maybe King Muwatallis wouldn't be able to understand my modern Turkish accent. But the things I'd have to learn, here—chemistry, physics, engineering, how to run analytic tests on steel girders and beryllosilver alloys and plastics and silicones. I'm more at home with a civilization that rode in chariots and fought with swords and was just learning how to work iron. Mars is for young people. This expedition is a cadre of leadership—not only the Space Force people, who'll be the commanders of the main expedition, but us scientists, too. And I'm just an old cavalry general who can't learn to command tanks and aircraft. You'll have time to learn about Mars. I won't."

His reputation as the dean of Hittitologists was solid and secure, too, she added mentally. Then she felt ashamed of the thought. He wasn't to be classed with Tony Lattimer.

"All I came for was to get the work started," he was continuing. "The Federation Government felt that an old hand should do that. Well, it's started, now; you and Tony and whoever come out on the *Schiaparelli* must carry it on. You said it, yourself; you have a whole new world. This is only one city, of the last Martian civilization. Behind this, you have the Late Upland Culture, and the Canal Builders, and all the civilizations and races and empires before them, clear back to the Martian Stone Age." He hesitated for a moment. "You have no idea what all you have to learn, Martha. This isn't the time to start specializing too narrowly."

They all got out of the truck and stretched their legs and looked up the road to the tall building with the queer conical cap askew on its top. The four little figures that had been busy against its wall climbed into the jeep and started back slowly, the smallest of them, Sachiko Koremitsu, paying out an electric cable behind. When it pulled up beside the truck, they climbed out; Sachiko attached the free end of the cable to a nuclear-electric battery. At once, dirty gray smoke and orange dust puffed out from the wall of the building, and, a second later, the multiple explosion banged.

She and Tony Lattimer and Major Lindemann climbed onto the truck, leaving the jeep stand by the road. When they reached the building, a satisfyingly wide breach had been blown in the wall. Lattimer had placed his shots between two of the windows; they were both blown out along with the wall between, and lay unbroken on the ground. Martha remembered the first building they had entered. A Space Force officer had picked up a stone and thrown it at one of the windows, thinking that would be all they'd need to do. It had bounced back. He had drawn his pistol —they'd all carried guns, then, on the principle that what they didn't know about Mars might easily hurt them—and fired four shots. The bullets had ricochetted, screaming thinly; there were four coppery smears of jacketmetal on the window, and a little surface spalling. Somebody tried a rifle; the 4000-f.s. bullet had cracked the glasslike pane without penetrating. An oxyacetylene torch had taken an hour to cut the window out; the lab crew, aboard the ship, were still trying to find out just what the stuff was.

Tony Lattimer had gone forward and was sweeping his flashlight back and forth, swearing petulantly, his voice harshened and amplified by his helmet-speaker.

"I thought I was blasting into a hallway; this lets us into a room. Careful; there's about a two-foot drop to the floor, and a lot of rubble from the blast just inside."

He stepped down through the breach; the others began dragging equipment out of the trucks—shovels and picks and crowbars and sledges, portable floodlights, cameras, sketching materials, an extension ladder, even Alpinists' ropes and crampons and pickaxes. Hubert Penrose was shouldering something that looked like a surrealist machine gun but which was really a nuclear-electric jackhammer. Martha selected one of the spike-shod mountaineer's ice axes, with which she could dig or chop or poke or pry or help herself over rough footing.

The windows, grimed and crusted with fifty millennia of dust, filtered in a dim twilight; even the breach in the wall, in the morning shade, lighted only a small patch of floor. Somebody snapped on a floodlight, aiming it at the ceiling. The big room was empty and bare; dust lay thick on the floor and reddened the once-white walls. It could have been a large office, but there was nothing left in it to indicate its use.

"This one's been stripped up to the seventh floor!" Lattimer exclaimed. "Street level'll be cleaned out, completely."

"Do for living quarters and shops, then," Lindemann said. "Added to the others, this'll take care of everybody on the *Schiaparelli*."

"Seem to have been a lot of electric or electronic apparatus over along this wall," one of the Space Force officers commented. "Ten or twelve electric outlets." He brushed the dusty wall with his glove, then scraped on the floor with his foot. "I can see where things were pried loose."

The door, one of the double sliding things the Martians had used, was closed. Selim von Ohlmhorst tried it, but it was stuck fast. The metal latch-parts had frozen together, molecule bonding itself to molecule, since the door had last been closed. Hubert Penrose came over with the jackhammer, fitting a spear-point chisel into place. He set the chisel in the joint between the doors, braced the hammer against his hip, and squeezed the trigger-switch. The hammer banged briefly like the weapon it resembled, and the doors popped a few inches apart, then stuck. Enough dust had worked into the recesses into which it was supposed to slide to block it on both sides.

That was old stuff; they ran into that every time they had to force a door, and they were prepared for it. Somebody went outside and brought in a power-jack and finally one of the doors inched back to the door jamb. That was enough to get the lights and equipment through; they all passed from the room to the hallway beyond. About half the other doors were open; each had a number and a single word, *Darfhulva*, over it.

One of the civilian volunteers, a woman professor of natural ecology from Penn State University, was looking up and down the hall.

"You know," she said, "I feel at home here. I think this was a college of some sort, and these were classrooms. That word, up there; that was the subject taught, or the department. And those electronic devices, all where the class would face them; audio-visual teaching aids."

"A twenty-five-story university?" Lattimer scoffed. "Why, a building like this would handle thirty thousand students."

"Maybe there were that many. This was a big city, in its prime," Martha said, moved chiefly by a desire to oppose Lattimer.

"Yes, but think of the snafu in the halls, every time they changed classes. It'd take half an hour to get everybody back and forth from one floor to another." He turned to von Ohlmhorst. "I'm going up above this floor. This place has been looted clean up to here, but there's a chance there may be something above," he said.

"I'll stay on this floor, at present," the Turco-German replied. "There will be much coming and going, and dragging things in and out. We should get this completely examined and recorded first. Then Major Lindemann's people can do their worst, here."

"Well, if nobody else wants it, I'll take the downstairs," Martha said.

"I'll go along with you," Hubert Penrose told her. "If the lower floors have no archaeological value, we'll turn them into living quarters. I like this building; it'll give everybody room to keep out from under everybody else's feet." He looked down the hall. "We ought to find escalators at the middle."

The hallway, too, was thick underfoot with dust. Most of the open rooms were empty, but a few contained furniture, including small seat-desks. The original proponent of the university theory pointed these out as just what might be found in classrooms.

There were escalators, up and down, on either side of the hall, and more on the intersecting passage to the right.

"That's how they handled the students, between classes," Martha commented. "And I'll bet there are more ahead, there."

They came to a stop where the hallway ended at a great square central hall. There were elevators, there, on two of the sides, and four escalators, still usable as stairways. But it was the walls, and the paintings on them, that brought them up short and staring.

They were clouded with dirt—she was trying to imagine what they must have looked like originally, and at the same time estimating the labor that would be involved in cleaning them—but they were still distinguishable, as was the word, *Darfhulva*, in golden letters above each of the four sides. It was a moment before she realized, from the murals, that she had at last found a meaningful Martian word. They were a vast historical panorama, clockwise around the room. A group of skin-clad savages squatting around a fire. Hunters with bows and spears, carrying the carcass of an animal slightly like a pig. Nomads riding long-legged, graceful mounts like hornless deer. Peasants sowing and reaping; mud-walled hut villages, and cities; processions of priests and warriors; battles with swords and bows, and with cannon and muskets; galleys, and ships with sails, and ships without visible means of propulsion, and aircraft. Changing costumes and weapons and machines and styles of architecture. A richly fertile landscape, gradually merging into barren deserts and bushlands—the time of the great planet-wide drought. The Canal Builders—men with machines recognizable as steam-shovels and derricks, digging and quarrying and driving across the empty plains with aqua-ducts. More cities—seaports on the shrinking oceans; dwindling, half-deserted cities; an abandoned city, with four tiny humanoid figures and a thing like a combat-car in the middle of a brush-grown plaza, they and their vehicle dwarfed by the huge lifeless buildings around them. She had not the least doubt; *Darfhulva* was History.

"Wonderful!" von Ohlmhorst was saying. "The entire history of this race. Why, if the painter depicted appropriate costumes and weapons and machines for each period, and got the architecture right, we can break the history of this planet into eras and periods and civilizations."

"You can assume they're authentic. The faculty of this university would insist on authenticity in the *Darfhulva*—History—Department," she said.

"Yes! *Darfhulva*—History! And your magazine was a journal of *Sornhulva!*" Penrose exclaimed. "You have a word, Martha!" It took her an instant to realize that he had called her by her first name, and not Dr. Dane. She wasn't sure if that weren't a bigger triumph than learning a word of the Martian language. Or a more auspicious start. "Alone, I suppose that *hulva* means something like science or knowledge, or study; combined, it would be equivalent to our 'ology. And *darf* would mean something like past, or old times, or human events, or chronicles."

"That gives you three words, Martha!" Sachiko jubilated. "You did it."

"Let's don't go too fast," Lattimer said, for once not derisively. "I'll admit that *darfhulva* is the Martian word for history as a subject of study; I'll admit that *hulva* is the general word and *darf* modifies it and tells us which subject is meant. But as for assigning specific meanings, we can't do that because we don't know just how the Martians thought, scientifically or otherwise."

He stopped short, startled by the blue-white light that blazed as Sid Chamberlain's Kliegettes went on. When the whirring of the camera stopped, it was Chamberlain who was speaking:

"This is the biggest thing yet; the whole history of Mars, stone age to the end, all on four walls. I'm taking this with the fast shutter, but we'll telecast it in slow motion, from the beginning to the end. Tony, I want you to do the voice for it—running commentary, interpretation of each scene as it's shown. Would you do that?"

Would he do that! Martha thought. If he had a tail, he'd be wagging it at the very thought.

"Well, there ought to be more murals on the other floors," she said. "Who wants to come downstairs with us?"

Sachiko did; immediately, Ivan Fitzgerald volunteered. Sid decided to go upstairs with Tony Lattimer, and Gloria Standish decided to go upstairs, too. Most of the party would remain on the seventh floor, to help Selim von Ohlmhorst get it finished. After poking tentatively at the escalator with the spike of her ice axe, Martha led the way downward.

The sixth floor was *Darfhulva*, too; military and technological history, from the character of the murals. They looked around the central hall, and went down to the fifth; it was like the floors above except that the big quadrangle was stacked with dusty furniture and boxes. Ivan Fitzgerald, who was carrying the floodlight, swung it slowly around. Here the murals were of heroic-sized Martians, so human in appearance as to seem members of her own race, each holding some object—a book, or a testtube, or some bit of scientific apparatus, and behind them were scenes of laboratories and factories, flame and smoke, lightning-flashes. The word at the top of each of the four walls was one with which she was already familiar—*Sornhulva*.

"Hey, Martha; there's that word," Ivan Fitzgerald exclaimed. "The one in the title of your magazine." He looked at the paintings. "Chemistry, or physics."

"Both," Hubert Penrose considered. "I don't think the Martians made any sharp distinction between them. See, the old fellow with the scraggly whiskers must be the inventor of the spectroscope; he has one in his hands, and he has a rainbow behind him. And the woman in the blue smock, beside him, worked in organic chemistry; see the diagrams of long-chain molecules behind her. What word would convey the idea of chemistry and physics taken as one subject?"

"*Sornhulva*," Sachiko suggested. "If *hulva's* something like science, *sorn* must mean matter, or substance, or physical object. You were right, all along, Martha. A civilization like this would certainly leave something like this, that would be self-explanatory."

"This'll wipe a little more of that superior grin off Tony Lattimer's face," Fitzgerald was saying, as they went down the motionless escalator to the floor below. "Tony wants to be a big shot. When you want to be a big shot, you can't bear the possibility of anybody else being a bigger big shot, and whoever makes a start on reading this language will be the biggest big shot archaeology ever saw."

That was true. She hadn't thought of it, in that way, before, and now she tried not to think about it. She didn't want to be a big shot. She wanted to be able to read the Martian language, and find things out about the Martians.

Two escalators down, they came out on a mezzanine around a wide central hall on the street level, the floor forty feet below them and the ceiling thirty feet above. Their lights picked out object after object below—a huge group of sculptured figures in the middle; some kind of a motor vehicle jacked up on trestles for repairs; things that looked like machine-guns and auto-cannon; long tables, tops littered with a dust-covered miscellany; machinery; boxes and crates and containers.

They made their way down and walked among the clutter, missing a hundred things for every one they saw, until they found an escalator to the basement. There were three basements, one under another, until at last they stood at the bottom of the last escalator, on a bare concrete floor, swinging the portable floodlight over stacks of boxes and barrels and drums, and heaps of powdery dust. The boxes were plastic—nobody had ever found anything made of wood in the city—and the barrels and drums were of metal or glass or some glasslike substance. They were outwardly intact. The powdery heaps might have been anything organic, or anything containing fluid. Down here, where wind and dust could not reach, evaporation had been the only force of destruction after the minute life that caused putrefaction had vanished.

They found refrigeration rooms, too, and using Martha's ice axe and the pistollike vibratool Sachiko carried on her belt, they pounded and pried one open, to find desiccated piles of what had been vegetables, and leathery chunks of meat. Samples of that stuff, rocketed up to the ship, would give a reliable estimate, by radio-carbon dating, of how long ago this building had been occupied. The refrigeration unit, radically different from anything their own culture had produced, had been electrically powered. Sachiko and Penrose, poking into it, found the switches still on; the machine had only ceased to function when the power-source, whatever that had been, had failed.

The middle basement had also been used, at least toward the

end, for storage; it was cut in half by a partition pierced by but one door. They took half an hour to force this, and were on the point of sending above for heavy equipment when it yielded enough for them to squeeze through. Fitzgerald, in the lead with the light, stopped short, looked around, and then gave a groan that came through his helmet-speaker like a foghorn.

"Oh, no! No!"

"What's the matter, Ivan?" Sachiko, entering behind him, asked anxiously.

He stepped aside. "Look at it, Sachi! Are we going to have to do all that?"

Martha crowded through behind her friend and looked around, then stood motionless, dizzy with excitement. Books. Case on case of books, half an acre of cases, fifteen feet to the ceiling. Fitzgerald, and Penrose, who had pushed in behind her, were talking in rapid excitement; she only heard the sound of their voices, not their words. This must be the main stacks of the university library—the entire literature of the vanished race of Mars. In the center, down an aisle between the cases, she could see the hollow square of the librarians' desk, and stairs and a dumb-waiter to the floor above.

She realized that she was walking forward, with the others, toward this. Sachiko was saying: "I'm the lightest; let me go first." She must be talking about the spidery metal stairs.

"I'd say they were safe," Penrose answered. "The trouble we've had with doors around here shows that the metal hasn't deteriorated."

In the end, the Japanese girl led the way, more catlike than ever in her caution. The stairs were quite sound, in spite of their fragile appearance, and they all followed her. The floor above was a duplicate of the room they had entered, and seemed to contain about as many books. Rather than waste time forcing the door here, they returned to the middle basement and came up by the escalator down which they had originally descended.

The upper basement contained kitchens—electric stoves, some with pots and pans still on them—and a big room that must have been, originally, the students' dining room, though when last used it had been a workshop. As they expected, the library reading room was on the street-level floor, directly above the stacks. It seemed to have been converted into a sort of common living room for the building's last occupants. An adjoining auditorium had been made into a chemical works; there were vats and distillation apparatus, and a metal fractionating tower that extended through a hole knocked in the ceiling seventy feet above. A good deal of plastic furniture of the sort they had been finding everywhere in the city was stacked about, some of it broken up, apparently for reprocessing. The other rooms on the street floor seemed also to have been devoted to manufacturing and repair work; a considerable industry, along a number of lines, must have been carried on here for a long time after the university had ceased to function as such.

On the second floor, they found a museum; many of the exhibits remained, tantalizingly half-visible in grimed glass cases. There had been administrative offices there, too. The doors of most of them were closed, and they did not waste time trying to force them, but those that were open had been turned into living quarters. They made notes, and rough floor-plans, to guide them in future more thorough examination; it was almost noon before they had worked their way back to the seventh floor.

Selim von Ohlmhorst was in a room on the north side of the building, sketching the position of things before examining them and collecting them for removal. He had the floor checkerboarded with a grid of chalked lines, each numbered.

"We have everything on this floor photographed," he said. "I have three gangs—all the floodlights I have—sketching and making measurements. At the rate we're going, with time out for lunch, we'll be finished by the middle of the afternoon."

"You've been working fast. Evidently you aren't being high-church about a 'qualified archaeologist' entering rooms first," Penrose commented.

"Ach, childishness!" the old man exclaimed impatiently. "These officers of yours aren't fools. All of them have been to Intelligence School and Criminal Investigation School. Some of the most careful amateur archaeologists I ever knew were retired soldiers or policemen. But there isn't much work to be done. Most of the rooms are either empty or like this one—a few bits of

furniture and broken trash and scraps of paper. Did you find anything down on the lower floors?"

"Well, yes," Penrose said, a hint of mirth in his voice. "What
would you say, Martha?"

She started to tell Selim. The others, unable to restrain their
excitement, broke in with interruptions. Von Ohlmhorst was
staring in incredulous amazement.

"But this floor was looted almost clean, and the buildings we've
entered before were all looted from the street level up," he said,
at length.

"The people who looted this one lived here," Penrose replied.
"They had electric power to the last; we found refrigerators full
of food, and stoves with the dinner still on them. They must have
used the elevators to haul things down from the upper floor. The
whole first floor was converted into workshops and laboratories.
I think that this place must have been something like a monastery
in the Dark Ages in Europe, or what such a monastery would have
been like if the Dark Ages had followed the fall of a highly developed scientific civilization. For one thing, we found a lot of
machine-guns and light auto-cannon on the street level, and all
the doors were barricaded. The people here were trying to keep
a civilization running after the rest of the planet had gone back
to barbarism; I suppose they'd have to fight off raids by the barbarians now and then."

"You're not going to insist on making this building into expedition quarters, I hope, colonel?" von Ohlmhorst asked
anxiously.

"Oh, no! This place is an archaeological treasure-house. More
than that; from what I saw, our technicians can learn a lot, here.
But you'd better get this floor cleaned up as soon as you can,
though. I'll have the subsurface part, from the sixth floor down,
airsealed. Then we'll put in oxygen generators and power units,
and get a couple of elevators into service. For the floors above,
we can use temporary airsealing floor by floor, and portable
equipment; when we have things atmosphered and lighted and
heated, you and Martha and Tony Lattimer can go to work systematically and in comfort, and I'll give you all the help I can

spare from the other work. This is one of the biggest things we've found yet."

Tony Lattimer and his companions came down to the seventh floor a little later.

"I don't get this, at all," he began, as soon as he joined them. "This building wasn't stripped the way the others were. Always, the procedure seems to have been to strip from the bottom up, but they seem to have stripped the top floors first, here. All but the very top. I found out what that conical thing is, by the way. It's a wind-rotor, and under it there's an electric generator. This building generated its own power."

"What sort of condition are the generators in?" Penrose asked.

"Well, everything's full of dust that blew in under the rotor, of course, but it looks to be in pretty good shape. Hey, I'll bet that's it! They had power, so they used the elevators to haul stuff down. That's just what they did. Some of the floors above here don't seem to have been touched, though." He paused momentarily; back of his oxy-mask, he seemed to be grinning. "I don't know that I ought to mention this in front of Martha, but two floors above we hit a room—it must have been the reference library for one of the departments—that had close to five hundred books in it."

The noise that interrupted him, like the squawking of a Brobdingnagian parrot, was only Ivan Fitzgerald laughing through his helmet-speaker.

Lunch at the huts was a hasty meal, with a gabble of full-mouthed and excited talking. Hubert Penrose and his chief subordinates snatched their food in a huddled consultation at one end of the table; in the afternoon, work was suspended on everything else and the fifty-odd men and women of the expedition concentrated their efforts on the University. By the middle of the afternoon, the seventh floor had been completely examined, photographed and sketched, and the murals in the square central hall covered with protective tarpaulins, and Laurent Gicquel and his airsealing crew had moved in and were at work. It had been decided to seal the central hall at the entrances. It took the French-Canadian engineer most of the afternoon to find all the ventilation-ducts and plug them. An elevator-shaft on the north side was found reaching clear to the twenty-fifth floor; this would give access to the top of the building; another shaft, from the center, would take care of the floors below. Nobody seemed willing to trust the ancient elevators, themselves; it was the next evening before a couple of cars and the necessary machinery could be fabricated in the machine shops aboard the ship and sent down by landing-rocket. By that time, the airsealing was finished, the nuclear-electric energy-converters were in place, and the oxygen generators set up.

Martha was in the lower basement, an hour or so before lunch the day after, when a couple of Space Force officers came out of the elevator, bringing extra lights with them. She was still using oxygen-equipment; it was a moment before she realized that the newcomers had no masks, and that one of them was smoking. She took off her own helmet-speaker, throat-mike and mask and unslung her tank-pack, breathing cautiously. The air was chilly, and musty-acrid with the odor of antiquity—the first Martian odor she had smelled—but when she lit a cigarette, the lighter flamed clear and steady and the tobacco caught and burned evenly.

The archaeologists, many of the other civilian scientists, a few of the Space Force officers and the two news-correspondents, Sid Chamberlain and Gloria Standish, moved in that evening, setting up cots in vacant rooms. They installed electric stoves and a refrigerator in the old Library Reading Room, and put in a bar and lunch counter. For a few days, the place was full of noise and activity, then, gradually, the Space Force people and all but a few of the civilians returned to their own work. There was still the business of airsealing the more habitable of the buildings already explored, and fitting them up in readiness for the arrival, in a year and a half, of the five hundred members of the main expedition. There was work to be done enlarging the landing field for the ship's rocket craft, and building new chemical-fuel tanks.

There was the work of getting the city's ancient reservoirs cleared of silt before the next spring thaw brought more water down the underground aquaducts everybody called canals in mistranslation of Schiaparelli's Italian word, though this was proving considerably easier than anticipated. The ancient Canal-Builders must have anticipated a time when their descendants would no longer be capable of maintenance work, and had prepared against it. By the day after the University had been made completely habitable, the actual work there was being done by Selim, Tony Lattimer and herself, with half a dozen Space Force officers, mostly girls, and four or five civilians, helping.

They worked up from the bottom, dividing the floor-surfaces into numbered squares, measuring and listing and sketching and photographing. They packaged samples of organic matter and sent them up to the ship for Carbon-14 dating and analysis; they opened cans and jars and bottles, and found that everything fluid in them had evaporated, through the porosity of glass and metal and plastic if there were no other way. Wherever they looked, they found evidence of activity suddenly suspended and never resumed. A vise with a bar of metal in it, half cut through and the hacksaw beside it. Pots and pans with hardened remains of food in them; a leathery cut of meat on a table, with the knife ready at hand. Toilet articles on washstands; unmade beds, the bedding ready to crumble at a touch but still retaining the impress of the sleeper's body; papers and writing materials on desks, as though the writer had gotten up, meaning to return and finish in a fifty-thousand-year-ago moment.

It worried her. Irrationally, she began to feel that the Martians had never left this place; that they were still around her, watching disapprovingly every time she picked up something they had laid down. They haunted her dreams, now, instead of their enigmatic writing. At first, everybody who had moved into the University had taken a separate room, happy to escape the crowding and lack of privacy of the huts. After a few nights, she was glad when Gloria Standish moved in with her, and accepted the newswoman's excuse that she felt lonely without somebody to talk to before falling asleep. Sachiko Koremitsu joined them the next evening, and before going to bed, the girl officer cleaned and oiled her pistol, remarking that she was afraid some rust may have gotten into it.

The others felt it, too. Selim von Ohlmhorst developed the habit of turning quickly and looking behind him, as though trying to surprise somebody or something that was stalking him. Tony

Lattimer, having a drink at the bar that had been improvised from the librarian's desk in the Reading Room, set down his glass and swore.

"You know what this place is? It's an archaeological *Marie Celeste!*" he declared. "It was occupied right up to the end— we've all seen the shifts these people used to keep a civilization going here—but what was the end? What happened to them? Where did they go?"

"You didn't expect them to be waiting out front, with a red carpet and a big banner, *Welcome Terrans,* did you, Tony?" Gloria Standish asked.

"No, of course not; they've all been dead for fifty thousand years. But if they were the last of the Martians, why haven't we found their bones, at least? Who buried them, after they were dead?" He looked at the glass, a bubble-thin goblet, found, with hundreds of others like it, in a closet above, as though debating with himself whether to have another drink. Then he voted in the affirmative and reached for the cocktail pitcher. "And every door on the old ground level is either barred or barricaded from the inside. How did they get out? And why did they leave?"

The next day, at lunch, Sachiko Koremitsu had the answer to the second question. Four or five electrical engineers had come down by rocket from the ship, and she had been spending the morning with them, in oxy-masks, at the top of the building.

"Tony, I thought you said those generators were in good shape," she began, catching sight of Lattimer. "They aren't. They're in the most unholy mess I ever saw. What happened, up there, was that the supports of the wind-rotor gave way, and weight snapped the main shaft, and smashed everything under it."

"Well, after fifty thousand years, you can expect something like that," Lattimer retorted. "When an archaeologist says something's in good shape, he doesn't necessarily mean it'll start as soon as you shove a switch in."

"You didn't notice that it happened when the power was on, did you?" one of the engineers asked, nettled at Lattimer's tone. "Well, it was. Everything's burned out or shorted or fused together; I saw one busbar eight inches across melted clean in two.

It's a pity we didn't find things in good shape, even archaeologically speaking. I saw a lot of interesting things, things in advance of what we're using now. But it'll take a couple of years to get everything sorted out and figure what it looked like originally."

"Did it look as though anybody'd made any attempt to fix it?" Martha asked.

Sachiko shook her head. "They must have taken one look at it and given up. I don't believe there would have been any possible way to repair anything."

"Well, that explains why they left. They needed electricity for lighting, and heating, and all their industrial equipment was electrical. They had a good life, here, with power; without it, this place wouldn't have been habitable."

"Then why did they barricade everything from the inside, and how did they get out?" Lattimer wanted to know.

"To keep other people from breaking in and looting. Last man out probably barred the last door and slid down a rope from upstairs," von Ohlmhorst suggested. "This Houdini-trick doesn't worry me too much. We'll find out eventually."

"Yes, about the time Martha starts reading Martian," Lattimer scoffed.

"That may be just when we'll find out," von Ohlmhorst replied seriously. "It wouldn't surprise me if they left something in writing when they evacuated this place."

"Are you really beginning to treat this pipe dream of hers as a serious possibility, Selim?" Lattimer demanded. "I know, it would be a wonderful thing, but wonderful things don't happen just because they're wonderful. Only because they're possible, and this isn't. Let me quote that distinguished Hittitologist, Johannes Friedrich: 'Nothing can be translated out of nothing.' Or that later but not less distinguished Hittitologist, Selim von Ohlmhorst: 'Where are you going to get your bilingual?' "

"Friedrich lived to see the Hittite language deciphered and read," von Ohlmhorst reminded him.

"Yes, when they found Hittite-Assyrian bilinguals." Lattimer measured a spoonful of coffee-powder into his cup and added hot water. "Martha, you ought to know, better than anybody, how little chance you have. You've been working for years in the Indus

Valley; how many words of Harappa have you or anybody else ever been able to read?"

"We never found a university, with a half-million-volume library, at Harappa or Mohenjo-Daro."

"And, the first day we entered this building, we established meanings for several words," Selim von Ohlmhorst added.

"And you've never found another meaningful word since," Lattimer added. "And you're only sure of general meaning, not specific meaning of word-elements, and you have a dozen different interpretations for each word."

"We made a start," von Ohlmhorst maintained. "We have Grotefend's word for 'king.' But I'm going to be able to read some of those books, over there, if it takes me the rest of my life here. It probably will, anyhow."

"You mean you've changed your mind about going home on the *Cyrano?*" Martha asked. "You'll stay on here?"

The old man nodded. "I can't leave this. There's too much to discover. The old dog will have to learn a lot of new tricks, but this is where my work will be, from now on."

Lattimer was shocked. "You're nuts!" he cried. "You mean you're going to throw away everything you've accomplished in Hittitology and start all over again here on Mars? Martha, if you've talked him into this crazy decision, you're a criminal!"

"Nobody talked me into anything," von Ohlmhorst said roughly. "And as for throwing away what I've accomplished in Hittitology, I don't know what the devil you're talking about. Everything I know about the Hittite Empire is published and available to anybody. Hittitology's like Egyptology; it's stopped being research and archaeology and become scholarship and history. And I'm not a scholar or a historian; I'm a pick-and-shovel field archaeologist— a highly skilled and specialized grave-robber and junk-picker—and there's more pick-and-shovel work on this planet than I could do in a hundred lifetimes. This is something new; I was a fool to think I could turn my back on it and go back to scribbling footnotes about Hittite kings."

"You could have anything you wanted, in Hittitology. There are a dozen universities that'd sooner have you than a winning football team. But no! You have to be the top man in Martiology, too. You can't leave that for anybody else—" Lattimer shoved his chair back and got to his feet, leaving the table with an oath that was almost a sob of exasperation.

Maybe his feelings were too much for him. Maybe he realized, as Martha did, what he had betrayed. She sat, avoiding the eyes of the others, looking at the ceiling, as embarrassed as though Lattimer had flung something dirty on the table in front of them. Tony Lattimer had, desperately, wanted Selim to go home on the *Cyrano*. Martiology was a new field; if Selim entered it, he would bring with him the reputation he had already built in Hittitology, automatically stepping into the leading role that Lattimer had coveted for himself. Ivan Fitzgerald's words echoed back to her— when you want to be a big shot, you can't bear the possibility of anybody else being a bigger big shot. His derision of her own efforts became comprehensible, too. It wasn't that he was convinced that she would never learn to read the Martian language. He had been afraid that she would.

Ivan Fitzgerald finally isolated the germ that had caused the Finchly girl's undiagnosed illness. Shortly afterward, the malady turned into a mild fever, from which she recovered. Nobody else seemed to have caught it. Fitzgerald was still trying to find out how the germ had been transmitted.

They found a globe of Mars, made when the city had been a seaport. They located the city, and learned that its name had been Kukan—or something with a similar vowel-consonant ratio. Immediately, Sid Chamberlain and Gloria Standish began giving their telecasts a Kukan dateline, and Hubert Penrose used the name in his official reports. They also found a Martian calendar; the year had been divided into ten more or less equal months, and one of them had been Doma. Another month was Nor, and that was a part of the name of the scientific journal Martha had found.

Bill Chandler, the zoologist, had been going deeper and deeper into the old sea bottom of Syrtis. Four hundred miles from Kukan, and at fifteen thousand feet lower altitude, he shot a bird. At least, it was a something with wings and what were almost but not quite feathers, though it was more reptilian than avian in general characteristics. He and Ivan Fitzgerald skinned and mounted it, and then dissected the carcass almost tissue by tissue. About seven-eighths of its body capacity was lungs; it certainly breathed air containing at least half enough oxygen to support human life, or five times as much as the air around Kukan.

That took the center of interest away from archaeology, and started a new burst of activity. All the expedition's aircraft—four jetticopters and three wingless airdyne reconnaissance fighters— were thrown into intensified exploration of the lower sea bottoms, and the bio-science boys and girls were wild with excitement and making new discoveries on each flight.

The University was left to Selim and Martha and Tony Lattimer, the latter keeping to himself while she and the old Turco-German worked together. The civilian specialists in other fields, and the Space Force people who had been holding tape lines and making sketches and snapping cameras, were all flying to lower Syrtis to find out how much oxygen there was and what kind of life it supported.

Sometimes Sachiko dropped in; most of the time she was busy helping Ivan Fitzgerald dissect specimens. They had four or five species of what might loosely be called birds, and something that could easily be classed as a reptile, and a carnivorous mammal the size of a cat with birdlike claws, and a herbivore almost identical with the piglike thing in the big *Darfhulva* mural, and another like a gazelle with a single horn in the middle of its forehead.

The high point came when one party, at thirty thousand feet below the level of Kukan, found breathable air. One of them had a mild attack of *sorroche* and had to be flown back for treatment in a hurry, but the others showed no ill effects. The daily newscasts from Terra showed a corresponding shift in interest at home. The discovery of the University had focused attention on the dead past of Mars; now the public was interested in Mars as a possible home for humanity. It was Tony Lattimer who brought archaeology back into the activities of the expedition and the news at home.

Martha and Selim were working in the museum on the second floor, scrubbing the grime from the glass cases, noting contents, and grease-penciling numbers; Lattimer and a couple of Space Force officers were going through what had been the administrative offices on the other side. It was one of these, a young second lieutenant, who came hurrying in from the mezzanine, almost bursting with excitement.

"Hey, Martha! Dr. von Ohlmhorst!" he was shouting. "Where are you? Tony's found the Martians!"

Selim dropped his rag back in the bucket; she laid her clipboard on top of the case beside her.

"Where?" they asked together.

"Over on the north side." The lieutenant took hold of himself and spoke more deliberately. "Little room, back of one of the old faculty offices—conference room. It was locked from the inside, and we had to burn it down with a torch. That's where they are. Eighteen of them, around a long table—"

Gloria Standish, who had dropped in for lunch, was on the mezzanine, fairly screaming into a radiophone extension:

". . . Dozen and a half of them! Well, of course they're dead. What a question! They look like skeletons covered with leather. No, I do not know what they died of. Well, forget it; I don't care if Bill Chandler's found a three-headed hippopotamus. Sid, don't you get it? We've found the *Martians!*"

She slammed the phone back on its hook, rushing away ahead of them.

Martha remembered the closed door; on the first survey, they hadn't attempted opening it. Now it was burned away at both sides and lay, still hot along the edges, on the floor of the big office room in front. A floodlight was on in the room inside, and Lattimer was going around looking at things while a Space Force officer stood by the door. The center of the room was filled by a long table; in armchairs around it sat the eighteen men and women who had occupied the room for the last fifty millennia. There were bottles and glasses on the table in front of them, and, had she seen them in a dimmer light, she would have thought that they were merely dozing over their drinks. One had a knee hooked over his chair-arm and was curled in foetus-like sleep. Another had fallen forward onto the table, arms extended, the emerald set of a ring twinkling dully on one finger. Skeletons covered with leather, Gloria Standish had called them, and so they were—faces like skulls, arms and legs like sticks, the flesh shrunken onto the bones under it.

"Isn't this something!" Lattimer was exulting. "Mass suicide, that's what it was. Notice what's in the corners?"

Braziers, made of perforated two-gallon-odd metal cans, the white walls smudged with smoke above them. Von Ohlmhorst had noticed them at once, and was poking into one of them with his flashlight.

"Yes; charcoal. I noticed a quantity of it around a couple of hand-forges in the shop on the first floor. That's why you had so much trouble breaking in; they'd sealed the room on the inside." He straightened and went around the room, until he found a ventilator, and peered into it. "Stuffed with rags. They must have been all that were left, here. Their power was gone, and they were old and tired, and all around them their world was dying. So they just came in here and lit the charcoal, and sat drinking together till they all fell asleep. Well, we know what became of them, now, anyhow."

Sid and Gloria made the most of it. The Terran public wanted to hear about Martians, and if live Martians couldn't be found, a room full of dead ones was the next best thing. Maybe an even better thing; it had been only sixty-odd years since the Orson Welles invasion-scare. Tony Lattimer, the discoverer, was beginning to cash in on his attentions to Gloria and his ingratiation with Sid; he was always either making voice-and-image talks for telecast or listening to the news from the home planet. Without question, he had become, overnight, the most widely known archaeologist in history.

"Not that I'm interested in all this, for myself," he disclaimed, after listening to the telecast from Terra two days after his discovery. "But this is going to be a big thing for Martian archaeology. Bring it to the public attention; dramatize it. Selim, can you remember when Lord Carnarvon and Howard Carter found the tomb of Tutankhamen?"

"In 1923? I was two years old, then," von Ohlmhorst chuckled. "I really don't know how much that publicity ever did for Egyptology. Oh, the museums did devote more space to Egyptian exhibits, and after a museum department head gets a few extra showcases, you know how hard it is to make him give them up. And, for a while, it was easier to get financial support for new excavations. But I don't know how much good all this public excitement really does, in the long run."

"Well, I think one of us should go back on the *Cyrano*, when the *Schiaparelli* orbits in," Lattimer said. "I'd hoped it would be you; your voice would carry the most weight. But I think it's important that one of us go back, to present the story of our work, and what we have accomplished and what we hope to accomplish, to the public and to the universities and the learned societies, and to the Federation Government. There will be a great deal of work that will have to be done. We must not allow the other scientific fields and the so-called practical interests to monopolize public and academic support. So, I believe I shall go back at least for a while, and see what I can do—"

Lectures. The organization of a Society of Martian Archaeology, with Anthony Lattimer, Ph.D., the logical candidate for the chair. Degrees, honors; the deference of the learned, and the adulation of the lay public. Positions, with impressive titles and salaries. Sweet are the uses of publicity.

She crushed out her cigarette and got to her feet. "Well, I still have the final lists of what we found in *Halvhulva*—Biology—department to check over. I'm starting on Sornhulva tomorrow, and I want that stuff in shape for expert evaluation."

That was the sort of thing Tony Lattimer wanted to get away from, the detail-work and the drudgery. Let the infantry do the slogging through the mud; the brass-hats got the medals.

She was halfway through the fifth floor, a week later, and was having midday lunch in the reading room on the first floor when Hubert Penrose came over and sat down beside her, asking her what she was doing. She told him.

"I wonder if you could find me a couple of men, for an hour or so," she added. "I'm stopped by a couple of jammed doors at the central hall. Lecture room and library, if the layout of that floor's anything like the ones below it."

"Yes. I'm a pretty fair door-buster, myself." He looked around the room. "There's Jeff Miles; he isn't doing much of anything.

And we'll put Sid Chamberlain to work, for a change, too. The four of us ought to get your doors open." He called to Chamberlain, who was carrying his tray over to the dish washer. "Oh, Sid; you doing anything for the next hour or so?"

"I was going up to the fourth floor, to see what Tony's doing."

"Forget it. Tony's bagged his season limit of Martians. I'm going to help Martha bust in a couple of doors; we'll probably find a whole cemetery full of Martians."

Chamberlain shrugged. "Why not. A jammed door can have anything back of it, and I know what Tony's doing—just routine stuff."

Jeff Miles, the Space Force captain, came over, accompanied by one of the lab-crew from the ship who had come down on the rocket the day before.

"This ought to be up your alley, Mort," he was saying to his companion. "Chemistry and physics department. Want to come along?"

The lab man, Mort Tranter, was willing. Seeing the sights was what he'd come down from the ship for. She finished her coffee and cigarette, and they went out into the hall together, gathered equipment and rode the elevator to the fifth floor.

The lecture hall door was the nearest; they attacked it first. With proper equipment and help, it was no problem and in ten minutes they had it open wide enough to squeeze through with the floodlights. The room inside was quite empty, and, like most of the rooms behind closed doors, comparatively free from dust. The students, it appeared, had sat with their backs to the door, facing a low platform, but their seats and the lecturer's table and equipment had been removed. The two side walls bore inscriptions: on the right, a pattern of concentric circles which she recognized as a diagram of atomic structure, and on the left a complicated table of numbers and words, in two columns. Tranter was pointing at the diagram on the right.

"They got as far as the Bohr atom, anyhow," he said. "Well, not quite. They knew about electron shells, but they have the nucleus pictured as a solid mass. No indication of proton-and-neutron structure. I'll bet, when you come to translate their scientific books, you'll find that they taught that the atom was the ultimate and indivisible particle. That explains why you people never found any evidence that the Martians used nuclear energy."

"That's a uranium atom," Captain Miles mentioned.

"It is?" Sid Chamberlain asked, excitedly. "Then they did know about atomic energy. Just because we haven't found any pictures of A-bomb mushrooms doesn't mean—"

She turned to look at the other wall. Sid's signal reactions were getting away from him again; uranium meant nuclear power to him, and the two words were interchangeable. As she studied the arrangement of the numbers and words, she could hear Tranter saying:

"Nuts, Sid. We knew about uranium a long time before anybody found out what could be done with it. Uranium was discovered on Terra in 1789, by Klaproth."

There was something familiar about the table on the left wall. She tried to remember what she had been taught in school about physics, and what she had picked up by accident afterward. The second column was a continuation of the first: there were forty-six items in each, each item numbered consecutively—

"Probably used uranium because it's the largest of the natural atoms," Penrose was saying. "The fact that there's nothing beyond it there shows that they hadn't created any of the transuranics. A student could go to that thing and point out the outer electron of any of the ninety-two elements."

Ninety-two! That was it; there were ninety-two items in the table on the left wall! Hydrogen was Number One, she knew; One, *Sarfaldsorn*. Helium was Two; that was *Tirfaldsorn*. She couldn't remember which element came next, but in Martian it was *Sarfalddavas*. *Sorn* must mean matter, or substance, then. And *davas*; she was trying to think of what it could be. She turned quickly to the others, catching hold of Hubert Penrose's arm with one hand and waving her clipboard with the other.

"Look at this thing, over here," she was clamoring excitedly. "Tell me what you think it is. Could it be a table of the elements?"

They all turned to look. Mort Tranter stared at it for a moment.

"Could be. If I only knew what those squiggles meant—"

That was right; he'd spent his time aboard the ship.

"If you could read the numbers, would that help?" she asked, beginning to set down the Arabic digits and their Martian equivalents. "It's decimal system, the same as we use."

"Sure. If that's a table of elements, all I'd need would be the numbers. Thanks," he added as she tore off the sheet and gave it to him.

Penrose knew the numbers, and was ahead of him. "Ninety-two items, numbered consecutively. The first number would be the atomic number. Then a single word, the name of the element. Then the atomic weight—"

She began reading off the names of the elements. "I know hydrogen and helium; what's *tirfalddavas*, the third one?"

"Lithium," Tranter said. "The atomic weights aren't run out past the decimal point. Hydrogen's one plus, if that double-hook dingus is a plus sign; Helium's four-plus, that's right. And lithium's given as seven, that isn't right. It's six-point-nine-four-oh. Or is that thing a Martian minus sign?"

"Of course! Look! A plus sign is a hook, to hang things together; a minus sign is a knife, to cut something off from something—see, the little loop is the handle and the long pointed loop is the blade. Stylized, of course, but that's what it is. And the fourth element, *kiradavas*; what's that?"

"Beryllium. Atomic weight given as nine-and-a-hook; actually it's nine-point-oh-two."

Sid Chamberlain had been disgruntled because he couldn't get a story about the Martians having developed atomic energy. It took him a few minutes to understand the newest development, but finally it dawned on him.

"Hey! You're reading that!" he cried. "You're reading Martian!"

"That's right," Penrose told him. "Just reading it right off. I don't get the two items after the atomic weight, though. They look like months of the Martian calendar. What ought they to be, Mort?"

Tranter hesitated. "Well, the next information after the atomic weight ought to be the period and group numbers. But those are words."

"What would the numbers be for the first one, hydrogen?"

"Period One, Group One. One electron shell, one electron in the outer shell," Tranter told her. "Helium's period one, too, but it has the outer—only—electron shell full, so it's in the group of inert elements."

"*Trav, Trav. Trav's* the first month of the year. And helium's *Trav, Yenth; Yenth* is the eighth month."

"The inert elements could be called Group Eight, yes. And the third element, lithium, is Period Two, Group One. That check?"

"It certainly does. *Sanv, Trav; Sanv's* the second month. What's the first element in Period Three?"

"Sodium, Number Eleven."

"That's right; it's *Krav, Trav*. Why, the names of the months are simply numbers, one to ten, spelled out."

"*Doma's* the fifth month. That was your first Martian word, Martha," Penrose told her. "The word for five. And if *davas* is the word for metal, and *sornhulva* is chemistry and/or physics, I'll bet *Tadavas Sornhulva* is literally translated as: 'Of-Metal Matter-Knowledge.' Metallurgy, in other words. I wonder what *Mastharnorvod* means." It surprised her that, after so long and with so much happening in the meantime, he could remember that. "Something like 'Journal,' or 'Review,' or maybe 'Quarterly.'"

"We'll work that out, too," she said confidently. After this, nothing seemed impossible. "Maybe we can find—" Then she stopped short. "You said 'Quarterly.' I think it was 'Monthly,' instead. It was dated for a specific month, the fifth one. And if *nor* is ten, *Mastharnorvod* could be 'Year-Tenth.' And I'll bet we'll find that *masthar* is the word for year." She looked at the table on the wall again. "Well, let's get all these words down, with translations for as many as we can."

"Let's take a break for a minute," Penrose suggested, getting out his cigarettes. "And then, let's do this in comfort. Jeff, suppose you and Sid go across the hall and see what you find in the other room in the way of a desk or something like that, and a few chairs. There'll be a lot of work to do on this."

Sid Chamberlain had been squirming as though he were afflicted with ants, trying to contain himself. Now he let go with an excited jabber.

"This is really it! *The* it, not just it-of-the-week, like finding the reservoirs or those statues or this building, or even the animals and the dead Martians! Wait till Selim and Tony see this! Wait till Tony sees it; I want to see his face! And when I get this on telecast, all Terra's going to go nuts about it!" He turned to Captain Miles. "Jeff, suppose you take a look at that other door, while I find somebody to send to tell Selim and Tony. And Gloria; wait till she sees this—"

"Take it easy, Sid," Martha cautioned. "You'd better let me have a look at your script, before you go too far overboard on the telecast. This is just a beginning; it'll take years and years before we're able to read any of those books downstairs."

"It'll go faster than you think, Martha," Hubert Penrose told her. "We'll all work on it, and we'll teleprint material to Terra, and people there will work on it. We'll send them everything we can . . . everything we work out, and copies of books, and copies of your word-lists—"

And there would be other tables—astronomical tables, tables in physics and mechanics, for instance—in which words and numbers were equivalent. The library stacks, below, would be full of them. Transliterate them into Roman alphabet spellings and Arabic numerals, and somewhere, somebody would spot each numerical significance, as Hubert Penrose and Mort Tranter and she had done with the table of elements. And pick out all the chemistry textbooks in the Library; new words would take on meaning from contexts in which the names of elements appeared. She'd have to start studying chemistry and physics, herself—

Sachiko Koremitsu peeped in through the door, then stepped inside.

"Is there anything I can do—?" she began. "What's happened? Something important?"

"Important?" Sid Chamberlain exploded. "Look at that, Sachi! We're reading it! Martha's found out how to read Martian!" He grabbed Captain Miles by the arm. "Come on, Jeff; let's go. I want to call the others—" He was still babbling as he hurried from the room.

Sachi looked at the inscription. "Is it true?" she asked, and then, before Martha could more than begin to explain, flung her arms around her. "Oh, it really is! You are reading it! I'm so happy!"

She had to start explaining again when Selim von Ohlmhorst entered. This time, she was able to finish.

"But, Martha, can you be really sure? You know, by now, that learning to read this language is as important to me as it is to you, but how can you be so sure that those words really mean things like hydrogen and helium and boron and oxygen? How do you know that their table of elements was anything like ours?"

Tranter and Penrose and Sachiko all looked at him in amazement.

"That isn't just the Martian table of elements; that's *the* table of elements. It's the only one there is," Mort Tranter almost exploded. "Look, hydrogen has one proton and one electron. If it had more of either, it wouldn't be hydrogen, it'd be something else. And the same with all the rest of the elements. And hydrogen on Mars is the same as hydrogen on Terra, or on Alpha Centauri, or in the next galaxy—"

"You just set up those numbers, in that order, and any first-year chemistry student could tell you what elements they represented," Penrose said. "Could if he expected to make a passing grade, that is."

The old man shook his head slowly, smiling. "I'm afraid I wouldn't make a passing grade. I didn't know, or at least didn't realize, that. One of the things I'm going to place an order for, to be brought on the *Schiaparelli*, will be a set of primers in chemistry and physics, of the sort intended for a bright child of ten or twelve. It seems that a Martiologist has to learn a lot of things the Hittites and the Assyrians never heard about."

Tony Lattimer, coming in, caught the last part of the explanation. He looked quickly at the walls and, having found out just what had happened, advanced and caught Martha by the hand.

"You really did it, Martha! You found your bilingual! I never believed that it would be possible; let me congratulate you!"

He probably expected that to erase all the jibes and sneers of the past. If he did, he could have it that way. His friendship would mean as little to her as his derision—except that his friends had to watch their backs and his knife. But he was going home on the *Cyrano,* to be a big shot. Or had this changed his mind for him again?

"This is something we can show the world, to justify any expenditure of time and money on Martian archaeological work. When I get back to Terra, I'll see that you're given full credit for this achievement—"

On Terra, her back and his knife would be out of her watchfulness.

"We won't need to wait that long," Hubert Penrose told him dryly. "I'm sending off an official report, tomorrow; you can be sure Dr. Dane will be given full credit, not only for this but for her previous work, which made it possible to exploit this discovery."

"And you might add, work done in spite of the doubts and discouragements of her colleagues," Selim von Ohlmhorst said. "To which I am ashamed to have to confess my own share."

"You said we had to find a bilingual," she said. "You were right, too."

"This is better than a bilingual, Martha," Hubert Penrose said. "Physical science expresses universal facts; necessarily it is a universal language. Heretofore archaeologists have dealt only with pre-scientific cultures."

Each writer creates his own Mars, but few have been as identified with their creation as Ray Bradbury. His clean, loose-limbed prose evokes an earth—or Mars—seen "through a glass darkly." It is nostalgic, redolent of an Earth that should have been and a Mars that may yet be if our best dreams come true, because Bradbury is an idealist who incarnates his vision into a Martian reality of his own creation. In so doing he has placed his own seal on Mars as no other writer. Burroughs' Mars, for example, is also Lowell's, and H. G. Wells's Martians are mythic monsters transformed by space. Bradbury's Mars, however, is like no other. In one very real sense, Bradbury's Mars is Bradbury.

This individuality poses a problem to anthologists. Which of his many Mars stories is most Bradbury-ian? And for that matter, which of *The Martian Chronicles* has not been overanthologized? We posed the problem to Ray, asking his help in selecting a story for *Mars, We Love You*. He plumped for "The Lost City of Mars," a recent tale which proves that the Bradbury verbal magic, like fine wine, mellows with age.

Ray Bradbury

THE LOST CITY OF MARS

The great eye floated in space. And behind the great eye somewhere hidden away within metal and machinery was a small eye that belonged to a man who looked and could not stop looking at all the multitudes of stars and the diminishings and growings of light a billion billion miles away.

The small eye closed with tiredness. Captain John Wilder stood holding to the telescopic devices that probed the Universe and at last murmured, "Which one?"

The astronomer with him said, "Take your pick."

"I wish it were that easy." Wilder opened his eyes. "What's the data on that last star?"

"Same size and reading as our sun. Planetary system, possible."

"Possible. Not certain. If we pick the wrong star, God help the people we send on a two-hundred-year journey to find a planet that may not be there. No, God help me, for the final selection is mine, and I may well send myself on that journey. So, how can we be sure?"

"We can't. We just make the best guess, send our starship out and pray."

"You are not very encouraging. That's it. I'm tired."

Wilder touched a switch that shut up tight the greater eye, this rocket-powered space lens that stared cold upon the abyss, saw far too much and knew little, and now knew nothing. The rocket laboratory drifted sightless on an endless night.

"Home," said the captain. "Let's go home."

And the blind beggar-after-stars wheeled on a spread of fire and ran away.

The frontier cities on Mars looked very fine from above. Coming down for a landing, Wilder saw the neons among the blue hills and thought, we'll light some worlds a billion miles off, and the children of the people living under these lights this instant, we'll make them immortal. Very simply, if we succeed, they will live forever.

Live forever. The rocket landed. Live forever.

The wind that blew from the frontier town smelled of grease. An aluminum-toothed jukebox banged somewhere. A junk yard rusted beside the rocketport. Old newspapers danced alone on the windy tarmac.

Wilder, motionless at the top of the gantry elevator, suddenly wished not to move down. The lights suddenly had become people and not words that, huge in the mind, could be handled with elaborate ease.

He sighed. The freight of people was too heavy. The stars were too far away.

"Captain?" said someone behind him.

He stepped forward. The elevator gave way. They sank with a silent screaming toward a very real land with real people in it, who were waiting for him to choose.

At midnight the telegram bin hissed and exploded out a message projectile. Wilder, at his desk, surrounded by tapes and computation cards, did not touch it for a long while. When at last he pulled the message out, he scanned it, rolled it in a tight ball, then uncrumpled the message and read again:

FINAL CANAL BEING FILLED TOMORROW WEEK. YOU ARE IN-
VITED CANAL YACHT PARTY. DISTINGUISHED GUESTS. FOUR-DAY
JOURNEY TO SEARCH FOR LOST CITY. KINDLY ACKNOWLEDGE.
                                          I. V. AARONSON.

Wilder blinked, and laughed quietly. He crumpled the paper again, but stopped, lifted the telephone and said:

"Telegram to I. V. Aaronson, Mars City I. Answer affirmative. No sane reason why, but still—affirmative."

And hung up the phone. To sit for a long while watching this night that shadowed all the whispering, ticking and motioning machines.

The dry canal waited.

It had been waiting 20,000 years for nothing but dust to filter through in ghost tides.

Now, quite suddenly, it whispered.

And the whisper became a rush and wall-caroming glide of waters.

As if a vast machined fist had struck the rocks somewhere, clapped the air and cried "Miracle!," a wall of water came proud and high along the channels, and lay down in all the dry places of the canal and moved on toward ancient deserts of dry bone surprising old wharves and lifting up the skeletons of boats abandoned countless centuries before when the water burnt away to nothing.

The tide turned a corner and lifted up—a boat as fresh as the morning itself, with new-minted silver screws and brass pipings, and bright new Earth-sewn flags. The boat, suspended from the side of the canal, bore the name Aaronson I.

Inside the boat, a man with the same name smiled. Mr. Aaronson sat listening to the waters live under the boat.

And the sound of the water was cut across by the sound of a hovercraft, arriving, and a motor bike, arriving, and in the air, as if summoned with magical timing, drawn by the glimmer of tides in the old canal, a number of gadfly people flew over the hills on jet-pack machines and hung suspended as if doubting this collision of lives caused by one rich man.

Scowling up with a smile, the rich man called to his children, cried them in from the heat with offers of food and drink.

"Captain Wilder! Mr. Parkhill! Mr. Beaumont!"

Wilder set his hovercraft down.

Sam Parkhill discarded his motor bike, for he had seen the yacht and it was a new love.

"My God," cried Beaumont, the actor, part of the frieze of people in the sky dancing like bright bees on the wind. "I've timed my entrance wrong. I'm early. There's no audience!"

"I'll applaud you down!" shouted the old man, and did so, then added, "Mr. Aikens!"

"Aikens?" said Parkhill. "The big-game hunter?"

"None other!"

And Aikens dived down as if to seize them in his harrying claws. He fancied his resemblance to the hawk. He was finished and stropped like a razor by the swift life he had lived. Not an edge of him but cut the air as he fell, a strange plummeting vengeance upon people who had done nothing to him. In the moment before destruction, he pulled up on his jets and, gently screaming, simmered himself to touch the marble jetty. About his lean middle hung a rifle belt. His pockets bulged like those of a boy from the candy store. One guessed he was stashed with sweet bullets and rare bombs. In his hands, like an evil child, he held a weapon that looked like a bolt of lightning fallen straight from the clutch of Zeus, stamped, nevertheless: MADE IN U. S. A. His face was sun-blasted dark. His eyes were cool surprises in the sun-wrinkled flesh, all mint-blue-green crystal. He wore a white porcelain smile set in African sinews. The earth did not quite tremble as he landed.

"The lion prowls the land of Judah!" cried a voice from the heavens. "Now do behold the lambs driven forth to slaughter!"

"Oh, for God's sake, Harry, shut up!" said a woman's voice.

And two more kites fluttered their souls, their dread humanity, on the wind.

The rich man jubilated.

"Harry Harpwell!"

"Behold the angel of the Lord who comes with Annunciations!" the man in the sky said, hovering. "And the Annunciation is——"

"He's drunk again," his wife supplied, flying ahead of him, not looking back.

"Megan Harpwell," said the rich man, like an entrepreneur introducing his troupe.

"The poet," said Wilder.

"And the poet's barracuda wife," muttered Parkhill.

"I am not drunk," the poet shouted down the wind. "I am simply *high*." And here he let loose such a deluge of laughter that those below almost raised their hands to ward off the avalanche.

Lowering himself, like a fat dragon kite, the poet, whose wife's mouth was now clamped shut, bumbled over the yacht. He made the motions of blessing same, and winked at Wilder and Parkhill.

"Harpwell," he called. "Isn't that a name to go with being a great modern poet who suffers in the present, lives in the past, steals bones from old dramatists' tombs, and flies on this new egg-beater wind-suck device, to call down sonnets on your head? I pity the old euphoric saints and angels who had no invisible wings like these so as to dart in oriole convolutions and ecstatic convulsions on the air as they sang their lines or damned souls to hell. Poor earthbound sparrows, wings clipped. Only their genius flew. Only their muse knew airsickness——"

"Harry," said his wife, her feet on the ground, eyes shut.

"Hunter!" called the poet. "Aikens! Here's the greatest game in all the world, a poet on the wing. I bare my breast. Let fly your honeyed bee sting! Bring me, Icarus, down, if your gun be sunbeams kindled in one tube, let free in single forest fires that escalate the sky to turn tallow, mush, candlewick and lyre to mere tarbabe. Ready, aim, fire!"

The hunter, in good humor, raised his gun.

The poet, at this, laughed a mightier laugh and, literally, exposed his chest by tearing aside his shirt.

At which moment a quietness came along the canal rim.

A woman appeared, walking. Her maid walked behind her. There was no vehicle in sight, and it seemed almost as if they had wandered a long way out of the Martian hills and now stopped.

The very quietness of her entrance gave dignity and attention to Cara Corelli.

The poet shut up his lyric in the sky and landed.

The company all looked together at this actress who gazed back without seeing them. She was dressed in a black jump suit that was the same color as her dark hair. She walked like a woman who has spoken little in her life and now stood facing them with the same quietness, as if waiting for someone to move without being ordered. The wind blew her hair out and down over her shoulders. The paleness of her face was shocking. Her paleness, rather than her eyes, stared at them.

Then, without a word, she stepped down into the yacht and sat in the front of the craft, like a figurehead that knows its place and goes there.

The moment of silence was over.

Aaronson ran his finger down the printed guest list.

"An actor, a beautiful woman who happens to be an actress, a hunter, a poet, a poet's wife, a rocket captain, a former technician. All aboard!"

On the afterdeck of the huge craft, Aaronson spread forth his maps.

"Ladies, gentlemen," he said. "This is more than a four-day drinking bout, party, excursion. This is a search!"

He waited for their faces to light properly, and for them to glance from his eyes to the charts, and then said:

"We are seeking the fabled Lost City of Mars, once called Dia-Sao, the City of Doom. Something terrible about it. The inhabitants fled as from a plague. The City left empty. Still empty now, centuries later."

"We," said Captain Wilder, "have charted, mapped and cross-indexed every acre of land on Mars in the last fifteen years. You can't mislay a city the size of the one you speak of."

"True," said Aaronson, "you've mapped it from the sky, from the land. But you have *not* charted it via water, for the canals have been empty until now! So we shall take the new waters that fill this last canal and go where the boats once went in the olden days, and see the very last new things that need to be seen on Mars." The rich man continued: "And somewhere on our traveling, as sure as the breath in our mouths, we shall find the most beautiful, the most fantastic, the most awful city in the history of this old world. And walk in that city and—who knows?—find the reason why the Martians ran screaming away from it, as the legend says, thousands of years ago."

Silence. Then:

"Bravo! Well done." The poet shook the old man's hand.

"And in that city," said Aikens, the hunter, "mightn't there be weapons the like of which we've never seen?"

"Most likely, sir."

"Well." The hunter cradled his bolt of lightning. "I was bored of Earth, shot every animal, ran fresh out of beasts, and came here looking for newer, better, more dangerous man-eaters of any size or shape. Plus, now, new weapons! What more can one ask? Fine!"

And he dropped his blue-silver lightning bolt over the side. It sank in the clear water, bubbling.

"Let's get the hell out of here."

"Let us, indeed," said Aaronson, "get the good hell out."

And he pressed the button that launched the yacht.

And the water flowed the yacht away.

And the yacht went in the direction toward which Cara Corelli's quiet paleness was pointed: beyond.

The poet opened the first champagne bottle. The cork banged. Only the hunter did not jump.

The yacht sailed steadily through the day into night. They found an ancient ruin and had dinner there and a good wine imported 100,000,000 miles from Earth. It was noted that it had traveled well.

With the wine came the poet, and after quite a bit of the poet came sleep on board the yacht that moved away in search of a city that would not as yet be found.

At three in the morning, restless, unaccustomed to the gravity of a planet pulling at all of his body and not freeing him to dream, Wilder came out on the afterdeck of the yacht and found the actress there.

She was watching the waters slip by in dark revelations and discardments of stars.

He sat beside her and thought a question.

Just as silently, Cara Corelli asked herself the same question, and answered it.

"I am here on Mars because not long ago for the first time in my life, a man told me the truth."

Perhaps she expected surprise. Wilder said nothing. The boat moved as on a stream of soundless oil.

"I am a beautiful woman. I have been beautiful all of my life. Which means that from the start people lied because they simply wished to be with me. I grew up surrounded by the untruths of men, women and children who could not risk my displeasure. When beauty pouts, the world trembles.

"Have you ever seen a beautiful woman surrounded by men, seen them nodding, nodding? Heard their laughter? Men will laugh at anything a beautiful woman says. Hate themselves, yes, but they will laugh, say no for yes and yes for no.

"Well, that's how it was every day of every year for me. A crowd of liars stood between me and anything unpleasant. Their words dressed me in silks.

"But quite suddenly, oh, no more than six weeks ago, this man told me a truth. It was a small thing. I don't remember now what it was he said. But he didn't laugh. He didn't even smile.

"And no sooner was it out and over, the words spoken, than I knew a terrible thing had happened.

"I was growing old."

The yacht rocked gently on the tide.

"Oh, there would be more men who would, lying, smile again at what I said. But I saw the years ahead, when beauty could no longer stomp its small foot, and shake down earthquakes, make cowardice a custom among otherwise good men.

"The man? He took back his truth immediately, when he saw that he had shocked me. But it was too late. I bought a one-way fare to Mars. Aaronson's invitation, when I arrived, put me on this new journey that will end . . . who knows where."

Wilder found that during this last he had reached out and taken her hand.

"No," she said, withdrawing. "No word. No touch. No pity. No self-pity." She smiled for the first time. "Isn't it strange? I always thought, wouldn't it be nice, someday, to hear the truth, to give up the masquerade? How wrong I was. It's no fun at all."

She sat and watched the black waters pour by the boat. When she thought to look again, some hours later, the seat beside her was empty. Wilder was gone.

On the second day, letting the new waters take them where it wished to go, they sailed toward a high range of mountains and lunched, on the way, in an old shrine, and had dinner that night in a further ruin. The Lost City was not much talked about. They were sure it would never be found.

But on the third day, without anyone's saying, they felt the approach of a great presence.

It was the poet who finally put it in words.

"Is God humming under His breath somewhere?"

"What a fierce scum you are," said his wife. "Can't you speak plain English even when you gossip?"

"Damnit, listen!" cried the poet.

So they listened.

"Don't you feel as if you stood on the threshold of a giant blast-furnace kitchen and inside somewhere, all comfortably warm, vast hands, flour-gloved, smelling of wondrous tripes and miraculous viscera, bloodied and proud of the blood, somewhere God cooks out the dinnertime of life? In that caldron sun, a brew to make the flowering forth of life on Venus, in that vat, a stew broth of bones and nervous heart to run in animals on planets ten billion light-years gone. And isn't God content at His fabulous workings in the great kitchen Universe, where He has menu'd out a history of feasts, famines, deaths and reburgeonings for a billion billion years? And if God be content, would He not hum under His breath? Feel your bones. Aren't the marrows teeming with that hum? For that matter, God not only hums, He sings in the elements. He dances in molecules. Eternal celebration swarms us. Something is near. Sh."

He pressed his fat finger to his pouting lips.

And now all were silent, and Cara Corelli's paleness search-lighted the darkening waters ahead.

They all felt it. Wilder did. Parkhill did. They smoked to cover it. They put the smokes out. They waited in the dusk.

And the humming grew nearer. And the hunter, smelling it, went to join the silent actress at the bow of the yacht. And the poet sat to write down the words he had spoken.

"Yes," he said, as the stars came out. "It's almost upon us. It has . . ." he took a breath, ". . . arrived."

The yacht passed into a tunnel.

The tunnel went under a mountain.

And the City was there.

It was a city within a hollow mountain with its own meadows surrounding it and its own strangely colored and illumined stone sky above it. And it had been lost and remained lost for the simple reason that people had tried flying to discover it or had unraveled roads to find it, when all the while the canals that led to it stood waiting for simple walkers to tread where once waters had trod.

And now the yacht filled with strange people from another planet touched an ancient wharf.

And the City stirred.

In the old days, cities were alive or dead if there were or were not people in them. It was that simple. But in the later days of life on Earth or Mars, cities did not die. They slept. And in their dreamful coggeries and enwheeled slumbers they remembered how once it was or how it might be again.

So as, one by one, the party filed out on the dock, they felt a great personage, the hidden, oiled, the metaled and shining soul of the metropolis slide in a landfall of muted and hidden fireworks toward becoming fully awake.

The weight of the new people on the dock caused a machined exhalation. They felt themselves on a delicate scales. The dock sank a millionth of an inch.

And the City, the cumbrous Sleeping Beauty of a nightmare device, sensed this touch, this kiss, and slept no more.

Thunder.

In a wall 100 feet high stood a gate 70 feet wide. This gate, in two parts, now rumbled back, to hide within the wall.

Aaronson stepped forward.

Wilder moved to intercept him. Aaronson sighed.

"Captain, no advice, please. No warnings. No patrols going on ahead to flush out villains. The City wants us in. It welcomes us. Surely you don't imagine anything's *alive* in there? It's a robot place. And don't look as if you think it's a time bomb. It hasn't seen fun and games in—what? Do you read Martian hieroglyphs? That cornerstone. The City was built at least twenty thousand years ago."

"And abandoned," said Wilder.

"You make it sound like a plague drove them——"

"Not a plague." Wilder stirred uneasily, feeling himself weighed on the great scales beneath his feet. "Something. Something . . ."

"Let's find out! In, all of you!"

Singly, and in pairs, the people from Earth stepped over the threshold.

Wilder, last of all, stepped across.

And the City came more alive.

The metal roofs of the City sprang wide like the petals of a flower.

Windows flicked wide like the lids of vast eyes to stare down upon them.

A river of sidewalks gently purled and washed at their feet, machined creekways that gleamed off through the City.

Aaronson gazed at the metal tides with pleasure. "Well, by God, the burden's off me! I was going to picnic you all. But that's the City's business now. Meet you back here in two hours to compare notes! Here goes!"

And saying this, he leaped out onto the scurrying silver carpet that treaded him swiftly away.

Wilder, alarmed, moved to follow. But Aaronson cried jovially back:

"Come on in, the water's fine!"

And the metal river whisked him, waving, off.

And one by one they stepped forward and the moving sidewalk drifted them away. Parkhill, the hunter, the poet and his wife, the actor, and then the beautiful woman and her maid. They floated like statues mysteriously borne on volcanic fluids that swept them anywhere, or nowhere, they could only guess.

Wilder jumped. The river seized his boots gently. Following, he went away into the avenues and around the bends of parks and through fiords of buildings.

And behind them, the dock and the gate stood empty. There was no trace to show they had arrived. It was almost as if they had never been.

Beaumont, the actor, was the first to leave the traveling pathway. A certain building caught his eye. And the next thing he knew, he had leaped off and edged near, sniffing.

He smiled.

For now he knew what kind of building he stood before, because of the odor that drifted from it.

"Brass polish. And, by God, that means only one thing!"

Theater.

Brass doors, brass rails, brass rings on velvet curtains.

He opened the door of the building and stepped in. He sniffed and laughed aloud. Yes. Without a sign or a light, the smell alone, the special chemistry of metals and dust torn free of a million tickets.

And above all . . . he listened. The silence.

"The silence that waits. No other silence in the world waits. Only in a theater will you find that. The very particles of air chafe themselves in readiness. The shadows sit back and hold their breath. Well . . . ready or not . . . here I come . . ."

The lobby was green velvet undersea.

The theater itself: red velvet undersea, only dimly perceived as he opened the double doors. Somewhere beyond was a stage.

Something shuddered like a great beast. His breath had dreamed it alive. The air from his half-opened mouth caused the curtains 100 feet away to softly furl and unfurl in darkness like all-covering wings.

Hesitantly, he took a step.

A light began to appear everywhere in a high ceiling where a school of miraculous prism fish swam upon themselves.

The oceanarium light played everywhere. He gasped.

The theater was full of people.

A thousand people sat motionless in the false dusk. True, they were small, fragile, rather dark, they wore silver masks, yet—people!

He knew, without asking, they had sat here for endless centuries.

Yet they were not dead.

They were—he reached out a hand. He tapped the wrist of a man seated on the aisle.

The hand tinkled quietly.

He touched the shoulder of a woman. She chimed. Like a bell.

Yes, they had waited some few thousand years. But then, machines have a property of waiting.

He took a further step and froze.

For a sigh had passed over the crowd.

It was like the sound, the first small sound a newborn babe must make in the moment before it really sucks, bleats and shocks out its wailing surprise at being alive.

A thousand such sighs faded in the velvet portieres.

Beneath the masks, hadn't a thousand mouths drifted ajar?

He moved. He stopped.

Two thousand eyes blinked wide in the velvet dusk.

He moved again.

A thousand silent heads wheeled on their ancient but well-oiled cogs.

They looked at him.

An unquenchable cold ran wild in him.

He turned to run.

But their eyes would not let him go.

And, from the orchestra pit: music.

He looked and saw, slowly rising, an insect agglomeration of instruments, all strange, all grotesquely acrobatic in their configurations. These were being softly thrummed, piped, touched and massaged in tune.

The audience, with a motion, turned their gaze to the stage.

A light flashed on. The orchestra struck a grand fanfare chord.

The red curtains parted. A spotlight fixed itself to front center, blazing upon an empty dais where sat an empty chair.

Beaumont waited.

No actor appeared.

A stir. Several hands were lifted to left and right. The hands came together. They beat softly in applause.

Now the spotlight wandered off the stage and up the aisle.

The heads of the audience turned to follow the empty ghost of light. The masks glinted softly. The eyes behind the masks beckoned with warm color.

Beaumont stepped back.

But the light came steadily. It painted the floor with a blunt cone of pure whiteness.

And stopped, nibbling, at his feet.

The audience, turned, applauded even louder now. The theater banged, roared, ricocheted with their ceaseless tide of approbation.

Everything dissolved within him, from cold to warm. He felt as if he had been thrust raw into a downpour of summer rain. The storm rinsed him with gratitude. His heart jumped in great compulsive beats. His fists let go of themselves. His skeleton relaxed. He waited a moment longer, with the rain drenching over his upthrust and thankful cheeks and hammering his hungry eyelids so they fluttered to lock against themselves, and then he felt himself, like a ghost on battlements, led by a ghost light, lean, step, drift, move down and along the incline, sliding to beautiful ruin, now no longer walking but striding, not striding but in full-tilted run, and the masks glittering, the eyes hot with delight and fantastic welcoming, the flights of hands on the disturbed air in upflung dove-winged rifle-shot flight. He felt the steps collide with his shoes. The applause slammed to a shutdown.

He swallowed. Then slowly he ascended the steps and stood in the full light with a thousand masks fixed to him and two thousand eyes watchful, and he sat in the empty chair, and the theater grew darker, and the immense hearth-bellow breathing softer out of the lyre-metal throats, and there was only the sound of a mechanical beehive thrived with machinery musk in the dark.

He held onto his knees. He let go. And at last he spoke:

"To be or not to be—"

The silence was complete.

Not a cough. Not a stir. Not a rustle. Not a blink. All waited.

Perfection. The perfect audience. Perfect, forever and forever. Perfect. Perfect.

He tossed his words slowly into that perfect pond and felt the soundless ripples disperse and gentle away.

"—that is the question."

He talked. They listened. He knew that they would never let him go now. They would beat him insensible with applause. He would sleep a child's sleep and arise to speak again. All of Shakespeare, all of Shaw, all of Molière, every bit, crumb, lump, joint and piece. *Himself* in repertory!

He arose to finish.

Finished, he thought: Bury me! Cover me! Smother me deep! Obediently, the avalanche came down the mountain.

Cara Corelli found a palace of mirrors.

The maid remained outside.

And Cara Corelli went in.

As she walked through a maze, the mirrors took away a day, and then a week, and then a month and then a year and then two years of time from her face.

It was a palace of splendid and soothing lies. It was like being young once more. It was being surrounded by all those tall bright glass mirror men who would never again in your life tell you the truth.

Cara walked to the center of the palace. By the time she stopped, she saw herself 25 years old, in every tall bright mirror face.

She sat down in the middle of the bright maze. She beamed around in happiness.

The maid waited outside for perhaps an hour. And then she went away.

This was a dark place with shapes and sizes as yet unseen. It smelled of lubricating oil, the blood of tyrant lizards with cogs and wheels for teeth, which lay strewn and silent in the dark, waiting.

A titan's door slowly gave a slithering roar, like a backswept armored tail, and Parkhill stood in the rich oily wind blowing out around him. He felt as if someone had pasted a white flower on his face. But it was only a sudden surprise of a smile.

His empty hands hung at his sides and they made impulsive and completely unconscious gestures forward. They beggared the air. So, paddling silently, he let himself be moved into the garage, machine shop, repair shed, whatever it was.

And filled with holy delight and a child's holy and unholy glee at what he beheld, he walked and slowly turned.

For as far as his eye could see stood vehicles.

Vehicles that ran on the earth. Vehicles that flew in the air. Vehicles that stood ready with wheels to go in any direction. Vehicles with two wheels. Vehicles with three or four or six or eight. Vehicles that looked like butterflies. Vehicles that resembled ancient motor bikes. Three thousand stood ranked here, four thousand glinted ready there. Another thousand were tilted over, wheels off, copper guts exposed, waiting to be repaired. Still another thousand were lifted high on spidery repair hoists, their lovely undersides revealed to view, their disks and tubes and coggeries all intricate and fine and needful of touching, unbolting, revalving, rewiring, oiling, delicately lubricating . . .

Parkhill's palms itched.

He walked forward through the primeval smell of swamp oils among the dead and waiting to be revived ancient but new armored mechanical reptiles, and the more he looked the more he ached his grin.

The City was a city all right, and, to a point, self-sustaining. But, eventually, the rarest butterflies of metal gossamer, gaseous oil and fiery dream sank to earth, the machines that repaired the machines that repaired the machines grew old, ill and damaging of themselves. Here then was the bestial garage, the slumberous elephant's bone yard where the aluminum dragons crawled rusting out their souls, hopeful of one live person left among so much active but dead metal, that person to put things right. One God of the machines to say, you Lazarus-elevator, rise up! You hovercraft, be reborn! And anoint them with leviathan oils, tap them with magical wrench and send them forth to almost eternal lives in and on the air and above the quicksilver paths.

Parkhill moved among 900 robot men and women slaughtered by simple corrosion. He would cure their rust.

Now. If he started now, thought Parkhill, rolling up his sleeves and staring off down a corridor of machines that ran waiting for a solid mile of garage, shed, hoist, lift, storage bin, oil tank and strewn shrapnel of tools glittering and ready for his grip; if he started now, he might work his way to the end of the giant's ever-constant garage, accident, collision and repair-works shed in 30 years!

A billion bolts to be tightened. A billion motors to be tinkered! A billion gross anatomical mysteries to lie under, a grand oil-dripped-upon orphan, alone, alone, alone with the always beautiful and never talking back hummingbird-commotion devices, accouterments and miraculous contraptions.

His hands weighed him toward the tools. He clutched a wrench. He found a 40-wheeled low running sled. He lay down on it. He sculled the garage in a long whistling ride. The sled scuttled.

Parkhill vanished beneath a great car of some ancient design.

Out of sight, you could hear him working on the gut of the machine. On his back, he talked up at it. And when he slapped it to life, at last, the machine talked back.

Always the silver pathways ran somewhere.

Thousands of years now they had run empty, carrying only dust to destinations away and away among the high and dreaming buildings.

Now, on one traveling path, Aaronson came borne like an aging statue.

And the more the road propelled him, the faster the City exposed itself to his view, the more buildings that passed, the more parks that sprang into sight, the more his smile faded. His color changed.

"Toy," he heard himself whisper. The whisper was ancient. "Just another," and here his voice grew so small it faded away, ". . . another toy."

A supertoy, yes. But his life was full of such and had always been so. If it was not some slot machine, it was the next-size dispenser or a jumbo-size razzmatazz hi-fi stereo speaker. From a lifetime of handling metallic sandpaper, he felt his arms rubbed away to a nub. Mere pips, his fingers. No, handless, and lacking wrists. Aaronson, the Seal Boy!!! His mindless flippers clapped applause to a city that was, in reality, no more and no less than an economy-size jukebox ravening under its idiot breath. And—he knew the tune! God help him. He *knew* the tune.

He blinked just once.

An inner eyelid came down like cold glass.

He turned and trod the silver waters of the path.

He found a moving river of steel to take him back toward the great gate itself.

On the way, he met Cara Corelli's maid, wandering lost on her own silver stream.

As for the poet and his wife, their running battle tore echoes everywhere. They cried down 30 avenues, cracked panes in 200 shops, battered leaves from 70 varieties of park bush and tree, and only ceased when drowned by a thundering fountain display they passed, like a rise of clear fireworks upon the metropolitan air.

"The whole thing is," said his wife, punctuating one of his dirtier responses, "you only came along so you could lay hands on the nearest woman and spray her ears with bad breath and worse poetry."

The poet muttered a foul word.

"You're worse than the actor," said his wife. "Always at it. Don't you ever shut up?"

"Don't you?" he cried. "Ah God, I've curdled inside. Shut up, woman, or I'll throw myself in the founts!"

"No. You haven't bathed in years. You're the pig of the century! Your picture will grace the *Swine Herder's Annual* next month!"

"That *did* it!"

Doors slammed on a building.

By the time she got off and ran back and fisted the doors, they were locked.

"Coward!" she shrieked. "Open up!"

A foul word came echoing out, dimly.

"Ah, listen to that sweet silence," he whispered, to himself, in the great shelled dark.

Harpwell found himself in a soothing hugeness, a vast womblike building, over which hung a canopy of pure serenity, a starless void.

In the middle of this room, which was roughly a 200-foot circle, stood a device, a machine. In this machine were dials and rheostats and switches, a seat and a steering wheel.

"What kind of junk is this?" whispered the poet, but edged near, and bent to touch. "Christ-off-the-cross and bearing mercy, it smells of what? Blood and mere guts? No, for it's clean as a virgin's frock. Still it does fill the nose. Violence. Simple destruction. I can feel the damn carcass tremble like a nervous highbred hound. It's full of *stuffs*. Let's try a swig."

He sat in the machine.

"What do I twig first? This?"

He snapped a switch.

The Baskerville-hound machine whimpered in its dog slumberings.

"Good beast." He flicked another switch. "How do you go, brute? When the damn device is in full tilt, where to? You lack wheels. Well, surprise me. I dare."

The machine shivered.

The machine bolted.

It ran. It dashed.

He held tight to the steering wheel.

"Holy God!"

For he was on a highway, racing fast.

Air sluiced by. The sky flashed over in running colors.

The speedometer read 70, 80.

And the highway ribboned away ahead, flashing toward him. Invisible wheels slapped and banged on an increasingly rough road.

Far away, ahead, a car appeared.

It was running fast. And——

"It's on the wrong side of the road! Do you see that, wife? The wrong side."

Then he realized his wife was not here.

He was alone in a car racing—90 miles an hour now—toward another car racing at a similar speed.

He veered the wheel.

His vehicle moved to the left.

Almost instantly, the other car did a compensating move and ran back over to the left.

"The damn fool, what does he think—where's the blasted brake?"

He stomped the floor. There was no brake. Here was a strange machine indeed. One that ran as fast as you wished, but never stopped until what? it ran itself down? There was no brake. Nothing but—further accelerators. A whole series of round buttons on the floor, which, as he tromped them, surged power into the motor.

Ninety, 100, 120 miles an hour.

"God in heaven!" he screamed. "We're going to hit! How do you like that, girl?"

And in the last instant before collision, he imagined she rather liked it fine.

The cars hit. They erupted in gaseous flame. They burst apart in flinders. They tumbled. He felt himself jerked now this way, now that. He was a torch hurtled skyward. His arms and legs danced a crazy rigadoon in mid-air as he felt his peppermint-stick bones snap in brittle and agonizing ecstasies. Then, clutching death as a dark mate, gesticulating, he fell away in a black surprise, drifting toward further nothings.

He lay dead.

He lay dead a long while.

Then he opened one eye.

He felt the slow burner under his soul. He felt the bubbled water rising to the top of his mind like tea brewing.

"I'm dead," he said, "but alive. Did you see all that, wife? Dead but alive."

He found himself sitting in the vehicle, upright.

He sat there for ten minutes thinking about all that had happened.

"Well now," he mused. "Was that not interesting? Not to say fascinating? Not to say almost exhilarating? I mean, sure, it knocked the stuff out of me, scared the soul out one ear and back the other, hit my wind and tore my seams, broke the bones and shook the wits, but, but, but, wife, but, but, but, dear sweet Meg, Meggy, Megeen, I wish you were here, it might tamp the tobacco tars out of your half-ass lungs and bray the mossy graveyard back-breaking meanness from your marrow. Let me see here now, wife, let's have a look, Harpwell-my-husband-the-poet."

He tinkered with the dials.

He thrummed the great hound motor.

"Shall we chance another diversion? Try another embattled picnic excursion? Let's."

And he set the car on its way.

Almost immediately, the vehicle was traveling 100 and then 150 miles per hour.

Almost immediately, an opposing car appeared ahead on the wrong side of the road.

"Death," said the poet. "Are you always here, then? Do you hang about? Is this your questing place? Let's test your mettle!"

The car raced. The opposing car hurtled.

He wheeled over into the far left lane.

The opposing car shifted, homing toward Destroy.

"Yes, I see, well, then, this," said the poet.

And switched a switch and jumped another throttle.

In the instant before impact, the two cars transformed themselves. Shuttering through illusory veils, they became jetcraft at take-off. Shrieking, the two jets banged flame, tore air, yammered back sound-barrier explosions before the mightiest one of all—as the two bullets impacted, fused, interwove, interlaced blood, mind and eternal blackness, and fell away into a net of strange and peaceful midnight.

I'm dead, he thought again.

And it feels fine, thanks.

He awoke at the touch of his own smile.

He was seated in the vehicle.

Twice dead, he thought, and feeling better each time. Why? isn't that odd? Curiouser and curiouser. Queer beyond queerness.

He thrummed the motor again.

What this time?

Does it locomote? he wondered. How about a big black choo-choo train out of half-primordial times?

And he was on his way, an engineer. The sky flicked over, and the motion-picture screens or whatever they were pressed in with swift illusions of pouring smoke and steaming whistle and huge wheel within wheel on grinding track, and the track ahead wound through hills, and far on up around a mountain came another train, black as a buffalo herd, pouring belches of smoke, on the same two rails, the same track, heading toward wondrous accident.

"I see," said the poet. "I do begin to see. I begin to know what this is used for; for such as me, the poor wandering idiots of a world, confused, and sore put upon by mothers as soon as dropped from wombs, insulted with Christian guilt, and gone mad from the need of destruction, and collecting a pittance of hurt here and scar tissue there, and a larger portable wife grievance beyond, but one thing sure, we do want to die, we do want to be killed, and here's the very thing for it, in convenient quick pay! So pay it out, machine, dole it out, sweet raving device! Rape away, death! I'm your very man."

And the two locomotives met and climbed each other. Up a black ladder of explosion they wheeled and locked their drive shafts and plastered their slick negro bellies together and rubbed boilers and beautifully banged the night in a single outflung whirl and flurry of meteor and flame. Then the locomotives, in a cumbrous rapine dance, seized and melted together with their violence and passion, gave a monstrous curtsy and fell off the mountain and took a thousand years to go all the way down to the rocky pits.

The poet awoke and immediately grabbed the controls. He was humming under his breath, stunned. He was singing wild tunes. His eyes flashed. His heart beat swiftly.

"More, more, I see it now, I know what to do, more, more, please, O God, more, for the truth shall set me free, more!"

He hoofed three, four, five pedals.

He snapped six switches.

The vehicle was auto-jet-locomotive-glider-missile-rocket.

He ran, he steamed, he roared, he soared, he flew. Cars veered toward him. Locomotives loomed. Jets rammed. Rockets screamed.

And in one wild three-hour spree he hit 200 cars, rammed 20 trains, blew up 10 gliders, exploded 40 missiles, and, far out in space, gave up his glorious soul in a final Fourth of July death celebration as an interplanetary rocket going 200,000 miles an hour struck an iron planetoid and went beautifully to hell.

In all, in a few short hours he figured he must have been torn apart and put back together a few times less than 500.

When it was all over, he sat not touching the wheel, his feet free of the pedals.

After a half hour of sitting there, he began to laugh. He threw his head back and let great war whoops. Then he got up, shaking his head, drunker than ever in his life, really drunk now, and he knew he would stay that way forever, and never need drink again.

I'm punished, he thought, really punished at last. Really hurt at last, and hurt enough, over and over, so I will never need hurt again, never need to be destroyed again, never have to collect another insult or take another wound, or ask for a simple grievance. God bless the genius of man and the inventors of such machines, that enable the guilty to pay and at last be rid of the dark albatross and the awful burden. Thank you, City, thank you, old blueprinter of needful souls. Thank you. And which way out?

A door slid open.

His wife stood waiting for him.

"Well, there you are," she said. "And still drunk."

"No," he said. "Dead."

"Drunk."

"Dead," he said, "beautifully dead at last. Which means, free. I won't need you anymore, dead Meg-Meggy-Megeen. You're set free, also, like an awful conscience. Go haunt someone else, girl. Go destroy. I forgive you your sins on me, for I have at last forgiven myself. I am off the Christian hook. I am the dear wandering dead who, dead, can at last live. Go and do likewise, lady. Inside with you. Be punished and set free. So long, Meg. Farewell. Toodle-oo."

He wandered away.

"Where do you think you're going?" she cried.

"Why, out into life and the blood of life, and happy at last."

"Come back here!" she screamed.

"You can't stop the dead, for they wander the Universe, happy as children in the dark field."

"Harpwell!" she brayed. "Harpwell!"

But he stepped on a river of silver metal.

And let the dear river bear him laughing until the tears glittered on his cheeks, away and away from the shriek and the bray and the scream of that woman, what was her name? no matter, back there, and gone.

And when he reached the gate he walked out and along the canal in the fine day, heading toward the far towns.

By that time, he was singing every old tune he had known as a child of six . . .

Behind him, by the strange building that had set him free, his wife stood a long while staring at the metal path that had floated him away. Then slowly she turned to glare at the enemy building. She fisted the door once. It slid open, waiting. She sniffed. She scowled at the interior.

Then, steadily, hands ready to seize and grapple, she advanced. With each step she grew bolder. Her face thrust like an ax at the strange air.

Behind her, unnoticed, the door closed.

It did not open again.

It was a church.

It was not a church.

Wilder let the door swing shut.

He stood in cathedral darkness, waiting.

The roof, if roof there was, breathed up in a great suspense, flowed up beyond reach or sight.

The floor, if floor there was, was a mere firmness beneath. It, too, was black.

And then the stars came out. It was like that first night of childhood when his father had taken him out beyond the city to a hill where the streetlights could not diminish the Universe. And there were a thousand, no ten thousand, no ten million billion stars filling the darkness. The stars were manifold and bright, and they did not care. Even then he had known: They do not care. If

I breathe or do not breathe, live or die, the eyes that look from all around don't care. And he had seized his father's hand and gripped tight, as if he might fall up into that abyss.

Now, in this building, he was full of the old terror and the old sense of beauty and the old silent crying out after mankind. The stars filled him with pity for small men lost in so much size.

Then yet another thing happened.

Beneath his feet, space opened wide and let through yet another billion sparks of light.

He was suspended as a fly is held upon a vast telescopic lens. He walked on a water of space. He stood upon a transparent flex of great eye, and all about him, as on a night in winter, beneath foot and above head, in all directions, were nothing but stars.

So, in the end, it was a church, it was a cathedral, a multitude of far-flung universal shrines, here a worshiping of Horsehead Nebula, there Orion's galaxy, and there Andromeda, like the head of God, fiercely gazed and thrust through the raw dark stuffs of night to stab his soul and pin it writhing against the backside of his flesh.

God, everywhere, fixed him with shutterless and unblinking eyes.

And he, a bacterial shard of that same Flesh, stared back and winced but the slightest.

He waited. And a planet drifted upon the void. It spun by once with a great mellow autumn face. It circled and came under him.

And he stood upon a far world of green grass and great lush trees, where the air was fresh, and a river ran by like the rivers of childhood, flashing the sun and leaping with fish.

He knew that he had traveled very far to reach this world. Behind him lay the rocket. Behind lay a century of travel, of sleeping, of waiting, and now, here was the reward.

"Mine?" he asked the simple air, the simple grass, the long simplicity of water that spilled by in the shallow sands.

And the world answered wordless: Yours.

Yours without the long travel and the boredom, yours without 99 years of flight from Earth, of sleeping in kept tubes, of intravenous feedings, of nightmares dreamed of Earth lost and gone, yours without torture, without pain, yours without trial and error, failure and destruction. Yours without sweat and terror. Yours without a falling down of tears. Yours. Yours.

But Wilder did not put out his hands to accept.

And the sun dimmed in the alien sky.

And the world drifted from under his feet.

And yet another world swam up and passed in a huge parade of even brighter glories.

And this world, too, spun up to take his weight. And here, if anything, the fields were richer green, the mountains capped with melting snows, far fields ripening with strange harvests, and scythes waiting on the edge of fields for him to lift and sweep and cut the grain and live out his life any way that he might.

Yours. The merest touch of weather upon the hairs within his ear said this. Yours.

And Wilder, without shaking his head, moved back. He did not say no. He thought his rejection.

And the grass died in the fields.

The mountains crumbled.

The river shallows ran to dust.

And the world sprang away.

And Wilder stood again in space where God had stood before creating a world out of chaos.

And at last he spoke and said to himself:

"It would be easy. Oh Lord, yes, I'd like that. No work, nothing, just accept. But . . . You can't *give* me what I want."

He looked at the stars.

"Nothing can be given, ever."

The stars were growing dim.

"It's really very simple. I must borrow, I must earn. I must take."

The stars quivered and died.

"Much obliged and thank you, no."

The stars were all gone.

He turned and, without looking back, walked upon darkness. He hit the door with his palm. He strode out into the City.

He refused to hear if the machine Universe behind him cried out in a great chorus, all cries and wounds, like a woman scorned.

The crockery in a vast robot kitchen fell. By the time it hit the floor, he was gone.

It was a museum of weapons.

The hunter walked among the cases.

He opened a case and hefted a weapon constructed like a spider's antennae.

It hummed, and a flight of metal bees sizzled out the rifle bore, flew away and stung a target-mannequin some 50 yards away, then fell lifeless, clattering to the floor.

The hunter nodded with admiration, and put the rifle back in the case.

He prowled on, curious as a child, testing yet other weapons here and there that dissolved glass or caused metal to run in bright yellow pools of molten lava.

"Excellent! Fine! Absolutely great!"

His cry rang out again and again as he slammed cases open and shut, and finally chose the gun.

It was a gun that, without fuss or fury, did away with matter. You pressed the button, there was a brief discharge of blue light and the target simply vanished. No blood. No bright lava. No trace.

"All right," he announced, leaving the place of guns, "we have the weapon. How about the game, the grandest beast ever in the long hunt?"

He leaped onto the moving sidewalk.

An hour later he had passed a thousand buildings and scanned a thousand open parks without itching his finger.

He moved uneasily from treadway to treadway, shifting speeds now in this direction, now in that.

Until at last he saw a river of metal that sped underground.

Instinctively, he jumped toward that.

The metal stream carried him down into the secret gut of the City.

Here all was warm blood darkness. Here strange pumps moved the pulse of the City. Here were distilled the sweats that lubricated the roadways and lifted the elevators and swarmed the offices and stores with motion.

The hunter half crouched on the roadway. His eyes squinted. Perspiration gathered in his palms. His trigger finger greased the metal gun, sliding.

"Yes," he whispered. "By God, now. This is it. The City itself . . . the great beast. Why didn't I think of that? The animal City, the dread carnivore that has men for breakfast, lunch and dinner, it kills them with machines, it munches their bones like bread sticks, it spits them out like toothpicks, and it lives long after they die. The City, by God, the City. Well now . . ."

He glided through dark grottoes of television eyes that showed him remote parkways and high towers.

Deeper within the belly of the underground world he sank as the river lowered itself. He passed a school of computers that chattered in maniac chorus. He shuddered as a cloud of paper confetti from one titan machine, holes punched out to perhaps record his passing, fell upon him in a whispered snow.

He raised his gun. He fired.

The machine disappeared.

He fired again. A skeleton strutwork under yet another machine vanished.

The City screamed.

At first very low and then very high, then, rising, falling, like a siren. Lights flashed. Bells began to ricochet alarms. The metal river shuddered under his feet. He fired at television screens that glared all white upon him. They blinked out and did not exist.

The City screamed higher until he raved against it, himself.

He did not see, until it was too late, that the road on which he sped fell into the gnashing maw of a machine that was used for some purpose long forgotten centuries before.

He thought that by pressing the trigger he would make the terrible mouth disappear. It did indeed vanish. But as the roadway sped on and he whirled and fell as it picked up speed, he realized at last that his weapon did not truly destroy, it merely made invisible what was there and what still remained, though unseen.

He gave a terrible cry to match the cry of the City. He flung out the gun in a last blow. The gun went into cogs and wheels and teeth and was twisted down.

The last thing he saw was a deep elevator shaft that fell away for perhaps a mile into the earth.

He knew that it might take him two minutes to hit the bottom. He shrieked.

The worst thing was, he would be conscious . . . all the way down . . .

The rivers shook. The silver rivers trembled. The pathways, shocked, convulsed the metal shores through which they sped.

Wilder, traveling, was almost knocked flat by the concussion.

What had caused the concussion he could not see. Perhaps, far off, there was a cry, a murmur of dreadful sound, which swiftly faded.

Wilder moved. The silver track threaded on. But the City seemed poised, agape. The City seemed tensed. Its huge and various muscles were cramped, alert.

Feeling this, Wilder began to walk as well as be moved by the swift path.

"Thank God. There's the gate. The sooner I'm out of this place the happier I'll——"

The gate was indeed there, not a hundred yards away. But, on the instant, as if hearing his declaration, the river stopped. It shivered. Then it started to move back, taking him where he did not wish to go.

Incredulous, Wilder spun about and, in spinning, fell. He clutched at the stuffs of the rushing sidewalk.

His face, pressed to the vibrant grillwork of the river-rushing pavement, heard the machineries mesh and mill beneath, humming and agroan, forever sluicing, forever feverish for journeys and mindless excursions. Beneath the calm metal, embattlements of hornets stung and buzzed, lost bees bumbled and subsided. Collapsed, he saw the gate lost away behind. Burdened, he remembered at last the extra weight upon his back, the jet-power equipment that might give him wings.

He jammed his hand to the switch on his belt. And in the instant before the sidewalk might have pulsed him off among sheds and museum walls, he was airborne.

Flying, he hovered, then swam the air back to hang above a

casual Parkhill gazing up, all covered with grease and smiling from a dirty face. Beyond Parkhill, at the gate, stood the frightened maid. Beyond even further, near the yacht at the landing, stood Aaronson, his back turned to the City, nervous to be moving on.

"Where are the others?" cried Wilder.

"Oh, they won't be back," said Parkhill, easily. "It figures, doesn't it? I mean, it's quite a place."

"Place!" said Wilder, hovered now up, now down, turning slowly, apprehensive. "We've got to get them out! It's not safe."

"It's safe if you like it. I like it," said Parkhill.

And all the while there was a gathering of earthquake in the ground and in the air, which Parkhill chose to ignore.

"You're leaving, of course," he said, as if nothing were wrong. "I knew you would. Why?"

"Why?" Wilder wheeled like a dragonfly before a trembling of storm wind. Buffeted up, buffeted down, he flung his words at Parkhill, who didn't bother to duck but smiled up and accepted. "Good God, Sam, the place is hell. The Martians had enough sense to get out. They saw they had overbuilt themselves. The damn City does everything, which is too much! Sam!"

And at that instant, they both looked round and up. For the sky was shelling over. Great lids were vising in the ceiling. Like an immense flower, the tops of buildings were petaling out to cover themselves. Windows were shutting down. Doors were slamming. A sound of fired cannons echoed through the streets.

The gate was thundering shut.

The twin jaws of the gate, shuddering, were in motion.

Wilder cried out, spun round and dived.

He heard the maid below him. He saw her reach up. Then, swooping, he gathered her in. He kicked the air. The jet lifted them both.

Like a bullet to a target he rammed for the gate. But an instant before he reached it, burdened, the gates banged together. He was barely able to veer course and soar upward along the raw metal as the entire City shook with the roar of the steel.

Parkhill shouted below. And Wilder was flying up, up along the wall, looking this way and that.

Everywhere, the sky was closing in. The petals were coming

down, coming down. There was only a last small patch of stone sky to his right. He blasted for that. And kicking, made it through, flying, as the final flange of steel clipped into place and the City was closed to itself.

He hung for a moment, suspended, and then flew with the woman down along the outer wall to the dock, where Aaronson stood by the yacht staring at the huge shut gates.

"Parkhill," whispered Wilder, looking at the City, the walls, the gates. "You fool. You damned fool."

"Fools, all of them," said Aaronson, and turned away. "Fools. Fools."

They waited a moment longer and listened to the City, humming, alive, kept to itself, its great mouth filled with a few bits of warmth, a few lost people somewhere hid away in there. The gates would stay shut now, forever. The City had what it needed to go on a long while.

Wilder looked back at the place, as the yacht took them back out of the mountain and away up the canal.

They passed the poet a mile farther on, walking along the rim of the canal. He waved them off. "No. No, thanks. I feel like walking. It's a fine day. Goodbye. Go on."

The towns lay ahead. Small towns. Small enough to be run by men instead of the towns running them. He heard the brass music. He saw the neon lights at dusk. He made out the junk yards in the fresh night under the stars.

Beyond the towns stood the silver rockets, tall, waiting to be fired off and away toward the wilderness of stars.

"Real," whispered the rockets, "real stuff. Real travel. Real time. Real space. No gifts. Nothing free. Just a lot of good brute work."

The yacht touched into its home dock.

"Rockets, by God," he murmured. "Wait till I get my hands on you."

He ran off in the night, to do just that.

Harry Harrison has the well-earned reputation of restoring the importance of *story* to science fiction. His many novels and shorter works are drenched with plot, action piling on action as his characters, often better realized than those of most writers, move through his fictional worlds.

This tale, "One Step From Earth," is one of the few in *Mars, We Love You* written since the Mariner photographs of 1969. Those pictures and their scientific implications gave us the Mars of reality and shattered the Mars of myth. In addition, this yarn demonstrates Harrison's sure touch with tone, dialogue, and situation. Thus it reveals what almost everyone knows: that Harry Harrison is one of the most professional science fiction writers around.

Harry Harrison

ONE STEP FROM EARTH

This landscape was dead. It had never lived. It had been born dead when the planets first formed, a planetary stillbirth of boulders, coarse sand, jagged rock. The air was thin and so cold that it was closer to the vacuum of space than to any habitable atmosphere. Though it was nearly noon and the pallid tiny disk of the sun was high overhead, the sky was dark, the wan light shining on the uneven plain that was unmarked by any footprint. Silent, lonely, empty.

Only the shadows moved. The sun paced its way slowly across the horizon until it set. Night came and with it an even greater cold. Silently the dark hours passed, the stars arched by overhead, until on the opposite horizon the sun appeared once again.

Then something changed. High above there was a tiny flicker of movement as the sun glanced from some shining surface, a motion where none had existed ever before. It grew to a spot of light that blossomed suddenly into a long tongue of flame. The flame continued, even brighter as it came close to the surface, dropped, hovering. Dust billowed out, rocks melted and the flame was gone.

The squat cylinder dropped the last few feet and landed on

wide-stretched legs. Shock absorbers took up the impact, giving way, then slowly leveling out the body of the device. It bobbed slightly for a few seconds and was still.

Minutes passed and nothing more happened. The dust had long settled and the molten slag hardened and cracked in the cold.

With sudden sharp explosions the side of the cylinder blew away and landed on the ground some yards distant. The capsule bobbed slightly in reaction to this but quickly came to rest. In the area uncovered by the discarded plate were a number of small devices, all ringed about a gray plate, some two feet in diameter, that resembled an obscured porthole.

Nothing else happened for quite a while, as though some hidden internal device were marking time. It reached some decision because, with a distant humming, an antenna began to emerge from its opening. At first it projected straight out from the side of the capsule, until a curved section emerged and it began to slowly rise until it towered into the air. Even as it was erecting itself a compact television camera moved jerkily into view on the end of a jointed arm. It hesitantly changed direction until it was above the circular plate and angled down towards it and the patch of ground below. Apparently satisfied it locked into this position.

With a loud *ping* the circular plate changed color and character. It was now a deep black and it seemed to shift without moving. A moment later a transparent plastic container appeared, coming from the surface of the plate as though emerging from a door, dropping forward and hitting the ground, rolling over.

The white rat inside the container was terrified at first, knocked off its feet as the tube struck the ground and dropped onto its side. The rat rolled onto its feet and scurried about trying to get a grip with its claws on the slippery walls, climbing up, then sliding back to the bottom again. In a few moments it settled down, blinking its pink eyes at the gray wastes outside. There was nothing moving, nothing to see. It sat and began to smooth its long whiskers with its paws. The cold had not yet penetrated the thick walls.

The picture on the television screen was very blurred, but considering the fact that it had been broadcast from the surface of

Mars to a satellite in orbit, had then been relayed to the Lunar station and from there sent to Earth—it wasn't really a bad picture. Through the interference and the snow the container could be clearly seen, with the rat moving about inside of it.

"Success?" Ben Duncan asked. He was a wiry, compact man with close-cropped hair and tanned leathery skin. There were networks of wrinkles in the corners of his eyes as though he had squinted a lot in very cold weather, or before a glaring sun. He had done both. His complexion was in direct contrast to that of the technicians and scientists manning the banks of instruments. Other than the few Negroes and one Puerto Rican, all of them were the fishbelly white of city dwellers.

"It looks good so far," Dr. Thurmond said. His degree was in physics from MIT. He was quite proud of it and insisted on its being used at all times. "Waves form fine, no attenuation, flat response, the trial subject went through with a one point three on the co-ord which can't be bettered."

"When can we go through?"

"In about an hour, maybe a little more. If biology gives the O.K. They'll want to examine this transmission on the first subject, maybe send another one through. If everything is in the green, you and Thasler will go through at once while conditions are optimum."

"Yes, of course, shouldn't wait," Otto Thasler said. Then, "Excuse me." He hurried away. A small man who wore thick-rimmed glasses. His hair was sandy and thin and he had a slouch from many hours over a laboratory bench so that he looked older than he was. And he was nervous. There was a fine beading of sweat on his face. Dr. Thurmond had noticed it, too.

"Otto is jumpy," he said. "But I don't think he will be any trouble."

"He'll be all right once we get there. It is the waiting that bothers people," Ben Duncan said.

"It doesn't bother you?" Dr. Thurmond was curious, but there was also a thin edge of malice to his words.

"Of course it does. But let's say that I have been over this waiting part many times before. I've never gone to Mars through a matter transmitter before, but I have been in some strange positions."

"I'm sure you have. Professional adventurer or some such." The malice was clear now; the distrust of the man who was used to giving orders towards the man who did not take them.

"Not quite. I'm a geologist and a petrologist. Some of the rare earths you use in this lab come from lodes I found. They are not always in the most accessible places."

"Well, that's fine." Dr. Thurmond's flat tone of voice did not reflect his words. "You have had plenty of experience taking care of yourself so you will be able to help Otto Thasler. He's the man in charge, the one who has to do the work, and you will assist him."

"Of course," Ben said and turned and walked away.

They were a clannish bunch and made no secret of the fact that he was an outsider. They would never have hired him if one of their own people could do the job. Transmatter Ltd. was richer than many governments, stronger than some as well. But they knew the value of the right man in the right job. A matter transmitter engineer for the trip was easy enough to find; just pick a suitable man from the staff and ask him to volunteer. Otto had had very little choice. But who would take care of him? In this overpopulated world of 1993 there were few frontiers left and even fewer men who knew their way around them. Ben had been in the Himalayas when the copter had come for him. His prospecting expedition was canceled, pressure from Transmatter, and a far better contract offered. He had been pressured into signing on, but that did not matter. Transmatter did not realize, and he had never told them, that he would have gone for one tenth the preposterous salary they offered—or even for free. These indoor types just could not realize that he *wanted* to make this trip.

There was a door nearby that opened onto a balcony and he went out to look over the city. He tamped tobacco into his pipe, but did not light it. There would be no smoking soon and he might as well begin to get used to it. The air was fairly fresh at this height, but the smog and haze closed in below. Mile after mile of buildings and streets stretched to the horizon, jammed, packed and turbulent with people. It could have been any city

on Earth. They were all like this—or worse. He had come out
through Calcutta and he still had nightmares about it.

"Mr. Duncan, come quickly, they are waiting for you."

The technician shifted from one foot to the other and wrung
his hands worriedly, holding the door open with his foot. Ben
smiled at him, in no hurry, then handed over his pipe.

"Hold that until I get back, will you?"

The dressers had almost finished with Otto by the time Ben
appeared and his own team rushed forward. They pulled off his
coverall, then dressed him from the skin out in layer after layer of
protective fabrics. Thermal underwear, a skintight silk cover over
that, an electrically heated suit next, electric socks. It was done
quickly. Dr. Thurmond came in while their outer suits were being closed and looked on approvingly.

"Leave the outer suit seals open until you get into the chamber," he said. "Let's go."

Like a mother hen with a parade of chicks, he led the way across
the cluttered transmission room, between the banks of instruments and under the high bus bars. The technicians and engineers
turned to watch when they passed and there was even one cheer
that was quickly stifled when Dr. Thurmond looked coldly towards the man. Two dispatchers were waiting for them in the
pressure chamber and they closed and sealed the door behind
Dr. Thurmond and the two heavily garbed men. They were beginning to sweat. Dr. Thurmond pulled on a heavy coat as the
cold air was pumped in.

"This is the final countdown," he said. "I'll repeat your instructions just one more time." Ben could have recited them equally
well, but he remained silent. "We are now lowering the air temperature and pressure until it matches the Martian atmosphere.
Readings just taken there show the temperature at twenty degrees below zero Fahrenheit and holding steady. Air pressure is
ten millimeters of mercury. We are dropping to that pressure now.
There is no measurable amount of oxygen in the air. Masks at
all times, that is never to be forgotten. We are breathing almost
pure oxygen in this chamber, but you will put on your masks
before you leave . . ." He stopped and yawned and his ears

popped, trying to equalize the pressure in his inner ear. "I will now go into the air lock."

He went and finished his lecture from there, watching them through the inset window. Ben ignored the drone of his voice and Otto seemed too paralyzed to listen. A thermostat closed in the battery case in the small of his back and Ben felt the heating elements grow warm inside his suit. The oxygen tank was slung onto his back and his face mask with built-in goggles was buckled into place. He automatically bit onto the oxygen tube and inhaled.

"Ready for the first man," Dr. Thurmond said, his voice squeaky and distant in the thin atmosphere.

For the first time Ben looked at the shining black disk of the matter transmitter set into the far wall. One of the dressers tossed a test cube into it as Ben lay face down on the table. While they were rolling the table forward the report came in. Everything in the green.

"Hold it," Ben said, and the table stopped. He turned to look at Otto Thasler who was sitting rigid, facing the opposite wall. Ben could imagine the terrified expression on the hidden face. "Relax, Otto, it's a piece of cake. I'll be waiting for you at the other end. Relax and enjoy it, man, we're making history."

There was no answer nor had he expected one. The quicker this part was over the better. They had been practicing the maneuver for weeks and he automatically took the position. Right arm straight forward ahead of him, left arm tight at his side. The matter transmitter screen grew like a great dark eye as the table rolled forward, until it was all he could see in front of him.

"Do it," he ordered, and they pushed smoothly against his feet.

Sliding. Hand, wrist, arm vanishing. Feeling nothing. A moment of recoil, of twisting pain, as his head went through, then he was looking at the coarse pebbles on the ground. He pushed aside the test cube and put his hand flat to break his fall. Then his other arm was through and his legs. Falling sideways in an easy roll his hip struck something hard.

Ben sat up, rubbing the sore spot and looked at the plastic container that he had landed on. Inside was a dying rat. A nice omen. He turned quickly away and went through the rest of the drill.

The microphone was hanging in the same spot as on the mockup and he switched it on.

"Ben Duncan to Control. Arrived O.K. No problems." He should say more than that on this historical moment, but his brain was empty of inspiration. He looked around at the low dark hills, the crater nearby, the tiny bright sun. There was nothing that really could be said.

"Send Otto through. Over and out."

He stood, brushing some dust from his side, and looked at the shining plate. Minutes passed before the loudspeaker rasped, the voice so distorted he had to strain for the meaning.

"We read you. Stand by for transmission. Thasler coming through."

Otto's hand appeared even before the voice ended. It took the radio waves nearly four minutes to reach Mars, but the matter transmission was almost instantaneous since it went through Bhattacharya space where time, as it is normally constituted, does not exist. Otto's arm dropped limply and Ben took him by the shoulders, a deadweight that he eased to the ground. Rolling him over Ben saw that his eyes were closed. But he seemed to be breathing regularly. He was probably unconscious. Transmission shock they called it. It wasn't uncommon. He should come to in a few minutes. Ben dragged him to one side and went back to the radio.

"Otto is here. Out cold, but he looks O.K. Send the junk through."

Then he waited. The wind made a thin whistling noise as it blew against his mask and he felt the cold of it touching his cheeks. He did not mind: there was something almost reassuring that the wind could blow, the hard ground push against his feet, that the sun still shone. For all the evidence of his senses he could still be on Earth, perhaps on one of the high plateaus in Assam that he had so recently left. Consciously he knew that the sunshine here was half as strong as back on Earth. But he could remember cloudy, misty days with far less sun. Gravity? With all the equipment he was burdened with he was aware of no difference. Rounded, red hills in the distance, thin bluish clouds drifting across the sun. A remote corner of Earth, that's all it was. He could not grip the reality of Mars. If he had crossed space in a ship, taken weeks or months, he would have believed it. But a few minutes before he had been standing on Earth. He scuffed at the gravel with his boot and saw the second plastic tube that had been sent through with the struggling rat inside.

It was cold, freezing to death. It would scratch pathetically at the containing walls, then huddle up and shiver. And it had its mouth open, gasping. It appeared to have an even chance of running out of air or freezing first. Just a laboratory animal; thousands like it died every day in the cause of science. On Earth. But this one was here, perhaps the only other living thing on the planet. Ben knelt and twisted the lid off the tube.

The end was quicker than he had thought possible. The rat took one breath of the Martian air and gave a convulsive contraction of its entire body—and died. Ben had not thought it would be like that. Of course he had been told on Earth that the great danger of the Martian atmosphere was its complete dryness, containing only an unmeasureable trace of water vapor. They had said that inhaling it would scorch the mucous membranes in the nose, throat and lungs so fiercely that it would be the same as breathing concentrated sulphuric acid. This had seemed a little preposterous. Then. The rat's staring dark eye filmed as it froze. Ben straightened up and pushed his face mask tighter against his face. He checked Otto to make sure his was correctly in place, too.

No, this was not Earth. He could believe it now.

"Attention! Please," the loudspeaker chattered. "Will you be able to handle equipment yourself? Is Thasler still unconscious? Loads were estimated for two-man manipulation. Report."

Ben grabbed the microphone.

"Send that stuff through! By the time you get this message twelve minutes will have been shot. Send it! If anything gets broken, you can send replacements. We're alone here, can you understand that, with just the oxygen we have and nothing else, stuck at the other end of a one-way door a couple of hundred million miles from Earth. Send everything—*now! Send it!*"

Ben paced up and down, hammering his fist into his palm, kicking the test blocks and the rat sarcophagus to one side. The fools!

He looked at Otto who seemed to be enjoying his rest. A wonderful beginning. He dragged Otto to one side where he wouldn't get stepped on and came back to the screen as the end of a canister emerged.

"And about time!"

Grabbing the end he ran forward until the other end appeared and clanged to the ground. OXYGEN—FOOD the painted letters on it read. Fine. He kicked it rolling to one side and jumped for the next one.

The demand regulator on his back was clicking regularly, feeding him an almost steady flow of pure oxygen, and his head was swimming with fatigue. The ground all about was littered with containers, tubes and bundles of all lengths, but with the same diameter. Otto tapped him on the shoulder and he dropped the case he was dragging.

"I passed out, I'm sorry. Is anything—"

"Shut up and grab that tube that is jamming up in front of the screen."

One, two more, then Ben looked on and blinked as a shining dural plate fell from the screen and clattered to the ground. He bent over and saw that someone had lettered on it with red grease pencil.

"SUGGEST YOU CHECK OXYGEN TANK LEVEL. ERECT SHELTER. CHANGE TANKS."

"Someone is thinking now," Ben muttered and jerked his thumb at the tank on his back. "What does it read?"

"Just a quarter left."

"They're right. Erecting the shelter gets priority."

Otto rooted about among the canisters while Ben stretched out the long and unwieldy fabric sausage. The fastenings snapped open easily and he spread it out flat just as he had done in training. Only during training he had not hovered on the edge of exhaustion, fighting the heavy shelter material with clumsy gloves. It was finally done and he looked up to see Otto fastening a tank to an inlet tube with the quick fastening attachment.

"What the hell do you think you are doing?" Ben said, the words rasping in his dry throat. He hit Otto on the shoulder knocking him sprawling.

Otto just lay there, wide-eyed and silent, as though he thought Ben had gone mad. Shaking with anger Ben pointed to the connection.

"Use your eyes. Stay alert. Or you will kill us both. You were attaching a green tank to a red pipe."

"I'm sorry—I didn't notice—"

"Of course you didn't, you stupid slob. But you *have* to here. Red is oxygen, what we breathe and what inflates the shelter. Green is the insulating gas that goes into the double wall. Not poisonous, but just as deadly because we can't breathe it."

Ben made the connections himself and would not let Otto come near, even threatening him with the wrench when he tried to. One tank of oxygen blew the shelter up to a pudding-shaped mound. The second erected it to a firm dome and the pressure valve on the inlet sealed shut automatically. Ben knew that he was almost out of oxygen, but he could not stop before he finished this. He attached the green tank and left it alone to fill the insulating layer by itself. Now the heater. He was dragging it towards the air lock on the shelter. Letting go he staggered one step, two, then dropped unconscious.

"Have more soup?" Otto asked.

"A good idea." He sipped the cup empty and passed it over. "I'm sorry about the names I called you. Particularly since you managed to save my life right afterwards." Otto looked uncomfortable and bent over the pressure stove.

"That's all right, Ben. I deserved what you called me and more. I must have panicked. I'm not used to this kind of thing the way you are."

"I've never been to Mars before!"

"You know what I mean. You've been everywhere else. I've been to college, and to the job, and holidays in the Bahamas. I'm a city boy, a real urban dweller."

"You did fine when I blacked out."

"Without you there to back me up I suppose I had to. Your tank was empty and I was sure it was anoxia. I knew the shelter had oxygen in it so I just dragged you in here as quick as I could. I pulled off your mask and you seemed to be breathing O.K., but it was cold so I went after the heater, then the food. That was all. I just did what had to be done." His words trickled off into silence and he looked owllike and frightened again behind his heavy-rimmed glasses.

"But that is all that *had* to be done. All that can be done." Ben leaned forward, hammering the words home. "No one could have done more. It is about time you stopped thinking of yourself as one more city boy and faced the fact that you are one of the only two Martian explorers in the whole solar system."

Otto thought about it and almost straightened up his shoulders. "That is true, isn't it?"

"Don't you forget it. The worst is over. We are safely through that box of tricks, which is always what troubled me, and we are at home on Mars. We have food, water, everything we need for months. All we have to do is take normal precautions, do your job, and then go back as heroes. Rich ones."

"We have to set up the transmitter first, but that should not be difficult."

"I'll take your word for it, thanks." Ben took the soup and sipped at it noisily because it was hot. "I have no idea why we even have to build another MT when we have one here. In fact I don't even know how the thing works and no one ever bothered to tell me."

"It's simple enough." Otto relaxed, on familiar ground, eager to explain, forgetting their situation for the moment. Which is just why Ben, who knew a good deal about MT theory, had asked him the question.

"The discovery of Bhattacharya space is what made matter transmission possible. Bhattacharya space—or B-space—is analogous to our three-dimensional continuum but nevertheless lies outside of it. But we can penetrate it. The interesting thing is that wherever we penetrate it, from whatever location in our own universe, we appear to come through in the same place there. So by careful alignment it is possible to have two screens sharing the same portion of B-space. The B-space, in effect, is allowed to penetrate into our space before each screen so that as far as we are concerned the screens no longer exist in our space-time continuum. Whatever enters one comes out of the other. That is it."

"Simple enough—as long as you leave out the details about how the gadget is built. But it doesn't explain why we can't leave Mars in the same manner that we came."

"There are a number of factors involved, but the more important ones are alignment power and physical distance."

"You told me distance doesn't affect the screens?"

"It doesn't, directly, but it makes alignment much more difficult. The screen out there that was rocketed here to Mars has a two-foot working diameter, about the very largest we could send. Almost all of its power goes to holding its existence. The transmitter on Earth reaches out and . . . it is difficult to describe . . . latches onto it. Holds it in shape, stabilizes it to receive transmission. But the same process won't happen in reverse."

"What would happen if something were sent back in the other direction?"

"There is no 'other direction'. Anything put into this transmitter would be converted to Y radiation and simply sprayed into Bhattacharya space."

"Doesn't sound healthy at all. What do you say we recharge our oxygen tanks and move the rest of the stuff in here that we are going to need? Then get some sleep."

"I'm with you."

They gathered only the immediate essentials, food, air-scrubbing equipment and the like, then crawled into their sleeping bags. The next day they were both feeling much better and finished setting up the camp. On the third day the first pieces of the big matter transmitter were sent through.

It was a component engineer's nightmare. All the units, whatever their function, had to have been designed to fit through a two-foot hole. A number of compromises had been made. After a good many sleepless nights over the drawing boards it had been finally decided that a diesel-electric generator could not be modified enough to get it through. Some nameless subengineer bestowed credit on his superiors by suggesting that enough high-charge batteries could be sent through to activate the big six-foot screen long enough to push the generator through in one piece.

The supporting frame had been set up and they had adapted a routine. Ben, who was in far better shape for the physical work, was doing most of the construction work, while Otto worked in the shelter assembling the electronic components. They helped each other when they had to. Ben finally tightened the last bolt on the steel frame, kicked it affectionately, and cycled through the air lock into the shelter. In the morning they could wire-in the screen-face elements.

Otto was slumped over the workbench, his face flattened against a printed circuit module, his skin red and flushed. His hand was resting on the hot soldering iron and the air stank with the smell of burnt flesh.

Ben dragged him over to his bunk, feeling the burning heat of his flesh all the while. "Otto," he said, shaking him, but the man was limp. His breathing was heavy and slow and he would not regain consciousness. Ben made a thorough job of bandaging the severely burnt hand and tried to order his thoughts. He was no doctor, but he had enough field training with medicine to be able to identify most severe diseases and traumatic injuries. This fitted no categories. His mind sheered away from any thoughts of what it really might be. He finally gave Otto a heavy shot of penicillin and made notes of the man's temperature, respiration and pulse. Sealing his suit he went to the capsule and called Earth.

"I want this transcribed. I am going to give you some information. Do not answer until I am finished and when I am done do not radio but type copy and send it through the MT. All right. Otto is hurt, sick, something, I'm not sure. These are the details."

He sent what he had observed and what he had done, then waited the slow minutes until his message was received and the answer had arrived. As he finished reading it he crumpled the paper in anger and grabbed the mike.

"Yes, I have considered the possibility of a Martian disease and no, I will not research and send reports. Get a doctor through at once. Offer enough and you'll get a volunteer. Start sending his equipment now while you are finding and dressing him. *Then* you can send through your microscope and sampling equipment and I will be glad to look for microorganisms in the dirt or where-ever you want. As we reported, we found some small plantlike growths, but we didn't bother them. The biologists can look into that. I'll look for your germs for you, but only after you have done what I tell you."

His message was understood. Transmatter Ltd. were just as eager as he was to insure the safety of the expedition; they had a lot of money tied up in it, and were not at all hesitant to risk some more lives in the effort. The doctor, a bewildered, young, staff medic—who had just signed papers that made his wife financially independent for life—dropped to the ground less than half an hour after the last of his equipment and supplies had arrived. Ben hurried him into the shelter and peeled off his outer clothing.

"I've set up all your stuff on the bench there. Your patient is waiting."

"My name is Joe Parker," the doctor said, but he lowered his extended hand when he saw the look on Ben's face. He hurried over to the sick man. Even after a complete examination he was reluctant to admit the truth.

"It could be an unusual disease—"

"Don't dodge the point. Have you ever seen anything like it before?"

"No, but—"

"That's what I thought."

Ben sat down heavily and poured himself a waterglass of the medicinal brandy, then hesitated and poured a smaller one for the doctor.

"A new disease, something really new? A Martian disease?"

"Probably. That's what it looks like. I'll do everything in my power, Ben, but I have no idea how it will turn out."

They both already knew, although they would not admit it out loud. In spite of all the medicines and supportive treatment Otto died two days later. Parker made a postmortem examination and discovered that most of the victim's brain had been destroyed by an unknown organism. He froze samples and made numerous slides while Ben worked on the large transmitter.

Word about what had happened must have circulated among the staff on Earth because it took four more days to get an engineer volunteer to finish the technical end of the MT. He was a frightened, silent man named Mart Kennedy and Ben did not talk to him about it because he did not really want to know what pressures had been used.

The work went quickly then, even though a dark shadow seemed to hang over their lives. They ate together without much conversation and pushed the construction. Dr. Parker had been working hard and thought that he had obtained a transparent liquid that contained the submicroscopic agent responsible for the disease. This was tightly stoppered and sealed in a case for transmission as soon as the screen was operating.

On the morning of the day operating tests were to begin, Mart Kennedy rose early to watch the sunrise. He had barely been aware of his surroundings since he had arrived, working with almost no rest on the big screen. That was all right, too; thinking about the Martian crud was avoided that way. It was a misapplied, supposedly funny, name that did not conceal the waiting horror. Certain death. Mars, it certainly was something. In his most wayout dreams, reading space fiction as a kid, he had never thought he would ever be here. He yawned and went to put the coffee on, then woke the others. Ben's eyes opened instantly and he nodded, fully awake. Parker wouldn't stir and he shook him by the shoulder—then jerked his hand away in sudden fear.

"Ben," he called out, stammering over the sounds as he did when disturbed. "S-something's wrong here."

"The same, the symptoms are all the same," Ben said, hitting his fists again and again against the head of the bed without realizing it. "He has it all right. We'll give him the shots and get the screen working. There's nothing else we can do."

The big matter transmitter had been ready to go the day before, but they had all been too tired to finish the job. Ben made the sick man as comfortable as he could, giving him the medication that had not worked before, then joined Mart Kennedy.

"Everything tests in the green," Mart said. "Ready to activate whenever you say."

"That is right now. The sooner the better."

"Right."

The screen flickered and darkened, then went black all over. Ben had scrawled SEND GENERATOR on a canister lid and he threw it into the screen. It vanished. To Earth—or into radiation in B-space. Nothing happened. Seconds trickled by. The batteries could only hold the screen for about a minute.

Then it appeared. The leading edge of the wheeled platform dropped to the ground and they pulled hard on the handles. The heavy motor-generator came through and they rolled it aside. Behind them the screen wavered and the field died.

"Hook up the leads while I fire it up," Ben said.

He cracked open the valves on the fuel and oxygen tanks and pressed the starter. It kicked over with the first turn. Prewarmed before it had been sent. As the power built up the transmitter screen was restored. A container with a frightened rat came through and they returned it at once. There were more tests, more rats, and Ben sent a message through with them about Dr. Parker. The answer came quickly enough.

"WE ARE PULLING YOU ALL OUT," the typed message read. "EQUIPMENT IS TO BE LOCKED ON AUTOMATIC AND WE WILL OPERATE FROM THIS END. THANK YOU FOR YOUR AID. TRANSMISSION WILL BEGIN. SEND DR. PARKER THROUGH FIRST."

Ben scrawled a quick note and sent it.

"WHAT WILL HAPPEN TO US?"

"A SEALED QUARANTINE UNIT HAS BEEN ESTAB-LISHED WITH ENTRANCE ONLY BY MT. YOU WILL BE CARED FOR. EVERYTHING POSSIBLE WILL BE DONE."

"Let's get Parker," Ben said after he had read the note.

They dressed the unconscious man, and Ben made sure that the oxygen tube could not slip out of his mouth. A stretcher had been sent through earlier and they rolled him onto it and strapped him into place.

"Take the front," Ben said and they started towards the air lock. It was cramped, even with the stretcher standing on end, but they got through. Ben took up his end of the stretcher without a word, without even looking back, and they went to the large transmitter. It was big enough for the three to go through together.

The light was stronger than they were used to, and Ben's legs felt heavier. When he opened his face mask the air was thick and had unusual smells in it. They stood in a bare hallway with a transparent wall. At least a hundred men were watching them from the other side.

"Dr. Thurmond speaking, here are your instructions," a loud-speaker said. "You will—"

"Can you hear me?" Ben broke in.

"Yes. You will wait until—"

"Shut up and listen closely. You now have two specimens, a sick man and a well one. That's enough. I'm going back to Mars. If I have to die, I might as well die there." He turned to the plate but Dr. Thurmond's voice stopped him.

"You cannot. It is forbidden. The screen is turned off. You will do as ordered."

"No, I won't," Ben said loudly, and even smiled a little. "I have taken my last order. Those weeks on Mars helped me understand a little about my life on Earth. I don't like people in crowds, in large stinking depressing numbers, eating and reproducing and polluting this Earth. It was a fine place before the people spoiled it. I'm going back to the world they haven't spoiled. Yet. With some luck perhaps they never will. I remember a dead rat, he came with me to Mars. A laboratory specimen. And that is all I am now in your eyes and I won't have it. I would far rather be the first Martian."

The crowd parted as Dr. Thurmond came forward and stood looking through the transparent wall at Ben, just inches away. He was angry, but he controlled it. He raised the wireless microphone and spoke.

"That is all very nice, but it does not bear on the case in hand. You are an employee and bound by contract and you will do as you are ordered. Your room is number three and you will go—"

"I will go back to Mars." Ben slipped the chrome steel pinch bar out of his pocket and tapped it against the window. Some of the men shrank back, but Dr. Thurmond did not move.

"This is a tool," Ben told them. "I will use it. I will find a door, or a crack, or a window gasket and I will lever away until I get through to your side. And then all the nice Martian crud germs will come out and eat you. So it is really you, Dr. Thurmond, who has no choice. Or rather a choice of two possibilities. You can kill me, or send me back to Mars. Now make up your mind."

Dr. Thurmond's face was drawn with hatred though his voice was calm as ever.

"I won't mention loyalty to you, Duncan, because you have none. But I will tell you that too much money has been spent to jeopardize things now. You will do as ordered."

"I will *not!*" Ben said, and swung the pinch bar so hard that a chip flew from the plastic surface. This time even Dr. Thurmond winced away.

"Can't you understand that I don't like it here and I am not staying here? And that just for once you have found someone whom you cannot order about? I'll be of immense value on Mars if the crud doesn't knock me over. Use that to convince yourself. But do it quick."

Another chip cracked off the window as he hit it. Dr. Thurmond did not speak but stood rigid. It wasn't until a third chip dropped to the floor that he turned his back suddenly.

"Activate the transmitter," he ordered, then turned off the microphone. The screen went dark. Ben looked at the shimmering surface, then back at the observers.

"Don't make any mistakes, Dr. Thurmond," Ben said. "I know you can have that screen out of sync and can send me through into B-space as a spurt of radiation. And that is that. But I sincerely hope that you are not going to be that wasteful. I won't ask you for any sympathy, since I know it would please you immensely to kill me in that fashion. But I must remind you that others have heard this talk we have had and you must have superiors who will resent the loss of a valuable man like myself, manager-to-be of your Martian settlement. Why I'll bet they could fire you just as fast as you fire your underlings."

Ben started towards the screen then looked back to face the still silent audience.

"I'll do a good job of running things on Mars. If I live, I'll keep on doing the work, so you lose nothing by it. But, if I don't do it, I imagine you'll find other applicants for the job pretty hard to come by."

Without waiting for an answer he sealed his face mask and stepped into the screen.

Save for the brilliant but unfortunately neglected *Holding Your Eight Hands* (Doubleday, 1969), most science fiction poetry is pretty miserable stuff. Exceptions do occur, however, and many writers who inject an occasional poem into their stories or novels find that verse can create a mood or sustain an emotion. One writer who has used the art of poetry as part of the genesis of prose creation is Frank Herbert. His fine novel *Dune* is structured like an epic poem, and entire individual chapters of the book often grew from a single *haiku*. The relationship between *Dune*, Mars, and poetry is simple. Herbert admits that he originally fashioned Arrakis after Mars—forbidding, beautiful, brutal, alluring. Here we are proud to present the first appearance in print of Herbert's poetic thoughts about another Marslike, desert civilization, Carthage. It is fine poetry, filled with the eerie melancholy of vanished desert-power. We follow Herbert's major production with the first printing of two shorter poems by two California writers, William Fox and Irene Jackson. Fox's *First Landing* is as provocative and illusive as the desert scene it suggests. Mrs. Jackson's *Earthbound* catches the spirit of all men and women for whom the moon and Mars have been magic symbols, perhaps only Apollo or Mariner photographs on the TV screen or pages in a book about Mars.

Frank Herbert

CARTHAGE: REFLECTIONS OF A MARTIAN

Thy expected alien
Am I.
Weird of shade
And doomfire face:
All thy senses
Cry to my
Mourning mysteries
Which yesterday
Were commonplace.

We sit at Sunday breakfast
And I smell the dust of Carthage.
It drowns the spang
Of our automatic toaster.

That strange woman across from me
Smiles, butters two slices.
Her smile arouses a multitude in me!
Her smile . . .
Frightens us.

I must look away!
Out the window beside my arm,
Sunglow warms a brick walk,
Grass, a tree, a planting of forsythia.
It is spring.
In the spring . . .
The earth is covered with dust.

Thy alien surprise
Hides beneath a gentle mask.
The melting death lime
Covers all this woman's yesterdays.
Where was she when the Martian came
And looked out through my eyes
Into this breakfastnook?

I sit at Sunday breakfast,
Sharing space and time
With a strange woman in a housecoat.
My trembling hands rustle the front page.
She smoothes Prince Valiant,
Not looking up.
I grow aware her hair's
Englazed . . .
From a spraycan!
Our terror solidifies this alien world.
I long for the button to push:
One long hissssss
And this englazed moment
Will be rendered tame, smooth, harmless.

My kind walked among Greeks and Romans.
We've been aliens here before, you know.
Taught the Romans arts and letters.
And, I recall,

Taught them other things before their fall:
The joys of little boys
And a way to breed bureaucracy onto itself.
Parthenogenesis, it's called—
From the Roman.
It spawns a durable kine
Which weathers inevitable decline.

Sunday breakfast
Smoothes eggs across my tongue.
I taste the clay of fate,
Which is only dust and spittle.
My mind aches from reading
A little late in the night.
I've read many books,
But last night, the subject
Was de la Molle,
Who exposed the shambles of Carthage.

En passant:
You archeologist of a time
When I'm dustier than Carthage—
Listen!
When you lift gently at fused green glass
And expose this breakfastnook,
To which translation will you attribute
Your ideas about conditions here—
Our mores, habits, artifacts?
About this toaster, now,
From which she takes two more—
Listen!
A collector of ancient gossip
Will need sensitive ears
To hear the scratch of a knife
Buttering toast.

Listen:
Conversation at Sunday breakfast
In the presence of loud sunlight on forsythia,
Flowers echoing in the corners of our eyes—

She: "What're the headlines today?"
Crystal flowers dissolve, shattered by that bright yellow noise.
Alien: "Ahhh, another crisis in the East."
She: "Must you bring the war to breakfast?"
Alien: "You asked."
She: "Well, you know it upsets me."
Hear how the platitudes tumble the toast crumbs from her mouth?
She says: "One consolation; this time, you won't have to go, my dear."
Ahhh, she thinks it's me, answering.
And I was always kind.
Martians aren't really kind.
But we often display patience,
Often mistaken for kindness.
Her smile, exposing lipstick'd incisors,
Demands a bloody answer—
But she gets quiet patience, instead,
And splashes words against such annoyance:
"Anyway, I don't think it'll come to war . . . do you?"
Silence.

Martian anger cannot be explained.
Alien vocal chords within my throat
Play a subtle tympany:
"Are you through with the funnies?"
Difficillimum est inimicos amare.
It's difficult to love enemies.
Ira est causa belli.
Anger the cause of war?
Is it now?
Indeed!
Always before
I thought it was the poor
Punishing the poor.

A wind speaks to the forsythia:
Busybody petals!
Hawking your seeds for tomorrow!
Can't you understand?
Nobody's listening.

En passant:
No doubt M. de la Molle
Uncovered friends of mine,
Their dust inextricably mingled
With some who wouldn't listen.
Why am I singled out, then,
For this alien role—
A wind ignored one more time?

The wind:
Shout me bureaucrats and bullyboys!
Howl with crime and the fall into darkness!
As translated from the Martian.
We've seen it all before, you know.
Carthage, Assyria . . .
Israel before the fright of flaming bush
And angry Moses.
"You are servants unto me! Not servants unto servants!"
God! What a voice from the storm that was!
But they didn't hear it in Knossos
Or Heliopolis.
And all through the long night of Rome,
The wind blew silently, full of ancient angers.
From the Inquisitional Jesuits
To laughing, stamping Hitler—
The wind could not be heard
Above the knouts and fires
And rampaging genitals
And official reports in quintuplicate.
Shout me official reports in quintuplicate!
Scream filing cabinets!
Howl thin, important, inflammable paper!
Si peccamus, puniemur.
If you sin, you will be punished.
Turn your back when the wind blows.
When exceptions multiply on the storm,
Agree that times are different.
A turned-back hides much.

What shames this time?
The usual.

Anything can be ignored . . .
If it's too upsetting.

Ceremonial-Sunday-breakfast-woman:
"That book you read so late last night—would I like it?"
I speak with the voice of de la Molle:
"Archeology. It's pretty dry."
"I thought you'd never turn off the light."
"Sorry if I . . ."
"Was it really that interesting?"
"It was about Carthage . . . the infant bones in the temple pottery."
"All that morbid, gruesome stuff!"
"They held a lottery, you know."
"What?"
"A lottery, to choose the ones they threw into Baal Ammon's jaws."
"I shudder sometimes at the things which interest you!"
"It was just their religion."
"To sacrifice children?"
"In the fiery furnace. Look it up in the Bible."

Her strange red lips encompass a bite of toast.
Teeth crunch and she swallows.
"I don't see why you read such things."

I must turn away and stare out the window.
How brightly the thin young tree
Dances beside the brick walk,
Singing to forsythia,
A song which says:
"Flowers cannot read."

Sunday breakfast peppered with Carthaginian dust!
Archeologist—
I wonder what you'll think
When you stir this breakfastnook
And find a toaster gone to rust?

Ahhhh, the shocking interpretations
Which will arise from things touched by us!

PART II

Time-intoxicated Sunday—
Dirty mounds of clouds drip ticks and tocks.
My morning sun, outglared by thunderheads,
Has fled the afternoon.
This day, an alien awoke in me.
He sits now in the artificial gloom,
In the skimmed-milk glimmer
Of a cathode livingroom.
We attend a face which booms through
The universal electronic view.
It's Pinocchio educating Pinocchios.
A Martian can see the strings, you know.
He's lecturing on economics,
And that strange female in this house
Pronounces this "cultural and elevating."
What a sad little two-dimensional creature, Pinocchio.
Puts me in mind of Cato,
Whose barracks voice echoed in the Senate:
"Ceterum censeo Carthaginem delendem esse."
As for the rest, I believe Carthage should be destroyed!
What a windy little bastard he was!
But he knew his economics—
A full credit balance in triremes
And interest-bearing Legionnaires.
Between then and now,
Banks note little change in men's affairs.
One rocket in its nest
Is worth two in the air.

Pinocchio didn't do his homework.
Listen to him, Cato!
Damn' fool!
He should've gone to school the way we did,
Hart-crouched, fearful,

Knowing what lurks out there beyond the fireflicker
They call civilization.
Times our own pulses sounded like tom-toms:
"Barroom-boom-boom!"
All those driving rhythms—
Carrier waves and harmonics
And harmonics on harmonics.
Poor slob of a Pinocchio!
He's masked all those clues
In his properly discredited mysteries—
Calls them all astrology.

He should become like the clam—
Listening with his guts
For the passage of sun and moon and planets.
He'd know then when to rise and when to sink,
When to bull and when to bear.
Even a willow bends before a gale,
Stupid little bastard Pinocchio!

Speak me the interest paid on those who seek
Their own kind the way a skipped rock touches a lake.
What do the rock and the lake share?
Pinocchio, I am your alien lake!
We have death in common and little else.
You lie about your manhood when that's not at stake.
You're always half-clothed in your furtive sex,
Forever hiding awareness of your mortality
In Sunday morning's barbiturituals.
All warnings have one exception, eh, Pinocchio?
You—posturing there in your grayness.
Life and Death make no exceptions.
That
Is basic economics.

You have forgotten, Pinocchio,
That Babylonian *lingua franca*
Served its merchant world for two thousand years
Before Jesus.

Jesus!
There's economics for you—
Gods, commerce and bureaucracy!
They endure, but you pass away, Pinocchio.
There is no interest-bearing Valhalla,
If we read God's deputy correctly . . .
As translated from the Martian.

Graeci et Romani plures deos habent.
But eternal flames were known to sear a careless virgin.
And you could always hear some foolishness in Minerva's wisdom.
Ahhhh, Pinocchio,
Hidden in your Trinity you've just as great a pantheon,
And just as many careless virgins.
You've merely Anglicized the names.
I remember rose garlands dripping blood petals
On Diana's altar.
And the God, Ea, creator of all things,
Possessor of unsearchable wisdom!
He's the one who struck fear into captive Jews.
But Ea was Sumerian, not naturalized
And certainly uncircumcised.

Naturalization:
Assur becomes Merodach.
And O'Brien comes out of Spain with a new name: Obreon.
Phoenician Astarte is Ashtaroth.
And Ishtar, moongoddess of Assyria,
Enters Athens as Artemis.
Aphrodite-Juno-Venus!
Who's to blame a goddess of fertility
For changing her middle name?
If you can't pronounce Czarnokofsky,
Make it Arno.
In some flame-lighted night,
She who comforted nomad sheepherders
Has been seen
On a movie screen.
The name of the game is faces.

Faces:
Before Roman ways etched their deltas
In the mind,
There were things the bowels knew
Which no brain could comprehend.
Knowledge flared to music of bowstrings,
Warcries and whimpers
And kite-shadowed silences.
I cannot forget a fair Gutian slave,
Coffled and herded into Babylon
In the time of Cabyses.
She was an Egyptian woman,
Taken with her child,
The spoil of the bow to be sacrificed
Before Nin-Girsu, who blessed commerce and litigation.
It was a simple economic equation:
Armies equal slavery and death.
The sum is greater than its parts.

Leave your screen, Pinocchio.
Make way for a better instructor—
Assur-nasir-apli, cruelest of the cruel,
Whose reign began with patricide.
I saw him yesterday, alive,
Striding across Rockefeller Plaza.
Genes remain, Pinocchio . . .
Timeless, carried in a spilling river
Of tadpole-sperm:
Omen tablets, the germ of yesterday,
Resurrecting bodies out of Babylon.
I see mighty Ur in a dirty village
Called Muqayyar.

Pause for station identification:
That woman!
There!
Advertising spray to extinguish body odor—
That's the daughter of Kallima-Sin
Given in marriage to Amenophis III!

And that was three thousand five hundred years ago,
The way Pinocchio reckons time.
Commercial, sans the blessing of Nin-Girsu:
Now playing at the Roxy—
A man who's really King Cyrus,
The one, you remember,
Who preferred archeology to a throne?

Tiglath-Pileser is not gone.
Sargon marches yet in Babylon—
Through Ishtar Gate,
Along Procession Street,
With Sennacherib,
Shalmaneser, Isem-Dagan
And Sin-sarra-iskun,
Whose walls were breached
By the Tigris flood.
They remember yet in Birs-Nimrud.

But when their names tangle the tongue,
The unpronounceable
Is unpronounced.

And now, back to our program:
Pinocchio, professor emeritus
Of someplace whose name will change,
Given time—
Your familiar face,
With its long, pretentious nose
Overhanging cold lips—
You've forgotten, but your genes have not.
Beyond blood exists that world pulse,
Sine-pounding timewave:
Diastole/systole.
Compelling blacksnake ripples
Whip across generations,
Generating a surfboard rider!
Does he feel a lift and thrust
Stronger than the sea?

That long breaker crashing white upon the coast—
What but a wavelet-harmonic,
Measured by the Martian scale!
Clams and stockmarket respond,
Counting sunspots and electrical charges
In the common air.
We Martians breathe out skipped rocks—
Where they touch, eons condense.

I bring you this message from our sponsor:
Start with Sheba's time
(She whose camel-station metropolis
Withstood Aelius Gallus,
But now, like Carthage, is reduced
To jetty walls of crumbled mud)
And count forward, hurling aside
The dustspume from every sandwave,
Count forward to this micro-instant
Of comprehension:
In all that time, there have been
The same gods and the same long rhythms
Booming out the centuries.

You've timed your breathing, Pinocchio,
And sunspot cycles,
And that fifty-one-year slackdrum
Throbbing in your economics.
You've heard the music.
Why haven't you learned the dance?

All that rhy-thm!
All that rhy-thm!
Clap your hands and stamp your feet,
Let your fingers feel that beat.
Workday traffic pumps along;
Listen to that bloodflow song.
Whoa!
And gee . . .
And haw.

Consider the artery of a country road,
Its diastaltic morningpulse
And systolic nightpulse.
Put your finger just so—there.
Feel it?
Now, over here—
Light, color!
How swift the fibrillation
Of a kerosene lantern!
Rhythms, rhythms—
Moon equals menstruation,
Floggings,
Crops,
Arson,
Sex . . .
Feel the erection/detumescence
In clouds and rain.
Sense the pulse of birth-death.
In the season of the winds,
There are wars and wars and wars . . .

From those moods conditioned by the chemistry
Ebbing and flowing in an amniotic sea,
Pinocchio vaguely senses
A peristaltic barroom-boom-boom.
Yet, when he looks upward
At variable stars and spinning galaxies,
At comets and eclipses,
He fails to recognize
That he's a bivalve on the tide-edge of the universe.

You must recall that I'm a Martian.
Which is vastly different in space and time
From Denubians and the people of Al Minhar.
We do not come as far to make our cruel observations.
I have my distant moods, though,
When your history collapses,
And I forget—
Not the day—

Not the year—
But the *age!*
Which eon is this?
That sad little man on circus-video
Blends all together with Censorius Cato!
Old Marcus Porcius himself!
Which newsreel is this
With Roman words tumbling
From a familiar, fat-lipped mouth?
"I say bury them before they bury us!"
And all around him I can see
Ghosts of Carthaginian judges.
"Rome! That confederacy of barbarians!
They claim they invented the trireme!"
My Martian brain throbs with an effort of translation.
I say: "Listen to him! Cato knows! He was our ambassador."

Economics lecture:
I marked the day when Romans taught
Their lesson of tens built on tens.
Ten cohorts equal a legion.
Behind each silver eagle march
Five thousand foot and three hundred cavalry.
As Cato remarked at the time:
"Fear kings whose slaves are crafty."
Simple figuring which can be traced
To a script passed along by the Phoenicians.
Commerce requires more than mumbling.
That was, you know, a time of accounting.
End of lecture.
If I'd only had a camera,
Even eight millimeter with sound,
Anything to record those two kings of Carthage
As they looked around them from Citadel-Byrsa.
How they smiled at Corthon, their inner harbor.
It was a beautiful view—
Two hundred and five warships there,
Safely sheltered while their crews enjoyed shoreleave.

Convoy duty can be a thankless job!
The merchantmen unloading in the outer bay,
Now, they had it easy and earned more pay.
What a day that was!
If I'd only had a camera,
Anything to show you that familiar scene.

I get time-drunk just thinking about it.
Take that guy Cato.
Before you can understand him,
You have to realize he's very religious.
He won't admit, of course,
That he shares his gods with Greece—
Those gawdamn' perverts!
Still, I've heard him say many times:
"Proper sacrifice and right thinking—
The gods reward such behavior with victory."

Let me tell you about one day
In the Senate caucus room—
Old Marcus Porcius was vetoing
A Triumph . . . I think it was for Nobilio.
Yes, Nobilio. Now, I recall.
Gods, what a voice old Marcus had!
"Nobilio indulges his troops!
He keeps *poets* in his camp!
And literary types . . .
If you ask me, Nobilio's as fruity as a Greek orchard!"
That was Marcus for you—
Old straight-arrow himself,
Really up tight—
Always recounting his victory at Thermopylae.
A plain, conservative Republican,
Dead set against Greek luxuries.
He was a strict Roman
And with morals like your maiden aunt.
You should've heard old Marcus
Carrying on about Manilius!
And all because poor Manilius

Kissed his own wife in broad daylight,
Right out there in front of God and everybody,
Including one of his own daughters!
"Immoral, by Jove!"
Just for that, Manilius lost Cato's vote
And, with it, command of the Fourth Legion.
Old Marcus put it just as bluntly as he could:
"I didn't earn my surname *Censorius*
By being soft and decadent!"

Yes, that was old Marcus Porcius Cato—
Patriotic, courageous, arrogant, avaricious, revengeful.
He was a legionnaire, through and through.
See him there in your cathode-arena:
"Carthage must be destroyed!"
As translated from the Martian.
I have to remember who I am
And when.
It's awfully easy to mix up two thousand years,
Just one big kaleidoscopic blur,
Confuses me all to hell!
That bald peasant with stainless steel teeth
Could be old *Censorius* in the flesh,
A Sabine farmer schooled in earthy frugality . . .
Or that earlier one, Shirmirab uhhh, whatsisname?
Minerva help me! I've forgotten all my Akkadian!
It's a damn' silly situation
For a Martian to have to go to bed
In a split-level suburban
Which sold originally for twenty-one-five.
If I told you what the taxes are on this place
You'd pass out cold from the shock.
No wonder I have trouble getting to sleep.
The night drags itself across my bed
Through a pulse of stale perfume.
What a fragile room this is,
Where expectancy in every light I see
Is a winkflare into burning darkness.

Did I lock the garage?
I should've told George
To have that Eaton report ready by noon.
This night congests my Martian soul
With drumsounds—
That infinite past!
And I have no book at last
In which to hide my mind.
M. de la Molle!
You and your damned infant bones
In the temple pottery!
I'm through with you,
But you're not through with me.
I want to slam a fist into eternity!
What new monsters lurk on another page?
Whose windy rage must I record for next eon's episode?
Martian sounds in my hidden voice
Fall silently on emptiness . . .
And somebody's left a TV on with a late-late movie.
If that damned Aelius Gallus had only taken the siege engines
With him the way I told him to!

You know what catches on my sleepless Martian memory?
A troop of Boy Scouts breaking step across a bridge.
The wrong rhythm could bring the whole structure crashing down.
And ruined Nazis straggling through ruined Munich—
Haunted eyes that I get all tangled up
With Hannibal's men,
Leaving their elephants and running . . .
When?

I remember a great financier at his table.
This man, mind you, helped frame atomic policy.
But I recall him at a garden-party luncheon
In some western valley—never mind where.
Around him in the cool shade
Sat crafty Democrats and Republicans . . .
"Fear kings whose slaves are crafty."
This time, I had a camera and a voice on tape.

How like a kindly father our financier appears.
Listen to the recording:
"FDR's big mistake was listening to Keynes."
(He means old John Maynard, Lord Tilton)
"We'll pay the economic consequences
Of listening to the spellbinder of Bretton Woods!"
(That's a veiled pun on one of Lord Tilton's early writings)

In the way such luncheons go,
You can hear the sound of crockery and a string orchestra . . .
Faintly, faintly—playing something from *Rose Marie*.
But it could just as well be
The slap of sandals
And *Censorius* deploring the cost of keeping foreign legions,
Or delivering a tirade against Greek advisers . . .

Outside these luncheon pleasantries,
You can see the servants gliding by
With delicacies: honey-dates and burnt cream.
The waiters wear white uniforms and black, pointed shoes
Which pinch their toes—
You can hear one of them complaining to a friend:
"Damn' shoes cost me sixteen bucks!
Oughta fit better'n this!"

Do they really hear?
You see them standing near
While the great sit at table.
A kitchen door opens creakingly,
Green leaves go slither among the potted palms.
The waiter comes and conversation hesitates,
Poised above the dishes . . .
The host, a gnome with angry face,
Whispers to his companion:
"Put it in chemicals. Not really a gamble, of course—
The world situation being what it is."

And the white-coated, obsequious, attendant-waiter
Murmurs to the financier:
"The fishcakes are very good, sir."

Is it any wonder I can't sleep?
This damn bedroom smells of salt!
History collapsing all around my Martian soul.
If I open the window, I'll smell the wind off Carthagae.
Salt!
You know, right there above that citadel,
We layered on the salt, sterilizing the place.
By order of the Commander, the citadel got an extra dose—
"To be covered with salt to the thickness of a foot soldier's toe!"
How about that?
Me, Private Flavius, one-time batman to Nobilio,
They call me out and have me hold my foot there
To get the proper thickness.
Took my sandal off and, Minerva pity me!
That sand was hot enough to feel right through
My marching callouses.
And you know what I was thinking?
About the booty, and a kind of vengeful joy
That we'd killed two more kings,
Destroyed two more palaces.
And underneath my thoughts, I suppose,
Lay that deep-soft-breath reflection
Any soldier knows:
    I've lived through another one.

William Fox

SOFT LANDING

red planet blink, red planet wink,
I pulled you down when I was child
on top of airports and t-v sets,

and now it seems you beat our dreams—
we came to you instead.

Irene Jackson

EARTHBOUND

He was one of Bradbury's kind of people
Who early took to wings—
Jumped first from the barn roof at home,
Then the church steeple;
And when his bones were finally out of slings
Took off from Baldy's snowy dome
Landing this time in a tree,

And still denied the pull of gravity.
Instead he dug the pull of endless time and space . . .

He gazed nightly at the stars,
Read Verne and Wells,
He was an active flying ace
Who dreamed of setting foot (where else?) on Mars
                    (or was it old Barsoom?).
He watched the astronauts return
Two times from landing on the moon,
And swore to break the bonds that held him, soon.

And then one day they came, out in the bog
Behind the Carter place.
Took him and his dog
For one swift silent spin in outer space

To Mars itself and back again!
He swears that he and his old hound,
After this Martian joyride, no longer are earthbound!

I only know they disappeared one day
And were a long, long time away.

Since they came back they mostly sit and look
At the green trees, the garden, and the brook.

Harlan Ellison is many things: winner of more Nebula and Hugo awards than you can count; prophet and harlequin of the "New Wave," and Hollywood script writer, to name only a few. But there is one other aspect of his character that he vainly tries to hide: the fact that he is a very generous human being. This story, "In Lonely Lands," is one example of that generosity. When we asked him to suggest a Mars story of his to reprint, he replied within a week by sending this original to us. This version is printed here for the first time, and we are happy to commend it to you. It's a different kind of Ellison story, one which shows him with an almost romantic talent, a far different tale than the gutsy, almost-hard-boiled speculation of some of his prize-winning efforts. Yet "In Lonely Lands" is really a poetic statement of one of Ellison's great themes: we must love one another or die, as poet W. H. Auden put it, and that love must transcend the differences of color or race, even of planet. And when we love, we will not die in lonely lands.

Harlan Ellison

IN LONELY LANDS

> "He clasps the crag with crooked hands;
> "Close to the sun in lonely lands,
> "Ring'd with the azure world he stands."
>
> ALFRED, LORD TENNYSON

Pederson knew night was falling over Syrtis Major; blind, still he knew the Martian night had arrived; the harp crickets had come out. The halo of sun's warmth that had kept him golden through the long day had dissipated, and he could feel the chill of the darkness now. Despite his blindness there was an appreciable *changing* in the shadows that lived where once, long ago, there had been sight.

"Pretrie," he called into the hush, and the answering echoes from the moon valleys answered and answered, *Pretrie, Pretrie, Pretrie*, down and down, almost to the foot of the small mountain.

"I'm here, Pederson old man. What do you want of me?"

Pederson relaxed in the pneumorack. He had been tense for some time, waiting. Now he relaxed. "Have you been to the temple?"

"I was there. I prayed for many turnings, through three colors."

It had been many years since Pederson had seen colors. But he knew the Martian's religion was strong and stable because of colors. "And what did the blessed Jilka foretell, Pretrie?"

"Tomorrow will be cupped in the memory of today. And other things." The silken overtones of the alien's voice were soothing. Though Pederson had never seen the tall, utterly ancient Jilkite, he had passed his arthritic, spatulate fingers over the alien's hairless, teardrop head, had seen by feeling the deep round sockets where eyes glowed, the pug nose, the thin, lipless gash that was mouth. Pederson knew this face as he knew his own, with its wrinkles and sags and protuberances. He knew the Jilkite was so old no man could estimate it in Earth years.

"Do you hear the Grey Man coming yet?"

Pretrie sighed, a lung-deep sigh, and Pederson could hear the inevitable crackling of bones as the alien hunkered down beside the old man's pneumorack.

"He comes but slowly, old man. But he comes. Have patience."

"Patience," Pederson chuckled ruminatively. "I got that, Pretrie. I got that and that's about all. I used to have time, too, but now that's about gone. You say he's coming?"

"Coming, old man. Time. Just time."

"How are the blue shadows, Pretrie?"

"Thick as fur in the moon valleys, old man. Night is coming."

"Are the moons out?"

There was a breathing through wide nostrils—ritualistically slit nostrils—and the alien replied, "None yet this night. Tayseff and Teei are below the horizon. It grows dark swiftly. Perhaps this night, old man."

"Perhaps," Pederson agreed.

"Have patience."

Pederson had not always had patience. As a young man, the blood warm in him, he had fought with his Presby-Baptist father, and taken to space. He had not believed in Heaven, Hell, and the accompanying rigors of the All-Church. Not then. Later, but not then.

To space he had gone, and the years had been good to him. He had aged slowly, healthily, as men do in the dark places between dirt. Yet he had seen the death, and the men who had died believing, the men who had died not believing. And with time had come the realization that he was alone, and that someday, one day, the Grey Man would come for him.

He was always alone, and in his loneliness, when the time came that he could no longer tool the great ships through the star spaces, he went away.

He went away, searching for a home, and finally came full circle to the first world he had known; came home to Mars, where he had been young, where his dreams had been born; Mars, for home is always where a man has been young and happy. Came home where the days were warm and the nights were mild. Came home where men had passed but somehow, miraculously, had not sunk their steel and concrete roots. Came home to a home that had changed not at all since he'd been young. And it was time. For blindness had found him, and the slowness that forewarned him of the Grey Man's visit. Blindness from too many glasses of vik and scotch, from too much hard radiation, from too many years of squinting into the vastnesses. Blind, and unable to earn his keep.

So alone, he had come home; as the bird finds the tree, as the winter-starved deer finds the last bit of bark, as the water quenches the thirst. He had come there to wait for the Grey Man, and it was there that the Jilkite Pretrie had found him.

They sat together, silently, on the porch with many things unsaid, yet passing between them.

"Pretrie?"

"Old man."

"I never asked you what you get out of this. I mean—"

Pretrie reached and the sound of his claw tapping the Formica table top came to Pederson. Then the alien was pressing a bulb of water-diluted vik into his hand. "I know what you mean, old man. I have been with you close on two harvestings. I am here. Does that not satisfy you?"

Two harvestings. Equivalent to four years Earth time, Pederson knew. The Jilkite had come out of the dawn one day, and stayed to serve the old blind man. Pederson had never questioned it. One day he was struggling with the coffeepot (he dearly loved old-fashioned brewed coffee and scorned the use of the coffee briquettes) and the heat controls on the hutch . . . the next he had an undemanding, unselfish manservant who catered with dignity and regard to his every desire. It had been a companionable relationship; he had made no great demands on Pretrie, and the alien had asked nothing in return.

He was in no position to wonder or question.

Though he could hear Pretrie's brothers in the chest-high floss brakes at harvesting time, still the Jilkite never wandered far from the hutch.

Now, it was nearing its end.

"It has been easier with you here. I—uh—thanks, Pretrie," the old man felt the need to say it clearly, without embroidery.

A soft grunt of acknowledgment. "I thank you for allowing me to remain with you, old man, Pederson," the Jilkite answered softly.

A spot of cool touched Pederson's cheek. At first he thought it was rain, but no more came, and he asked, "What was that?"

The Jilkite shifted—with what Pederson took for discomfort— and answered, "A custom of my race."

"What?" Pederson persisted.

"A tear, old man. A tear from my eye to your body."

"Hey, look . . ." he began, trying to convey his feelings, and realizing *look* was the wrong word. He stumbled on, an emotion coming to him he had long thought dead inside himself. "You don't have to be—uh—you know, sad, Pretrie. I've lived a good life. The Grey Man doesn't scare me." His voice was brave, but it cracked with the age in the cords.

"My race does not know sadness, Pederson. We know grat-itude and companionship and beauty. But not sadness. That is a serious lack, so you have told me, but we do not yearn after the dark and the lost. My tear is a thank you for your kindness."

"Kindness?"

"For allowing me to remain with you."

The old man subsided then, waiting. He did not understand. But the alien had found him, and the presence of Pretrie had made things easier for him in these last years. He was grateful, and wise enough to remain silent.

They sat there thinking their own thoughts, and Pederson's mind winnowed the wheat of incidents from the chaff of life spent.

He recalled the days alone in the great ships, and how he had at first laughed to think of his father's religion, his father's words about loneliness: "No man walks the road without companionship, Will," his father had said. He had laughed, declaring he was a loner, but now, with the unnamable warmth and presence of the alien here beside him, he knew the truth.

His father had been correct.

It was good to have a friend. Especially when the Grey Man was coming. Strange how he knew it with such calm certainty, but that was the way of it. He knew, and he waited placidly.

After a while, the chill came down off the hills, and Pretrie brought out the treated shawl. He laid it about the old man's thin shoulders, where it clung with warmth, and hunkered down on his triple-jointed legs once more.

"I don't know, Pretrie," Pederson ruminated, later.

There was no answer. There had been no question.

"I just don't know. Was it worth it all? The time aspace, the men I've known, the lonely ones who died and the dying ones who were never lonely."

"All peoples know that ache, old man," Pretrie philosophized. He drew a deep breath.

"I never thought I needed anyone. I've learned better, Pretrie."

"One never knows." Pederson had taught the alien little; Pretrie had come to him speaking English. It had been one more puzzling thing about the Jilkite, but again Pederson had not questioned it. There had been many spacers and missionaries on Mars.

"Everybody needs somebody," Pederson went on.

"You will never know," Pretrie agreed, then added, "Perhaps you will."

Then the alien stiffened, his claw upon the old man's arm. "He comes, Pederson old man."

A thrill of expectancy, and a shiver of near fright came with it. Pederson's grey head lifted, and despite the warmth of the shawl he felt cold. So near now. "He's coming?"

"He is here."

They both sensed it, for Pederson could feel the awareness in the Jilkite beside him; he had grown sensitive to the alien's moods, even as the other had plumbed his own. "The Grey Man," Pederson spoke the words softly on the night air, and the moon valleys did not respond.

"I'm ready," said the old man, and he extended his left hand for the grasp. He set down the bulb of vik with his other hand.

The feel of hardening came stealing through him, and it was as though someone had taken his hand in return. Then, as he thought he was to go, alone, he said, "Good-by to you, Pretrie, friend."

But there was no good-by from the alien beside him. Instead, the Jilkite's voice came to him as through a fog softly descending.

"We go together, friend Pederson. The Grey Man comes to all races. Why do you expect me to go alone? Each need is a great one.

"I am here, Grey Man. Here. I am not alone." Oddly, Pederson knew the Jilkite's claw had been offered, and taken in the clasp.

He closed his blind eyes.

After a great while, the sound of the harp crickets thrummed high once more, and on the porch before the hutch, there was the silence of peace.

Night had come to the lonely lands; night, but not darkness.

Bruce McAllister's "World of the Wars," which was written especially for this volume, is an "original" in the best sense of the word. As its title suggests, the story looks back to H. G. Wells's *War of the Worlds*: on one level "World of the Wars" modernizes and intensifies Wells's vision, picturing a Martian attack on smog-choked twentieth-century Southern California. McAllister's evocation of contemporary America packs a satiric punch rivaling that of the Victorian masterpiece. But "World of the Wars" is even more compelling on its second level, where it does not extend but rather reverses Wells's sense of things. Instead of Wells's adult's eye view of the Martian invasion, McAllister gives us the child's perspective. Deftly utilizing Jungian symbolic patterns, he centers his tale in the consciousness of his boy-hero Timmothy, a latter-day fusion of Twain's Huck Finn and Henry James's Maisie. Through Timmothy's innocent, partly uncomprehending eyes we discover the horrible truth: the Martians are right here, present in every racially prejudiced man, active on the bloody streets of every riotous ghetto, Watts, Beverly Hills, La Puente. The editors are proud to present this remarkable work by Mr. McAllister, an experienced short-story writer and critic, whose first novel, *Humanity Prime*, has just been published by Ace.

Bruce McAllister

WORLD OF THE WARS

"Not even lichen," Mr. Turner said to his wife, and Timmothy listened carefully. "All they found was a kind of rust—no lichen."

Timmothy knew they were talking about Mars and the astronauts, but he didn't understand it.

"What about the Martians?" he asked, his arms crossed on the dinner table in boyish imitation of his father's. His blond head returned his parents' stares.

"No Martians, Tim," his father mumbled. "And no one ever thought there'd be."

"But Jimmy says there are Martians."

Neither his mother nor father answered.

"Jimmy has four books about Martians."

His father smiled the kind of smile that always made Timmothy red-faced.

"Those books are made-up stories," his mother said.

"Jimmy says there are Martians. They're also called 'aliens.'"

"No aliens in the solar system," his father said, then paused, and laughed. "Just the black, brown and yellow aliens moving in next door."

His mother gave back a short laugh, and started to get up with the dishes.

"I want to see Mars," Timmothy said quickly. "Can I see it at night?"

His mother sat back down. "No. We could at one time, about five years ago. It looked like an ordinary star—but it was reddish. You can't see any stars these days, Timmothy, because of the smog."

"Jimmy says you can see Mars at night."

"Has he ever seen it?" His father asked the question, and his white face formed a frown.

"No, but it says in his books that you can see it in the sky."

"Smog says you can't," his father mumbled, waiting for his wife to clear the table.

They were right. You couldn't see any stars at all. Just a hazy yellowish light reflected back down from the smogbanks over Puente. The famous Los Angeles smog.

Timmothy stood in the bare back yard of the stucco house and looked up at the night, first toward the southern tract-housing hills, then west toward Los Angeles, then north toward the factory where his father worked.

"We could see stars once, about five years ago," he remembered. Five years ago he had been three years old, and he hadn't been interested in Mars then. He had never looked up at the night then.

Returning to the house, through the screen door, and into the living room, he found his father swearing.

"Who was it?" his mother was saying, standing over the stuffed chair occupied by his father.

"Cartwright, calling from the plant. Someone started a fire over there at about eight o'clock. It was arson, no doubt about it."

"Have there been any demonstrations at the plant recently, Sam?"

"Around a *shoe* factory? No. But it's the same kind of people. They wrote things on the walls with red paint, and then started the fire."

"What did they say, those things?" asked the boy, remaining by the back door.

His father looked toward him—but not at him.

"What did the writing say?" his mother echoed.

"Two things. 'Soon your cities will fall.' And 'Sabotage is love.'"

"Can you see the fire from here?" Timmothy asked quietly.

His father didn't answer, and his mother said quickly, "I'm sure it's been put out by now, Timmothy."

Outside, Timmothy looked toward the factory again. No, there wasn't any fire to be seen. Not even any smoke. No sirens of fire engines either.

He started to look away, and a tiny something flashed before his eye—out in the night sky.

He looked back, harder, and found it again. High above the factory, barely visible in the night-yellowed smog, was a red star blinking very red.

Jonathan wanted to be a member of the club. He had said so a dozen times, before Timmothy finally let him in.

"How many guys are in the club, do you think?" Timmothy asked, beginning Jonathan's initiation.

"There's you, and Jimmy, and Charlie."

"*And* Billy."

"And Billy . . ." Jonathan was shaking a little, as Timmothy could see under the street lamp's light. Jonathan stopped shaking only when they started walking toward Jimmy's house.

"There has to be another guy around when I make you a member, Jonathan."

Jonathan nodded and didn't stop nodding until Jimmy left his house and joined them for the walk back to Timmothy's yard.

"If there aren't two guys with you," Timmothy added, "you won't be able to see it. It's a secret, and no one knows about it."

On the dying summer grass in the back yard Timmothy stood by the new member and pointed up at the sky.

"There! Can you see it *now*? Over my dad's factory."

Jonathan couldn't see it. Timmothy pointed again. "It's not very bright, but you *should* be able to see it."

Jonathan shook his head slowly.

He was younger, and in a moment was almost crying. Then he saw it.

To let the other two boys know that he *really* did see it, Jonathan said, "There it is! It kind of blinks and is very, very red."

"Okay, now you're a member," Timmothy said, then added, "You can't see them from here, but there are Martians on it—weird-looking *aliens.*"

Jimmy nodded now. He was the oldest, and he had the books, and he wanted to remind the other two of those facts. He said, "Yes, I've read a lot about those Martians."

Timmothy knew he had chosen a bad night to show his father Mars. He had been out staring at the red star, and he realized now that he had missed most of the discussion his parents were having at the table, long after dinner was over.

". . . underground newspapers said so," his father was saying when Timmothy entered the dining room.

"Did you read them yourself, Sam?" his mother asked, sighing. She sighed again.

"I didn't have to. The supervisor keeps track of them, and gets the word to the rest of us. Those kind of newspapers have been talking about today as *the* day—"

"Dad?" Timmothy asked it as quietly as he could.

"Well," his mother ignored him, "maybe you should call the police and see what they think, Sam."

"Don't have to! Carlyle says the police are already ready for it. They think it'll be tonight too."

"Dad?"

"What!" His father turned as if the boy had bitten him.

"I can see Mars, Dad."

"Oh for God's sake!" Turning back to his mother, his father said, "I'll keep in phone contact with the plant tonight. Remember, we did get hit with arson last month. If anything happens there tonight, we'll know for sure they weren't kidding."

"I *really* can see Mars."

His father stared at the table, his lips in a rubberlike frown.

"Go ahead, Sam," his mother said, sighing again. "Find out what it is he's seeing."

Like a big dog his father struggled up from the chair—sighing like his mother, but longer and deeper—and followed the boy toward the back door.

As they opened the screen and started out, his father stopped and looked down at him.

"I don't think I've mentioned this before, but keep it in mind. If there's ever any trouble—guns or fires started around here—go hide in a closet, please."

Timmothy was already pointing happily up at the sky, above the factory.

His father squinted. "Where? What . . ."

The boy pointed harder, wanting and trying to make his finger so thin and sharp that his father couldn't possibly miss the red star, the only star in the sky.

His father kept squinting, then started and grunted. "Oh for God's sake!" He began, "That's just the light on the tower for—"

He was interrupted by the lights going out in the house. The street lights around in front of the house went out. The light reflected off the smog cloud over Puente went out. In the sudden darkness his father cried, "Oh God."

Timmothy couldn't see him, but could hear his father's heavy footsteps pounding back to the house, now stumbling around the screen door.

"Tim! Get the hell in the house!"

His father's voice was different now. It had the pitch of a woman's voice. Timmothy started trembling.

As he ran to the house, he looked back once at the red star, and stopped.

Mars had gone out.

And then the factory blew up, and for a long minute there was too much light everywhere.

He was hiding in the living-room closet, in darkness that embraced the whole house. He could hear his parents running from room to room, stumbling.

"The blacks! Of course it's them!" his father was shouting. "And they'll have guns!"

"Please don't shout, please don't." His mother was crying.

So the "blacks"—those "aliens" his father had always talked about, afraid that they would live nearby—were powerful enough to destroy the red star, the planet. It was unbelievable, the boy knew, but it was true. He was afraid of wetting his pants, it was so true.

Something crashed at the front door. In a minute he realized it was the sound of a bullet hitting wood. His mother screamed then, as if she had just realized it too.

His father was bellowing now. His mother kept crying. Neither one said a single word Timmothy could understand.

After an hour of closet darkness, the front door crashed open, and Timmothy wet his pants. Had his father left the house?

In the distance there were popping sounds, sirens, boomings, and maybe shouting.

He was wet, and had to get out.

He was afraid that if he opened the closet door slowly someone would reach in and grab him. So he opened it quickly and ran out—over to the living-room window.

Outside, in the red light of a police car zooming by, he could see his mother. She was leaning over a man on the ground, his father. Another red light went by, and the wetness on his father's T-shirt shone red.

Even without the red light, the wetness would have been red.

There was nothing left in him to wet his pants with, but his body tried, and he whimpered and stepped back from the window.

He understood it slowly now. He was on Mars. That was what had happened. The *red* lights, the *red* fires burning at the factory and down the street, and the *red* wetness on his father's shirt. This was the Red Planet.

The red star was no longer in the sky because he and his parents had been carried to it. He was on Mars. The Martians were angry, and they were attacking, burning everything, causing *redness* everywhere.

He and his mother and father were trespassers. The Martians, the aliens, hated them. "Don't go into other people's yards," he remembered his mother had always said.

Back in the closet, he quietly wished he were a Martian. He wished he were black, because this was Mars, the aliens' home, and they had the right. They would win.

I want to be a winner too, the boy thought to himself.

In the darkness of the closet he looked at his arm, and it was black. For a brief moment he was a crouching Martian, and happy.

Barry Malzberg's "Exploration" has the panoramic scope of a novel, the bold character contrasts of a play, and the lyricism and density of a poem. Yet "Exploration" is neither novel, play, nor poem, but rather a beautifully made short story, with a fascinating new approach to man's old friend, the Red Planet. In "Exploration" Malzberg gives us a triple perspective on Mars: resolutely sensible technician, passionate poetess, alarmed colonizer, each presents his very different sense of their common destination, the Mars they are separately to explore. The result of fusing these three strangely dissimilar views is that Malzberg's story becomes an extraordinarily rich and complex study of both the human mind and the Martian territory. For this reason, "Exploration" is also a kind of summary of this entire volume, *Mars, We Love You,* which contains so many different Marsscapes. We are indeed proud to be the first to publish this outstanding original work by our distinguished colleague.

Barry N. Malzberg

EXPLORATION

1. DEIMOS: He sees it as if from a great distance but it is really close, close on to him, the shallow surfaces of that sphere no more than three or four miles dead ahead, it looks like machinery. All of it is machinery, he has consoled himself to remember that, the satellites, the planet, the ship that takes him there, his own wicker and sniff of blood is nothing but a question of engineering and so he invokes this knowledge against the more ancient dreads which pursue him, trying to stifle the merry, mad monologue which has assaulted him throughout this trip: *we do not belong here, we do not have any business here, we are trespassing on some unity we do not understand. We do not understand/the very land/ which we walked on earth, that stricken turf* he sings, conscious of the fact that he is probably going insane but this, after all, is only a natural phenomenon, a concomitant, as it were, of the great ride itself. *Oh you buggers, oh you muggers,* he mutters and cuts the drive, cuts all power in the void, lets himself drift into some kind of stationary orbit looking down (or is it up?) at that damned moon, trying to reconcile himself with the feelings that

he knows will surely come: awe, mystification, fear, etc. But there are no such feelings at all, only a kind of vague dismay which is instantly subsumed in its more technological overlay and he remembers what he is there to do, he is to take findings, certain mappings and adjustments which will lead the project forward one more transient step and so he does so, going to work with computer and graphs, letting the technology take over for him, all singing now stifled. He does not even remember what he was singing about. Perhaps it was only some refraction of a popular tune he learned on earth, the leading hit in recent months and therefore only a nervous reflex, nothing more. *Oh, we can conquer space, but not the inward depths, that can only be done by yoo-hoo,* he sings while the machinery titters and squeaks in the background and the slow guiding huff of the sensors assesses all that has to be known about Deimos, the major satellite of Mars.

2. PHOBOS: In the tracking device she has picked it up clearly now, moving its wavering way across the path of the heavens, stars strewn to the back of it, the front of it, the sides of it. *Oh it's beautiful, beautiful to behold,* she murmurs, trying to construct some kind of poem which will both show her appreciation of the moment and communicate to the others, later, what it all means on some abstract, metaphysical level, *passenger of the night, child of the unborn, scepter of the red planet;* she will get all this down on her typewriter as soon as she is relieved and try it on the quarterlies when she returns to earth. In the meantime, however, there is very little to do but to relax and let the instruments perform their work; they have Phobos on a dead set and in due course will tell her everything she needs to know about the dimensions of its orbit, the characteristics of its mode. She struggles against the renewed realization that she is nothing but an adjunct, that the project runs in such a fashion as to make their presence only audacious, certainly irrelevant and then finally gives up, mutters the hell with it, allows the speculations to come, and gloomy they are, fine and gloomy, there is poetry in them to say nothing of various levels of apperception and she knows that, whatever else, she has been served well by her time on this project because when

she returns she will no longer be a technician but a poetess. Somewhere she has read that Phobos and the other one, whatever its name is, are supposed to be artificial satellites, not natural creatures of the heavens at all but rather constructions that might have been tossed into orbit eons ago by a decadent or dying Martian race that needed them as sentinels, or perhaps they were only interceptors. It is difficult to remember all of this, it is not her specialty, it is all very dull and depressing anyway because the origin of the satellites has nothing to do now with her condition or her ambitions; in any event they are only meaningful as they relate to her own inner terrain, her own inner space as it were and the rest of the project, the entire governmental swindle that sent them up here can only be in a kind of unwitting sanctification to that knowledge. Once some boy—she forgets his name and face—had swung over her and in the heat of necessity had made a fast penetration-and-orgasm, so rapid that his semen felt then as her slight cold sweat does now, a slight trickle both centrifugal and peripheral to her purposes, a pulse of irrelevance in the bending night; yes that too she thinks and reminds herself that she will have to include this image in the poem she will be writing. She has no fear now; the *Carolina Quarterly* or *Epoch* certainly cannot reject her now; she will be the only lady poet who has gone to Mars: there will even be the possibility of an anthology or a grant or two, and at the thought of how far she has had to go to make some minuscule connection between the layers of self, she smiles and quickens while Phobos swims slowly across the channel of sight and the stars themselves, nothing but a blanket, seem to swaddle down upon her.

MARS: THEREFORE YOU MUST UNDERSTAND THAT THERE IS SOME BASIC MISAPPROPRIATION HERE, THE WHOLE PURPOSE OF THE SURVEY IS NULLIFIED, he writes but it is the tenth time that he has tried this approach and he is not satisfied, not satisfied at all, in fact he is disgusted because there is no way that he will be able to impress upon the bureaucracy, either by code or wire, the true horror of what is happening here. GENTLEMEN: WE RETAIN OUR

HUMANNESS ALWAYS, he has written and THE FURTHER WE GO THE MORE LIMITED WE BECOME: IT IS THE ONLY JUST COMPENSATION FOR FEAR OF ENDLESS FROZEN NIGHT and this had been a good beginning, he had been pleased with it, almost moved, but now he has no way of knowing how to proceed and he knows that if he sends this kind of wire his career will be finished. They will not even allow him to participate with the rest of the group in the parades, the luncheons, the congressional ceremonies and the rest of it, that is how isolated he will become. But nevertheless, he must struggle with it: the intimation has come upon him in these last days that he is dealing with a situation so momentous and final by turns that if he does not take the responsibility for its explication no one ever will, besides, he is the Commander. YOU MUST BE MADE AWARE OF THIS DELIMITATION, THE FURTHER WE GO, THE LESS WE ARE, he continues, AND IN ANY EVENT THE TERRAIN HERE IS NO MORE INTRINSICALLY DISMAYING THAN THE FAR ANTARC-TIC, IT MUST BE OTHER THINGS, OTHER CONSIDERA-TIONS WHICH ARE DRIVING ALL OF US QUITE MAD. YOU MUST, GENTLEMEN, BE PREPARED TO EM-BRACE SOME KIND OF METAPHYSIC IF YOU WISH TO CONTINUE, and then with a flare of revulsion he picks up everything he has written and throws it into his wastebasket because it is no good, he knows that now, there is no way that he can possibly make it clear to them: the whole thing has been mad and nothing madder but the voyage itself which shakes slowly toward disaster on the shoulders of the fifteen men and five women who have been sent there. *Inner space is outer space is middle earth and we've no birth* he hums, one of the popular hits when the expedition left the earth, and he reflects that in the popular culture at least, the more complex things have appeared, the more simple they have been made. He feels a trembling in his shoulder blades or is it merely an itch, a difficult discrimina-tion to make and then palpates a hand against his forehead, yes, he has a fever. Moving from the bunk, moving out of the room, seeking the medic for a diagnosis, he is unaware of the man tracking Deimos, the woman tracking Phobos, but this will end, this too will end, everything will come together in the long or short run and of this he would in any event be convinced: they have plans for him and have always had, only the enactment remains unsure.

A Discussion

DOUBLE STAR BY ROBERT A. HEINLEIN

Mention Mars and someone will say "Robert A. Heinlein." Mention it again and someone else will respond "*Stranger in a Strange Land*." Mention a Martian and he'll say "Valentine Michael Smith." Mention the Martian language and he'll show you his "Grok" button.

Probably no science fiction novel of the last ten years has had the impact on society of *Stranger in a Strange Land*. Despite a slow start, some discouraging reviews, and a brief life in hard-back, the novel gradually moved out of the Doubleday Science Fiction Book Club circles and fans' enthusiasms to the serious consideration of the "love children" for whom grokking became almost a way of life.

Yet the intensity with which the novel was received did little to answer many of the questions it raised. What were the Martians like? What were their ethical codes? What did the Martian nest really resemble? What about the young Martians, the "nymphs" or "eggs," as Heinlein called them? Astute readers of Heinlein could have provided many of the answers to these questions, because he had earlier written at least two major novels in which Martians play a major role. There was *Podkayne of Mars* with Podkayne and her quiz-kid bright, *wunderkind* brother. But they cavorted on Venus, not Mars, and the novel, while about human

Martians, gave no new insights into other, earlier inhabitants of the fourth planet.

But there was also Heinlein's *Double Star*, that greatly underrated novel which told of the successful lifelong impersonation of Federation Supreme Minister John Joseph Bonforte—did his name mean *good deeds?*—by one Lorenzo Smythe, unemployed ham actor. On one level *Double Star* is a profound search for self, the story of the art of becoming, rather than being. On a very mythic level it is also the story of the search for a father. Against these compound, personal tensions, Heinlein chooses to clash at least two of his favorite themes: the identity of life or humanity, regardless of the external form into which it is incarnated, and the necessity for a man—or all mankind—to have liberty within the restraints imposed only by the nature of man. Man's freedom to act is always crucial to Heinlein.

Set into this nexus are some tantalizing descriptions of the native Martians. While they appear at first examination to be quite similar to the Martians of *Stranger in a Strange Land*, they actually belong to a different order of fictional reality. The Martians of *Double Star* reproduce by conjugate fission, while in *Stranger* reproduction is sexual. There are other differences, of course, but the thematic similarities between the two novels are more enlightening than any others. If the theme of paternity seems only accidental or casual in *Double Star*, it becomes theological in *Stranger in a Strange Land*, for paternity is the great crux upon which the later novel ultimately rests. If the Martian sense of obligation receives only cursory attention in the early book, expansions of that concept provide a foundation for the profound treatment of the multilevel meanings of *grok* in the later novel. So also with linguistic analysis or the search for personal identity. *Double Star*, then, indicates some of the literary areas that Heinlein will explore further, if differently, in *Stranger in a Strange Land*.

Early in Double Star *John Joseph Bonforte recalls his life as Lorenzo Smythe. While being hired to undertake a brief impersonation, he is left in a bar where some Martians are sitting:*

I didn't like Martians. I did not fancy having a thing that looks like a tree trunk topped off by a sun helmet claiming the privileges of a man. I did not like the way they grew pseudo limbs; it reminded me of snakes crawling out of their holes. I did not like the fact that they could look all directions at once without turning their heads—if they had had heads, which of course they don't. And I could not *stand* their smell!

Nobody could accuse me of race prejudice. I didn't care what a man's color, race, or religion was. But men were men, whereas Martians were *things*. They weren't even animals to my way of thinking. I'd rather have had a wart hog around me any day. Permitting them in restaurants and bars used by men struck me as outrageous. But there was the Treaty, of course, so what could I do?

These four had not been there when I came in, or I would have whiffed them. For that matter, they certainly could not have been there a few moments earlier when I had walked to the door and back. Now there they were, standing on their pedestals around a table, pretending to be people. I had not even heard the air conditioning speed up.

The free drink in front of me did not attract me; I simply wanted my host to come back so that I could leave politely. It suddenly occurred to me that he had glanced over that way just before he had left so hastily and I wondered if the Martians had anything to do with it. I looked over at them, trying to see if they were paying attention to our table—but how could you tell what a Martian was looking at or what it was thinking? That was another thing I didn't like about them.

However, Lorenzo Smythe is given an intensive education about Martian customs, particularly their ethical system with its complex standards of debts and obligations:

"Do you know the legend of Kkkahgral the Younger?"

"Eh? I'm afraid I don't."

"You must study it; it will give you insight into what makes a Martian tick. Briefly, this boy Kkkah was to appear at a certain time and place, thousands of years ago, for a very high honor—

like being knighted. Through no fault of his own (the way we would look at it) he failed to make it on time. Obviously the only thing to do was to kill him—by Martian standards. But because of his youth and his distinguished record some of the radicals present argued that he should be allowed to go back and start over. But Kkkahgral would have none of it. He insisted on his right to prosecute the case himself, won it, and was executed. Which makes him the very embodiment, the patron saint, of propriety on Mars."

"That's crazy!"

"Is it? We aren't Martians. They are a very old race and they have worked out a system of debts and obligations to cover every possible situation—the greatest formalists conceivable. Compared with them, the ancient Japanese, with their *giri* and *gimu*, were outright anarchists. Martians don't have 'right' and 'wrong'—instead they have propriety and impropriety, squared, cubed, and loaded with gee juice. But where it bears on this problem is that the Chief was about to be adopted into the nest of Kkkahgral the Younger himself. Do you scan me now?"

I still did not. To my mind this Kkkah character was one of the more loathsome items from *Le Grand Guignol*. Broadbent went on, "It's simple enough. The Chief is probably the greatest practical student of Martian customs and psychology. He has been working up to this for years. Comes local noon on Wednesday at Lacus Soli, the ceremony of adoption takes place. If the Chief is there and goes through his paces properly, everything is sweet. If he is not there—and it makes no difference at all why he is not there—his name is mud on Mars, in every nest from pole to pole—and the greatest interplanetary and interracial political coup ever attempted falls flat on its face. Worse than that, it will backfire. My guess is that the very least that will happen is for Mars to withdraw even from its present loose association with the Empire. Much more likely there will be reprisals and human beings will be killed—maybe every human on Mars. Then the extremists in the Humanity Party would have their way and Mars would be brought into the Empire by force—but only after every Martian was dead. And all set off just by Bonforte failing to show up for the adoption ceremony . . . Martians take these things very seriously."

The Martian language also receives Smythe's attention:

The Martian language gave me my greatest worry. Like most actors, I had picked up enough Martian, Venerian, Outer Jovian, etc., to be able to fake in front of a camera or on stage. But those rolled or fluttered consonants are very difficult. Human vocal cords are not as versatile as a Martian's tympanus, I believe, and, in any case, the semi-phonetic spelling out of those sounds in Roman letters, for example "kkk" or "jjj" or "rrr," have no more to do with the true sounds than the g in "Gnu" has to do with the inhaled click with which a Bantu pronounces "Gnu." "Jjj," for instance, closely resembles a Bronx cheer.

Human languages fall into four groups: inflecting ones as in Anglo-American, positional as in Chinese, agglutinative as in Old Turkish, polysynthetic (sentence units) as in Eskimo—to which, of course, we now add alien structures as wildly odd and as nearly impossible for the human brain as non-repetitive or emergent Venerian. Luckily Martian is analogous to human speech forms. Basic Martian, the trade language, is positional and involves only simple concrete ideas—like the greeting: "I see you." High Martian is polysynthetic and very stylized, with an expression for every nuance of their complex system of rewards and punishments, obligations and debts. It had been almost too much for Bonforte; Penny told me that he could read those arrays of dots they use for writing quite easily but of the spoken form of High Martian he could say only a few hundred sentences.

Smythe's concern with language and behavior prefigures a major theme of Stranger in a Strange Land. *What if ignorance of the language or some pattern of behavior causes him inadvertently to commit a breach of propriety, he wonders:*

"I see what you mean. But that, too, is tied up with Martian notions about 'propriety.' " (He used the Martian word.) "Death is the one acceptable excuse for not carrying out an obligation. If he were simply killed, they would adopt him into the nest after his death—and then the whole nest and probably every nest on Mars would set out to avenge him. They would not mind in the least if the whole human race were to die or be killed—but to kill this one human being to keep him from being adopted, that's another kettle of fish entirely. Matter of obligation and propriety—in some ways a Martian's response to a situation is so automatic as to remind one of instinct. It is not, of course, since they are incredibly intelligent. But they do the damnedest things."

Finally, Lorenzo Smythe, now become John Joseph Bonforte, enters the nest:

I looked out and saw my audience and I wanted to run. I had stage fright for the first time in thirty years.

The siblings of the nest were spread out before me as far as I could see. There was an open lane in front of me, with thousands on each side, set close together as asparagus. I knew that the first thing I must do was slow-march down the center of that lane, clear to the far end, to the ramp leading down into the inner nest.

I could not move.

I said to myself, "Look, boy, you're John Joseph Bonforte. You've been here dozens of times before. These people are your friends. You're here because you want to be here—and because they want you here. So march down that aisle. Tum tum te *tum!* 'Here comes the bride!' "

I began to feel like Bonforte again. I was Uncle Joe Bonforte, determined to do this thing perfectly—for the honor and welfare of my own people and my own planet—and for my friends the Martians. I took a deep breath and one step.

That deep breath saved me; it brought me that heavenly fragrance. Thousands on thousands of Martians packed close together—it smelled to me as if somebody had dropped and broken a whole case of Jungle Lust. The conviction that I smelled it was so strong that I involuntarily glanced back to see if Penny had followed me in. I could feel her handclasp warm in my palm.

I started limping down that aisle, trying to make it about the speed a Martian moves on his own planet. The crowd closed in behind me. Occasionally kids would get away from their elders and skitter out in front of me. By "kids" I mean post-fission

Martians, half the mass and not much over half the height of an adult. They are never out of the nest and we are inclined to forget that there can be little Martians. It takes almost five years, after fission, for a Martian to regain his full size, have his brain fully restored, and get all of his memory back. During this transition he is an idiot studying to be a moron. The gene rearrangement and subsequent regeneration incident to conjugation and fission put him out of the running for a long time. One of Bonforte's spools was a lecture on the subject, accompanied by some not very good amateur stereo.

The kids, being cheerful idiots, are exempt from propriety and all that that implies. But they are greatly loved.

Two of the kids, of the same and smallest size and looking just alike to me, skittered out and stopped dead in front of me, just like a foolish puppy in traffic. Either I stopped or I ran them down.

So I stopped. They moved even closer, blocking my way completely, and started sprouting pseudo limbs while chittering at each other. I could not understand them at all. Quickly they were plucking at my clothes and snaking their patty-paws into my sleeve pockets.

The crowd was so tight that I could hardly go around them. I was stretched between two needs. In the first place they were so darn cute that I wanted to see if I didn't have a sweet tucked away somewhere for them—but in a still firster place was the knowledge that the adoption ceremony was timed like a ballet. If I didn't get on down that street, I was going to commit the classic sin against propriety made famous by Kkkahgral the Younger himself.

But the kids were not about to get out of my way. One of them had found my watch.

I sighed and was almost overpowered by the perfume. Then I made a bet with myself. I bet that baby-kissing was a Galactic Universal and that it took precedence even over Martian propriety. I got on one knee, making myself about the height they were, and fondled them for a few moments, patting them and running my hands down their scales.

Then I stood up and said carefully, "That is all now. I must go," which used up a large fraction of my stock of Basic Martian.

The kids clung to me but I moved them carefully and gently aside and went on down the double line, hurrying to make up for the time I had lost. No life wand burned a hole in my back. I risked a hope that my violation of propriety had not yet reached the capital offense level. I reached the ramp leading down into the inner nest and started on down.

*   *   *   *   *   *   *   *   *   *   *   *   *

That line of asterisks represents the adoption ceremony. Why? Because it is limited to members of the Kkkah nest. It is a family matter.

Put it this way: A Mormon may have very close gentile friends —but does that friendship get a gentile inside the Temple at Salt Lake City? It never has and it never will. Martians visit very freely back and forth between their nests—but a Martian enters the inner nest only of his own family. Even his conjugate-spouses are not thus privileged. I have no more right to tell the details of the adoption ceremony than a lodge brother has to be specific about ritual outside the lodge.

Oh, the rough outlines do not matter, since they are the same for any nest, just as my part was the same for any candidate. My sponsor—Bonforte's oldest Martian friend, Kkkahrrreash—met me at the door and threatened me with a wand. I demanded that he kill me at once were I guilty of any breach. To tell the truth, I did not recognize him, even though I had studied a picture of him. But it had to be him because ritual required it.

Having thus made clear that I stood four-square for Motherhood, the Home, Civic Virtue, and never missing Sunday school, I was permitted to enter. 'Rrreash conducted me around all the stations, I was questioned and I responded. Every word, every gesture, was as stylized as a classical Chinese play, else I would not have stood a chance. Most of the time I did not know what they were saying and half of the time I did not understand my own replies; I simply knew my cues and the responses. It was not made easier by the low light level the Martians prefer; I was groping around like a mole.

I played once with Hawk Mantell, shortly before he died, after he was stone-deaf. There was a trouper! He could not even use a hearing device because the eighth nerve was dead. Part of the time he could cue by lips but that is not always possible. He directed the production himself and he timed it perfectly. I have seen him deliver a line, walk away—then whirl around and snap out a retort to a line that he had never heard, precisely on the timing.

This was like that. I knew my part and I played it. If *they* blew it, that was their lookout.

But it did not help my morale that there were never less than half a dozen wands leveled at me the whole time. I kept telling myself that they wouldn't burn me down for a slip. After all, I was just a poor stupid human being and at the very least they would give me a passing mark for effort. But I didn't believe it.

After what seemed like days—but was not, since the whole ceremony times exactly one ninth of Mars' rotation—after an endless time, we ate. I don't know what and perhaps it is just as well. It did not poison me.

After that the elders made their speeches, I made my acceptance speech in answer, and they gave me my name and my wand. I was a Martian.

I did not know how to use the wand and my name sounded like a leaky faucet, but from that instant on it was my legal name on Mars and I was legally a blood member of the most aristocratic family on the planet—exactly fifty-two hours after a ground hog down on his luck had spent his last half-Imperial buying a drink for a stranger in the bar of Casa Mañana.

I guess this proves that one should never pick up strangers.

I got out as quickly as possible. Dak had made up a speech for me in which I claimed proper necessity for leaving at once and they let me go. I was nervous as a man upstairs in a sorority house because there was no longer ritual to guide me. I mean to say even casual social behavior was still hedged around with airtight and risky custom and I did not know the moves. So I recited my excuse and headed out. 'Rrreash and another elder went with me and I chanced playing with another pair of the kids when we were outside—or maybe the same pair. Once I reached the gates the two elders said good-by in squeaky English and let me go out alone; the gates closed behind me and I reswallowed my heart.

The only non-fiction selection of this anthology, if one excludes the selections from Schiaparelli and Lowell, is the article which follows. Rather than reprint a passage or two from *Stranger in a Strange Land* and perhaps damage the essential unity of the novel, the editors thought it best to present the only serious analysis of Heinlein's novel yet published in a "mainstream" journal, *The CEA Critic* of The College English Association. While the editors cannot achieve toward the author of the article that Olympian objectivity which is the goal of scholarship, at least one of the editors liked it well enough to include here.

Willis E. McNelly

LINGUISTIC RELATIVITY IN MIDDLE HIGH MARTIAN

At a recent cocktail party in Berkeley, a corporation lawyer bemoaned the generation gap. "These kids of mine act as if they live in another world and as if I'm from another planet. I can't get across to them. I might as well be speaking Martian."

His companion, an editor of an avant-garde journal, but cursed by the "over-thirty" stigma, replied enthusiastically, "You are absolutely right. I grok you. My daughter's a go-go dancer."

Ten minutes later after some animated discussion about go-go dancing, someone thought to ask the editor what "grok" meant. Only one other person had heard the term before, but if the rapidity of dissemination at the cocktail party is an indicator of a larger acceptance, we will all be "grokking" within a year or so.

The word was created by Robert A. Heinlein, dean of American science fiction writers, in his provocative novel *Stranger in a Strange Land* (first publ. in 1961 and reprinted by Berkley, N1571). It is the story, told in detail with sardonic humor, of Valentine Michael Smith, a Mars-born earth child. Raised by Martians after the death of his parents and all other members of the first Martian expedition, Smith is returned to earth by crewmen of the second expedition twenty-five years later. Having been nurtured by the Martians, who are so non-earthly as to confound earthly analysis, Mike Smith is a Martian in an earth body. He thinks in Martian.

The rest of the novel is well-written—perhaps "slick" is the best adjective to describe Heinlein's style—as a variation on the noble-savage theme, coupled with some intriguing variations of the Whorf-Sapir theory of linguistic relativity. You can't really appreciate Mike Smith or the Martians until you learn to think in Martian, and you begin to think in Martian when you begin to grok. As one character put it, "I grok it. Language itself shapes a man's basic ideas." *Grok* is the only Martian word used in the novel,[1] but it is so basic to the Martian character, according to Heinlein, that an understanding of *grok* comes before an understanding of every other word in the Martian tongue.

As Heinlein handles the concept, the notion of grokking is crucial to the enlightened pantheism which is the religious construct of *Stranger in a Strange Land*. *Grok* means *drink* in basic Martian, and on a desert planet the sharing of water, or drinking together, becomes almost the highest, the only, religious sacrament. Those who share water become "water brothers," a unity so elevated that mistrust is impossible to one so internally baptized. *Grok* also means, in the words of one of the characters,

> . . . even antithetical concepts. It means 'fear,' it means 'love,' it means 'hate,'—for by the Martian 'map' you cannot have anything unless you grok it, understand it so thoroughly that you merge with it and it merges with you—then you can hate. . . . Grok means to understand so thoroughly that the observer becomes a part of the observed—to merge, blend, intermarry, lose identity in group experience. (p. 204)

If we benighted Terrans cannot grok *grok* completely until we learn to think in Martian, we can at least follow some of the extensions Heinlein gives the word. For example, Martians are

---

[1] Advance copies of Jubal Harshaw's A *Basic Martian Dictionary* (Marsport, Caxton Press, 2063) have not yet been received for review.—Ed.

sexless. They apparently reproduce by some sort of conjugate fission.

By a process of extension of meaning drawn from its earthly context, Heinlein adds a number of Terran modifications to the wildly alien Martian concept of *grok*. *Grok* seems first to mean *know, understand, appreciate, comprehend*. It resembles the hipster "dig." Gradually it comes to include *love, cherish, create*.[2] The Terrans in the novel do have sex, of course (they "grok growing closer," to use the terminology of the book). Thus the unsexual Martian *grok* becomes modified in the minds of the living Terrans: it broadens to include the fullest and most intimate communication humanly possible, the very essence of life itself, sexual intercourse. Thus transmuted, *grok* becomes a quasi-assonantal surrogate for its common Anglo-Saxon equivalent, and it revitalizes the archaic meaning of the Biblical *know* as well as emphasizes the ambiguity of the Terran word *intercourse*.

There are several further extrapolations of the term as Heinlein handles it. *Grok* also means *life*, as a logical extension of its meaning *drink*. In a most logical Martian way, all that groks is God. This concept leads Heinlein to build a quasi-pantheistic religious system with Mike Smith, man by ancestry but Martian by environment and thought processes, as its major prophet. The water ceremony is the sole sacrament: "Share water, drink deep, never thirst." In basic Martian this translates, approximately, into "Grok, grok, grok."

The salutation among water brothers is "Thou art God," with the central message of the novel being, as noted earlier, "All that groks is God." Alternately, God groks, in every sense of the word thus defined: God loves, drinks, creates, cherishes, infuses every being.

Heinlein carries the religious message of the novel even further by advancing the thoroughly Martian concept of ritual cannibalism. When a Martian groks death, he "discorporates," and the surviving water brothers eat the remains, grokking him in fullness. The custom on Mars is formalized and deeply religious. The

2 Cf. the classic religious admonition: "You cannot love what you do not know."

survivors would, by eating the discorporated one, thereby acquire some of his characteristics, attributes, or even eccentricities. One character expresses it this way, "If I chopped you up and made a stew, you and the stew, whatever was in it, would grok—and when I ate you, we would grok together and nothing would be lost and it would not matter which one of us did the eating." Of course, Heinlein does not evaluate any qualitative or quantitative differences between the symbolic cannabalism of most Terran religious sects and the actual cannibalism of the Martians. He leaves those discussions to his readers.

One of Benjamin Whorf's great contributions in his studies of Hopi which led in turn to the thesis of linguistic relativity was his analysis of Hopi time perception. Heinlein has apparently read his Whorf well, because this concept of temporal discontinuity is another of the major theses of *Stranger in a Strange Land*. He puts it this way, "With eternity to draw on there could be no reason for hurrying—'hurry' was not a concept in Martian. Speed, velocity, simultaneity, acceleration, and other abstractions of the pattern of eternity were part of Martian mathematics, but not of Martian emotion" (p. 126).

Heinlein is quick to point out, as did Whorf in a similar connection, that ". . . the unceasing rush of human existence came not from mathematical necessities of time but from the frantic urgency implicit in human sexual bipolarity" (p. 126). Thus the Whorfian conclusion inevitable in the novel: the realities of time, space, and matter are almost totally dependent upon the verbal system one uses to speak of time, space, and matter. When we learn to think in another language, our entire perception of reality changes. What is more important, reality itself changes. Grok?

Accomplished literary craftsman that he is, Heinlein skillfully utilizes almost every technique to communicate his ideas. One specific device is Mike Smith's constant use of the participle or progressive verb form to indicate the eternal present of the Martian now. "I am been saying so." "We are growing closer." "I am savoring and cherishing." Further examples could be multiplied, but only one more need be cited. It is used so often in the novel that it becomes almost a ritualistic theme song: "Waiting is."

Not "Waiting is necessary," or "Waiting is important," or "Waiting is inevitable." Simply, "Waiting *is*." The phrase, a curious juxtaposition of tense forms, implies that one will wait, until eternity if necessary, before grokking in fullness.

In one of the most moving parts of the novel, Mike comes to understand that merely speaking about love is meaningless. If all that groks is God, Mike must demonstrate this truth, not simply repeat it. He says in a striking parallelism with the Crucifixion, "I'm ready to show them now—I grok the fullness. Waiting is ended" (p. 396).

But this is not the place to note the number of Christian parallels in *Stranger in a Strange Land*, nor to evaluate if they are wholly successful. From a standpoint of linguistic relativity, however, similarities of Martian grokking and English thought find a union in Mike's last benediction as he is being stoned to death. Rocks have given him a "crown of blood." "The Truth is simple but the Way of Man is hard. First learn to control your *self*. The rest follows. Blessed is he who knows himself and commands himself, for the world is his and love and happiness and peace walk with him wherever he goes. Thou art God. Know that and the Way is opened" (p. 400).

Implicit in this Martian-Terran-Christian-Buddhist-Hindu benediction is the ultimate concept that "Love," however extrapolated from whatever widely divergent culture, will find an identity of expression. Many anthropological linguists will find this thesis highly debatable. In fact, the identity of expression seems to contradict the thrust of the novel: that a language "map" will alter reality—any reality, including that of love.

The appeal of *Stranger in a Strange Land* is not limited to its intriguing development of Martian thought, or even to its more than adequate descriptions of the "growing closer" ceremony.[3] The sugar-coated, over-simplistic romanticism of the story has become almost a cult in certain areas of the country. Psychedelic bookstores in the Haight-Ashbury district of San Francisco have

[3] Heinlein's humor should not remain unnoted. One of the major characters of the book is a journalist, Ben Caxton, who is a lippman, not a winchell. He is joined by a happy medium, Madame Allie Vesant, whose late husband was Professor Simon Magus.

sold dozens of lapel buttons engraved, "Are you a stranger in a strange land: Grok or share water." Martian-Terran nests of water brothers are grokking wherever grokking needs to be grokked. There is no doubt that the sense of alienation or anomie which troubles the flower children has caused many of them to turn to *Stranger*, as the cult calls it, with the same emotion that causes them to wear buttons reading "Frodo Lives" or "Go, Go, Gandalf!" Heinlein is almost Swiftian in his attack on some of the same American folkways that the hippies reject. His analysis of the hypocrisies of religion, politics, economics, and, explicitly, the Protestant ethic, seems to supplement the strictures which the flower children themselves maintain against our society. Whether grokking is an adequate substitute for involvement or commitment is conjectural, but a certain vociferous element in our society has seized upon it as a way of life. Fiction has become reality.

Stranger in a Strange Land may not be a great novel. Perhaps science fiction has yet to produce one. Yet when a writer skillfully combines the varied themes of any work as well as Heinlein has done, science fiction has at least come of age.

Grok what I mean?